Macomber "retells the parable of women's
age-old concerns with gentle humor and charm."
—*Publishers Weekly*

"Debbie Macomber's name on a book
is a guarantee of delightful, warmhearted romance.
She crafts endearing characters and
stories that leave readers feeling good."
—*New York Times* bestselling author Jayne Ann Krentz

❤ ❤ ❤

"Tara Taylor Quinn's deeply felt stories
of romance and family will warm your heart."
—national bestselling author Jennifer Crusie

"Tara Taylor Quinn writes with wonderful assurance...
Her handling of male viewpoint is exceptional;
she manages to make her heroes both intriguing
and human, which isn't always easy. She seems to
genuinely like and understand men,
an attitude as refreshing as it is unusual."
—*New York Times* bestselling author Jennifer Blake

DEBBIE MACOMBER

New York Times bestselling author Debbie Macomber
always enjoyed telling stories—first to her baby-sitting
clients, and then to her own four children. As a full-time
wife and mother and an avid romance reader, she dreamed
of one day sharing her stories with a wider audience. In
the autumn of 1982 she sold her first book, and then began
making regular appearances on the *USA Today* bestseller
list. Now her heartwarming stories have conquered the *New
York Times* bestseller list, and there are over forty million
copies of her books in print worldwide!

TARA TAYLOR QUINN

worked as a journalist and an English teacher before she
finally realized her dream of becoming a Harlequin writer—
a dream she'd nursed ever since buying her first Harlequin
Romance novel at the age of fourteen. Her first novel,
Yesterday's Secrets, was a finalist for the Romance Writers
of America RITA Award. She has now written more
than fifteen novels, including the popular Shelter Valley
trilogy, and her contribution to the TRUEBLOOD, TEXAS
continuity series, *The Rancher's Bride*, will appear next year.

DEBBIE

The First Man You Meet

MACOMBER

Jacob's Girls

TARA TAYLOR QUINN

HARLEQUIN®

TORONTO • NEW YORK • LONDON
AMSTERDAM • PARIS • SYDNEY • HAMBURG
STOCKHOLM • ATHENS • TOKYO • MILAN • MADRID
PRAGUE • WARSAW • BUDAPEST • AUCKLAND

ISBN 0-373-83454-3

HARLEQUIN SPECIAL Vol. 2

Copyright © 2001 by Harlequin Books S.A.

The publisher acknowledges the copyright holders
of the individual works as follows:

THE FIRST MAN YOU MEET
Copyright © 1992 by Debbie Macomber

JACOB'S GIRLS
Copyright © 1995 by Tara Lee Reames

Visit us at www.eHarlequin.com

Printed in U.S.A.

CONTENTS

The First Man You Meet

Debbie Macomber

Chapter One

IT HAD BEEN one of those days.

One of those hellish, nightmarish days in which nothing had gone right. Nothing. Shelly Hansen told herself she should have seen the writing on the wall that morning when she tripped over the laces of her high-top purple tennis shoes as she hurried from the parking lot to her dinky office. She'd torn a hole in the knee of her brand-new balloon pants and limped ingloriously into her building. The day had gone steadily downhill from there.

By the time she returned to her apartment that evening she was in a black mood. All she needed to make her day complete was to have her mother pop in unannounced with a man in tow, convinced she'd found the perfect mate for Shelly.

That was exactly the kind of thing Shelly had come to expect from her dear, sweet *desperate* mother. Shelly was twenty-eight now and single, and her mother tended to view her unmarried status as something to be remedied.

Never mind that Shelly felt content with her life just the way it was. Never mind that she wasn't interested in marriage and children...at least not yet. That time would come, she was sure, not now, but someday soon—or rather, some *year* soon.

For the moment, Shelly was absorbed in her career. She was proud of her work as a video producer, although she continually suffered the cash-flow problems of the self-employed. Her relaxation videos—seascapes, mountain scenes, a flickering fire in a brick fireplace, all with a background of classical music—were selling well. Her cat-baby-sitting video had recently caught the attention of a major distributor, and she couldn't help believing she was on the brink of being discovered.

That was the good news.

Her mother hounding her to marry was the bad.

Tossing her woven Mexican bag and striped blue jacket onto the sofa, Shelly ventured into the kitchen and sorted through the packages in her freezer until she found something to strike her fancy for dinner. The frozen entrée was in the microwave when the doorbell chimed.

Her mother. The way her day was going, it *had* to be her mother. Groaning inwardly, she decided she'd be polite but insistent. Friendly but determined, and if her mother began talking about husbands, Shelly would simply change the subject.

But it wasn't Faith Hansen who stood outside her door. It was Elvira Livingston, the building manager, a warm, delightful but insatiably curious older woman.

"Good evening, dear," Mrs. Livingston greeted her. She wore heavy gold earrings and a billowing, bright yellow dress, quite typical attire. She clutched a large box protectively in both hands. "The postman dropped this off. He asked if I'd give it to you."

"For me, Mrs. L.?" Perhaps this day wasn't a total waste, after all.

Elvira nodded, holding the package as though she wasn't entirely sure she should surrender it until she got every bit of relevant data. "The return address is California. Know anyone by the name of Millicent Bannister?"

"Aunt Milly?" Shelly hadn't heard from her mother's aunt in years.

"The package is insured," Mrs. Livingston noted, shifting the box just enough to examine the label again.

Shelly held out her hands to receive the package, but her landlady apparently didn't notice.

"I had to sign for it." This, too, seemed to be of great importance. "And there's a letter attached," Mrs. Livingston added.

Shelly had the impression that the only way she'd ever get her hands on the parcel was to let Mrs. Livingston open it first.

"I certainly appreciate all the trouble you've gone to," Shelly said, gripping the sides of the box and giving a firm tug. Mrs. Livingston released the package reluctantly. "Uh, thanks, Mrs. L. I'll talk to you soon."

The older woman's face fell with disappointment as Shelly began to close the door. Obviously, she was hoping for an invitation to stay. But after such a frustrating day, Shelly wasn't in the mood for company, especially not the meddlesome, if well-meaning, El-vira Livingston.

Shelly sighed. This was what she got for renting an apartment with "character." She could be living in a modern town house with a sauna, pool and work-out room in an upper-class yuppie neighborhood. In-stead she'd opted for a brick two story apartment building in the heart of Seattle. The radiators hissed at all hours of the night in perfect harmony with the plumbing that groaned and creaked. But Shelly loved the polished hardwood floors, the high ceilings with their delicate crystal light fixtures and the bay win-dows that overlooked Puget Sound. She could live without the sauna and the other amenities, even if it meant occasionally dealing with an eccentric busy-body like Mrs. Livingston.

Eagerly she carried the package into the kitchen and set it on her table. Although she wondered what Aunt Milly had sent her, she carefully peeled the let-ter free, then just as carefully removed the plain brown wrapper.

The box was an old one, she noted, the cardboard heavier than that currently used by stores. Shelly gently pried off the lid and set it aside. She found thick layers of tissue paper wrapped around…a dress. Shelly pushed aside the paper and painstakingly lifted the garment from its box. She gasped in surprise as the long white dress gracefully unfolded.

This wasn't just any dress. It was a wedding dress, an exquisitely sewn lace-and-satin wedding dress.

Surely it couldn't have been Aunt Milly's wedding dress... No, that couldn't be... It wasn't possible.

Anxious now, her heart racing, Shelly carefully refolded the dress and placed it back in the box. She reached for the letter and discovered that her hands were trembling as she tore open the envelope.

My Dearest Shelly,

I trust this letter finds you happy and well. You've frequently been in my thoughts the past few days. I suppose you could blame Mr. Donahue for that. Though now that I think about it, it may have been Oprah. As you'll have gathered, I often watch those talk shows these days. John would have disapproved, but he's been gone eight years now. Of course, if I wanted to, I'd watch them if he were still alive. John could disapprove all he wanted, but it wouldn't do him a damn bit of good. Never did. He knew it and loved me, anyway.

I imagine you're wondering why I'm mailing you my wedding dress. (Yes, that is indeed my infamous wedding dress.) I suspect the sight of it has put the fear of God in you. I wish I could be there to see your face when you realized what I was sending you. No doubt you're familiar with its story; everyone in the family's known about it for years. Since you're fated to marry the first man you meet once the dress is in your hands, your first instinct is probably to burn the thing!

Now that I reconsider, I'm almost certain it was Donahue. He had a show recently featuring pets as companions to the elderly, lifting their spirits and the like. The man being interviewed brought along a cute little Scottish terrier pup and that was when the old seamstress drifted into my mind. I must have fallen asleep, because the next thing I knew the six o'clock news was on.

While I slept I had a dream about you. This was no ordinary dream, either. I saw you plain as day, standing beside a tall young man, your blue eyes bright and shining. You were so happy, so truly in love. But what amazed me was the wedding dress you were wearing.

Mine.

The very dress the old Scottish woman sewed for me all those years ago. It seemed to me I was receiving a message of some sort and that I'd best not ignore it. Neither had you! You're about to embark on the grandest adventure of your life, my dear. Keep me informed!

Believe me, Shelly, I know what you're thinking. I well remember my own thoughts the day that Scottish seamstress handed me the wedding dress. Marriage was the last thing on my mind! I had a career, back in the days when it was rare for a woman to attend college, let alone graduate from law school.

You and I are a great deal alike, Shelly. We value our independence. It takes a special kind of man to be married to women like us. And you, my dear niece, are about to meet that one special man just the way I did.

All my love,
Aunt Milly

P.S. You're only the second person to wear this dress, my dear. Never before have I felt like this. Perhaps it's the beginning of a tradition!

With hands that trembled even more fiercely now, Shelly folded the letter and slid it into the envelope. Her heart was pounding loud and fast, and she could feel the sweat beading her forehead.

The phone rang then, and more from instinct than any desire to talk, Shelly reached for the receiver.

"Hello." It hadn't dawned on her until precisely that moment that the caller might well be her mother, wanting to bring over a man for her to meet. Any man her mother introduced would only add to the growing nightmare, but—

"Shelly, it's Jill. Are you all right? You sound...a bit strange."

"Jill." Shelly was so relieved that her knees went weak. "Thank heaven it's you."

"What's wrong?"

Shelly hardly knew where to begin. "My aunt Milly's wedding dress just arrived. I realize that won't mean anything to you unless you've heard the family legend about my aunt Milly and uncle John."

"I haven't."

"Of course you haven't, otherwise you'd understand what I'm going through,'' Shelly snapped. She immediately felt guilty for being short-tempered with her best friend. Making an effort to compose herself, she explained, ''I've just been mailed a wedding dress—one that's been in my family for nearly fifty years—with the clear understanding that I'll be wearing it myself soon.''

''I didn't even realize you were dating anyone special.'' Jill hadn't managed to disguise the hurt in her voice.

''I'm *not* getting married. If anyone should know that, it's you.''

''Then your aunt simply intends you to wear it when you do get married.''

''There's far more to it than that,'' Shelly cried. ''Listen. Aunt Milly—who's really my mother's aunt, a few years younger than my grandmother—became an attorney just after the Second World War. She worked hard to earn her law degree and had decided to dedicate her life to her career.''

''In other words, she'd planned never to marry.''

''Precisely.''

''But apparently she did.''

''Yes, and the story of how that happened has been in the family for years. It seems that Aunt Milly had all her clothes professionally made. As the story goes, she took some lovely white material to an old Scottish woman who had a reputation as the best seamstress around. Milly needed an evening dress for some formal event that was coming up—business related, of course. The woman took her measurements and told her the dress would be finished within the week.''

"And?'' Jill prompted when Shelly hesitated.

This was the part of the tale that distressed her the most. "And...when Milly returned for the dress the old woman sat her down with a cup of tea.''

"The dress wasn't ready?''

"Oh, it was ready, all right, only it wasn't the dress Aunt Milly had ordered. The Scottish woman explained she was gifted with the 'sight.'''

"She was clairvoyant?''

"So she claimed,'' Shelly said, breathing in deeply. "The old woman told my aunt that when she began the dress a vision came to her. A clear vision that involved Milly. This vision apparently showed Milly getting married. The old woman was so convinced of it that she turned what was supposed to be a simple evening dress into an elegant wedding gown, with layers of satin and lace and lots of pearls.''

"It sounds beautiful,'' Jill said with a sigh.

"Of course it's beautiful—but don't you see?''

"See what?''

It was all Shelly could do not to groan with frustration. "The woman insisted that my aunt Milly, who'd dedicated herself to her career, would marry within the year. It happened, too, just the way the seamstress said it would, right down to the last detail.''

Jill sighed again. "That's the most romantic story I've heard in ages.''

"It isn't romance,'' Shelly argued, "it's fate interrupting one's life! It's being a...pawn in the game of life! I know that sounds crazy, but I've grown up hearing this story. It was as though my aunt Milly didn't have any choice in the matter."

"And your aunt Milly mailed you the dress?"

"Yes," Shelly wailed. "*Now* do you understand why I'm upset?"

"Frankly, no. Come on, Shelly, it's just an old dress. You're overreacting. You make it sound as if you're destined to marry the next man you meet."

Shelly gasped audibly. She couldn't help herself. "How'd you know?" she whispered.

"Know what?"

"That's exactly what happened to Aunt Milly. That's part of the legend. She tried to refuse the dress, but the seamstress wouldn't take it back, nor would she accept payment. When Aunt Milly left the dress shop, she had car problems and needed a mechanic. My uncle John was that mechanic. And Aunt Milly married him. She married *the first man she met*, just like the seamstress said."

Chapter Two

"SHELLY, THAT doesn't mean *you're* going to marry the next man you meet," Jill stated calmly, far too calmly to suit Shelly.

Perhaps Jill didn't recognize a crisis when she heard about one. They were talking about destiny here. Predestination. Fate. Okay, maybe, just maybe, she was being a bit melodramatic, but after the ghastly day she'd had, who could blame her?

"Aunt Milly came right out and said I'm going to get married soon," Shelly explained. "The family legend says that the first man you meet when you get the dress is the man you'll marry."

"It's just coincidence," Jill reassured her. "Your aunt probably would have met her husband *without* the dress. It would've happened anyway. And don't forget, she's an old woman now," Jill continued soothingly. "I know this wonderful old lady who comes into the pharmacy every few weeks and she always insists *I'm* going to get married soon. I smile and nod and fill her prescription. She means well, and I'm sure your aunt Milly does, too. She just wants you to be happy, the way she was. But I think it's a mistake for you to take any of this prediction nonsense seriously."

Shelly exhaled sharply. Jill was right; Aunt Milly

was a sweetheart, who had Shelly's happiness at heart. She'd had a long, blissful marriage herself and wanted the same for her great-niece. But Shelly had a career. She had plans and goals, none of which included meeting and marrying a stranger.

The story of Aunt Milly's wedding dress had been handed down from one generation to the next. Shelly had first heard it as a child and had loved it. In her young romantic heart, she'd ranked the story of her aunt Milly and uncle John with her favorite fairy tales of Cinderella and Sleeping Beauty, barely able to distinguish truth from fantasy. However, she was an adult now. Her heart and her life weren't going to be ruled by something as whimsical as a "magical" wedding dress or a fanciful legend.

"You're absolutely right," Shelly announced emphatically. "This whole thing is ridiculous. Just because this wedding dress supposedly conjured up a husband for my aunt Milly fifty years ago doesn't mean it's going to do the same thing for me, no matter what she claims."

"Well, thank goodness you're finally being sensible about this."

"No one bothered to ask me what I thought before shipping off a so-called magic wedding gown. I don't want to marry just yet, so I certainly don't need the dress. It was a nice gesture, but unnecessary."

"Exactly," Jill agreed.

"I'm not interested in playing déjà voodoo." She paused to laugh at her own joke.

Jill chuckled, too. "I wouldn't be, either."

Shelly felt greatly relieved and sighed expressively. The tight muscles along the back of her neck began to relax. Jill was, as usual, full of sound, practical advice. Aunt Milly was a wonderful old lady, and the legend was a delightful bit of family lore, but it would be laughable to take any of this seriously.

"How about meeting me for lunch tomorrow?" Jill suggested. "It's been ages since we got together."

"That sounds good to me," Shelly said eagerly. Although they'd been good friends since college, it took some effort on both their parts these days to make time in their hectic lives to see each other. "When and where?"

"How about the mall?" Jill asked. "That would be easiest for me since I'm scheduled to work tomorrow. I can get off a few minutes before twelve."

"Great. I'll see you at noon at Patrick's," Shelly promised. Meeting her friend for lunch was just the antidote she needed after the terrible day she'd suffered through. But then what did she expect on Friday, April thirteenth?

SHELLY OVERSLEPT, then got caught in a traffic jam on her way to meet Jill the following morning. She detested being late, although she often was. Rather than fight for a convenient parking spot in the vast lot that surrounded the mall, she took the first available space and rushed toward the nearest entrance. Patrick's, a cozy, charming restaurant on the mall's upper level, was deservedly popular for business lunches. Shelly had eaten there often and especially enjoyed the spinach-and-shrimp salad.

A glance at her watch told her it was already after twelve, and not wanting to keep Jill waiting, she hurried toward the escalator. The shopping center was especially busy on weekends, she noted, as she weaved her way around several people.

Her mind must have been on the salad she intended to order for lunch instead of the escalator because the moment she placed her foot on the first tread, she lost her balance.

"Oh...oh!" Swinging her arms out at both sides in a futile effort to remain upright, she groped at thin air. She tried frantically to catch herself as she fell backward.

Landing in someone's arms shocked her as much as having lost her balance. Incredulous, she twisted around to thank her rescuer but this proved to be a mistake. Her action caught the man off guard, and before he could prevent it, they both went crashing to the floor. Once again Shelly expected to experience pain. Instead, her waist was surrounded by arms that were surprisingly strong. His grip was firm but gentle, protective. As they fell, he maneuvered himself to take the brunt of the impact when they landed. Sprawled as she was above him, Shelly found herself staring down at the most attractive man she'd ever seen. Her heart thrummed. Her breath caught. Her body froze.

For a moment neither of them spoke. A crowd had gathered around them before Shelly managed to

speak. When she did, her voice was weak and breathless. "Are you all right? I'm so sorry…"

"I'm fine. What about you?"

"Fine. I think."

She lay cushioned by his solid chest, their faces
scant inches apart. Shelly's long hair fell forward,
framing his face. He smelled of mint and some clean-
scented soap. Her gaze wandered curiously over his
features; at such close range she could see the tiny
lines that fanned out from the edges of his sapphire-
blue eyes as well as deep grooves that bracketed his
mouth. His nose was classically straight, his mouth
full and sensuous. At least his lower lip was. It didn't
take her long to recognize that this man was uncompromisingly male. His eyes held hers reluctantly, as
if he, too, was caught in the same powerful trance.

Neither of them moved, and although Shelly was
convinced the breathless sensation she felt was a result of the fall, she couldn't seem to breathe properly
even now.

"Miss, are you hurt?"

Reluctantly Shelly glanced up to find a security
guard standing over her.

"Um…I don't think so."

"Sir?"

"I'm fine."

The arms that were holding hers securely loosened.

"If we could have you both sit over here for a
moment," the guard instructed, pointing at a bench.
"We have an ambulance on the way."

"An ambulance? But I told you I'm not hurt," she objected.

The guard gently helped Shelly to her feet. Her legs were shaky and her breathing a bit uncertain, but otherwise she was unhurt.

"Officer, there's really no need—" the man who'd fallen with her protested.

"Mall policy," the guard interrupted. He hooked his thumbs into the wide leather belt and rocked gently back on his feet. "It's standard procedure to have all accident victims checked immediately."

"If you're worried about a lawsuit—"

"I don't make the rules," the guard interrupted her rescuer once again. "I just see that they're carried out. Now, if you'd both sit over here, the medical team will be here in a couple of minutes."

"I don't have time to wait," Shelly cried. "I'm meeting someone." She glanced longingly at the upper level, wondering how she could get word of her delay to Jill. It didn't reassure her to notice the number of people clustered by the railing, staring down at her. Her little escapade had attracted quite a bit of attention.

"I've got an appointment, as well," the man said, looking pointedly at his watch.

The security guard ignored their protests. He removed a small notebook from his shirt pocket and flipped it open. "Your names, please."

"Shelly Hansen."

"Mark Brady."

He wrote down the information and a brief account of how they happened to fall.

"I won't have to go to the hospital, will I?" Shelly demanded.

"That depends," the guard answered.

This whole thing was ridiculous. She was perfectly fine. A little shaken, true, but uninjured. She suddenly realized that she hadn't thanked this man—Mark, was it?

"I'm terribly sorry about all this," she offered. "I can't thank you enough for catching me."

"In the future, you might be more careful." Mark glanced at his watch a second time.

"I will be. But if it ever happens again, might I suggest you just let me fall?" This delay was inconvenient for her, too, but that wasn't any reason to be quick-tempered. She studied her rescuer and shook her head slightly, wondering why she'd been so impressed. He looked as if he'd stepped off the Planet Square. Dark blue suit and tie, crisp white shirt with gold cufflinks. This guy was as original as cooked oatmeal. About as personable, too.

If she was giving him the once-over, she discovered he was eyeing her, too. Apparently he was equally unimpressed. Her sweatshirt was a fluorescent orange and her jeans as tight as a second skin. Her ankle-high boots were black, her socks the same shade of orange as the sweatshirt. Her hair cascaded about her shoulders in a layer of dark frothy curls. Mark was frowning in obvious disapproval.

The wide glass doors at the mall entrance opened,

and two paramedics hurried inside. Seconds later, when the ambulance arrived, two more medical people entered the building. Shelly was mortified that such a minor accident would result in all this attention.

The first paramedic knelt down in front of her while the second concentrated on Mark. Before she completely understood what was happening, her shoe was off and the man was examining her ankle. Mark, too, was being examined, a stethoscope pressed over his heart. He didn't seem to appreciate the procedures any more than she did.

It wasn't until he stood up that she realized how tall he was. Close to six-five, she guessed. A good match for her own five feet ten inches, she thought automatically.

It hit her then. Bull's-eye. Aunt Milly's letter had mentioned her standing beside a tall young man. Mark Brady was tall. Very tall. Taller than just about any man she'd ever met.

Aunt Milly's letter had also said something about Shelly's blue eyes. She'd ignored it at the time, but her eyes weren't blue. They were hazel. Mark had blue eyes, though. The kind of vivid blue eyes women generally found striking... Nor could she forget her initial reaction to him. She'd been attracted. Highly attracted. It'd been a long while since a man had interested her this much. Until he stood, anyway. When she got one good look at him, she'd known immediately that they had nothing in common. Mark Brady probably didn't own a single article of clothing that wasn't blue, black or tan. Clearly the man had no imagination.

On a sudden thought, she glanced worriedly toward his left hand. No wedding ring. Closing her eyes, she sagged against the back of the bench and groaned.

"Miss?" The paramedic was studying her closely.

"Excuse me," she said, straightening. She jerked impatiently on Mark's suit jacket. He was involved in a conversation with the ambulance attendant who was interviewing him and didn't turn around.

"Excuse me," she said again, louder this time.

"Yes?" Mark turned to face her, his gaze impatient.

Now that she had his attention, she wasn't sure she should continue. "This may sound like a silly question, but, uh…are you married?"

He frowned again. "No."

"Oh, no," Shelly moaned and slumped forward. "I was afraid of that."

"I beg your pardon."

"Surely you've got a girlfriend—I mean, you're a tall, handsome kind of guy. There's got to be someone important in your life. Anyone? Please, just think. Surely there's someone?" She knew she was beginning to sound desperate, but she couldn't help it. Aunt Milly's letter was echoing in her mind and all of last night's logic had disappeared.

The four paramedics, as well as Mark, were staring at her. "Are you sure you don't want to come to the hospital and talk to a doctor?" one of them asked gently.

Shelly nodded. "I'm sure." Then before she could stop herself, she blurted out, "What do you do for a living?"

"I'm a CPA," he answered wearily.

"An accountant," she muttered. She should have guessed. He was obviously as staid and dignified as he looked. And as boring. The type of man who'd probably never even heard of videos for entertaining bored house cats. He probably wouldn't be interested in purchasing one, either.

Surely her aunt Milly couldn't have seen Mark and Shelly together in her dream. Not Mark Brady. The two of them were completely ill-suited. A relationship between them wouldn't last five minutes! Abruptly she reminded herself that she wasn't supposed to be taking Aunt Milly's prediction seriously.

"May I go?" she asked the paramedic. "I'm not even bruised."

"Yes, but you'll need to sign here."

Shelly did so without bothering to read the statement. Mark, however, seemed to scrutinize every sentence. He would, of course.

"Uh, Mark…" Shelly hesitated, and Mark glanced in her direction.

"Thank you," she said simply.

"You're welcome."

Still she delayed leaving.

"You wanted something else?"

She didn't know quite how to say this, but she felt the need too strongly to ignore it. "Don't take offense at this—I'm sure you're a really great guy…. I just want you to know I'm not interested in marriage right now."

Chapter Three

JILL WAS SEATED at the table, doodling on the paper place mat, when Shelly arrived. "What kept you?" she asked. "I've been here for almost half an hour."

"I—I fell off the escalator."

Jill's eyes widened in alarm. "My goodness, are you all right?"

Shelly nodded a bit sheepishly. "I'm fine...I think."

"Shouldn't you see a doctor?"

"I already have," she explained, avoiding eye contact with her friend. "Well, sort of. The security guard called in the paramedics. A whole bunch of them."

"No wonder you're late."

"I would have been, anyway," Shelly admitted as she reached for a menu, though she'd decided an hour earlier what she intended to order.

"This has really got you flustered, hasn't it?"

"It's more than the fall that's unsettled me," Shelly explained, lowering the menu. "It's the man who caught me."

Jill arched her eyebrows jokingly. "Aha! I should have guessed there was a man involved."

"You might try to understand how I felt," Shelly

said reproachfully. "Especially since I haven't recovered from receiving Aunt Milly's wedding dress yet."

"Don't tell me you're still worried about that first-man-you-meet nonsense."

"Of course not. That would be ridiculous. It's just...it's just I can't help feeling there might be something to that silly wedding dress."

"Then mail it back."

"I can't," Shelly said, slapping the menu down on the table. "Aunt Milly warned me not to—though not exactly in those words, mind you. She said I shouldn't ignore the dress. I mean, how can I? It's like an albatross hanging around my neck."

"I still think you're overreacting to this whole thing."

"That's the crazy part. I *know* I am, but I can't seem to stop myself. I grew up hearing the legend of that wedding dress, and now it's in my possession. I've got a piece of family history hanging in the back of my closet. Heaven forbid if my mother should hear about this." She shuddered at that thought.

"So you hung the dress in your closet."

"I couldn't very well keep it under my bed. I tried that, but I couldn't sleep, so I finally got up and stuck it in the back of the closet." She closed the menu and set it aside. "That bothered me, too. I tossed and turned half the night, then I remembered Aunt Milly had done the same thing when the seamstress gave her the dress."

"She stuck it under her bed?"

Shelly nodded slowly. "I seem to remember hear-

ing something like that. She'd tried to refuse it, but
the old woman insisted Aunt Milly take the gown
home with her. By the time she arrived at her apartment she'd already met my uncle John although she
still didn't know she was going to marry him.''

Jill raised a skeptical eyebrow. "Then what? After
she put it under her bed and couldn't sleep, I mean?''

"Well, she did the same thing I did," Shelly admitted. "She shoved it into her closet." Shelly felt as
if she were confessing to a crime. "I didn't want the
thing staring me in the face so I hung it in the back.''

"Naturally." Jill was trying, unsuccessfully, to disguise a smile. Shelly could see how someone else
might find her situation humorous, but she personally
didn't think any of this was too amusing. Not when
it was her life, her future, being tossed around like
some cosmic football. At this rate, she'd be married
and with child by nightfall!

"That's not the worst of it," Shelly added. She
exhaled slowly, wondering why her heart was still
beating so fiercely.

"You mean there's more?''

She nodded. The waitress arrived just then and took
their orders, returning quickly with tall glasses of iced
tea. Shelly breathed in deeply before she continued.
"I literally fell into that man's—Mark Brady's—
arms.''

"How convenient.''

"It's all very nice of him to have broken my fall,''
she said sternly, "but I wish he hadn't.''

"Shelly!''

"I mean it," she insisted. She glanced around, as if to make sure no one was listening, then added, "The man's an accountant."

Jill reacted in mock horror, covering her mouth with both hands and widening her eyes. "No! An accountant?"

"Think about it. Could you honestly picture me married to an accountant?"

Jill took a moment or two to mull over the question. "Hmm, a CPA," she repeated slowly. "You still haven't memorized your multiplication tables, have you? You freeze up whenever you have to deal with numbers. No, I guess you're right, I can't honestly see you with an accountant."

Shelly raised both hands, palms up, in a dramatic gesture. "I rest my case."

Jill reached for some bread, carefully selecting a whole-wheat roll. "Just because you fell into his arms doesn't mean you're going to marry him," she said in a matter-of-fact voice.

"I know that."

"Then what's the problem?"

"I can't make myself *believe* it," Shelly said. "I feel like one tiny pin fighting the force of a giant magnet."

"That's preposterous."

"I know," Shelly agreed readily. "I just wish I hadn't said anything to Mark."

Jill set the roll on her plate with exaggerated care. "You told him the story about your aunt Milly's wedding dress?"

"Of course not." Shelly was horrified her friend would suggest such a thing. "I just told him I couldn't marry him."

Jill's mouth dropped. "You didn't! Did you?"

Shelly nodded hesitantly. "I don't know what made me say anything so ludicrous. I honestly don't. I can't imagine what he must think of me. Not that I plan on seeing him again, of course. Unless—"

"Unless what?"

Their lunches were served. Jill had ordered a hot spinach salad with slices of chicken simmering in soy sauce sprinkled with sesame seeds. Shelly's spinach salad was piled high with shrimp, egg slices and black olives.

"Go on," Jill urged once the waitress had left the table. "You don't plan on seeing Mark again unless—"

"Unless it's unavoidable."

"I take it this means your aunt Milly's first encounter with your uncle John wasn't her last." Jill giggled. "Silly of me. Obviously it wasn't."

"No. Aunt Milly felt the same reluctance I do. My uncle was a wonderful man, don't get me wrong, and he was absolutely perfect for Aunt Milly, as it turned out, but the two of them were as different as night and day. Aunt Milly was a college graduate and Uncle John never completed high school."

Shelly sighed wistfully. At one time the story of their romance had been like her own personal fairy tale. But now Shelly didn't find it nearly as enthralling. "He helped Milly fix her car the night it broke down. The very next day she was in court defending a client in a lawsuit—''

"Let me guess," Jill interrupted, "your uncle John was the man suing her client."

Shelly nodded. "Yes, and that was only the beginning. Every time they turned around they were bumping into each other."

"How long after they met were they married?"

This was the question Shelly had dreaded most. She closed her eyes and whispered, "Ten days."

"Ten days," Jill echoed with an incredulous look.

"I know. It seems that once they kissed they both realized there wasn't any use fighting it."

"Did your aunt tell John about the seamstress and the wedding dress?"

Shelly shrugged. "I don't know, but my guess is she didn't…at least not at first." She hadn't touched her salad yet and paused long enough to savor a forkful of her favorite seafood. Then she said abruptly, "They eloped without telling anyone."

"Children?" Jill wanted to know.

"Three boys. My mother's cousins."

"What about granddaughters? You'd think your aunt Milly would want to hand the dress down to one of them."

"All three of her sons had boys themselves. I guess you could say I'm the closest thing she's got to a granddaughter."

"Ten days," Jill repeated. "That's really something."

Forking up another succulent shrimp, Shelly continued her story. "That old Scottish woman knew about the wedding even before the family did. When Aunt Milly and Uncle John returned from their honeymoon, there was a wedding card from the seamstress waiting for them at the house."

Jill propped her elbows on the table and gazed at Shelly. "Tell me what Mark Brady looks like."

Shelly frowned, trying to form her impressions of him into some kind of reasonably articulate description. He was compelling in ways she didn't quite understand. Principled and headstrong, but how she knew that, Shelly couldn't explain. "He's tall," she began slowly.

"How tall?"

"Basketball-player tall. He must be about six five."

"Brown hair?"

Shelly nodded. "With blue eyes. *Really* blue eyes. I can't remember the last time I met a man with eyes that precise color. They seemed to..." She hesitated, unsettled by the emotion that stirred within her when she thought about Mark. Although their encounter had been brief, Shelly was left feeling oddly certain that she could trust this man, trust him implicitly. It wasn't a sensation she could ever remember experiencing with any other man. She didn't like the feeling; it made her uncomfortable. Until Jill had started asking her about Mark, Shelly didn't realize she'd experienced any emotion toward him—except for embarrassment, of course.

"Why do you want to know?" she asked.

Jill gave her a silly, knowing grin. "Because if he's as tall as you say, with dark brown hair and deep blue eyes, then the man you described just walked into this restaurant."

"What?" Shelly felt her stomach sink. "Mark's here? Mark Brady?"

"That's not so amazing, is it? This is, after all, the same shopping mall in which you, uh, met—" Jill made a show of glancing at her watch "—thirty or so minutes ago."

"He's here." She reminded herself that Jill was right: Mark's choosing to have lunch at Patrick's was just a logical coincidence. Too bad she couldn't convince her racing heart to believe that.

"He's sitting on the other side of the room," Jill whispered.

"Has he seen me yet?"

"I don't think so."

Without being obvious—or at least Shelly hoped she wasn't being obvious—she turned to look in his direction. At that same instant, Mark happened to glance up. Their eyes met. Despite herself, she gasped. Her hands shook and she felt herself break out in a cold sweat.

Mark scowled and quickly looked away.

She couldn't blame him. He seemed surprised to see her there. Unpleasantly surprised.

"Well, is it him?" Jill demanded.

Shelly couldn't find her voice, so she answered with a quick nod.

"I thought it might be. What are you thinking?"

"That I've lost my appetite." Shelly doubted she'd be able to finish her lunch.

"You want my advice?" Jill asked, grinning broadly. "I don't have a lot of experience in the area of magic wedding dresses, but I recently read a fascinating book on home remedies."

"Sure." At this point Shelly was feeling reckless enough to try just about anything.

"Garlic," Jill said solemnly. "Wear a garlic rope around your neck. Not only does it deter vampires, but it just might ward off potential husbands conjured up by a magic wedding dress."

Chapter Four

HARD THOUGH SHE TRIED, Shelly had a difficult time ignoring Mark Brady. He sat there, stiff and unapproachable, at the other side of the small restaurant. Just as stiff and unapproachable as she was. Jill wanted to linger over her coffee before returning to her job at the PayRite Pharmacy in the mall, but Shelly was eager to be on her way. The sooner she left, the sooner she could put this bothersome encounter out of her mind.

"Don't forget Morgan's baby shower on Tuesday night," Jill said as Shelly reached for her purse.

Shelly had completely forgotten about their friend's party, which was understandable given her present state of mind. Most of their college friends were married and several were now having babies. Rather than admit how absentminded she'd suddenly become, Shelly asked, "Do you want to drive over together?"

"Sure," Jill agreed. "I have to go directly from work so I'll stop off at your place and we can leave from there."

"Sounds good to me." She tried to imagine their blond, scatterbrained classmate as a wife and mother. It was Morgan who'd gotten the entire dorm hooked on daytime soap operas. Before anyone could figure out how it had occurred, all the girls were obsessed with the characters and their lives. It became as important as mealtimes to learn if Jessie would ever find true love. To the best of Shelly's knowledge, she hadn't.

But then, Jessie didn't have an aunt Milly. The unexpected thought flashed through her mind.

Irritated with herself, Shelly dropped her share of the bill and a tip on the table. "I'll see you Tuesday, then."

"Right. And Shelly, don't look so worried. No enchanted wedding dress is going to disrupt your life unless you allow it to happen."

Easy for Jill to say, since it wasn't her life and her great-aunt's wedding dress. Nevertheless, her advice was sound. Aunt Milly might have had some fanciful dream about Shelly's marring a tall man with blue eyes, but that didn't mean it was going to happen, especially when Shelly was so determined that it wouldn't.

"You're absolutely right," she stated emphatically. "I know I keep saying that, but...well, I seem to need reminding. So, thanks. Again." With a final wave, she wandered out of the restaurant, barely noticing the colorful shop windows as she passed them. As Jill had pointed out, Aunt Milly meant well, but the letter and the wedding dress shouldn't be taken too seriously. Shelly was content with her life, and the last thing she needed right now was a man. Especially a staid, conventional man like Mark Brady.

Shelly knew exactly what kind of man she'd fall in love with. He'd be intelligent, and fervent about life, and as passionate as she was herself. Naturally, he'd appreciate her work and take pride in his own. He'd need to be a free spirit, like her. Unconventional. She'd like a man with gumption, too—someone who possessed a bit of initiative. It'd be nice if he was a little better at organizational skills than she was, but that wasn't absolutely necessary.

With thoughts of marriage so prominent in her mind, Shelly soon found herself standing in front of a jeweler's display window. A large assortment of wedding bands had captured her attention. Scanning the selection, she found one ring that stood out from the rest: three small rows of diamond chips, bracketed on each side by a thin band of gold. The ring was striking in its simplicity, its uncontrived beauty.

For the longest moment Shelly stared at the rings as her mind wove whimsical dreams around the happy bride and the tall groom. *Tall groom.* Her thoughts came to a skidding halt.

What on earth had come over her? She didn't know, but whatever it was, she didn't like it. Self-consciously she glanced around, fearful that someone was watching her. Well, a very specific someone, to be honest. Someone who definitely shouldn't see her gazing with open longing at a collection of absurdly high-priced wedding rings. Mark Brady.

With a sense of urgency, Shelly hurried toward the mall exit, her feet barely able to move fast enough. It was all she could do to keep from breaking into a run. No matter how fast she walked, however, she couldn't shake the feeling that *he* was there, watching

her. Twice she whirled around, convinced she'd find
Mark Brady strolling behind her, sneering and making
contemptuous remarks.

He wasn't there.

Shelly felt herself relax as she neared her apartment. She parked her car, then stopped in the lobby
to collect her mail. As soon as she opened the small
box, Mrs. Livingston's head poked out her door.

"Good afternoon, Shelly," she chirped, gazing at
her expectantly.

It took Shelly a moment to realize that Mrs. L. must
have been waiting to hear about the contents of her
package.

"It's a lovely day," Shelly said conversationally,
sorting through her mail. Two bills, a flyer and something from the Internal Revenue Service. The way her
luck had been going, it was probably an audit notice.
A quick inspection revealed exactly that. She closed
her eyes and groaned inwardly.

"A lovely day indeed," Mrs. Livingston echoed
cheerfully.

Muttering under her breath, Shelly stuffed the IRS
notice back inside the envelope. When she glanced
up, she noticed that the older woman was now standing in the hallway, wearing another vividly colored
outfit—turquoise and purple this time.

"I suppose you're wondering about the package,"
Shelly said resignedly, tucking her mail inside her
purse. "It was a gift from my aunt Milly."

"Something from the past, I guess?" Mrs. Livingston asked.

"Why...yes, how'd you know?"

"I'd take whatever it was very, very seriously if I were you," Mrs. Livingston continued in a solemn voice. "Wizard wouldn't go anywhere near that box. Think what you want, but my cat has always had a sixth sense when it comes to this sort of thing."

"It's a dress, Mrs. L." Shelly explained, hiding behind a falsely bright smile. "How am I supposed to take a dress seriously?"

Mrs. Livingston opened her apartment door and scooped the large black-and-white cat into her arms. "That I wouldn't know," she returned, her eyes narrowed and mysterious. "All I can tell you is that Wizard felt skittish around that package. You don't suppose there's...magic in it, do you?"

Somehow Shelly managed a reply, although she felt certain it was unintelligible. Taking the stairs two at a time, she hurried into her apartment, leaning breathlessly against the door once she was inside. Even Mrs. Livingston's cat knew there was something strange about Aunt Milly's wedding dress!

WHEN JILL ARRIVED late Tuesday afternoon, Shelly was ready and waiting for her, brightly wrapped baby gift in hand. She was eager to get out and socialize—eager to get out, period. Anything to escape another phone call from her mother, who'd recently heard from Aunt Milly. Now Faith Hansen was calling daily for updates on the romantic prospects in her daughter's life.

"Well," Jill demanded as she entered the apartment. "Are you going to show it to me?"

"Show what to you?"

Jill gave her a look that seemed to question her friend's intelligence. "The wedding dress, of course."

For several hours Shelly had managed to put the dress out of her mind. "No," she said forcefully. "I want to forget about the whole thing."

"Met any tall blue-eyed men lately?" Jill couldn't resist asking.

"None," Shelly answered shortly. Checking her watch, she noted that they were early but suggested they leave, anyway. "Shouldn't we go now?"

"We've got lots of time," Jill countered, moving toward Shelly's bedroom. "Come on, it isn't going to hurt to let me look at the dress."

"Oh, all right," Shelly conceded ungraciously. Leading the way, she opened the closet door and reached into the back of the closet.

She brought out the lace-and-satin gown, holding it up for Jill's inspection. She'd barely looked at the dress the day she'd received it, and now she was almost shocked by how breathtakingly beautiful it actually was.

The laughter drained from Jill's dark brown eyes as she stared at the gown. "Oh, Shelly, it's...lovely." She gently touched the Elizabethan sleeve and ran her finger along the delicate layer of pearls that decorated the cuff. The high neckline was also trimmed with an intricate design of pearls, so that it resembled a choke collar. "I don't know what I expected," Jill continued in an awed whisper, "but certainly nothing as beautiful as this."

Shelly nodded wordlessly. The dress was far more exquisite than she'd realized. Her heart swelled with unexpected emotion, and to her dismay, tears filled her eyes as she thought about the old Scottish woman who had so lovingly constructed the gown. Each pearl had been sewn into place by hand. She thought of her aunt Milly, as tall and statuesque as Shelly herself, wearing the dress. Then she recalled her uncle John, such a determined man. She imagined him, standing tall and proud beside Milly. Shelly thought fondly of those two, who'd been so completely different, yet had loved each other so well....

For a moment neither she nor Jill spoke. "Have you tried it on?" Jill asked finally.

Shelly shook her head adamantly, not wanting her friend to realize how emotional she'd become. "Heavens, no, but you can if you want."

"I don't think I could resist if I were you," Jill whispered, obviously affected by the dress, too. "Just seeing it...makes me long to be a bride myself."

"There's always Ralph," Shelly teased. Jill had been dating Ralph, a computer programmer, for several months, but frankly she couldn't understand what her friend saw in him.

Jill tossed her an irritated look. "The dress is for you, not me."

"But I don't want it," Shelly insisted, though she was no longer sure what she felt. Not since she'd really examined the dress and allowed herself to remember the wonder of John and Milly's romance.

"You're sure you don't mind?" Jill asked, slipping off her shoes. "I mean, if you'd rather I didn't try it on, I'll understand."

"No, feel free." Shelly strove for a flippant air. "As far as I'm concerned the dress is nothing but bad luck. It arrived on Friday the thirteenth. The next day I had that minor accident on the mall escalator. Now I'm being audited by the IRS."

It was as if Jill didn't hear. "I doubt it'll fit," she said as she cautiously removed the gown from the padded hanger. "I'm a good five inches shorter than you and heavier on top."

"Maybe the dress was meant for you in the first place," Shelly ventured. Perhaps Aunt Milly had been confused and it was Jill she'd viewed in her dream. After all, Milly's eyes weren't what they used to be....

"Does your mother know?" Jill asked as she stepped into the dress. She raised it over her hips and turned around to let Shelly fasten the buttons that ran down the back.

"That's another thing," Shelly moaned. "Mom's been calling me every day since the dress arrived, wanting to know if I've met anyone special yet."

"What did you tell her?" Jill asked, looking at Shelly over her shoulder.

"What's there to tell?" she asked irritably.

"Well, you might have mentioned Mark."

"Mark," Shelly repeated. She shrugged elaborately. "I haven't given him a thought in days." Not strictly true, but she'd been *trying* not to think about him. Even if he was interested in her—and he'd made very clear that he wasn't—she couldn't imagine two more ill-suited people. "I haven't seen him since last Saturday and I doubt I'll ever see him again."

"You're sure of that?"

"Positive."

"Well, what do you think?" Jill asked next, pirouetting slowly in front of her. "My hair's a mess and I've got hardly any makeup on, but..."

Shelly looked at her friend and sighed audibly. Never had she seen Jill look lovelier. It was as if the dress had been made for her. "You look absolutely enchanting. It fits like a dream."

"I feel like I am dreaming," Jill admitted softly. "Here," she said, turning around, "undo me before I start longing for a husband and 2.5 children."

"Don't forget the house with the white picket fence," Shelly teased, unfastening the buttons.

Jill slipped out of the dress. "Your turn," she said as she laid it carefully across the bed. "If it fits me, then it can't possibly fit you. You've got the perfect excuse to mail it back to your aunt Milly."

"I...don't know." Shelly bit her lip. She felt an inexplicable urge to keep the dress, and at the same time she would've willingly express-mailed it back to her aunt. Even while she hesitated, Shelly found herself undressing. She couldn't explain her sudden eagerness to try on the wedding gown any more than she could fathom its growing emotional appeal.

The dress slid easily over her hips. She turned around so Jill could secure the back, then glanced toward the mirror, expecting to find the skirt miles too short. It would have to be in order to fit Jill as perfectly as it had.

"Shelly," Jill whispered, then cupped her hand over her mouth. "My goodness...you look beautiful...really beautiful."

The sentiment was what Shelly had felt when she'd viewed her friend in the dress. "Something's wrong," she said once she found her voice. "Something's very wrong."

"No," Jill countered, "it's very right. It's as if the dress was made for you."

"Then answer me this," Shelly whispered. "How is it possible for the same dress to fit two women who wear totally different sizes?"

Chapter Five

SHELLY STRUGGLED to open the door of the Internal Revenue office, her arms weighted down with a huge box stuffed full of receipts and records she'd need for the audit. By bracing the box against the wall with her knee, she freed one hand to open the door. For the first time ever, she'd completed her tax return early—all by herself, too—and *this* was where it got her. She grumbled righteously and bit her lip, more in anxiety than annoyance.

She'd just managed to grasp the door handle, when the door unexpectedly opened and she staggered into the room, nearly colliding with an end table. She did a quick pirouette, convinced she'd ruined a new pair of panty hose. With a heartfelt sigh, she set her box of records on the floor and sank into the first available chair, neatly arranging her unaccustomed skirt around her knees. Only then did she bother to look around. There was one other person in the large reception area.

Shelly's heart did a nosedive, landing somewhere in the pit of her stomach. The man who'd opened the door for her, the man sitting in this very waiting room, was none other than Mark Brady—the man she'd hoped to avoid for the rest of her natural life. She gave an involuntary gasp.

Mark was leafing through the dog-eared pages of a magazine when he happened to glance her way. The automatic smile quickly faded from his face, and his gaze narrowed as if he strongly suspected Shelly had purposely arranged this meeting.

"What are you doing here?" Shelly demanded.

"I might ask you the same thing."

"I didn't follow you here, if that's what you're implying!"

"Listen, Ms....Hansen, I really couldn't care less." With that he returned to his magazine as if he were reading the fine print in a million-dollar contract. "*You're* the person who blurted out to everyone within hearing distance that you weren't marrying me. As if I'd even asked! As if I even *knew* you!"

Shelly felt the heat rising up her neck and quickly offered the first excuse she could think of. "I...was distraught."

"Obviously," he muttered from behind his magazine.

A few minutes of strained silence passed. Shelly shifted uncomfortably in her chair, checking her watch every couple of minutes. For the first time in recent history she was early for an appointment, but if this was where promptness got you, she'd prefer to be late.

"All right, I apologize," Shelly said when she couldn't tolerate the silence any longer. "I realize it was utterly ridiculous and...and out of turn—"

"Out of turn," Mark echoed, slapping the magazine down on the table. "I repeat—I don't even know you."

"I realize that."

He inhaled deeply, which drew her attention to his broad, muscular chest. She noticed that he was as meticulously dressed as he'd been at their first encounter. His dark suit and silk tie, however conventional, added a touch of sophistication to his natural good looks.

"If there's anyone to blame for this it's Aunt Milly," Shelly said, more to herself than to him.

"Aunt Milly?" Mark repeated, sounding unsure. He eyed her warily.

She'd said this much; she might as well launch into the whole ridiculous tale.

"Actually, it has more to do with the wedding dress than with my aunt Milly, although by now the two of them are inseparable in my mind. I don't usually dabble in this sort of thing, but I'm beginning to believe there just might be something supernatural about that silly dress, after all."

"Supernatural?"

"Magic, if you prefer."

"Magic in a wedding dress?" Mark gazed hopefully at the door that led to the inner offices of Internal Revenue, as though he was anxious to be called away.

"It's unbelievable, but the dress fits both Jill and me—which is virtually impossible. You saw Jill— she's the friend I was having lunch with last Saturday. I know we were halfway across the room from you, but you couldn't help noticing how much shorter she is than I am. We're completely different sizes.''

Mark hurriedly reached for the magazine as if he wanted to shut her out again before she said anything else.

"I know it sounds crazy. I don't like this any better than you do, but I'm honestly afraid it was you Aunt Milly mentioned in her letter.'' Well, it was only fair to tell him that.

Mark glanced in her direction again, blue eyes suspicious. "Your aunt Milly mentioned me in a letter?''

"Not by name—but she said she had a clear vision of me in the wedding dress and I was standing with a tall man. She also mentioned blue eyes. You're tall and you have blue eyes and the legend says I'm going to marry the first man I meet after receiving the dress.''

"And I just happened to be that man?''

"Yes,'' Shelly cried. "Now do you understand why I was so disturbed when we met?''

"Not entirely,'' Mark said after a moment.

Shelly rolled her eyes. How obtuse could the man be? "You're tall, aren't you? And you have blue eyes.''

He flipped intently through the magazine, not looking up at her as he spoke. "Actually, I really don't care what the letter said, nor am I concerned about this wedding dress you keep mentioning.''

"Of course you don't care,'' Shelly said indignantly. "Why should you? It must all seem quite absurd to you. And I'm aware that I'm overreacting, but

I do have a tendency to get emotional about things. If it helps any, I want you to know I'm content with my life just the way it is. I don't want to get married now—to anyone." When she'd finished, she sucked in a deep breath and began leafing idly through a magazine, doing her utmost to ignore him.

Silence returned. Silences had always bothered Shelly. It was as if she felt personally responsible for filling them. "If you want something to be grateful about, you can thank your lucky stars I didn't mention you to my mother."

"Your mother," Mark repeated, briefly glancing at her. "Does she know about Aunt Milly sending you this...dress?"

"Naturally she does," Shelly answered, closing the magazine. "She's phoned me every day since she heard, because she thinks I'm going to meet that special someone any minute."

"And you didn't mention me?"

"How could I? The instant I do that, she'll be contacting the caterers."

"I see." The edges of his mouth lifted as though he was beginning to find the situation amusing. "She believes in the power of this dress, too?"

"Unfortunately, yes. You have to understand where my mother stands on this marriage business," Shelly continued, undaunted.

"I'm not sure I want to," Mark muttered under his breath.

Shelly disregarded his comment. "By age twenty-eight—my age now, coincidentally—Mom had been married for eight years and already had three children. She's convinced I'm letting the best years of my life slip away. There's nothing I can say to make her believe differently.''

"Then I'll add my gratitude that you didn't mention me.''

Mollified, Shelly nodded, then glanced at her watch. Her meeting was in ten minutes and she was nervous, since this was the first time she'd done her own taxes. She should have known there'd be a problem.

"I take it you're here for an audit?'' Mark asked.

She nodded again, studying her tax return, sure she'd be in jail by nightfall without even understanding what she'd done wrong.

"Relax.''

"How can I?''

"Have you knowingly hidden something from the government? Lied about the income you received, or claimed expenditures you've never made?''

"Oh, no!''

"Then you don't have anything to worry about.''

"I don't?'' Shelly stared at him, soaking up his confidence. She'd been restless for days, worrying about this meeting. If it wasn't the wedding dress giving her nightmares, it was the audit.

"Don't volunteer any information unless they ask for it.''

"All right.''

"Did you prepare your own tax return?''

"Well, yes. It didn't seem that complicated, and

well, I realize this sounds silly but Jill bet me I couldn't do it. So I did. Back in February. You see, usually numbers boggle my mind and I decided to accept the challenge, and..." She realized she was chattering, something she did when she was nervous. Forcing herself to stay quiet, she scanned her return for the hundredth time, wondering what she could have possibly done wrong.

"Do you want me to check it over for you?"

Shelly was surprised by his generosity. "If you wouldn't mind. Are you being audited yourself?"

Mark smiled and shook his head. "A client of mine is."

"Oh."

Mark crossed the room and sat next to her. When Shelly handed him her tax return, his gaze ran quietly down the row of figures, then he asked her several questions.

"I've got everything right here," she assured him, gesturing toward the carton she'd lugged in with her. "I really am careful about saving everything I should."

Mark glanced down at the large cardboard box. "This is all for one year?"

"No," she admitted sheepishly. "I brought along everything I had for the past six years. I mean, it made sense at the time."

"That really wasn't necessary."

"I'd rather be safe than sorry," Shelly said, managing a small grin. She watched Mark as he scrutinized her return. At such close range, she saw that his eyes were even bluer than she'd thought. Blue as the sky on a bright July afternoon, she told herself fancifully. Her heart felt heavy in her chest, and hard as she tried, she couldn't keep from staring.

Mark handed back her return. "Everything looks fine. I don't think you'll have a problem."

It was amazing how relieved she felt at hearing that. No, at hearing that from *him*. Mark smiled at her and Shelly found herself responding readily with a smile of her own. The fluttery sensation returned to her stomach. She knew her eyes were wide and questioning and although she tried to look away, she couldn't make herself do it.

A look of surprise mingled with gentleness came over Mark's features, as if he were seeing her for the first time, really seeing her. He liked what he saw— Shelly could read that in his eyes. Slowly his gaze traveled over her features, and she felt her pulse tripping into double time. The letter she'd received from Aunt Milly flitted across her mind, but instead of dismissing the memory, she wondered, *Could there really be something to all this?*

Mark was the one to break eye contact. He stood abruptly and hurried back to his seat. "I don't think you have much to be concerned about."

"Yes, you told me."

"I mean about your aunt Milly's wedding dress."

"I don't have anything to worry about?" Shelly wasn't sure she understood.

"Not with me, at any rate."

"I don't quite follow..." If he was even half-aware

of the way her heart was clamoring as they gazed into
each other's eyes, he wouldn't be nearly as confident.

"I'm engaged."

"Engaged?" Shelly felt as though someone had
slugged her in the stomach. Her first reaction was
anger. "You couldn't have mentioned this sooner?"
she snapped.

"It's not official yet. Janice hasn't picked out a
diamond. Nor have we discussed our plans with her
family."

The irritation faded, swallowed by an overwhelming sense of relief. "Engaged," she repeated, reminding herself that she really had no interest in marriage.
And this proved there was no such thing as a
"magic" wedding dress. If Mark was involved with
Janice, he wouldn't be free to marry her. It was that
simple. Shelly leaped to her feet and started to pace.

"Are you all right?" Mark asked. "You're looking
pale."

She nodded and pressed her hands to her cheeks,
which suddenly felt hot. "I'm so relieved," she whispered hoarsely. "You have no idea how relieved I
am. You're engaged... My goodness, I feel like I've
got a new lease on life."

"As I explained," Mark said, frowning, "it isn't
official yet."

"That doesn't matter. You're committed to someone else and that's all that matters. However—" she
forced a smile "—you might have said something
sooner and saved me all this anxiety."

"You did ask that day at the mall, but I was more

concerned with avoiding a scene than revealing the personal details of my life.''

''I'm sorry about that.''

''No problem,'' Mark was quick to assure her.

Shelly settled back in the chair and crossed her legs, hoping to stroke a relaxed pose. She even managed to skim through a couple of magazines, although she barely knew what she was reading.

Finally, the receptionist opened the door and called her name. Eager to get this over with, Shelly stood, picking up the large box she'd brought in with her. She paused on her way out of the reception area and turned to Mark. ''I wish you and Janice every happiness,'' she said formally.

''Thank you,'' he answered, then grinned. ''The same to you and whomever the wedding dress finds for you to marry.''

Chapter Six

SHE SHOULD BE HAPPY, Shelly told herself early the following morning. Not only had she survived the audit—in fact she'd come away with an unexpected refund—but she'd learned that Mark was practically engaged.

Yes, she should be dancing in the streets, singing in the aisles... Instead she'd been struggling with a strange melancholy ever since their last encounter. She seemed to have lost her usual vitality, her sense of fun.

And now it was Saturday, and for once she had no looming deadlines, no appointments, no pressing errands. Remembering the exhilaration and solace she'd experienced when she videotaped an ocean storm sequence recently, Shelly decided to see if she could recapture some of those feelings. She headed toward Long Beach, a resort town on the Washington coastline. The sky was clear and almost cloudless; the sun was bright and pleasantly warm—a perfect spring day. Once she drove onto the freeway, the miles sped past and two hours later she was standing on the sandy beach with the breeze riffling her long hair.

She walked around for a while, enjoying the sights and sounds about her, the chirping of the sea gulls, the salty spray of the Pacific Ocean and the scent of wind and sea. She was satisfied with the end product, her beach video, and started to work out plans for a whole series—the ocean in different seasons, different moods. That would be something special, she thought, something unique.

She wandered down the beach, kicking at the sand with the toe of her tennis shoes. Tucking her fingertips in the pockets of her jeans, she breathed in the vivid freshness around her. After an hour or so, she made her way back to the concession stands, where she bought a hot dog and a cold drink.

Then, just because it looked like such fun, she rented a moped.

She sped along the shore, thrilled with the sensation of freedom, reveling in the solitude and the roar of pounding surf.

The wind tossed her hair about her face until it was a confusion of curls. Shelly laughed aloud and listened as the galloping breeze carried off the sound.

Her motorized bike rushed forward, spitting sand in its wake. She felt reckless with exhilaration, as though there was nothing she couldn't do. It was that kind of afternoon. That kind of day.

When she least expected it, someone else on a moped raced past her. Shelly hadn't encountered anyone during her ride and this person took her by surprise. She glanced quickly over her shoulder, amazed by how far she'd traveled. The only other person she could see was the one who'd passed her.

To her surprise, the rider did an abrupt turnaround and headed back in her direction. With the sun in her eyes and the wind pelting against her, Shelly slowed to a crawl and she shaded her eyes with one hand.

It wasn't until he was nearly beside her that Shelly recognized the other rider.

Mark Brady.

She was so shocked that she allowed the engine to die, her feet dropping to the sand to maintain her balance. Mark appeared equally shocked. He braked abruptly.

"Shelly?" He seemed not to believe it was her.

Shelly shook her head and blinked a couple of times just to make sure she wasn't fantasizing. The last person she'd expected to encounter on a beach two hours out of Seattle was Mark Brady. Mr. Conservative on a moped! This time, though, he wasn't wearing a dark suit. He didn't have his briefcase with him, either. And he looked even handsomer than usual in worn jeans and a University of Washington sweatshirt.

"Mark?" She couldn't prevent the astonishment from creeping into her voice.

"What are you doing here?" She heard the hostility in his and answered him coolly.

"The same thing as you, apparently." She pushed the hair from her face, and the wind promptly blew it back.

Mark's blue gaze narrowed suspiciously. "You didn't happen to follow me, did you?"

"Follow you?" she repeated indignantly. She'd rarely been more insulted. "Follow you!" she repeated, starting her moped and revving the engine.

"May I remind you that I was on the beach first? If anyone was doing any following, it was *you* following me." She was breathless by the time she finished. "In light of our previous encounters, you're the last person I'd seek out."

Mark scowled at her. "The feeling's mutual. I'm not in the mood for another story about your aunt Martha's damn wedding dress, either."

Shelly felt an unexpected flash of pain. "I was having a perfectly wonderful afternoon until you arrived," she said stiffly.

"I was having a good time myself," Mark muttered.

"Then I suggest we go our separate ways and forget we ever met."

Mark looked as if he were about to say something more, but Shelly was in no frame of mind to listen. She twisted the accelerator on the handlebar of her moped and took off down the beach. Although she knew it was unreasonable, she was furious. Furious at the surge of joy she'd felt when she recognized him. Furious at Mark, because he didn't seem even a little pleased to see her. She bit her lower lip, remembering the comment he'd made about not wanting to hear anything more about her "damn wedding dress." Now, that was just rude, she told herself righteously. She could *never* be interested in a man who was not only conventional but rude.

Squinting, Shelly hunched her shoulders against the wind, in a hurry now to return to the boardwalk area. She hadn't meant to go nearly this far.

The wet, compact sand made for smooth, fast riding and Shelly stayed close to the water's edge in an effort to outdistance Mark. Not that he was likely to chase her, but she wanted to avoid any possibility of another embarrassing encounter.

Then it happened.

A large wave came in, sneaking its way up the sand, creating a thin, glistening sheen. Shelly hardly noticed, as her front tire ripped through the water, spraying it out on both sides. Then the moped's front wheel dipped precariously. One minute she was sailing down the beach at breakneck speed and the next she was cartwheeling over her handlebars.

She landed heavily in a patch of wet sand, too paralyzed with shock to know if she was hurt or not.

Before she could move, Mark was crouching at her side. "Shelly? Are you all right?"

"I...don't know." Carefully she flexed one arm and then the other. Sitting up, she tested each leg and didn't feel pain there, either. Apparently she'd survived the experience unscathed.

"You crazy fool!" he yelled, leaping to his feet. "What are you trying to do, kill yourself?"

"Ah..." It was painful to breathe just yet, otherwise she would have answered him.

"Can you imagine what I thought when I saw you flying through the air like that?"

"Good riddance?" she suggested.

Mark closed his eyes and shook his head. "I'm in no mood for your jokes. Here, let me help you up."

He moved behind her, sliding his arms around her waist and gently raising her up.

"I'm fine," she protested the instant his arms surrounded her. The blood rushed to her head, but Shelly didn't know if that was because of her tumble or because Mark was holding her as though he never intended to let go. Even when she was on her feet, he didn't release her.

"Are you sure you're not hurt?"

Shelly nodded, not trusting her voice. "I'm less confident about the moped, though." Her bike seemed to be in worse shape than she was.

"It doesn't look good to me, either," Mark said. He finally dropped his arms and retrieved the moped, which was lying on its side, the waves lapping over it. There were regular hissing sounds as the cold water splashed against the heated muffler. Steam rose from the engine.

Mark did his best to start the bike for her, but to no avail. "I'm afraid it's hopelessly wet. It won't start now until it's had a chance to dry. A mechanic should check it over to be sure nothing's wrong."

Shelly brushed the hair from her face and nodded. There was no help for it; she was going to have to walk the bike back to the rental shop. No small feat when she considered she was about three miles down the beach.

"Thank you very much for stopping," she said a bit primly. "But as you can see I'm not hurt...."

"What do you think you're doing?" Mark asked as she began pushing the moped. It made for slow progress, the bulky machine was far more difficult to transport under her own power than she'd realized. At this rate, she'd be lucky to return it by nightfall.

"I'm taking the bike back to the place where I rented it."

"That's ridiculous."

"Do you have any better ideas?" she asked in a reasonable tone of voice. "I don't understand what you're doing here in the first place," she said, sounding far calmer than she felt. "You should be with Janet."

"Who?" he demanded. He tried to take the moped away from her and push it himself, but she wouldn't let go.

"The woman you're going to marry. Remember?"

"Her name is Janice and as I said before, the engagement's unofficial."

"That doesn't answer my question. You should be with her on a beautiful spring day like this."

Mark frowned again. "Janice couldn't get away. She had an important meeting with a client—she's a lawyer. Listen, quit being so stubborn, I'm stronger than you. Let me push the bike."

Shelly hesitated; his offer was tempting. She hadn't gone more than a few feet and already her side ached. She pressed one hand against her hip and straightened, her decision made. "Thanks, but no thanks," she answered flatly. "By the way, it's Aunt Milly who sent me the wedding dress, not Aunt Martha, so if we're going to get names straight, let's start there."

Mark rolled his eyes skyward, as though he'd

reached the end of his limited reserve of patience. "Fine, I'll apologize for what I said back there. I didn't mean to insult you."

"I didn't follow you," she said.

"I know, but I didn't follow you, either."

Shelly nodded, finding that she believed him.

"Then how do you explain that we've inadvertently stumbled into each other twice in the last week?" Mark asked. "The odds of that happening have got to be phenomenal."

"I know it sounds crazy, but...I'm afraid it's the dress," Shelly mumbled.

"The wedding dress?" Mark repeated.

"I'm really embarrassed about all this. I'm not sure I believe any of it myself. And I do apologize, especially since there's been an apparent mix-up—"

"Why's that?" Mark asked.

"Well...because you're involved with Janice. I'm sure the two of you are a perfect match and you'll have a marvelous life together."

"What makes you assume that?"

His question caught her off guard. "Well, because...didn't you just tell me you're about to become officially engaged?"

"Yes," Mark muttered, frowning.

Although she was reluctant to admit it, Shelly found pushing the moped extremely taxing, so she stopped to rest for a moment. "Listen," she said a little breathlessly, "there's no need for you to walk with me. Why don't you just go on ahead?"

"There most definitely is a need," Mark answered

sharply. He didn't seem too pleased with her suggestion. "I'm not going to desert you now."

"Oh, Mark, honestly, you don't have to be such a gentleman."

"You don't like gentlemen?"

"Of course I do—but it's one of the reasons you and I would never get along for any length of time. You're very sweet, don't get me wrong, but I don't need anyone to rescue me."

"Forgive me for saying so, but you *do* appear to need rescuing." The look he gave her implied that he was referring to more than the moped.

"I was the one foolish enough to get the engine wet," she said brightly, ignoring his comment. "So I should be the one to pay the consequences."

Mark waited a moment, as if debating whether to continue arguing. "Fine, if that's the way you feel," he said finally, straddling the moped and starting his engine, which roared to life with sickening ease. "I hope you don't tire out too quickly."

"I'll be okay," she said, hardly able to believe he was actually going to leave her.

"I hope you're right about that," he said, revving the engine.

"You...you could let someone know," she ventured, hoping the rental agency might send someone out with a truck to find her.

"I'll see what I can do," he agreed, then grinning broadly, took off at top speed down the beach.

Although she'd made the suggestion that he go on ahead without her, Shelly had assumed he wouldn't take it seriously. She'd said it more for the sake of dignity, of preserving her pride. She had actually been enjoying his company, enjoying the banter between them.

As he vanished into the distance, Shelly squared her shoulders, determined to manage on her own—particularly since she didn't have much choice in the matter. She'd been dragging the moped along for several minutes when she noticed a moped racing toward her. It didn't take her long to identify the rider, with his lithe, muscular build, as Mark. She picked up her pace, unreasonably pleased that he'd decided to return. He slowed as he approached her.

"Still eager to be rid of me?"

"No," she admitted, smiling half in relief, half in pleasure. "Can't you tell when a woman means something and when she's just being polite?"

"I guess not." He smiled back, apparently in a jovial mood. "Rest," he said, parking his own moped and taking hers. "A truck will be along any minute."

Shelly sank gratefully into the lush sand. Mark lowered himself onto the beach beside her. She picked several blades of grass and began weaving them industriously together. That way, she wouldn't have to look at him.

"Are you always this stubborn?" he asked.

"Yes," she said quietly, giving him a shy smile. Shelly couldn't remember being shy in her life. But something about Mark made her feel shaky inside, and oddly weak. An unfamiliar sensation, but she dared not analyze it, dared not examine it too closely.

She turned away from him and closed her eyes, trying to picture Janice, the woman he was going to marry. Despite her usually creative imagination, Shelly couldn't seem to visualize her.

"Shelly, what's wrong?"

"Wrong?"

"It's not like you to be quiet."

She grinned. They were barely more than acquaintances, and he already knew her. "Nothing."

"I think there must be." His finger against the side of her face guided her eyes toward him. Their lips were so close. Shelly's breath seemed to be caught somewhere in her throat as she stared helplessly into the bluest eyes she'd ever seen....

His forehead touched hers, then he angled his face gently, brushing her cheek. Shelly knew she should break away, but she couldn't make herself do it. Gently, deliberately, he pressed his mouth to hers, his lips warm and moist.

Shelly moaned at the shock of sensation. Her eyes drifted shut as his mouth moved hungrily over hers, and soon their arms were wrapped tightly around each other, their bodies straining closer.

The sound of the approaching truck intruded into their private world and broke them apart. Mark's eyes met hers, then he scowled darkly and glanced away. But Shelly didn't know whether he was more angry with her or with himself. Probably her.

Chapter Seven

"HEY," SHELLY SAID reassuringly, "don't look so concerned. It was just an ordinary, run-of-the-mill kiss." She stood indignantly and brushed the wet sand from her jeans. "Besides, it didn't mean anything."

Mark's scowl darkened. "Didn't mean anything?" he echoed.

"Of course it didn't! I mean, we were both wondering what it would be like, don't you think? Good grief, we seem to be running into each other every other day and it only makes sense that we should want to, you know, experiment."

"In other words, you think the kiss was just a means of satisfying our mutual curiosity?"

"Sure. All this nonsense about the wedding dress overcame our normal good sense, and we succumbed to the temptation." Thank goodness Mark seemed to understand her rambling. Shelly's knees were shaking. It was a wonder she could still stand upright. Although she'd tried to minimize the effects of his kiss, it left her feeling as though she'd never been kissed before. Her entire body had been overwhelmed by a feeling of rightness. Now all she felt was the crushing weight of confusion. She shouldn't be feeling any of these things for Mark. A CPA! An almost-engaged CPA, to boot.

"And was your curiosity satisfied?" he demanded. His blue eyes probed and waited.

"Uh...yes. And yours?"

"Yes," he muttered, but he was frowning again.

The youth from the rental agency leaped out of the truck and loaded Shelly's moped into the back. "You're not supposed to get the engine wet," he scolded. "It's in the rental agreement. You'll have to pay a fine."

Shelly nodded. She didn't have an excuse; she doubted the agency would accept her trying to escape Mark as a legitimate reason for damaging one of their vehicles.

Mark hefted his own bike onto the truck as well, and the three of them got into the pickup's cab and rode silently down the long stretch of beach.

Shelly went to the office to deal with her fine and was surprised to find Mark waiting for her when she'd finished. "You hungry?" he asked in an offhand invitation.

"Uh..." She would have thought he'd be anxious to see the last of her.

"Good," he said immediately, not giving her a chance to reply. His hand grasped her elbow firmly as he led her to a nearby fish-and-chips stand. Shelly couldn't recall the last time a man had taken her elbow. Her first reaction was to object to what she considered an outdated gesture but she was surprised to find it oddly comfortable, even pleasant.

They ordered their fish and chips, then carried the small baskets to a picnic table.

"I should have paid for my own," she said once they were seated, vaguely guilty that he'd paid for both meals. Janice might be the jealous type, and Shelly didn't want her to hear about this.

His eyes met hers, steady and direct. "When I ask you to join me, I pick up the bill."

Any argument she had vanished before it reached her lips.

After that, Shelly concentrated on her fish and chips, which were fresh and absolutely delicious. Mark seemed preoccupied with his meal, as well.

"What brought you to the beach today?" Shelly asked, finishing the last few French fries in her basket. Perhaps if they could figure out what had brought them both to a lonely stretch of beach two hours out of Seattle, they might be able to make sense of how they'd happened upon each other a third time.

"I have a beach house here. After tax time I generally try to get away for a few days, to come down here and relax."

"I had no idea." She found it inordinately important that he understand she hadn't somehow managed to stalk him across the state. Their meeting was pure coincidence…again.

"Don't worry about it, Shelly. You couldn't possibly have known about the beach house or that I intended to be here today. I didn't know it myself until this morning."

Shelly suddenly wished that Mark hadn't kissed

her. Everything was becoming far too complicated now.

"You're very talented," he told her out of the blue. "I bought one of your videos the other day."

"How did you know what I do?" Shelly felt flustered by his praise; she was at a complete loss to understand why it meant so much to her.

"I saw it on the income tax form and I was curious about your work."

"Curiosity seems to have gotten us both into a great deal of trouble," she said.

Mark grinned, a shameless irresistible grin. The kind of grin that makes a woman forget all sorts of things. Like the fact that he was practically engaged. And that he was a tall, blue-eyed stranger who, according to Aunt Milly's letter, would soon become her husband....

Shelly scrambled to her feet, hurrying toward the beach. Mark followed.

"You shouldn't look at me like that," she said, her voice soft and bewildered.

"You said it was just a kiss. Was it?"

"Yes," she boldly lied. "How could it be anything more?"

"You tell me."

Shelly had no answers to give him.

"While you're at it, explain why we keep bumping into each other or why I can't stop thinking about you."

"You can't?" She hadn't been able to stop thinking about him, either, but she wasn't ready to admit it.

"No." He stood behind her, his hands caressing her shoulders. Leisurely he stroked the length of her arms. His touch was so light that she thought she was imagining it, and she felt both excited and afraid.

He turned her around and gazed at her lips. "If that was just a run-of-the-mill kiss, then why do I feel the need to do it again?"

"I don't know."

His lips brushed hers. Briefly, with a whisper-soft touch, as though he was testing her response. Shelly closed her eyes and moaned. She didn't want to feel any of this. They were so far apart, such different people. Besides, *he* was involved with another woman and *she* was involved with her career.

When the kiss ended and he slowly released her, it was all Shelly could do to keep from sinking to the sand. "I have...to get back to Seattle," she managed to say, backing away from him. She turned and took four or five wobbly steps before she realized she was headed toward the Pacific Ocean.

"Shelly?"

"Yes?"

"Seattle is due north. If you continue going west, you'll eventually land in Hawaii."

"Oh, yeah, right," she mumbled, reversing her direction abruptly, eager now to escape.

THE FIRST PERSON Shelly called when she got home was Jill. "Can you come over?" Shelly asked without preamble. She could barely keep the panic out of her voice.

"Sure, what's wrong?"

"I saw Mark again."

"And?"

"Let me put it like this. We kissed and I haven't stopped trembling since."

Jill's romantic sigh came over the receiver as her breath softly caught. "This I've got to hear. I'll be there in ten minutes."

Actually it was closer to seven minutes. Shelly hadn't stopped pacing from the moment she got off the phone. She checked her watch repeatedly, waiting desperately for a dose of Jill's good sense.

"Shelly," Jill said, smiling as she breezed into the apartment, "what happened to your hair?"

Shelly smoothed down the errant curls. "I was at Long Beach."

"That's where you saw Mark? Good grief, that's something of a coincidence, isn't it?"

"I saw him earlier in the week, too.... Remember I told you I was being audited by the IRS? Lo and behold, guess who was in their waiting room when I arrived?"

"I don't need to be a rocket scientist to figure that one out. Mark Brady!"

"Right." Shelly rubbed her damp palms along her jeans in agitation. They, at least, had finally dried.

"And?"

Shelly groaned. "Can't you see what's happening? This is the third time we've been thrown together in the past few days. I'd never seen the man before, and all of a sudden he's around every corner. Then the wedding dress fit. It fit you...and it fits me."

"I agree that's all rather odd, but I wouldn't put too much stock in it, if I were you."

"Put too much stock in it... Listen, Jill, I've never had a man make me feel the way Mark does—all weak inside and, I don't know, special somehow. To be perfectly honest, I don't like it." She closed her eyes, hoping to chase away the memory of his touch, but it did no good. "You want to know the real kicker?" she asked abruptly, turning to face her friend. "He's engaged."

"Engaged," Jill echoed, her voice as startled as her expression.

"He keeps insisting it's not official yet. Nevertheless he's involved with someone else."

"But it was you he kissed," Jill pointed out.

"Don't remind me." Shelly covered her eyes with both hands. "I don't mind telling you, I find this whole thing unnerving.

"Obviously. Here," Jill said, directing Shelly toward the kitchen. "Now sit down. Let me make us some tea, then we can try to reason this out. Honestly, Shell, I don't think I've ever seen you so upset."

"I'm not upset," she cried. "I'm confused. There's a big difference. I'm...I'm trapped." Despite all logic to the contrary, she couldn't help fearing that the entire course of her life was about to change because her aunt Milly had fallen asleep watching "Donahue" one day and had some nonsensical dream.

"Trapped?" Jill repeated. "Don't you think you're being a bit dramatic?"

"I don't know anymore." Shelly rested her elbows on the table, buried her face in her hands and breathed in deeply. She had a tendency to become emotional, especially over family issues; she realized that. But this was different. This was scary.

"Calm down," Jill advised. "Once you think it through in a rational manner, you'll realize there's a perfectly ordinary explanation for everything."

Jill's serenity lent Shelly some badly needed confidence. "All right, you explain it."

"I can't," Jill admitted matter-of-factly, pouring boiling water into Shelly's teapot. "I'm not even going to try. My advice to you is to quit taking all this so seriously. If a relationship develops between you and Mark, just enjoy it—providing the other woman's out of the picture, of course! Just forget about that dress."

"Easy for you to say."

"That's true," Jill agreed readily. "But you're going to have to accept it for your own peace of mind."

Shelly knew good advice when she heard it. "You're right. I'm unnecessarily leaping into the deep end with this."

"A dress can't make you do anything you don't want to do. The same applies to Mark."

Shelly always counted on her friend's levelheadedness. Although Jill had given her basically the same advice several days earlier, Shelly needed to hear it again.

Jill prepared two cups of tea and carried them to the table. "Are you going to be all right now?"

Shelly nodded. "Of course. I just needed a friend to remind me that I was overreacting." She took a sip of the tea, surprised by how much it revived her. "You're still planning to see *Street Suite* with me tomorrow afternoon, aren't you?"

The recent Broadway hit was showing locally, and Shelly and Jill had purchased their tickets several weeks earlier.

"That's not tomorrow, is it?" Jill looked stricken, her teacup poised midway to her mouth.

"Jill…"

"I promised I'd work for Sharon Belmont. She's got some family thing she has to attend. She was desperate and I completely forgot about the play. Oh, dear, you'll just have to go without me."

"You're sure you can't get out of it?" Shelly couldn't help feeling disappointed.

"I'm sure. I'm really sorry, Shell."

Although frustrated that Jill couldn't come with her, Shelly decided to go to the theater alone. She wasn't pleased at the prospect and given her proclivity for running into Mark Brady, she didn't feel entirely convinced that this wasn't another attempt by the fates to regulate their lives.

However, if she stayed home, she'd be missing a wonderful play. Not only that, she'd be giving in to a nebulous and irrational fear, allowing it to take over her life.

The following afternoon, Shelly dressed carefully,

in the type of conservative outfit her mother would have approved of. Mark, too, would approve of her rose-colored linen dress with its matching jacket.... The minute the thought flashed through her head, she rejected it.

She was on her way out the door when her phone rang. For a split second she toyed with the idea of not answering. More than likely it was her mother, checking in to see if Shelly had met a prospective husband yet. Her calls had become more frequent and more urgent since Aunt Milly's dress had arrived.

Years of habit prompted her to reach for the telephone.

"Shelly." Mark's voice came over the line. "I was about to leave for the afternoon's performance of *Street Suite*. Since we seem to have this tendency to run into each other everywhere we go, I thought I should probably clear it with you. If you're going to be there, I'll go another time."

Chapter Eight

"ACTUALLY I WAS PLANNING to see the play this afternoon myself," Shelly admitted hesitantly. "Jill had to cancel out at the last minute."

"It seems Janice can't attend, either."

Hearing the other woman's name, the woman Mark loved, had a curious and unexpected effect on Shelly. Her heart sank, and she felt a sharp pang of disappointment. She rebounded quickly, however, forcing a lightness into her voice, a blitheness she didn't feel. "Listen, there's no need for you to miss the play. I'll call the ticket office and see about an exchange."

"No, I will," Mark offered.

"That's ridiculous. Jill really wanted to see this play and—"

"Would it really be so terrible if we both decided to attend the same performance?"

"Uh..." The question caught Shelly unprepared. Mark was the one who'd suggested they avoid each other.

"What could it possibly hurt? You have your ticket and I have mine. It'd be absurd to let them go to waste because we're afraid of seeing each other again, don't you think?"

Forming a single, coherent thought seemed beyond Shelly at that moment. After her long talk with Jill the day before, followed by the pep talk she'd given herself, she'd recovered a degree of composure. Now, all of a sudden, she wasn't sure of anything.

"I don't think it should matter," she said finally, although it did matter, greatly.

"Good. Enjoy the play."

"You, too."

The theater was within walking distance of her apartment building, and Shelly left as soon as she'd finished talking to Mark. He was right. Just because they each had tickets to the same play was no reason for either of them to be penalized.

So Mark was going to see *Street Suite*. It wasn't the type of play she would have thought he'd enjoy. But the man was full of surprises. Riding mopeds on the beach, kissing so spectacularly, and now this...

Shelly's mind was full of Mark as she hurried down the steep hill on Cherry Street. The theater was only a block away when she saw him. Her pulse soared and she wasn't sure if she should smile and wave or simply ignore him.

She didn't need to do either. He stood on the sidewalk, waiting for her.

"You're late," he said, glancing at his watch. "But then you traditionally are." His grin was wide and welcoming. "I couldn't see any reason not to watch the play together," he went on. "What do you say?"

"You're sure?"

"Positive." He offered her his arm, and she reflected that it was the kind of old-fashioned courtesy, the kind of gentlemanly gesture, she'd expected from Mark.

The usher seated them and smiled constantly as if to say they were a handsome couple. Shelly was terribly tempted to explain that Mark was engaged to someone else; luckily she managed to hold her tongue. Minutes after they'd settled into their seats, the curtain rose.

The play, a clever satire about urban life, was as good as the reviews claimed, and Shelly enjoyed herself thoroughly. Throughout the performance, however, she was all too aware of Mark sitting next to her. She found herself wondering if he was equally aware of her. She also found herself wondering how long it would be before they "bumped" into each other again—and hoped it was soon.

By the end of the play Shelly felt inspired and full of enthusiasm, eager to start a new project of her own. As she and Mark left the theater, she talked excitedly about her idea for the "ocean moods" series. He asked a few questions and even suggested some shots. Before she realized it, they were several blocks past the theater, headed in the opposite direction from her apartment building. Shelly paused and glanced around.

"There's an excellent Chinese restaurant in this neighborhood," was all Mark said. Without giving her the opportunity to decline, he gently guided her toward the place he'd mentioned.

It was early for dinner, and they were seated immediately. Although they'd been talking comfortably during their walk, Shelly found herself suddenly self-conscious. She toyed with the linen napkin, smoothing it across her lap.

"I hadn't expected to like the play as much as I did," he said after a while.

Shelly thought it a bit off that he'd ordered tickets for this production, but perhaps he'd gotten them because Janice had wanted to see *Street Suite*.

"It's a little frightening the way we keep finding each other, isn't it?" she ventured.

"I can see how *you'd* find it disconcerting," Mark answered.

"You don't?"

Mark shrugged. "I haven't given it much thought."

"I'll admit all these…coincidences do throw me," she said, running her index finger along the outline of the fire-breathing dragon on the menu cover. Chancing a glance in his direction, she added, "But I'm learning to deal with it."

"So you feel you've been caught in something beyond your control?" Mark surprised her by asking.

Shelly lifted her gaze to his, amazed by the intensity she read in his eyes. "No, not really. Well…a little bit, maybe. Do you?"

"It wasn't *my* aunt Milly who had the dream."

Shelly smiled and dropped her gaze. "No, but as my friend Jill reminded me recently, no fifty-year-old dress is going to dictate my life. Or yours," she felt obliged to add. Then she realized why he'd asked the question. "You must feel overwhelmed by all of this.

All of a sudden I've been thrust into your life. There's no escaping me, is there?'' she said wryly. ''Every time you turn around, there I am.''

''Are you going to stand up and announce to everyone in the restaurant that you refuse to marry me?''

''No.'' Shelly was appalled at his remark until she remembered that she'd done exactly that the first time they met.

''If you can resist doing that, then I think I can bear up under pressure.''

Shelly ignored his mild sarcasm. ''I'm not interested in marriage yet,'' she told him seriously—just in case he'd forgotten. ''I'm content with my life. And I'm too busy for a husband and family.''

She hadn't noticed how forcefully she was speaking until she saw several of the people at other tables glancing in her direction. Instantly she lowered her voice. ''Sorry, my views on marriage seem to be more fervent than I realized. But I'm not about to let either my mother or my dear aunt Milly determine when I decide to settle down and marry.''

''Personally, I can't see you ever settling down,'' Mark said with a small grin. ''You don't have to worry. When you're ready, you'll know it.''

''Did you?'' She hadn't meant to bring up Janice, but now seemed as good a time as any to remind him—and her—that there was someone else in his life.

Mark shrugged casually. ''More or less. I took a good, long look at my life and discovered I'd already achieved several of my professional goals. It was time to invest my energy in developing the personal aspects of my life. Marriage, children and the like.''

Mark made marriage sound as if it were the next chapter in a book he was reading or a connect-the-dots picture. Shelly couldn't stop herself from frowning.

''You have a problem with that?''

''Not a problem, exactly. I happen to think of marriage a bit differently, that's all.''

''In what way?''

He seemed genuinely interested, otherwise she would have kept her opinions to herself. ''People should fall in love,'' she said slowly. ''I don't think it's necessary or even possible to plan for that to happen. Love can be unexpected—it can take a couple by surprise, knock them both off their feet.''

''You make falling in love sound like a bad case of the flu.''

Shelly smiled. ''In some ways, I think that's exactly how it should be. Marriage is one of the most important decisions in anyone's life, so it should be a *deeply felt* decision. It should feel inevitable. It's the union of two lives, after all. So you can't simply check your watch and announce 'it's time.''' She was suddenly concerned that she'd spoken out of turn and might have offended him, but one quick glance assured her that wasn't the case.

''You surprise me,'' Mark said, leaning forward. ''I would never have guessed it.''

''Guessed what?'' She was beginning to feel a little foolish now.

"That a woman who gives the impression of being a scatterbrain is really quite reflective. Beneath those glow-in-the-dark sweatshirts lies a very romantic heart."

"I seem to have a tendency to get emotional about certain things," she answered, studying the menu, eager to change the subject. "I've heard hot-and-sour soup is wonderful. Have you ever tried it?"

Their conversation over dinner remained light and amusing. Shelly noticed that Mark avoided any more discussion of a personal nature, as did she.

After they'd finished their dinner and Mark had paid the bill, they leisurely strolled back toward the theater. Mark offered to drive her home when they reached his parked car, but Shelly declined. Her apartment was only a couple of blocks north and she preferred to walk.

Walk and think. Their time together had given her plenty to think about.

"Thank you for dinner," she said as he unlocked the car.

"You're welcome," he answered. "Well, good night for now," he said, grinning. "I suspect I'll be seeing you soon."

She grinned back. "Probably within a day or two. Maybe we should synchronize our schedules," she teased.

"That wouldn't bother you, would it?"

"Oh, no. What about you?" She hated the way her voice rose expectantly with the question. She certainly wasn't bothered by the prospect of seeing him again. In fact, she was downright eager to see what tricks fate would play on them next.

Mark's eyes found hers then, and he slowly pocketed his car keys. His look was so potent, so full of emotion, that Shelly took a step in retreat. "I had a wonderful afternoon, a wonderful evening. Thanks again," she said nervously.

Mark didn't say a word as he continued to gaze at her.

"The play was great, wasn't it? And dinner…fabulous." Shelly's throat seemed to close as Mark stepped onto the curb and walked toward her.

The whole world seemed to come to a sudden, abrupt halt when she realized he intended to kiss her. *Not again,* her mind shouted. *Please hurry,* her heart sang.

Her heartbeat tripped wildly as Mark lowered his head, his mouth seeking hers. Despite the fierce battle inside her, Shelly was forced to admit how much she wanted this kiss. If for no other reason, she told herself, than to prove that the first time had been an accident, a fluke.

Only it happened again. But this kiss was a hundred times more compelling than the first one they'd shared. A hundred times more exciting.

Shelly wanted to cry out at the unfairness of it all. If a man's kiss was going to affect her this acutely, why did it have to be Mark Brady's?

He broke away from her reluctantly, his warm breath fanning her cheek. His eyes were filled with questions, filled with surprise. Shelly wasn't sure what her own eyes were saying to him. She didn't even want to know.

"Take care," he whispered as he turned away.

SHELLY STAYED home from work on Monday. She wasn't sick, just confused and puzzled. Nothing about her relationship with Mark seemed to make sense. He was everything she *didn't* want in a man—and everything she did.

Shelly didn't realize how despondent she was until she found herself standing barefoot in front of her closet, carrying on a conversation with Aunt Milly's wedding dress.

"I'll have you know I had a perfectly good life until you arrived," she muttered disparagingly. "Now it seems my whole world's been turned upside down." She slammed the door closed, then jerked it open. "No wonder Mrs. Livingston's cat wouldn't go near you. You're *dangerous*."

Chapter Nine

"THE PLAY WAS GREAT," Shelly told Jill over coffee Wednesday afternoon. She'd stopped off at PayRite, hoping Jill could get away for lunch. "Even Mark—"

"Mark?" Jill's coffee cup hit the saucer with a clang. "He was at the play?"

Shelly nodded sheepishly. "I guess I forgot to mention I ran into him, didn't I? Actually he called me first and since we both had plans to attend the same performance, we decided to go together."

"Is there anything else you haven't told me?" Jill's eyes narrowed astutely.

Shelly tried to hide her uneasiness behind a relaxed shrug, but how well she succeeded in fooling Jill remained to be seen. "We had dinner afterward...as friends. It didn't mean anything. I did tell you he's engaged, didn't I?"

"*Unofficially* engaged." Jill was studying her closely and Shelly felt distinctly uneasy under the scrutiny.

"We've been friends for a long time," Jill reminded her. "In some ways I know you as well as I do myself. There's something troubling you."

Shelly nodded, knowing it wouldn't do any good to hide the truth from Jill. Her need to confide in a sympathetic, understanding person was the very reason for her impromptu visit to Jill's workplace. Lunch had been a convenient excuse.

"You won't believe this," Shelly said, cradling the warm coffee cup in both hands and keeping her gaze lowered. "I can hardly believe it myself."

"You're falling in love with Mark."

Shelly's gaze shot upward. "It shows that much?"

"No," Jill said softly. "But you look like you're about to break into tears."

"If I wasn't so darn irritated I would. Good grief, think about it. Can you imagine two people less suited to each other? Mark is so…so responsible…"

"So are you."

"Not in the same way," Shelly argued. "He's so sincere and…"

"Shelly, so are you."

"Perhaps, but I'm such a scatterbrain. I'm disorganized and always late and I like to do things my own way. You know that better than most."

"I prefer to think of you as creative."

Shelly tossed Jill a smile of appreciation. "That's the reason you're my best friend. I don't mind telling you, Jill, I'm worried. Mark Brady may be the Rock of Gibraltar, but I sincerely doubt he's got an original thought in his head. Everything is done by the book or according to schedule."

"You need someone like Mark in your life," Jill returned kindly. "Don't look so shocked. It's true. The two of you balance each other. He needs you because you're fun and crazy and imaginative, and you need him because he knows his times tables by heart and will remind you when it's time for meals.''

"The problem is, Mark's the type of man who would expect a woman to *cook* those meals."

Jill chuckled.

"If the fates are determined to match me up with someone," Shelly moaned, "couldn't it be with someone other than an accountant?"

"Apparently not."

"What really angers me about this is that I allowed it to happen. The first time he kissed me—"

"He *kissed* you?" Jill feigned a look of horror.

Shelly ignored it. "Yes. A couple of times. It's only natural—our being curious about each other, don't you think?"

"I suppose," Jill said quickly, no longer teasing. "So tell me what happened."

"Fireworks bigger than the Fourth of July. I've never experienced the feelings I do with Mark, and all because of a simple kiss. I can't even begin to imagine what would happen if we ever made love."

"And does Mark feel the same thing?"

"I—I can't speak for him, but I think it must be equally disturbing for him. He certainly looked as if he'd been taken by surprise."

"How do you get along with him otherwise?"

"Fine, I guess." Shelly paused long enough to take a sip of her coffee. "I'm sure I amuse him. But someone like Mark isn't looking for a woman to entertain him, any more than I'm looking for a man to balance my checkbook."

"His opinion of you has mellowed, hasn't it?" Jill asked, then answered her own question. "There was a time when he thought you were a little bizarre, remember?"

Shelly did, all too well. "At first I thought he was about as exciting as oatmeal, but I've altered my opinion of him, too."

"So what's the problem?"

"I don't *want* to fall in love," Shelly said pointedly. "I've got bigger plans for my life than to tie myself down to a committed relationship right now."

"Then don't. It shouldn't be that difficult. Decide what you want and ignore everything else. There's no law that says you have to fall in love this minute. For that matter, no one can regulate when and who you marry, either. Not even your aunt Milly."

Jill was saying everything Shelly wanted to hear. Everything she needed to hear. But it didn't make any difference; her heart was already involved. If she could forget she'd ever met Mark, she would. But it was too late. She was in love with him. With Mark, who was in love with someone else. Mark, who saw love and marriage as goals to be achieved within a certain time frame. He'd probably never done anything impulsive in his life.

A lasting relationship would never work between them. If he wasn't smart enough to figure that out, she was. Something had to be done and soon, and Shelly knew it would be up to her to do it.

SHELLY DIDN'T HAVE LONG to wait before she saw Mark again. They met at the main branch of the Se-

attle Public Library Wednesday evening. She was returning ten overdue books. Six months' overdue. The
library had sent her three warnings, each one pro-
gressively less friendly.

She was half-afraid the buzzer just inside the library entrance would go off the moment she walked
through the hallowed doors and armed officers would
haul her away.

"I wondered how long it would take for us to find
each other again," Mark said, strolling up to her at
the counter. She'd seen him almost immediately and
tried to pretend she hadn't.

Shelly acknowledged him with a quick nod and
ordered her heart to be still. She managed a small
smile. "Hello again," she said, drawing the checkbook out of her purse. The fine for the books was
sure to be monstrous. It might be cheaper to buy
them.

Mark set the two volumes he was borrowing on the
counter. Shelly noted the titles—*Tools for Time Man-
agement* and *The State of the Language,* and groaned
inwardly. To someone like her accountant friend,
these books were probably easy reading. Her own
tastes leaned more toward mystery and romance, with
a little nonfiction.

"Have you got time for a cup of coffee?" Mark
asked as she wrote out the check to pay her fine.

Her heart was gladdened by the invitation, but she
knew she had to refuse it. Before he could say or do

anything to change her mind, she shook her head. "Not tonight, thanks."

His smile faded as though her refusal took him by surprise. "You're busy?"

She nodded, smiling at the librarian as she tore the check free and handed it to the woman, who smiled pleasantly in return. It had been a civilized exchange, Shelly thought, and her library card had *not* been confiscated, despite her transgressions.

"A date's waiting for you?"

It took Shelly a second to understand that Mark was referring to her refusal to join him for coffee.

"Not exactly." She turned away from the counter and headed toward the exit. To her surprise Mark followed her outside.

"Something's wrong," he said, standing at the top of the steps. She stopped her descent and stood below him, looking up. Pretense had never suited Shelly; she was too innately honest to hide her feelings. "Mark, I think you're a very nice man—"

"But you don't want to marry me," he concluded for her. "I've heard that line before, remember? Actually half the mall heard it, too."

"I've already apologized for that. It's just that...all right, if you must know, I'm beginning to like you...really like you, and frankly that terrifies me." She stood facing him, two steps below.

Her candid response seemed to unnerve him. He frowned and rubbed the side of his jaw. "I know what you mean. I'm beginning to like you, too."

"See!" she cried, tossing her hands in the air. "If

we don't take care of this problem now, heaven only knows what could happen. It has the potential of ruining both our lives. We're mature adults, aren't we?'' At the moment, though, she felt singularly lacking in maturity.

All her senses were clamoring, telling her to enjoy their brief time together and damn the consequences. It was what her heart wanted, but she couldn't allow her life to be ruled by her heart. Not when it came to Mark.

''Liking each other doesn't have to be a federal crime,'' he said, advancing one step toward her.

''You're right, of course, but I know myself too well. I could easily fall in love with you, Mark.'' She didn't dare admit she already had. ''Before we knew how it happened, we'd be spending more and more time with each other. We might even become seriously involved.''

He remained suspiciously silent.

''You're a wonderful man. If my mother were to meet you she'd be shouting from the rooftops, she'd be so grateful. For a while I might convince myself that we could really make something of this relationship. I might even consider taking cooking classes because you're the kind of man who'd expect a woman to know how to make a roast and mashed potatoes.''

''It'd probably come in handy someday,'' he admitted.

''That's what I thought,'' she murmured, disheartened. ''I'm not a traditional woman. I never will be.

The only time I ever baked a pie I ended up throwing it in the garbage disposal—and it broke the disposal.''

"A pie ruined your garbage disposal?" Mark repeated, then shook his head. "Never mind, don't bother explaining how that happened. It seems to me you're getting ahead of yourself here. You're talking as though coffee together means a lifetime commitment."

Shelly wasn't listening. "What about Janice?" she demanded. "She's the one you should be inviting to coffee, not me."

"What's Janice got to do with this?" he asked impatiently.

"Janice," Shelly snapped, her own temper short. "The woman you've decided to marry. Remember her? The love of your life? The woman you're unofficially engaged to marry."

"It's not unofficial any longer," Mark explained evenly.

"Oh great, you're taking me out to dinner, kissing me and at the same time picking out engagement rings with another woman." She had to admit he'd never lied to her about his relationship with the faceless Janice. From the beginning he'd been forthright and honest about the other woman. But it hurt, really hurt, to learn that he was going ahead with his plans to marry Janice.

For a moment she'd been shocked into stillness. "Then..." She struggled to force some enthusiasm into her voice. "Congratulations are in order. I wish you both the very best." With that she turned and bounded down the stairs, taking them recklessly fast.

"Shelly!"

She could hear Mark calling after her, but she ignored him, desperate to get away before the lump in her throat made it impossible to breathe. Tears had formed in her eyes and she cursed herself for being so ridiculous, for caring so much. Her vision blurred and she wiped a hand across her face, furious with herself for the lack of control. This marriage was what she'd hoped would happen. What she wanted for Mark. *Wasn't it?*

"Shelly, for heaven's sake, will you wait?"

When she reached the bottom of the steps, Shelly moved quickly into a side street, hoping to disappear in the crowd, praying Mark wouldn't pursue her.

She thought she'd escaped until a hand on her shoulder whirled her around.

"Shelly, please listen," Mark pleaded breathlessly, his shoulders heaving with the effort of catching up with her. "The engagement isn't official, because there isn't an engagement. How could I possibly marry Janice after meeting you?"

Chapter Ten

"YOU BROKE OFF your engagement with Janice?" Shelly demanded furiously. Something inside, some reservoir of emotion, felt as if it had burst wide open. "You fool," she cried. "You idiot!" Her eyes brimmed over with tears and deep, deep inside her heart began its stirrings of glad excitement. "That was the worst thing you could have done!"

"No," he said. "It was the smartest move I've ever made."

"How can you say that?" she wailed.

"Shelly?"

He reached for her as though to offer comfort, but Shelly jerked her arms away and stepped back, freeing herself from his grasp. "Janice was perfect for you," she lamented.

"How do you know that?" he asked calmly, much too reasonably to suit Shelly. "You never met her."

"I didn't need to. I know she was right for you. You'd never have asked her to marry you if she wasn't."

"Janice is a wonderful woman and she'll make some lucky man a good wife, but it won't be me."

"You're crazy to break off your engagement. Crazy!"

"No, I'm not," Mark returned confidently. "I'm

absolutely certain I did the right thing. Do you know why?''

Shelly could only shake her head, wiping away the tears with the back of her hand. She was ecstatic—and yet she was so frightened. She loved him, she was sure of it. Then why had everything become confused and difficult?

''What you said about love the other day changed my mind.''

''You listened to me?'' she cried in real horror. ''Do I look like an expert on love? I've never been in love in my life!'' Not counting what she felt for him, of course. She'd always thought love would clarify her life, not make it more complicated.

Mark ignored her outburst. ''You helped me understand that I was marrying Janice for all the wrong reasons. I'd decided it was time to settle down. Janice had come to the same conclusion. She's thirty and figured if she was going to marry and have a family, the time was now. It wasn't a love match, and we both knew it.''

''This is none of my business,'' Shelly said, frantically shaking her head as if to chase the words away. ''I don't want to hear any of it.''

''You are going to hear it,'' Mark insisted, gripping her elbows and gently drawing her closer to him. ''You claimed people shouldn't plan love. It should take them by surprise, you said, and you were right. Janice and I are fond of each other, but—''

''There's nothing wrong with fond!''

His eyes widened in obvious surprise. ''No, there

isn't," he agreed, "but Janice isn't a zany video producer. I like spending time with you. I've come to realize there's a certain thrill in expecting the unexpected. Every minute with you is an adventure."

"A relationship between us would never last," Shelly insisted, drawing on the most sensible argument. "It would be fine for a while, but then we'd drift apart. We'd have to. In case you haven't noticed, we're nothing alike."

"Why wouldn't a relationship last?" Mark asked patiently.

"For all the reasons I listed before!" Mark was so endearing, and he was saying all the words she'd secretly longed to hear, but nothing could change the fundamental differences between them.

"So you aren't as adept in the kitchen as some women. I'm a fair cook."

"It's more than that."

"Of course it is," he concurred. "But there's nothing we can't overcome if we're willing to work together."

"You know what I think it is?" she said desperately, running her splayed fingers through her hair. "You're beginning to believe there's magic in Aunt Milly's wedding dress."

"Don't you?"

"No," she cried. "Not anymore. I did when I was a little girl...I loved the story of how Aunt Milly met Uncle John, but I'm not a child anymore, and what seemed so romantic then just seems unrealistic now."

"Shelly," Mark said in exasperation. "We don't

need to do anything right away. All I'm suggesting is we give this thing between us a chance."

"There's nothing between us," she denied vehemently.

Mark's eyes narrowed. "You don't honestly believe that, do you?"

"Yes," she lied. "You're a nice guy, but—"

"If I hear any more of this nice-guy stuff I'm going to kiss you and we both know what will happen."

His gaze lowered to her mouth and she unconsciously moistened her lips with anticipation.

"I just might, anyway."

"No." The threat was real enough to cause her to retreat a couple of steps. If Mark kissed her, Shelly knew she'd be listening to her heart and not her head. And then *he'd* know… "That's what I thought." His grin was downright boyish.

"I think we should both forget we ever met," she suggested next, aware even as she said it how ludicrous she sounded. Mark Brady had indelibly marked her life and no matter how much she denied it, she'd never forget him.

"Are you forgetting you threw yourself into my arms? *You* can conveniently choose to overlook the obvious, but unfortunately that won't work for me. I'm falling in love with you, Shelly."

She opened her mouth to argue that he couldn't possibly love her…not yet, not on such short acquaintance, but he pressed his finger to her lips, silencing her.

"At first I wasn't keen on the idea," he admitted,

"but it's sort of grown on me since. I can see us ten years in the future and you know what? It's a pleasant picture. We're going to be very happy together."

"I need to think," she cried, placing her hands on either side of her head. Everything was happening much too quickly; she actually felt dizzy. "We'll leave it to fate…how does that sound?" she offered excitedly. It seemed like the perfect solution to her. "The next time we bump into each other, I'll have more of a grasp on my feelings. I'll know what we should do." She might also take to hibernating inside her apartment for a month, but she wasn't mentioning that.

"Nope," Mark returned, slowly shaking his head. "That won't work."

"Why not?" she demanded. "We bump into each other practically every day."

"No, we don't."

He wasn't making any sense.

"*Street Suite* was a setup," he informed her. "I made sure we bumped into each other there."

"How? When?"

"The day at the beach I saw the play ticket sticking out of your purse. Our meeting at the theater wasn't any accident."

Mark couldn't have shocked her more if he'd announced he was an alien from outer space. For the first time in recent memory, she was left speechless. "Tonight?" she asked when she could get the words out. "The library?"

"I'd decided to stop off at your apartment. I was

prepared to make up some story about the wedding dress luring me into your building, but when I drove past, I saw you coming down the front steps loaded down with library books. It didn't take a whole lot of figuring to know where you were headed. I found a parking space and waited for you inside.''

"What about...the IRS office and the beach?" She didn't know how he'd managed those chance meetings.

Mark shook his head and grinned. "Coincidence, unless you had anything to do with those. You didn't, did you?"

"Absolutely not," she replied indignantly.

Still grinning, he said, "I didn't really think you had."

Shelly started walking, her destination unclear. She felt too restless to continue standing there; unfortunately the one action that truly appealed to her was leaping into his arms.

Mark matched his own steps to hers.

"It's Aunt Milly's wedding dress, I know it is," Shelly mumbled under her breath. She'd tried to bring up the subject earlier, but Mark had refused to listen. "You broke off an engagement because you believe fate has somehow thrown us together."

"No, Shelly, the dress doesn't have anything to do with how I feel," Mark responded calmly.

"But you'd already decided to marry someone else!"

"I'm choosing my own destiny, which is to spend the rest of my life with you."

"You might have consulted with me first. I have no intention of getting married...not for years and years."

"I'll wait."

"You can't do that," she cried. He didn't understand because he was too respectable and adorable and so much of a gentleman. The only thing that would work would be to heartlessly send him away before he wasted the better part of his life waiting for her.

She stopped and turned to face Mark. She was careful to wear just the right expression of remorse and regret. "This is all very flattering, but I don't love you. I'm sorry, Mark. You're the last person in the world I want to hurt."

For a moment Mark said nothing, then he slowly shrugged and looked away. "You can't be any more direct than that, can you? There's no chance you'll ever fall in love with me?"

"None." Her breath fell harshly, painfully, from her lips. It shouldn't hurt this much to do the right thing. It shouldn't hurt to be noble. "You're very nice, but..."

"So you've said before."

Falteringly, as though the movement caused him pain, he lifted his hand to her face, his fingers tenderly caressing the delicate curve of her jaw.

Until that moment, Shelly hadn't understood how fiercely proud Mark was. He could have dealt with every argument, calmed every doubt, answered every question, but there was nothing he could say when she denied all feeling for him.

"You mean it, don't you?" he asked huskily. He was standing so close that his breath warmed her face.

Shelly had schooled her features to reveal none of her clamoring emotions. His touch, so light, so potent, seemed to clog her throat with anguish, and she couldn't speak.

"If that's what you want—" he dropped his hand abruptly "—I won't trouble you again." With those words, he turned and walked away. Before she fully realized what he intended, Mark had disappeared around a corner.

"You let him go, you idiot!" she whispered to herself. A lone tear escaped and she smeared it across her cheek.

Mark meant what he said about not bothering her. He was a man of his word. He'd never try to see her again—and if they did happen upon each other, he'd pretend he didn't know her.

He might eventually decide to marry Janice. Hadn't he admitted he was fond of the other woman?

Shelly's heart clenched painfully inside her chest. Before she could stop herself, before she could question the wisdom of her actions, she ran after Mark.

She turned the corner and was halfway down the sidewalk when she realized he wasn't anywhere to be seen. She came to a skidding halt, then whirled around, wondering how he could possibly have gotten so far in so short a time.

Mark stepped out from the side of a building, hands

on his hips, a cocky, jubilant smile on his face. "What took you so long, darlin'?" he asked, holding out his arms.

Shelly didn't need a second invitation to throw herself into his embrace. His mouth feasted on hers, his kiss hungry and demanding, filled with enough emotion to last a lifetime.

Shelly slid her arms around his neck and stood on her tiptoes, giving herself completely to his kiss, to his love. The only thing that mattered was being in his arms—where she was supposed to be.

"I take it this means you love me, too?" he whispered close to her ear. His voice was rough with emotion.

Shelly nodded. "I'm so afraid."

"Don't be. I'm confident enough for both of us."

"This is crazy," she said, but she wouldn't have moved out of his arms for the world. Breathing deeply, she buried her face in his chest.

"But it's a good kind of crazy."

"Aunt Milly saw us together in her dream. She wrote me about a tall, blue-eyed man."

"Who knows if it was me or not?" Mark whispered into her hair, and brushed his lips over her temple. "Who cares? If fate had anything to do with me finding you or if your aunt Milly's wedding dress is responsible, I can't say. Personally, I couldn't care less. I love you, Shelly, and I believe you love me, too."

She glanced up at this man who had altered the course of her life and smiled, her heart too full for words. "I do love you," she said when she could. "An accountant! In a suit! Hardly the husband I imagined for myself."

Mark chuckled. "I'd never have guessed I could find myself head over heels in love with a woman who wears the kind of clothes you do, but I am."

"I do love you," Shelly repeated and closed her eyes.

THE MORNING of her wedding day, Shelly, who was rarely nervous, couldn't sit still. Her mother was even worse, pacing in front of her, dabbing her eyes and sniffling.

"I can't believe my baby's getting married."

Shelly had to restrain herself from reminding her dear mother that less than a month before, she'd been desperate to marry her daughter off. Thank goodness Jill was around. Without her best friend there to re-assure her, Shelly didn't know what she would have done. While her mother fussed with the caterers, complained to the florists and fretted about who had a key to the kitchen in the reception hall, Jill led Shelly upstairs to her childhood bedroom and helped her dress. When Shelly was finished, Jill stood back to examine her.

"Well?" Shelly asked, smoothing her hand down the antique dress, loving the feel of the satin and lace against her fingers. It was probably her imagination but now that she was wearing the dress, really wearing it, she could almost feel a magic quality.

Tears gathered in Jill's eyes as she stared at her friend.

"That bad?" Shelly teased.

Jill pressed her fingertips to her lips. "You're beautiful," she whispered. "Mark isn't going to believe his eyes when he sees you."

"Do you really think so?" Shelly hated sounding so insecure, but she wanted everything perfect for this day. She was crazy in love—and crazy enough to give her mother free rein planning her wedding. Crazy enough to go through with a formal wedding in the first place. If it had been up to her, they'd have eloped weeks ago. But Mark had wanted the wedding and her mother certainly wasn't going to be cheated out of this moment. So Shelly had gone along with it.

Mark and her mother had defeated the majority of her ideas. She'd wanted to hire clowns to entertain at the reception, but her mother didn't seem to think that was a good idea.

Shelly had never been that fond of white wedding cake, either. She wanted something a bit less traditional, like Cherries Jubilee, but Mark was afraid something might catch on fire and so in the interests of safety, Shelly had agreed to a traditional cake, decorated with pink roses.

A knock sounded on her bedroom door and Jill opened it. In walked Aunt Milly, looking absolutely delighted with herself.

She introduced herself to Jill, then turned to gaze lovingly at Shelly. "So I see the dress worked."

"It worked," Shelly agreed.

"You love him?"

Shelly nodded. "Enough to eat white wedding cake."

Milly laughed softly and sat on the edge of the bed. Her hair had faded to gray, but her eyes were still blue and clear. It was difficult to tell that she was a woman well into her seventies. She clasped both of Shelly's hands in her own.

"Nervous?"

Shelly nodded again.

"I was, too, although I knew to the very bottom of my heart that I'd made the right decision in marrying John."

"I feel the same way about Mark."

Aunt Milly hugged her tightly. "You're going to be very happy, my dear."

AN HOUR LATER Shelly and Mark stood at the front of a packed church with Pastor Johnson, who'd known her most of her life. He smiled warmly as he spoke a few words, then asked Shelly to repeat her vows.

Linking hands with Mark, she raised her eyes to his. Everyone else faded away. Aunt Milly. Jill. Her mother. There were only the two of them. She felt a jolt of pure joy at the love that radiated from Mark's eyes. He stood tall and proud, his gaze eagerly holding hers, the love shining through without doubt, without question, shining through for her to read. Shelly knew her eyes told him the same thing.

Later, Shelly couldn't remember speaking her vows

aloud, although she was sure she did. The words came directly from her heart. Directly from Mark's.

They'd been drawn to this place and this time by forces neither fully understood. Shelly wasn't entirely sure she believed Aunt Milly's wedding dress was responsible, but it didn't matter. They were there out of love. She didn't know exactly when it had happened. Perhaps that day on the beach, when Mark first kissed her. Something had happened then, something that touched them both.

The love that began as a small spark had grown and flared to life until they'd been brought here, to stand before God and family, pledging their lives to one another.

To love. To cherish. All the days of their lives.

It was enough. More than enough.

Jacob's Girls
Tara Taylor Quinn

CHAPTER ONE

"I DON'T KNOW about you, but that woman can sing to me anytime. That was Celine Dion with 'The Power of Love' on KOLR as we get you to work on time. I'm Jacob Ryan…"

"…and I'm Michelle Colby, on 'color,' your station at the end of the rainbow."

"You wanna do the weather or shall I?"

"You go ahead. You do it so well."

"So I've been told."

"The weather, Jacob, the weather."

"Yeah, well, it looks like it's going to be a hot one today, folks…" He grinned at Michelle. She grinned back. What the…? Hell, it was happening again.

Jacob finished the weather report, but he was shaken. For a second there he'd actually wished their sexual banter was more than an act for the show. The prospect of his upcoming meeting this morning must have had him more off kilter than he'd realized.

While Michelle announced a giveaway, he glanced at the AP bulletin that had just come over the wire. Then he leaned toward his mike. "For all of you heading into work this gorgeous Monday morning, let's check in with Officer Barb Jansen in the traffic 'copter. You there, Barb?" he asked.

"I'm here, Jacob, and we've got some good news this morning..." Barb's voice piped into the sound booth. Jacob shut her off. They had three minutes until they were on again. He needed some peace and quiet.

"YOU OKAY?"

Michelle was watching him, a pair of scissors in one hand as she clipped an article out of the local newspaper spread in front of her.

"Couldn't be better," he said. It wasn't true, but confiding in people wasn't something that came easily to him. He picked up the *Wall Street Journal*, looking for anything that might interest their listeners.

"You seem a little preoccupied."

Damn her for noticing. And damn her even more for letting him know she'd noticed. They were casual friends, workmates, but that was all. "Hey, who wouldn't seem a little preoccupied at six o'clock in the morning? It's called 'not awake yet,'" he said lightly.

She gave him a pointed look, telling him she wasn't buying it, but she went back to clipping news articles for them to use on the show. And that was when he realized he was actually tempted to tell her about Friday's phone call, to ask her opinion. What the hell was wrong with him these days?

"IT'S EIGHT-O-NINE on this gorgeous January morning, and in just a few minutes we'll be talking with football superstar Joe Montana, so keep your dial right where it is on ninety-four-point-five, KOLR. But first we have a special anniversary wish to send out...." Jacob clicked off his mike and half listened while Michelle took over to congratulate a couple of Los Angeles natives on their fiftieth wedding anniversary.

Only another hour and he'd be on his way to Lomen Elementary School to tackle whatever crisis awaited him there. The next time they called him from school asking for a conference he was going to insist on meeting with the principal immediately. He'd been driving himself crazy all weekend with possible scenarios of the triple trouble his daughters could have concocted. But really, how bad could it be? They were only seven years old. It wasn't as if they were at an age to skip classes or be caught smoking in the locker room....

"What do you think, Jacob? A day at the beach sound good?" Michelle's voice cut into his ruminations.

He reached automatically for the button that would turn on his mike. "With you?" he asked, a standard comeback. But for once he really thought about what he was saying. He could imagine a lot worse things than a day at the beach with Michelle.

"That depends," she said.

"On what?" he asked, reminding himself that they'd been trading this kind of banter for almost three years, that it meant nothing.

"On whether or not you plan to wear those ridiculous boxer trunks you wore to the company picnic last summer. I gotta tell you, they didn't do anything for your legs.''

"They hung down to my knees. You couldn't see my legs." She was looking at him, but she wasn't laughing the way she usually did when they played their on-air roles. For the first time in three years, the sound booth seemed small to him.

"My point exactly." She stuck out her tongue and grinned. So that was that. She'd just been playing with him—as usual.

"Well, I'd love to fill you in on this little racing suit I've got, but it's time to get Joe Montana on the line," Jacob said, a tad peeved. Which was ridiculous. Michelle was doing the same professional job she'd done ever since they'd started cohosting the morning show. He was the one acting weird.

He punched in the blinking button on the phone and looked to Michelle.

"Joe? Michelle Colby here on KOLR. We're on the air...."

Jacob sat back, disgusted with himself. Not only was Michelle his partner, she was a married woman. And while Jacob enjoyed the company of many women, he stayed away from the married ones—always. Besides, however casual, Michelle was his friend, and Jacob never slept with his friends—ever.

HE STOPPED HOME after the show to change his sweats for a pair of off-white cotton slacks. Stepping over three little pairs of sandy beach shoes in the garage, he was glad to be away from the station. His reaction to Michelle that morning was still bothering him. They worked well together. And no matter how beautiful she was, he wasn't going to let his libido mess up a good thing.

He passed through the kitchen, clean except for the cereal bowls, through the living room cluttered with Dr. Seuss books, past a huge bedroom with three unmade beds, to the master bedroom in the back of his beach house. Of course if he was to be honest with himself he'd have to admit that what was bothering him most was how close he'd come to pouring out his concerns over the triplets to Michelle when he was perfectly capable of handling his children's problems on his own.

His sweats landed in the general vicinity of the laundry basket. He tucked the KOLR T-shirt into the waistband of his slacks and slipped on a pair of canvas loafers. Glancing in the mirror over his sink, he wondered if he looked as tired as he felt. His hair, dark and a little too long, was slightly mussed but it would do. He was ready to take whatever the school principal had to dish out.

MICHELLE SPED along the 405 toward Long Beach, weaving in and out of the traffic with the ease of a California native. She had to get home, far away from Jacob Ryan.

Not once, in all the years since she'd met Brian Colby, had she been seriously tempted by another man. She was in love with her husband, and damn

Jacob's cocky, sexy-as-hell attitude for making her forget that—even for a minute.

She exited the 405, past the car dealership where Brian had taken her to buy her first new car, the Thunderbird she still drove. He'd planned the car as a surprise for her college graduation, and he'd preened like a rooster as he'd handed her the keys. They'd driven for hours that night, taking turns at the wheel as they'd traveled along the California coastline.

And then, sometime after midnight, they'd pulled into a deserted cove, climbed into the back seat and made love till dawn. Brian was a tender lover, always thinking about her pleasure as much as his own. He'd made love to her slowly, savoring every second, and afterward they'd fallen asleep in each other's arms, cramped in the back seat. Michelle could still almost feel that warm safe haven they'd created, with Brian on one side of her, and the seat back, smelling of new leather, on the other. And then, when the sky had changed from black to purple to a hazy gray, he'd made love to her again, caressing every inch of her body, telling her with his hands how much he adored her. Their bodies had still been linked when the sun finally rose, and Brian had teased her that nice girls didn't romp all night in the back seats of cars. Then, his eyes having grown serious, he'd whispered her name. And he'd promised to love her forever.

Tears blurred Michelle's vision as she turned into her neighborhood, and she hurriedly blinked them away. She'd promised to love Brian forever, too. Which was why she had no business flirting with another man—especially not Jacob Ryan. If there was one thing Michelle had learned from her parents long happy marriage it was that loyalty was everything. Jacob didn't know the meaning of the word. As much as she valued his friendship, she despised his womanizing. His liaisons were too casual to be considered relationships. He never dated the same woman twice in a row—twice in a week, perhaps, but not twice in a row.

Maybe that was why her body had responded to him this morning. After five years of silence, she finally had a small lead on Brian's whereabouts. She was geared up, coming alive again. And Jacob was safe. Lusting after him was safe. He'd never take her up on it. He never slept with women he had to see in the morning.

She pulled the Thunderbird into her cracked driveway, trying not to notice how run-down the neighborhood had become in the past couple of years. She'd had the house painted. She had her lawn mowed once a week. But while she could certainly afford to have the driveway repaved, she knew that any money she put into the place was money wasted. It was time to move. And she would—just as soon as she found Brian. Until then, she wasn't budging from the tiny home they'd bought together.

Fumbling with the dead bolt on her front door, she swore softly, anxious to get inside and check her answering machine. Frank Steele, the private detective she'd hired several months before was in Egypt. Brian had been working as a foreign correspondent in Cairo at the time of his disappearance, and Frank thought he'd found someone who might have a lead on his whereabouts. It was the first time she'd heard anything of her husband since he'd ordered breakfast from room service five years ago.

The minute she was in the door her fluffy white cat wrapped herself around Michelle's legs. No one had ever told Noby that cats were supposed to be standoffish. Michelle scooped the Persian up, rubbing her face in Noby's soft fur as she hurried to the little bedroom she'd converted into a den.

The red light on her answering machine wasn't blinking. No messages. Michelle ran the machine through its cycle, anyway, just to be certain it was still working.

"This is the Colbys. We're not here right n—"

Noby put her soft front paws on Michelle's cheeks, kneading and purring, as Michelle clicked off the message Brian had recorded so many years ago. Frank had said he'd call as soon as he had something. And unlike the government officials who'd finally given up and pronounced Brian legally dead, Frank Steele *had* to call her. She was paying him a good portion of her salary to do so. It was just a matter of waiting until he had something to report.

JACOB LOVED WOMEN. They intrigued him. Introduce him to a woman, young or old, fat or skinny, and he could usually find something about her to like.

Not this time. From the moment Lomen Elementary School principal Eleanor Wilson ushered him into her office, Jacob didn't like her. She reminded him of his mother—impossible to please.

But unlike his mother, Ms. Wilson had the power to make Jacob's life difficult. Which was why he immediately took the seat she indicated, a hard-backed, walnut-colored torture device set directly in front of her slate gray desk. Feeling like he was twelve again, he folded his hands in his lap.

"Mr. Ryan, there are several situations I feel I must make you aware of concerning your daughters."

Ms. Wilson's short dark hair looked as stern as she did. Jacob sat up straight and smiled encouragingly. After all, they were on the same side, weren't they?

"In the past month, Alison, Jessica and Meghan have been to the nurse's office a total of thirteen times."

"Thirteen times? That's crazy. They haven't been sick."

"A couple of times Allie brought Jessie in from the playground."

Jacob tried to relax. "She fell out of the swing again, right? That kid can't hold on and pump at the same time. She's too busy creating fairy tales in her head. I swear that Jessie's going to be a writer some day."

Ms. Wilson pursed her pale lips. "She didn't fall out of a swing, Mr. Ryan. They've all three been complaining about stomachaches...."

"But that's ridiculous. They've never once told me their stomachs hurt and they're eating like a pack of hogs," Jacob said, thoroughly confused.

"They've also had sore throats, headaches, cramps and fatigue."

Jacob's hands fell to his sides. "Cramps and fatigue? Fatigue? Are we talking about the same bundles of energy that have my house trashed ten minutes after they come home from school?"

Ms. Wilson tapped a pencil against the top of her desk. "They're a little young for cramps, too, unless you know something we don't?"

"What? Oh," Jacob said, feeling stupid. "No, I mean, yes, they're too young for that."

"Well, as you can imagine, we've become quite concerned—"

"Wait just a minute here." Jacob leaned forward, placing his palms on the edge of her desk. "Are you implying that I'm not taking proper care of my daughters? Because if you are you can stop right there. Meggie, Allie and Jessie are all healthy as horses. You just have to spend an hour playing with them to know that. Even the sea gulls run for cover when the girls are on the beach. And why am I just hearing about this now after it's already reached the point where you're *concerned?* Isn't it standard to notify a child's parent when the child isn't feeling well?"

Ms. Wilson's lips softened, her eyes filling with something close to sympathy as she nodded. So maybe he'd been mistaken about her resemblance to his mother. "And we would have called, but each time we started to the symptoms mysteriously disappeared, leaving us no reason to contact you."

"Disappeared?" Jacob sat back, frowning. The hard wooden slats of the chair dug into his back.

"Your daughters aren't sick, Mr. Ryan. They're looking for attention."

Jacob froze. He knew he wasn't good at relationships, but surely he wasn't failing his own daughters.

"I give the girls more attention than most kids receive in a household with two parents," he said, knowing he was right. He spent all of his free time with them. It had to be enough.

"I know you do. You're to be commended for the effort you put into being a father. The girls benefit greatly from your guidance and love. But they're girls. And I suspect that they need some feminine influence, too."

Jacob gritted his teeth. "Before you suggest it, I'm not about to go out and find another wife just to be a companion to my daughters. They've done all right without one for the past four years. This is probably just another stage they're going through. I'm sure it'll pass like the others have." Jacob stood up. "I'll talk to them about visits to the nurse. I can assure you it won't happen again."

"Sit down, Mr. Ryan."

Jacob took one look at the woman's serious expression and sat.

"Alison is organizing her teacher to death. As you know, this is the first year she's been separated from her sisters, and she's lost without them. Instead of playing with the kids in her class, she spends her days making suggestions about what the other students should be doing and trying to help the teacher give them their instructions.''

"She's always had a lot of initiative. That, combined with her incessant drive to organize, is going to serve her well in life." He knew he sounded rather pompous, but he didn't need this. His triplets were the one thing he'd done right.

"Initiative is good, I agree, but not when it's taken to such an extreme. Not only is it disruptive to the rest of the class, but we'd be remiss to ignore what appears to us to be Alison's cry for help. Last Friday, she sneaked out of the lunch room, tricked her way into the staff lounge by saying she had an emergency and proceeded to inform her teacher that they needed to rearrange the classroom seating—put the students in alphabetical order, she said—and if the teacher liked, she'd be willing to stay in at recess to help her do it."

Jacob shrugged, wondering if the principal wasn't overreacting a bit. "So she's a little obsessive. We'll work on it. I fail to see how this points to a need for female guidance."

"Not even when Alison's plan would've given her a recess period alone with her teacher *and* put her in the seat right next to the teacher's desk?"

Jacob rubbed his forehead. He hadn't realized that Allie was so fond of her teacher. "Like I said, I'll talk to them."

"Jessica's crying has become much too frequent."

There was more? Jacob stared at the principal as worry crept past his defenses and started to knot his stomach. He was facing what every parent dreaded—a child with problems. Only apparently he had three of them.

Ms. Wilson came around to the front of the desk, crossing her arms. "The reasons for her tears are always different—bumping her leg on a desk, catching her finger in the pencil sharpener, getting a bad grade on a paper—but the pattern is always the same. With a hug from her teacher, the tears stop immediately. Lately it's been happening almost daily. We believe that Jessica, like her sister, is reacting to a need for a woman's love."

"Maybe. Or maybe—"

"She's more forgetful than normal, too. She's had to get her lunch money from Alison three times in the past week, and she's forgotten several assignments. I'm afraid her grades are dropping, Mr. Ryan."

"Jessie's a normal seven-year-old girl. She's taken up with fantasies right now, but just wait until she masters reading. She'll be more studious than both of her sisters, mark my words."

"I'm not saying any of your children are abnormal, Mr. Ryan. I'm saying they're sending out signs and it's our job to recognize. Meghan has become almost reclusive. In class she refuses to work or play with anyone but Jessica. And if Jessica's busy, Meghan occupies herself on her own. She resists any attempts her teacher makes to include her in games with the other children."

Jacob's gut clenched. This wasn't something he

could rationalize away. He'd been concerned for a while now about Meggie's holding herself apart. He'd tried to give her some extra attention, to cuddle her a little more, but nothing seemed to be working.

At a complete loss he stared at Ms. Wilson. Meggie's behavior worried him. Unlike Jessie, who lived in a dreamworld much of the time, Meggie seemed just plain lonely to him, which was ridiculous considering she had two identical sisters around her practically twenty-four hours a day.

"A couple of weeks ago, the teacher put her arm around Meghan while she was explaining a math problem," Ms. Wilson continued. "Meghan jerked away and told her teacher not to touch her—ever."

Jacob studied the pearl buttons running the length of Ms. Wilson's blue-flowered dress. He had a problem. Okay, he'd faced that much. Now what in hell was he going to do about it?

"Have the girls said anything to you about the try-outs for the spring play?" Ms. Wilson asked, returning to her seat.

Jacob shook his head, surprised by the change in subject. "Come to think of it, they haven't. Which is odd, since that's all they talked about over Christmas break. They love acting."

"They're very good at it, too," Ms. Wilson said with a nod. "And that's why it concerned us when they started telling anyone who'd listen that acting is dumb."

"My girls are saying that? But why?"

"I suspect it has to do with the costumes. The

school doesn't have money for costumes this year. Instead of canceling the play, we decided that each actor or actress would be responsible for his or her own costume. And to keep things fair, they all have to be homemade.''

Jacob was beginning to get the picture. Out of necessity he'd mastered a lot of skills over the past several years. But he knew nothing about sewing. And his daughters were well aware of it. He'd made it into something of a joke so they wouldn't feel as if he was incapable of caring for them.

''You got any suggestions?'' Jacob asked, meeting Ms. Wilson's concerned gaze. The bottom line was, he'd do whatever it took to keep his girls happy.

She folded her hands together. ''One you may not want to hear, Mr. Ryan. Your daughters need a woman in their lives. From several things the girls have said, their teachers and I believe they're blaming themselves for the fact that there isn't one. I'm not suggesting you rush out and get married, but apparently you aren't even in the habit of bringing your dates home to meet them. They think it's because they're too much trouble.''

Jacob felt sick. All he'd hoped to do was protect his girls from further desertion. He'd had no idea they'd misconstrued things so completely. ''I'll talk to them,'' he said again.

''You need to do more than talk, Mr. Ryan. If you don't have a current woman friend to introduce them to, hire a housekeeper, but I wouldn't put this off.''

''I have a perfectly good housekeeper. Nonnie

Moore has been keeping house for fifty years and she's damn good at it. She comes in twice a week like clockwork, and any other time I need her to help out. They have a baby-sitter, too. Laurie's a nice responsible teenager and she loves the girls.''

''They've mentioned Laurie, and I've seen Nonnie a time or two when she's come for the girls. I assumed she was their grandmother. Apparently she doesn't hear as well as she used to.''

''She's seventy-five years old, but she takes excellent care of us.''

''I'm not doubting that, Mr. Ryan. But a seventy-five-year-old woman is hardly companion material for three lively seven-year-olds. And a teenager, however sweet, can't give the guidance of a grown woman. I must tell you, the next step we take here on an official level is the school counselor.''

''Are you threatening me?'' Jacob asked, rising to his full six foot one.

''Absolutely not,'' Ms. Wilson said, not intimidated by Jacob's glare.

''No one's going to take my daughters away from me. You can call in all the officials in the state. Call in the whole damn army if you want but my daughters stay with me. I'm a damn good father, and I'll hire the best lawyer in the country if I have to to prove it.''

Ms. Wilson's thin hand descended on Jacob's arm, giving it a gentle squeeze. ''I wish all fathers were as conscientious, as caring, as you are, Mr. Ryan. The last thing the school wants to do is break up your home. We're only trying to help avoid more serious behavioral problems somewhere down the road. Your daughters are young. They're psyches are still being molded. Now's the time to give them the very best in all possible ways.''

Jacob nodded, covering the principal's hand with his own. ''I'll talk to them,'' he said.

Ms. Wilson sighed as she watched him leave her office. The man was what her older students would call a hunk. His chocolate brown eyes and irresistible grin exuded sex appeal and charm with every breath he took. There must be thousands of women in L.A. who'd be only too happy to set up housekeeping with him, even it meant taking on a set of triplets as impish as the Ryan girls. Jacob Ryan even made *her* heart beat a little faster, and it had been more years than Eleanor could count since that had happened.

She liked Mr. Ryan. She admired and respected him for raising those three girls on his own. But more importantly she was fond of his daughters, and worried about them. It wasn't proper for a school principal to play favorites, but Eleanor knew that, just this once, she was. Still, there was only so much she could do. The rest was up to their father.

CHAPTER TWO

MICHELLE KEPT HER EYE on the little black ball. Her arms ached, her lungs were burning, but her gaze never wavered. The court echoed as the ball smacked against the front wall. Michelle dove, flinging her racket out to her right just in time to see the ball fly over her outstretched arm. Damn! He'd put a back spin on it. She landed with a crash on the wooden floor.

"Nice match, sweetheart. You gave me a run for my money on that last set." James Walker reached out a hand to help his daughter up off the floor.

Michelle grinned ruefully. He was barely even sweating.

"Someone's got to keep you in your place," she said, rising and giving him a quick kiss on the cheek before she gathered her gear. "Meet you out front in twenty minutes?" she asked, water bottle, racket and towel in hand.

He held the door open for her. "Make it fifteen, and I'll buy you a soda."

"You're on."

Michelle turned toward the women's locker room but not before she'd seen the appreciative glance a young woman in the hall had sent her father's way. At forty-eight, James Walker would have been considered quite a catch if he hadn't already been caught thirty years before. Tall and lean, he still had a full head of blond hair that blended well with the few strands of gray that were starting to filter through it. Ever since Michelle could remember he'd attracted attention from the opposite sex, but not once had it crossed Michelle's mind to wonder if he might be interested in following up on some of the more overt glances. After thirty years of marriage, James Walker was still so entranced with his wife it would have been laughable if it weren't so darn sweet.

"HOW WAS YOUR GAME?" Grace Walker asked as her family came in through the back door forty-five minutes later. Gray-haired and plain, she was busy at the counter chopping vegetables for the Mexican feast the three of them shared every Tuesday evening after James wore Michelle out on the racquetball court.

"I would've beat him, but I decided to be nice today," Michelle said, giving her mother a kiss.

Grace's gaze met her husband's, her soft blue eyes alight with humor. "Did you trounce her?"

He smiled, leaning down to kiss his wife before helping himself to the pile of shredded cheese. "It won't be long before she's trouncing *me*," he said, stealing one more lingering kiss from his wife before he left the room.

"Right," Michelle said. "The day I win my first game with Dad, I'm going to announce it on the air."

She filled a glass with ice and popped the top on a can of diet cola.

Then she hoisted herself onto one of the stools at the breakfast bar and asked, "So how were things at the clinic?" Every Tuesday afternoon, while Michelle and her father battled it out on the racquetball court, Dr. Grace Walker donated her time to a free clinic in a part of L.A. that tourists never saw.

"Busy as usual, but nothing too terrible turned up. A couple of ear infections, a strep infection and the usual cases of head lice. All easily remedied."

"Did Amanda Blake show up for her prenatal check?"

"Yep. That's three in a row. We just may get that baby born healthy yet."

"So you think she's staying clean?"

Grace shrugged her slim shoulders. "She's either clean or hiding the evidence miraculously well. The baby's heartbeat is steady and strong. I think we have a fighting chance."

"And afterward?" Michelle knew her mother wouldn't be able to deliver the baby and then just forget it.

"Amanda wants this baby. That's half the battle won. If she stays clean for the next four months, we're well on our way to winning the second half."

Grace finished chopping the onions and lettuce, popped the tortillas in the oven and stirred the refried beans. Michelle got up to set the table.

"Any more word from Frank Steele?" Grace asked.

"Nope."

Grace brought the condiments, arranged in a sectioned serving tray, to the table. "How much longer are you going to give him?"

"As long as it takes," Michelle said, putting out napkins.

"Do you think that's wise?"

Michelle stared at her mother. "How can you ask that, Mom? You of all people know I don't have any other choice."

Grace's brow creased with concern and she reached out to smooth Michelle's hair back from her face. "I don't like what this is doing to you, honey. You have no life anymore, no friends."

"I have a life, Mom. I work out at the gym three times a week, I play racquetball every Tuesday, I have a job I love—a job that lets me go places and meet people—I have my crafts, and I have Noby."

"Noby aside, those are just *activities,* honey. They may fill up your time, but they won't fill you up inside. I'm afraid your soul is going to wither, and one day you'll wake up and find out it's gone."

"I have you and Dad."

Grace's lips tightened. "It's not the same, Michelle. You know it's not. You used to have so many friends I couldn't keep track of them. Every time I talked to you, you were running off to help one of them or on your way to a party. You thrive on people, just like I do. Needlework, no matter how beautiful, and jobs, no matter how satisfying, can't take the place of people in your heart."

"I gave my heart to Brian. As long as there's a chance he's alive, it's not mine to take back."

"He has only a part of your heart, honey. What about the rest? What happened to Sarah and Jaime? I haven't heard you mention either of them in months."

"I still talk to Sarah, but with her new job, any free time she has she likes to spend with Roger. It's the same with Jaime. She's on a husband hunt again and inevitably has some guy in tow. I'm always the odd one out. Believe me, I'm happier at home with Noby than feeling like a fifth wheel every time I leave my house. Besides, I don't think they understand about Brian. Ever since he was declared dead they've been after me to start dating again."

Grace bent to take the tortillas out of the oven. "And maybe you should."

"What?" Michelle's shock was evident in her voice.

"You're twenty-eight years old, Michelle. Brian's been missing for more than five years. At some point you're going to have to either get on with your life or die right along with him."

Michelle paled. "How can you say that? I finally have word on Brian and all of a sudden you want me to give up on him?"

"The word is three years old, honey."

"But it's still more than I had a month ago."

"I'm just afraid this is going to drag out forever, Michelle, with a word here and there, just enough to keep you hoping. And then one day you'll realize your whole life has passed you by. You've always wanted a family more than anything else—you'd be a wonderful mother. But it's never going to happen if you don't lay the past to rest and start building a future for yourself.''

"You're saying I should just call Frank Steele and tell him thanks but no thanks. That I should forget Brian, forget the vows I made to him, the love we shared, and go find some other man to father my children?" Michelle's voice was clogged with tears.

"I'd never suggest that you forget any of it, sweetheart. I know how much you loved Brian. Your father and I loved him, too. I'm only saying that maybe it's time for you to consider the possibility that Brian isn't coming back.''

Michelle looked at her mother. "Would you, Mom? If it was Dad missing, would you give up, ever, if there was one iota of hope?''

Grace held her daughter's gaze for a long second and then turned away. "If you run low on money to pay Frank's fees, let us know. Your father and I will give you whatever you need.''

JACOB WAS WAITING, already in his swim trunks, when the girls got home from school. He knew they'd want to take advantage of the unseasonably warm weather with a swim in the ocean.

"What's for a snack?" Allie asked as she led the line coming in through the front door of the beach house. Her long dark hair was falling loose from the ponytail he'd put it in that morning.

"I want peanut butter," Jessie said, following right behind her sister. She was missing a barrette.

"Hi, Daddy," Meggie said, dropping her book bag on the floor as she headed for the refrigerator. She'd braided her hair sometime after he'd left them that morning. There were straggling pieces sticking out all over her head.

"How was school?" Jacob asked, depositing three granola bars on the table. He reached past Meggie to grab the milk, then shut the refrigerator.

"Okay. Billy Martin spilled his juice at lunch and cried. Only babies cry, don't they, Daddy?" Allie said as the three girls slipped into their chairs at the table. He used to have a smoked-glass tabletop. Now he had Formica. It was a breeze to clean and easily replaceable.

"It's not babyish to cry, is it, Daddy?" Jessie asked, waiting while Jacob opened her granola bar for her.

"Babies *do* cry," Meggie said, using her teeth to rip open her snack.

First talk, coming up. Jacob poured three glasses of milk, glad he could start with an easy one. "Of course babies cry. It's their only form of communication. But there are other reasons for crying, too. If you're sad or lonely or hurt you might cry. There are times when it's best to get those feelings out, so they don't bother you anymore. But sometimes people cry just because they don't control their feelings very well, like if they're mad or embarrassed or disappointed. If all goes well you learn to express those emotions differently as you grow up.''

"We're grown-up, Daddy, aren't we, you guys?'' Allie looked at her sisters, her mouth full of granola bar.

Jessie and Meggie nodded dutifully. And suddenly Jacob was faced with three sets of solemn brown eyes as the girls waited for his confirmation.

"Well, darlin's, grown-ups work before they play, so I guess that means you have to make your beds *before* you put on your bathing suits. You better hurry up if you want to be outside while it's still high tide.''

Jacob smiled at the three identical little faces scowling up at him. His daughters slid from their chairs and left the room, clearly unamused. He rinsed the milk glasses and wiped the crumbs from the table. And two minutes later he was shaking his head in resignation. The noise coming from the triplets' room was only one level below deafening. They were singing, if you could call it that, the L.A. Lakers Jam Session rap song at the top of their lungs.

THE OCEAN WAS TOO COLD, in spite of the January heat wave, for any real swimming, but the girls managed to get soaked, anyway. They did a fairly good job of soaking their father, too. Jacob finally retreated to sit well out of reach of their splashing. He watched his daughters play for a while, grinning at their happy squeals as they ran from the waves. All three of them wore fluorescent green, one-piece swimsuits; he remembered when he'd bought them. The girls had complained about the "gross" color. "All the better to see you with, my dears," he'd growled, and they'd giggled, just like he'd expected them to do. They didn't need to know how serious he'd been about his reason for the blindingly bright suits.

Jacob stretched his legs out in front of him, leaning back on his hands, watching while Allie organized a sand-castle construction crew. Jessie and Meggie played along, apparently content to be her laborers. God, how he loved them.

The muscles in his gut tightened as he watched them play together. How did a man tell his daughters that he wasn't as perfect as they thought he was? That he'd driven his wife away just as he had his parents before her? How did he convince them that their mother loved them, even though she'd left them? Eleanor Wilson had said that the girls thought they were too much trouble, but that wasn't true. Not to him. Never to him. Somehow he had to convince them of that.

Jessie darted over, bobbing up and down in front of him. "I have to go."

"Be sure to clean your feet before you go in," he said. He kept one eye on Allie and Meggie at the edge of the ocean while he watched Jessie run up the beach to their cottage. She stepped into the small tub of clean water he kept by the door, wiped one foot on the mat beside the tub and raced into the house. Oh, well, the floor could withstand a few wet footprints.

"What's for supper?" Allie asked half an hour

later. She plopped down in the sand beside Jacob, playing with the dark hairs on his forearm.

"Macaroni and cheese, but I want to talk to you guys first. Get your sisters for me, please?"

"JESSIE! MEGGIE! DADDY WANTS YOU!" Allie hollered.

Jacob covered his ears. "I could've done that myself," he told Allie, giving her what he hoped was a look of disapproval.

Jessie ran over and sat on Jacob's other side, spraying him with sand and seawater as she leaned her arm against his outspread thigh. "Wadja want?" she asked, grinning at him.

"What?" Meggie asked, bringing up the rear. She sat in front of Jacob, her expression serious.

"I've been thinking, since you guys are so grownup now and all, that maybe it was time we talked about your mother."

His stomach sank when he intercepted the worried looks that passed between his daughters. Ms. Wilson had been right on the mark. The girls' motherless state was bothering them more than they'd let on to him.

They stared up at him silently, expectantly.

"Your mother is a very beautiful woman," he said, wondering where on earth he was going to go from there. "You guys take after her."

Jessie smiled. Allie fiddled with the hair on his arm again. Meggie still stared silently. Jacob would've given just about anything to know what they were thinking.

"She loves all of you very much," he said, telling the lie without flinching. He'd grown up without the security of his parents' love. His children weren't going to suffer the same fate.

"Then why doesn't she ever come to see us?" Allie asked, her brows drawn together in a frown.

"She lives and works very far away from here."

"How far?" Meggie asked.

"All the way across the United States. She's a senator's, um, aide, at the White House."

Jessie tapped his leg. "What's an umaide, Daddy?"

Jacob took a deep breath. He should have guessed that the girls wouldn't be satisfied with the vague answers he'd hoped to give them.

"Aide, Jess. It's someone who stays close to a senator and helps him with things so that he can do his job better." At least Jacob hoped Ellen helped Senator Keller with something more than undressing at night.

"What kind of things?"

"Well, Al, things like entertaining prominent people and maybe writing important letters. Stuff like that."

"Can we go visit her sometime?" Meggie's small face was virtually expressionless.

"Maybe sometime. When you get a little older and don't need a baby-sitter, in case she has to go out and meet someone important for dinner or something."

"Weren't we important enough, Daddy? Is that why she left us?" Jessie's big brown eyes were filling with tears. Jacob felt sick, and he floundered for words as he hugged Jessie against his side. Her wet, sand-covered suit grated against his skin, but he couldn't have cared less about the discomfort.

"You guys are the most important people I know," he said, pinning each of them with his "I mean it" stare. "Your mommy didn't leave you. She left *me*. I wanted her to be someone she wasn't. Senator Keller liked her just as she was."

"Didn't you like her at all?"

Jacob pulled Meggie onto his lap and hugged Allie to his other side. "Of course I liked her, honey. I chose her to be your mommy, didn't I? But I wanted a different kind of wife than she wanted to be, and I guess I'm just a little too hardheaded sometimes. I wouldn't give in, and as much as she tried, your mommy couldn't be happy with me," Jacob wondered if he was making any sense.

"You're not hard in the head, Daddy. You're the best daddy in the whole world," Meggie said, laying her cheek against him. Her long black hair fell around her shoulders, tickling his chest.

"And I love being your daddy more than anything in the world, Meg, but your mommy and I just wanted to live our lives in two different ways. My way made her unhappy. You wouldn't want her to be unhappy would you?"

All three girls shook their heads. "Well, I didn't want to make her unhappy, either. So when Senator Keller asked her to go to Washington and she wanted to go, I told her it was okay with me."

"Did you miss her when she was gone?" Jessie's question was soft, hesitant.

"For a while, but I had you guys to keep me company, and we've done all right, don't you think?"

Meggie sat up. "Did you love Mommy a lot?"

"Not like I love you three," he said, though in his heart he didn't know how he could have loved a woman more than he had Ellen McCormick.

"Maybe we were bad, Daddy. Maybe we cried too much and she just didn't want to tell you," Allie said, her little face dejected.

"And we probably didn't pick up our toys, either," Jessie added.

"Yeah, and I'll bet we spilled stuff a lot, 'cause we were only babies then," Meggie said.

Impotent rage swept through Jacob as he realized that his words were falling on three sets of deaf ears. The thoughts the girls were expressing were obviously not new to them. And worse, in spite of all he'd said, they still believed them. So how the hell did he convince them of anything different?

"You guys were great babies. You loved to eat. And you slept a lot, too, giving us lots of time to keep up with stuff. Your mother used to love to take you out and show you off." The showing-off part was true. If only Ellen hadn't been so overwhelmed by getting three babies ready to go and in their car seats all at once.

"Where did she take us, Daddy?"

"To the mall. She liked to shop."

"Then why didn't she get a job at the mall and

take us there every day? Wouldn't that have made her happy?''

I'm blowing it. ''Because she couldn't work all the time, and when she came home to me she would've been unhappy. If we'd been madly in love like mommies and daddies should be, then she wouldn't have left even if we had a whole houseful of kids.

''Don't you love your girlfriends enough, either, Daddy? Is that why you never bring them home?''

''It's because of us, Jess,'' Meggie said, sounding far more adult than a seven-year-old had any business sounding. ''Remember Jennie? She didn't want to be our mommy, either.''

''That's not true!'' Jacob said, knowing he was failing miserably, but still finding himself without divine inspiration. The girls had taken his breakup with Jennie, his former on-air partner, hard at the time—she'd been the first woman he'd dated after Ellen left—but he'd had no idea they still remembered her.

''Yes, it is true, Daddy. Katie Walters's mother says we're a handful. She said if she'd had three to take care of all at once, she'd probably have left, too. We heard her tell that to Bobbie's mommy.''

Jacob bit back the curse that sprang to his lips. Just wait until he saw Katie Walters's mother.

''Katie Walters's mother doesn't know what she's talking about,'' he said. ''Jennie just wasn't in love with me. That's why we quit seeing each other. Believe me, it had nothing to do with you guys. Doing for three is just as easy as doing for one. It takes a little longer, that's all.''

Allie stood up suddenly. "Can we eat now, Daddy? My stomach's shocking it's so hungry.''

Jacob knew they weren't finished, not by a long shot, but it was probably best to do these things in small doses. He figured the girls had had enough for now; he knew he had.

"Last one to the shower has to load the dishwasher," he called, jumping up to race his daughters to the house.

Meggie was the first one to reach the outside shower head he'd installed right after the girls had learned to walk. It had only taken one houseful of sand to convince him he'd either have to rig up some outdoor plumbing or move. Meggie stood under the stinging spray, offering only a token argument when her sisters crowded in on her. Jacob knew she had to have an awful lot on her mind to put up with that without a fuss. He was in for a long haul.

ALLIE ENDED UP having to load the dishwasher, but only after Jacob declared that he didn't count since he'd made the dinner. At Jacob's urging, Jessie and Meggie helped their sister by clearing the table and rinsing the dishes. Jacob had the job of storing the leftovers.

"What's happening with that play—*Cinderella*—everyone was so excited about after Christmas?" he asked as he opened the refrigerator.

Jessie dropped a fork and looked at Allie. Meggie

stopped spraying and looked at Allie. Allie stood with a dripping plate in her hand.

Jacob found a place for the container of macaroni. "Did they call it off or something?"

"Uh-uh," Allie finally found her voice. "The trying-out part is next week."

"So who's trying out for what?"

Jessie and Meggie resumed their duties, glancing furtively at Allie.

"We're not sure yet," Allie said. Her voice was an octave higher than usual.

"We don't have costumes, Daddy," Jessie blurted, then dropped a knife covered with butter in the middle of the floor. Jacob watched as she took a wadded up napkin from the table and smeared the butter over the linoleum. Thank God for washable floors.

"If you get a part, we'll get you a costume," he told her.

"They have to be homemade, Daddy," Meggie said. She and Allie exchanged glances.

"Then we'll make them."

"They have to be *sewn*," Allie said.

"We'll handle it, girls. Have I ever let you down before?"

Three heads shook vigorously.

"Now, what parts are you trying out for?"

"Cinderella," Jessie said.

"And her two evil stepsisters," Allie and Meggie chorused.

LIGHTS-OUT WAS at eight o'clock sharp. It used to be at seven o'clock, but Daddy had added an hour after they turned seven. They were almost all grown-up now, and everybody knew that staying up late was part of the deal. Allie snuggled under her covers and waited for Daddy to kiss Jessie and Meggie goodnight. He'd already done her. He would turn off their light on his way out the door, and then he'd tell them that he was right down the hall if they needed him. She never had figured what he thought they might need him for when they were sleeping, but it was kinda good hearing him say it, anyway.

"I'm right down the hall if you need me." The words came just as Allie had known they would.

"'Night, Daddy," she said.

"'Night, Daddy." Jessie was always next.

"'Night, Daddy," Meggie said last, just like every night.

Allie waited until she heard Daddy's shower start and then climbed out of bed. She tapped Jessie on the shoulder.

"What?" Jessie's eyes looked funny, like she'd been asleep already.

"Come on." Allie tugged Jessie up and pulled her over to Meggie's bed. They always had their meetings on Meggie's bed.

Meggie sat up and made room for them.

"Daddy seemed pretty sad today," Allie said.

"Probably because he was talking about Mommy," Meggie said, picking at the foot of her sleeper.

"Do you think he's mad at us for making Mommy

leave him?'' Jessie asked, her lips all shaky like she was gonna cry. Allie exchanged a glance with Meggie. Daddy would get them for sure if they made Jessie cry.

"Shh." Allie scooted over to give Jessie a hug. "You don't want Daddy to hear us. I don't think he's mad at us, but we better really be gooder just in case." Allie looked at both of her sisters, making sure they were paying close attention to her. "We don't want to make him mad enough to leave us, too."

Meggie and Jessie nodded. Allie patted Jessie's hair. "And if we're going to have to do the trying outs, then we're just gonna have to try not to be too good."

Jessie frowned. "But, Allie, it's okay now. Daddy said he'd make—"

"Daddy can't sew, Jess, you know that." Meghan frowned at her sister.

"But he said—"

"Jessie—" Allie drew out the name like she'd heard Daddy do "—it's Daddy's job to say those things."

Meggie nodded and after a couple of seconds Jessie did, too. But she didn't seem convinced.

Allie hoped her sister wasn't going to screw things up. She didn't even want to think about making more trouble for Daddy. She just wanted Daddy to be happy living with her and Jessie and Meggie. She lay back down in her own bed, wishing she hadn't messed up Daddy's tuck-in. She wondered if Daddy knew that she'd been wishing for a mother. Feeling guilty and ashamed, she looked across at her sisters. She was afraid her wish might ruin everything.

JACOB STOOD under the shower until the water turned cold, but it did nothing to ease his worries. Ms. Wilson's suggestion that he find a woman for the girls sounded valid, but he knew in his heart that a woman wasn't the answer to his problems. He'd already tried that route shortly after Ellen had left him. And all he'd managed to accomplish was to confuse his daughters more. Maybe he'd wanted it too badly. Maybe he'd tried too hard. Or maybe he'd just expected more than anyone could give him. All he knew for sure was that he wasn't going to expose his girls to the possibility of further rejection. Twice in seven years was already too much, or they wouldn't be having the problems they were having now.

Walking into his bedroom, he rummaged in his drawer for a pair of boxer shorts and pulled them on, thinking back to the years of his own growing up. He still had scars from those years, albeit invisible ones. His real mother, a teen-pregnancy statistic, had given him up at birth. And after his adoptive parents divorced and subsequently remarried, they'd each had children of their own. They'd passed him back and forth between them as if they couldn't get rid of him fast enough.

Wandering out to the deck off his bedroom, he looked out at a light blinking on the ocean, remembering. The time he'd asked for a first-baseman's mitt had been one of the worst. He'd been so excited when his Little League coach had given him, a fifth grader, the honor of playing first base. Everyone knew a first baseman was one of the most important players on the defensive team. But when he'd asked his mom for a mitt, she'd told him to wait for his father to get it the following week. And when he'd been with his father, he'd been told that his mother would have to handle that one. As it turned out, the coach had lent him a mitt. He'd only been eleven at the time, but Jacob had felt the humiliation clear to his bones. He'd been barely able to make himself go to practice once his coach knew he wasn't worth enough to warrant a stupid baseball mitt.

He'd learned the lesson over and over again through his teenage years. There were celebrations for his half siblings' birthdays, while his were either forgotten or acknowledged with a card. There were school trips he couldn't take because his parents' "real" children always came first. By the time his high school graduation arrived, it hardly hurt at all when the seats reserved for his family were empty.

Jacob left the deck, walking through his silent house to the kitchen. He reached into the cupboard above the refrigerator, pulled out his bottle of scotch and poured himself a shot. Stopping only long enough to wipe the butter from the floor, he carried the glass back to his bedroom, looking in on the girls as he passed their open door. They hadn't been asleep long. Jessie's bear was still tucked in beside her and Meggie's covers were on top where they belonged. Satisfied that everything was as it should be, he returned to the deck and stretched out on the padded lounge. His kids were not going to grow up the way he had. They might have only one parent, but at least that parent loved them to distraction.

He took a sip of the scotch, savoring the taste, thinking suddenly of Michelle. Now there was a woman worth having. She was loyal to the core. It was too bad that the man she honored with her loyalty wasn't around to know what a lucky son of a bitch he was. If Jacob could ever find a woman who loved him the way Michelle loved Brian Colby…

Jacob stood up and tossed the rest of the scotch over the deck rail. He was getting maudlin. He had all the women he could handle, in miniature, sleeping right down the hall from him. They needed him and he needed to be there for them. He'd long since given up wanting anything more.

CHAPTER THREE

"I'M GOING TO BE a little late getting home today, but I'll make it up to you, Noby, I promise." Michelle gazed into the blue eyes across the table from her and refused to allow their unblinking stare to make her feel guilty. She took a sip of diet cola, her version of morning coffee, and picked up the Wednesday-morning newspaper. It was a rare treat for her to still be at home when the paper was delivered.

She read one headline before the newspaper was smashed to her lap. Those eyes were a lot closer—and demanding an explanation.

"Jacob and I are doing a remote broadcast at the new mall off La Cienega. I'm meeting him at the station at eight, we're driving over together, and we'll be done by two. That should put me home before four—in plenty of time for dinner."

Michelle took another sip of cola. The blue-eyed stare was relentless.

"You're not going to let me read my paper, are you?"

Still nothing but that silent stare.

"You're spoiled rotten." Michelle leaned over to plant a kiss between Noby's knowing blue eyes. "And I don't know what I'd do without you."

"AND THERE YOU HAVE IT, folks. Jacob Ryan and Michelle Colby are secretly involved in a wildly passionate relationship, which is open now for your viewing pleasure," Jacob muttered under his breath.

"Jacob." Michelle punched him playfully in the shoulder as they cleared the papers off their table in the main entrance of the mall. "It wasn't that bad."

Jacob unplugged their microphones, handing them to one of the KOLR technicians. "Admit it, Michelle. You just like having all those people drooling over me and envying you for having me."

"In your dreams, Ryan."

"Yeah, there, too," Jacob mumbled, reminded all too clearly of the dreams he'd had Monday night. Erotic dreams he could deal with. They came with the territory of the single man. But erotic dreams featuring Michelle Colby were something else entirely. As he'd told himself in no uncertain terms early Tuesday morning.

They finished clearing up, stopping several times to sign autographs, and in a matter of minutes were saying goodbye to the technicians who would drive the KOLR van back to the station. Jacob had to admit, if only to himself, that the broadcast had come off better than he'd hoped. Not because he'd had any doubts about his or Michelle's performance, but because for the past two days he'd had doubts about himself.

After all these years of working with Michelle, he was suddenly finding her more attractive than filet mignon. It made no sense. She certainly wasn't encouraging him. Hell, she wore her wide gold wedding band like a suit of armor. The woman was so tied up with a memory she probably wouldn't know what to do with a flesh-and-blood man if she had one. Or at least that was what he told himself.

And this morning it seemed to have worked. His libido was practically asleep.

"Would you mind if we made a quick stop before heading back?" he asked Michelle as she waved off the van. "I need to pick up something for the girls."

"I'm not in a hurry," Michelle replied, as easygoing as ever. Her blond hair swung over her shoulders as she turned toward the mall. In Jacob's dream it had been spread over his pillow.

He made a beeline for the department store where he did all his shopping for the girls. They'd had a minor crisis this morning, and he'd promised Allie he'd take care of it today.

"What are we looking for?" Michelle asked as she followed him into the store. He seemed to know exactly where he was going.

"Wednesday panties."

She looked to see if he was pulling her leg. "Pardon me?" she asked, trying to keep the laughter out of her voice when she saw he was serious.

"Allie couldn't find any Wednesday panties this morning. I don't know what happened to them, but they weren't in her drawer or in the laundry. I had a hell of a time getting her to go to school."

She could see the girls' department straight ahead.

"Uh, Jacob? What are Wednesday panties?"

"They're underwear with Wednesday written on them. There's a pair for every day of the week. Allie's obsessive about wearing the right pair on the right day."

"Oh." If anyone had ever told Michelle that she would be following Jacob Ryan into the girls' department to buy underwear, she'd have laughed them out of the city. "So how'd you get her to go to school?"

"Convinced her that if she wore both Tuesday and Thursday they'd average out to Wednesday."

Michelle burst out laughing and Jacob sent her an understanding grin. "I know. It's not the smartest thing I've ever come up with, but it was the best I could do on short notice."

He stopped in front of a rack of packages of pastel-colored underwear. Michelle watched as Jacob chose two packages of size-seven panties and four size-six ones. He obviously didn't realize that each package had an entire week's worth. Michelle smiled.

"Jacob? That's forty-two pairs of underwear," she said, trying to be gentle about educating him.

He just nodded as he moved through the department carrying all six packages. "I only go through each crisis once if I can help it. I'm going to put an extra day per person away in *my* underwear drawer."

Shying from thoughts of Jacob's underwear, Michelle wasn't sure which touched her the most, the ease with which he moved among the racks of miniature feminine apparel or the competent way he handled being a single father to three little girls. She did know that she envied him more than she'd have thought possible.

"Look at these." Jacob stopped by a rack of child-size Lakers jerseys. "They're great! The girls'll love them. Help me find two six-X's and a seven," he said, riffling through the shirts on the rack.

Michelle helped him find the sizes he needed and then followed along as he searched for three pairs of jeans to match. She was seeing a whole new side to Jacob Ryan. A side she liked far too much.

He took his choices to the register and handed over his credit card. "How are you today, Mr. Ryan?" the middle-aged clerk asked.

"Just fine, Joan, and you? Did you enjoy your trip to Florida?"

The clerk kept up her end of the conversation as she completed the transaction, but Michelle couldn't help but notice the glances she kept sending her. The glances weren't surprising. After all, she was used to speculation about Jacob and her. What shocked her was how disappointed she felt that there was absolutely nothing for the clerk to speculate about. Michelle had no business wishing she and Jacob *were* an item, and buying clothes for *their* children.

"You know, Jacob, if you end up with all this when you're just going after a single pair of underwear, I'd hate to see what happens when you shop for school clothes," Michelle said as they headed to his vehicle.

Unlocking Michelle's door before storing his package in the back of the Explorer, Jacob said, "A way

to a woman's heart is through the clothes department.'' At least he hoped the new clothes would help.

"Where'd you ever hear something like that?'' Michelle asked, grinning at him as he climbed behind
the wheel.

"God knows Ellen sure bought enough of them.
And I can remember my half sister's pleasure every
time my mother surprised her with something new.''
He turned his key in the ignition. He'd always told
himself it was because girls loved getting new clothes
that none of those surprises had ever been for him.

"So what have you done to upset your daughters?''

Jacob shot her a startled glance. "Why would you
think I've upset them?'' he asked, turning out into the
city traffic. Was he that transparent? Or worse, did
she know him that well?

"Why else would you think you need to buy your
way into their hearts?''

He could feel her looking at him. Really looking
at him. And he found himself wanting to tell her.
What could it hurt? She'd been a good buddy over
the years. And she was so tenaciously married to her
memory she was no threat to *him*.

"I think my place in their hearts is pretty much a
given. Though I'm not so sure it'll still be that way
a few years from now when they want to start wearing
crap on their faces and talk on the phone all the
time.'' He paused, wondering if he should stop right
there. He couldn't remember the last time he'd confided in anyone—not about something that mattered.

"So you just like to spoil them?'' she asked.

Jacob shook his head, well aware of the danger of overindulgence. "As a general rule they think I'm stingy with the goodies. But right now I don't want them feeling like they're missing out on anything." He turned onto La Cienega Boulevard, heading back toward the station. "I guess the jeans were a little overboard, considering that they already have enough clothes to get us through two weeks without doing laundry. I just wanted to do something to make them feel special."

Michelle was surprised by the concerned tone in Jacob's voice. He always seemed so invulnerable. She'd pretty much figured that if life ever did dare throw him problems, he'd just tackle them—or hire someone else to do it for him. But he'd been unusually preoccupied on Monday, too.

"Are you having some difficulties with the girls?" she asked, feeling rather tentative. Jacob wasn't the type one usually offered a shoulder to.

He shifted in his seat. "I don't know that I'd call it that exactly, but there seems to be a misunderstanding or two we need to clear up. The girls' principal called me last Friday. It seems there've been a few minor problems at school which they're attributing to a lack of feminine guidance in the girls' lives. Ms. Wilson seems to think that my daughters are blaming themselves for my divorce and subsequent single state."

"Did you talk with them about it?"

"Yeah. I talked. But I'm not sure they heard. In fact, I'm pretty sure they didn't."

"Did their principal have any suggestions?"

"Not really."

"She referred you to someone else?"

"No, though she did mention calling in a school counselor if things don't get better."

"So how does she expect that to happen?"

"The most obvious answer would be for me to marry again."

"Oh." Michelle didn't know why she should feel so deflated. "I guess that wouldn't be too difficult. Considering the number of women you've dated in the past year, you should have at least a hundred to choose from."

Jacob glanced at her oddly, and Michelle realized how she must have sounded. After all, why should she care if Jacob dated every eligible woman in the state of California? "I haven't dated a hundred women in the past *five* years, Colby."

"Fifty then."

"Thirty. Maybe. And since when have you been counting?"

"I'm not counting obviously." Michelle flushed with embarrassment, glad that at least half his attention was on the traffic. "So what'd you tell the principal?"

"That I'd talk to the girls."

"Which didn't work."

"Not yet, but it will. Like everything else, these things take time."

"I'd be glad to help out if they need anything meanwhile, Jacob. You know that, don't you?"

Jacob glanced over at her, his sexy brown eyes piercing. "What, you wanna marry me?"

For a split second the idea held way too much appeal, leaving her strangely depressed as she replied, "I'm already married."

"Hey, I was only teasing, Colby. Lighten up."

"I know you were. But I meant it about your girls, Jacob. I've only met them a couple of times, but they seem like great kids. I could spend some time with them. You know, do girl things. It'd be fun."

"Thanks, but that won't be necessary." Jacob answered so quickly Michelle knew he hadn't even considered her suggestion. "We've managed on our own thus far and we'll get through this, too. All they need is a little extra love and attention, and their insecurities will vanish just like their wet diapers did."

"Hey, I never meant to imply that you won't do just fine. It's obvious you have things well under control. But until Brian's home I've got time on my hands, and I can see where three little girls might benefit from having a woman around now and then. There are bound to be things that are understood differently from a female point of view. You know, like the importance of feeling pretty and falling in love with teddy bears."

"Just because I'll never feel some things doesn't mean I can't recognize or understand them. I'm not the first single father on earth, Michelle, and I damn sure won't be the last. Others have coped. So can I. But thanks for the offer. I appreciate it."

Michelle knew a brick wall when she smacked into

one. After all, she knew Jacob. What she hadn't realized until right then was just how much she would've enjoyed doing something for his children. For a brief moment there, when she'd heard herself offering to take Jacob's daughters under her wing, she'd felt almost excited. She had a gaping hole inside her that could use some filling up. And Jacob's children were safe. They belonged to him, not to her. She couldn't lose what she didn't have.

ELEANOR WILSON'S JOB was her life. She felt more at home in the school building than she did in her little two-bedroom bungalow a couple of blocks away. And as for her students, she loved them all, though admittedly some more than others. But she'd never felt as deep a fondness for any of them as she felt for the Ryan girls. Being triplets was enough of an oddity to make them stand out. Being beautiful, precious little girls made them easy to like. But being motherless bought them their special place in Eleanor's heart.

Which was the only reason she made it a point to attend the auditions for the spring play. Normally Eleanor avoided these auditions like the plague. In most cities children grew up encouraged to be doctors or lawyers. Not in L.A. Eleanor hated what the lure of Hollywood did to her students, but mostly she hated what it did to their parents. It seemed that for some, no sacrifice was too great if it meant their child might one day be on TV or in the movies. Several students at Lomen Elementary had agents already and missed school to go on auditions. And the parents of those who were just starting out weren't necessarily above attempting to bribe the school principal to get their children stage experience.

To be fair, some of the children were good. It wasn't that uncommon for Eleanor to see one of her students on a television commercial while she sat at home in the evenings. She'd watch with a twinge of pride while they tried to sell her cereal or tennis shoes or clothes freshener. Some of them were even convincing. But never had she seen three children just plain love acting the way Allie, Meggie and Jessie did. She wanted them in the school play.

She sneaked into the back of the auditorium and sat in the last row, not wanting to draw attention to herself. Slipping off her half-inch pumps, she swore to herself she'd just be an observer. She wasn't going to play favorites. She had faith that the triplets would win their parts all by themselves.

She watched myriad Prince Charmings amble onto the stage, some of them shy and quiet, some of them shouting lines that should have been heartfelt. But there were a couple of boys who were perfect for the part. She was glad she wasn't the one who had to decide between them.

And then it was time to look for Cinderella's two evil stepsisters. The first pair of girls out on the stage did nothing but giggle. The next two couldn't read all their lines. Two more little girls came out and read the lines in a monotone. Eleanor couldn't find anything wrong with the next pair, except that they just weren't right for the parts. And then Allie and Meggie Ryan came onstage. Eleanor felt as stiff as the starch in her collar as she waited for them to begin. So much rested on the outcome of this afternoon. Jacob Ryan would be forced to provide his daughters with a little female companionship if they got the parts. She'd seen the panic flare in his eyes when she'd mentioned costumes. He might have mastered things a lot of men never tackle, but she'd bet ten years of her life that he couldn't sew.

Allie stumbled over her first line. Ms. Thomas, this year's casting director, had to help her with the word "and." Eleanor's brow creased. For a second Allie seemed more interested in the stage lights than the play, but then she started to read again. The word "sister" came out without a hitch, yet she couldn't sound out "but." Eleanor slipped her feet back into her shoes. Allie continued, getting caught up in her part for a line or two. Then, as if remembering something, she faltered briefly. When she began again, she imposed enough sugar on an evil passage to raise the casting director's eyebrows. Meggie giggled throughout the audition, a forced unnatural sound. Eleanor stood up.

Jessie Ryan was onstage, a potential Cinderella, by the time Eleanor made it backstage. She watched Jessie trip over her feet, pick a fight with her prince and lose her place in her script. Ms. Thomas had to tell Jessie to speak up at least twice, and Eleanor was frustrated enough to cry.

The auditions were finally completed; as the children were leaving, Ms. Thomas reminded them that she'd be making her choices within the week. Eleanor couldn't stand still another minute. She grabbed Jessie as the little girl walked past, then rounded up Allie and Meggie. One look at their principal, and their guilt was written all over their young faces. They stood in a line before her, shoulders slumped.

"Okay, gang. Who wants to tell me what's going on?"

Meggie and Jessie looked toward Allie, whose face wore her determination like a cloak. "We just did our trying outs, Ms. Wilson," Allie said innocently enough. But her lips were so tightly pursed her chin was solid dimples.

Eleanor looked from one pair of big brown eyes to the next and almost gave in. Blowing the auditions meant a lot to them. But they were wrong if they thought that was going to solve their problems.

She pinned Jessie with her sternest stare, knowing that the affectionate little girl would be the one most likely to cave in. Jessie's lips started to tremble and she burst into tears. But she honored whatever pact she'd made with her sisters.

"Meggie?" Eleanor said, going for the other sibling who wasn't quite as forceful as their leader.

Meggie stared back solemnly, doing a perfect imitation of a deaf mute.

Eleanor's heart ached as she faced the threesome, but she reminded herself, not for the first time, that sometimes tough love was the only answer.

"Girls," she said in a no-nonsense tone, "I know

what you're doing here. And I think I have pretty good idea why. But do you really think your daddy will be happy to hear that you didn't get picked for the play?''

"He won't be mad at us," Allie said, looking at her sisters.

"He will be when he realizes that you blew the auditions on purpose."

Three horrified gazes locked onto Eleanor's face. "Please don't tell him, Ms. Wilson," Allie begged, confirming Eleanor's suspicions. "Daddy's got troubles right now. Please don't make him worried. We'll be good, we promise. Won't we, you guys?" Allie looked at her siblings.

Meggie and Jessie both nodded, Jessie's eyes flooding with tears again. Meggie studied her tennis shoes.

Eleanor wanted to hug all three of them. "Do you promise me you'll always try your best at whatever you do from now on?" she asked, keeping her tone properly firm.

"Yes, ma'am," Allie answered, nodding vigorously.

Eleanor looked at the most independent one of the trio. "Meghan?"

"Yes, ma'am."

"I promise, too, Ms. Wilson," Jessie said in a wobbly little voice, wiping her tears away with the back of her hand.

Before she could give in to the temptation to pull them all into her arms, Eleanor saw an older woman enter the back of the auditorium. Wearing a flowered dress that hung halfway down her calves and black low-heeled shoes, Nonnie Moore made her way slowly toward the girls. Ryan's housekeeper was favoring her left hip more than she had the last time Eleanor had seen her.

The triplets danced around Nonnie, eager to be gone, and Eleanor watched uneasily as the elderly woman led them away. All three were talking at once while Mrs. Moore nodded occasionally. Eleanor didn't doubt that the grandmotherly woman loved the girls. How could she not? But she suspected that the housekeeper didn't hear even a third of what the triplets were telling her. Which may have been why they weren't telling her anything important.

Eleanor went in search of Barbara Thomas.

"PICK YOU UP at seven?" Jacob asked Michelle the following Wednesday as they cleared off their workstation after the show.

"What?" Did Jacob have her confused with his date of the week?

"Childfair America's tonight." He'd stopped shuffling papers and was looking at her rather oddly.

"Oh. Right. I knew that," Michelle said. "Seven's fine." She'd been the one to suggest that she and Jacob emcee the charity gala that was to benefit the fight against child abuse in Los Angeles.

"See you then," Jacob said, and with one last look in her direction, left the studio.

"Yeah, see you," Michelle said to the empty room. Why was she becoming so obsessed about Jacob

Ryan these days? So he had a body to die for. He'd had it all the years she'd known him and it had never bothered her before. One trip to the girls' department with him didn't change things. She was still very much married, very much in love with her husband. And Jacob was still the world's worst womanizer. She needed to get a grip. Of course a little sleep might not hurt, either. If she wasn't careful she was going to drive herself right back into the emotional mess she'd been in when Brian first disappeared.

THE RED LIGHT on her answering machine was blinking when, with Noby in her arms, she walked into her den an hour later. With trembling fingers, she reached out to activate the machine.

"You know it's just Mom," she warned the cat.

"Frank Steele here, Mrs. Colby." There was a pause, as if the detective was waiting to see if Michelle was going to pick up the phone.

"I'm on my way to a village in Yemen where your husband lived for almost a year about three years ago. No one's saying yet why he was there or, for that matter, why he left. I'll be in touch."

Noby's ears flicked when the machine clicked off, as if the sound were offensive to her. But the cat could just as easily have been reacting to the tears that were soaking her fur.

JACOB'S MIND was on his girls as he drove to Michelle's that evening. They'd auditioned for *Cinderella* two days before and had been suspiciously quiet ever since—except to tell him that they didn't get the parts. They'd obviously forgotten the flyer they'd brought home the Friday before the auditions. Not only had it listed their audition times, it had also stated it would be at least Thursday before any definite decisions were posted.

They were up to something. And Jacob was having a hell of time trying to stay two steps ahead of them. Damn Eleanor Wilson and her suspicions. She had Jacob second-guessing every move he made. If she'd just left him alone Jacob would simply have asked Allie what was up. He and the girls had always kept everything out in the open. At least *he* had. And until recently he'd thought they had, too. Now he had to try to be a mind reader.

Shelving his worries for the moment, he pulled into Michelle's driveway and honked, just as he always did when he picked her up for their occasional evening functions. Equally predictably he looked around at the run-down condition of her neighborhood, wondering why she didn't move. It couldn't be a matter of money. KOLR showed ample appreciation to both of them.

Curious when she didn't come out, Jacob turned off the ignition and headed to her front door. He'd never been any farther than her driveway and was a little startled when he saw her doormat. Printed on it in large letters was "The Colbys." And beneath that was "Brian and Michelle." The mat was as faded and frayed as the rest of the neighborhood.

Jacob knocked and then, when there was no answer, knocked again. He was getting concerned. This wasn't like Michelle. Wasn't she home? He was just about to pound on her door for a third time when he heard the lock slide open. He waited for her to open the door, ready to tease her about spending hours primping for him. The words never got past his lips. Michelle was a wreck.

CHAPTER FOUR

STUNNED, JACOB STARED at Michelle's tear-ravaged face. He was going to kill whoever had done this to her.

"I'm s-sorry. Come in," she said, stepping back to let him by her.

Jacob strode in and grasped her arms. "What happened? Do I need to call a doctor?" he asked, looking her over from head to foot.

Michelle attempted to smile as she shook her head, but the gesture was too weak to do anything except concern Jacob more. "I'm okay. Really. I just need a couple of extra minutes." Jacob might have believed her if her voice hadn't cracked on the last word, and if she hadn't still been wearing the jeans and shirt she'd had on at the station that morning. She was the one who'd insisted they dress to the nines for this evening. It had taken her several days of fresh doughnuts to talk him into pulling out his tuxedo for the occasion.

She turned away with an embarrassed toss of her head.

"What happened, Michelle?" he asked, following her into the living room. She had to turn on a light so they could see, and Jacob wondered if she'd been sitting there in the dark.

"Nothing, really. I had a phone call…" Her words trailed off. "Everything's fine. It wasn't bad news or anything. Please, have a seat. I'll be ready in a minute."

Jacob seriously doubted that.

He reached out to her again, grabbing her hand when she would have walked away from him.

"Michelle. It's okay. So we'll be a little late. Our part of the show doesn't start until after dinner, anyway. So what was this phone call?"

She looked down at their interlocked hands, up at him and then down again. He'd never seen her anything but calm and unruffled before, and the misery he glimpsed in her eyes unnerved him.

"Come on. I don't do too badly when the girls need a shoulder to cry on. Why don't you give me a try?"

Tears sprang to her eyes, but she started to smile. "You're not supposed to be this nice, Ryan. Where's your sarcastic wit when I need it?"

He reached out a thumb to wipe the tears from her cheeks. "I guess these knocked it clear out of me. What caused them?"

She looked at him for a long moment and then sat on the edge of the couch. A fluffy white cat slipped out from behind a chair and jumped into her lap. Michelle stroked it tenderly. "About a year ago I hired a private detective to find Brian."

"But I thought the government was trying to find him."

She took a deep breath. Her frustration ran so deep he could feel it across the small room. "The government didn't want to spend any more money or waste any more time looking for him. But he's never been found, Jacob. Five years ago he ordered room service, somebody ate it, and that's the last anybody's ever seen or heard of him. He's not dead. I know he's not."

Jacob wasn't so sure, but what did he know? "So you hired a detective."

She nodded, still stroking the cat. "He called a couple of weeks ago to say he'd finally found someone who might know where Brian had been taken five years ago."

"Taken? Does that mean he knows for sure that your husband was abducted?"

"No. Until today nothing was for sure."

Jacob's gut knotted. Was Brian Colby dead, after all? Was that what she was about to tell him?

"Until today?"

"There was a message from Frank Steele, the detective, when I got home from work this morning. He's on his way to a village where Brian lived for at least a year."

"Does he suspect Brian might still be there?"

Her lips started to tremble again as she shook her head. "Not for the last three years. I know the news isn't very hopeful, but don't you see?" Her eyes pleaded with Jacob to understand. "It's the first real news I've had about him since he disappeared. Now I know that he wasn't just robbed and murdered like the government said. For some reason he was living in this village for at least a year. Two years after his disappearance he was alive. I've been hoping for so long, Jacob. And when I heard from Frank today it was like touching Brian. For the first time in five years I touched him.'' Her last words were barely audible through her tears.

Jacob couldn't stand to see her so torn up. But he didn't know how to help her. She was holding on to hope on the basis of three-year-old information. It seemed to him that her life was slipping away while she waited around for a man who could very well never be coming back to her. She was too beautiful, too sweet, too giving and funny to waste her life loving only a memory. And yet who was he to tell her that?

He watched her bowed head for as long as he could stand it, and then he pulled her to her feet.

"Come here," he said, tugging her awkwardly toward him.

She came willingly, almost innocently, like a child seeking comfort, burrowing her face against his neck, wrapping her arms around him. Her tears stopped almost instantly, but still he held her. He kept thinking of her sitting on her couch, in the dark all alone, and he couldn't let her go.

And as the minutes passed, as the tempest inside her calmed and she softened against him, it came to Jacob why he'd never held her before. There was no running from it, no more denying the hard truth. She was his partner. She was his buddy. But he wanted her. He wanted another man's wife.

"AND NOW, LADIES and gentlemen, I want to introduce two of L.A.'s favorites. They've appeared at countless charity functions over the years, giving their time generously to help build Los Angeles into the kind of city we all want it to be. Best known for their witty repartee that gets us all going in the morning, one of L.A.'s most beloved couples—except they claim they aren't one—Michelle Colby and Jacob Ryan."

Jacob ushered Michelle up onto the podium to the accompaniment of thundering applause, his hand burning where it touched her back. It had taken her an amazingly short time to change from the distraught woman who'd met him at the door to the elegant, self-assured woman who now walked beside him. Some fresh makeup, a few rhinestones and a backless black evening gown, and she was once again the buddy he'd always known. Or so he kept telling himself.

When he looked closely, though, he could see her tension. Her smile was forced, her bare shoulders a little too stiff.

"I think I just split the seat of my pants coming up the steps," he whispered as the applause died down. "And damned if I'm not wearing red polka-dot boxers."

Michelle glanced at him, humor replacing the strain in her eyes as she stepped up to the microphone. No one looking at her would have any idea of the heartache she was hiding.

"Good evening, ladies and gentlemen." Her husky voice flowed clear and easy. "I'm Jacob Ryan—"

"No, *I* want to be Jacob tonight," Jacob interrupted before she could falter at her mistake. "There are a lot of beautiful women here."

Laughter filled the ballroom. Michelle joined in and Jacob knew she was going to be okay.

"Yeah, on second thought, I'd probably be crushed if I had to carry your ego around," she said. "Though I wouldn't mind the paycheck."

The audience laughed again.

Jacob leaned one elbow on the podium and leered at Michelle. "It looks like you could use it to buy the other half of that dress."

Michelle's eyes promised retribution, and Jacob relaxed. Work had begun.

"We've got a great evening ahead of us, ladies and gentlemen, dancing to the sounds of Huey Michaels's band—" Jacob waited for the applause to stop "—but first we have a treat for you. As you all know we're gathered here tonight to honor the children of our city. Most of us were fortunate enough to grow up in loving homes, but many of the children living in our city today are not so fortunate, which is why we're all here—to help those children. We have hotlines young people can call, but not enough qualified people to man them. We have buildings to use as shelters, but no way to pay the utilities. These programs take money. Lots of it. And tonight the donations you've contributed have already totaled more than two hundred and fifty *thousand* dollars—'' A burst of applause interrupted him. ''You've just saved some lives, folks,'' Jacob said, stepping back as the audience stood as a whole, applauding their cause.

''And now for that treat Jacob mentioned,'' Michelle said, when the noise had died down.

''I know the one I'd like,'' Jacob said, as he eyed Michelle's bare shoulders.

The audience laughed, relieving some of the tension in the room.

''Tonight for your entertainment we have with us eight youngsters whose hard work and ability have won them positions as 'Talent Quest' finalists. Judges will select which four will compete on national television on 'Rising Stars'...''

Jacob and Michelle took turns at the microphone, introducing the acts before they came onstage. The children sang, danced, and one little guy even did a stand-up routine. Jacob was as awed as everyone else by the talent. He just wished he hadn't glanced at Michelle during one of the acts. The longing in her eyes as she watched the children on stage unsettled him. It dawned on him that she'd probably planned to be a mother by now. And probably would have been, if she wasn't so adamant about living in the past. He'd thought of several different explanations for Brian Colby's disappearance, not all of them involuntary. None of them had happy endings. But maybe the worst scenario was no ending at all.

JACOB NURSED his scotch, watching the women on
the dance floor, waiting for one to spark his interest.
There was certainly a bevy of lovelies here tonight.
Maybe that was why he was still standing on the side-
lines alone. There were too many choices.

He caught a glimpse of honey gold skin as a couple
sailed past and he looked the other way. He was glad
Michelle was having a good time. He just didn't think
her current partner needed to have his hand pressed
so intimately in the small of her back. Her bare back.
The tip of her shoulder would have done fine.

Taking another sip of his scotch, he looked around
for a partner for himself. A brunette across the room
caught his eye and smiled a come-hither smile that
men the world over could translate in a second. She
was available. He looked again. And she was beautiful. Her figure was model perfect in her shimmering
gold lamé gown. She was young enough not to have
that look that said she'd seen it all, yet old enough to
know the score. And she wanted to score. With Jacob.
He looked away.

He was sipping ice water and making small talk
with the bartender when he saw Michelle again. She
was with some guy who was so smooth-looking Jacob
wondered why her hands didn't just slip right off him.
He oozed money and position and just a little too
much confidence for Jacob's liking. And he was holding Michelle far too close.

Jacob set his glass down on the bar. It was time to
go. Michelle might not have to get up early in the
morning, but just because they didn't have to go to

work tomorrow didn't mean that *he'd* be able to sleep in. He had three little terrors who would be bouncing into his room by seven in the morning. If he was lucky. If not, they'd be jumping on the end of his bed by six.

He strode onto the dance floor for the first time that night, tapped Michelle's partner on the shoulder and, when they turned, grabbed Michelle's wrist.

"It's time to go."

Michelle's partner glared at him. She didn't look too pleased, either. Neither did the five or six couples who bumped into them in the middle of the crowded dance floor.

"I've got a headache," Jacob said, wondering what in the hell he was doing creating a scene just because some man had been dancing a little more closely than necessary with Michelle. A few hours ago he'd been encouraging her to have a good time, knowing that it was the best thing for her.

"You're not feeling well?" Michelle asked solicitously.

"No." Jacob was surprised to hear himself continuing the lie. Her concern was making him feel like a heel. But he still didn't let go of her wrist.

"Just let me get my purse," Michelle said.

Jacob cursed himself every way he knew how while he waited for Michelle to return. Being jealous of her dance partners was ludicrous. He was way out of line, overstepping the boundaries that governed their friendship—the boundaries that he himself needed if he and Michelle were going to remain partners.

MICHELLE WAS QUIET on the drive home, and Jacob welcomed the distance their silence placed between them. She stared out the window and he wondered if she was thinking about Brian Colby. Was she wondering where he was or remembering a night spent dancing in his arms? Envy welled up inside Jacob, although he'd long passed the days when he wanted a woman to care for him as loyally as Michelle cared for Brian. He knew better. And as much as he wished it could be different for Michelle, he suspected that someday she'd know better, too.

"Mind if we stop for something to eat?" he asked, breaking the silence that was suddenly deafening in the darkened vehicle.

"Not at all. I'm starving. I'll even buy, since we missed dinner on my account."

"In that case, I'll have two of everything," Jacob said, pulling into an all-night restaurant famous for its breakfasts.

The young, long-haired host who seated them at a cozy booth for two eyed Michelle appreciatively. She wasn't the only woman in the restaurant in evening clothes, but she was definitely the most beautiful. The young man glanced at Jacob with envy.

"You're one lucky dude," he muttered as Jacob waited for Michelle to slide into the booth. Jacob didn't bother correcting him.

"You feeling better?" Michelle asked half an hour later as they finished their breakfast.

Jacob nodded. The food had definitely helped improve his mood.

"You probably just needed something to eat," she said, smiling at him.

"Probably."

"So what'd you think of the show tonight?"

Jacob grinned at her. "Are you fishing for a chance to say, 'I told you so'?"

"Well, I did tell you it was worth our time, and I was right, wasn't I?"

"I'm not sorry we went," he said.

"After all the doughnuts I had to buy to get you to come tonight, I think I at least deserve the chance for an 'I told you so,' Ryan."

"You were absolutely correct, Ms. Colby. Our time was well spent and I'm glad you talked me into going. I had no idea how much one evening could accomplish."

"Those kids were really something, weren't they?" she asked, getting serious on him all of a sudden.

Jacob agreed that the kids had been remarkable. Remembering the yearning he'd seen on her face when she'd watched the talent show that evening, he was once again struck with how much she was cheating herself out of as the years rolled by without her.

"Did you and Brian plan to raise a family?" he asked before he could stop himself. What he needed right then was more distance, not more familiarity.

"I was six weeks pregnant when he left to go overseas."

"You were? But…" She'd said the words so softly Jacob wondered if maybe he'd misunderstood. But as he looked across the table into her pain-filled eyes, he knew he hadn't. "God, Michelle. I'm sorry."

She shrugged, looking down at her empty plate.

Jacob cradled his coffee cup in his palms. "What happened?" he asked.

"I lost the baby the day after they told me Brian was missing. It was a boy."

He could tell she was trying hard not to cry again. She looked up finally, a sad tremulous smile on her lips, and Jacob admired the hell out of her. He was amazed how she could come to work every day, be cheerful and optimistic, when her life had held so much tragedy. Until tonight, he'd had no idea how much.

"Did Brian know? About the baby, I mean?" he asked.

She looked down at her diet cola, stirring the near-empty glass with her straw, and shook her head.

"I wanted to wait until I was completely sure. It was going to be a homecoming surprise." Her words were little more than a whisper.

Silence stretched between them as her words hung in the air.

"How do you do it?" he finally asked. "How do you find so much good in this world when it treats you like it does?"

She shrugged and looked up at him. "I don't always find good. But I know it doesn't help any to focus on the bad. When I lost the baby I almost lost myself, as well. It hurt so badly I didn't have the strength to get up in the morning. I kept thinking I'd be okay when Brian came home. The loss was as much his as it was mine. He'd be as devastated by it as I was, and together, sharing that, we'd get through it. I didn't think things could get any worse. But they did.''

Jacob wished he were someplace he could take her into his arms. ''You mean not finding Brian?''

She shook her head. ''No. I was staying with my mom and dad after the miscarriage, and one morning a couple of weeks later, the first time I'd been alone since leaving the hospital, I got a phone call. It was a government official wanting me to identify a corpse that had washed up on the shore of the Gulf of Suez near Cairo. Brian had been staying in Cairo. The body was still intact and they were certain it was Brian. When I hung up the phone I promised myself, and God, that if I was spared that—if it wasn't Brian, if only I could still hope he was alive—I would handle anything else. They brought the body back here, my dad drove me to the airport to meet the plane, I looked into the body bag, and it wasn't Brian. I'd never been so thankful in my life. I knew then that I had to get a grip on my grieving or it was going to kill me before Brian made it home. Ever since then, I just do what I have to do to get through and look for whatever good I can find to make the waiting easier.''

''I think you're a remarkable, woman, Michelle

Colby," Jacob said softly, holding her gaze with his own.

She looked down. "I'm not really. Sometimes I think maybe I'm just taking the easy way out, doing nothing but waiting. But I just don't know any other way. So I wait." She shook her head. "Anyway, I don't even know why I'm telling you all this, except that tonight I needed a friend and you seemed different somehow, more human."

Jacob frowned. "More human? What have I been up to now? An alien?"

"You always seem so invincible. In all the years I've known you I've never heard you ask anyone for anything."

"Maybe you weren't listening," he said lightly, reaching for his wallet as he picked up their bill.

"And maybe you weren't asking." She snatched the bill from his fingers. "I said I'd pay. See if you can handle having someone do that much for you." Her tone was teasing, but her eyes told a different story.

Jacob drove her home, waiting until she'd waved at him from her living room window before he pulled away. Michelle might think he needed to reach out to people more. But she was wrong.

HE WALKED his baby-sitter to the end of his driveway, watched while she ran across the street to her mother's bungalow and went slowly back inside, locking up for the night. Looking in on the girls on the way to his bedroom, he tucked in a stray limb here and there. As he bent to put Jessie's teddy bear back into bed with her, he was surprised to see his daughter's big brown eyes gazing up at him. Her brow was puckered, her lower lip quivering.

Jacob sat down on her bed and lifted her onto his lap. "What is it, precious? Did you have a bad dream?"

She sniffled and shook her head. "Tomorrow's Valentine Day," she said softly. Her little voice was so forlorn Jacob had to struggle not to smile.

"Is that a problem?" he whispered back.

Her head moved against his chest as she nodded. Jacob loved the feel of her slight weight leaning on him, trusting him. Needing him.

"I forgot to tell you that me and Meggie are s'posed to bring cookies to the party."

"That's easy enough, punkin. We'll stop at the store on our way to school in the morning. Okay?"

"'Kay." She didn't sound any happier.

"Jess? Is there something else wrong?"

She sat up and studied him for a moment, then settled back against him. "Meggie says not to say," she said barely above a whisper.

While Jacob was concerned to hear that his daughters were deliberately keeping things from him, he was even more concerned about the reason for their silence. Picking Jessie up, he carried her out to the living room, reaching to flip on the light by the couch as he sat down with her on his lap.

"Okay, sport. Get this once and for all. There is never, *ever*, anything you can't tell me and there never will be—got that?" He took hold of her shoulders, turning her so that she was looking at him.

Wide-eyed, she nodded.

"I can't keep you and your sisters safe unless I know what's happening, Jess. So it's important that you guys don't keep secrets from me."

She fiddled with one of his shirt studs. "It's just that when I said me and Meggie'd bring cookies to the party, some of the kids said we always bring yucky store kinds, so I said uh-uh and they said uh-huh, 'cause we didn't have a mommy to make cookies for us to bring and I said we had you and they said daddies couldn't make cookies, so I said you could and now we're going to be bringing yucky store ones, anyway 'cause I forgot to tell you about making them," she finished in a rush.

Jacob would have loved to have a talk with each and every kid in Jessie's class. "I'm not glad you forgot to tell me about the cookies, Jess, but I think we can solve this pretty easily. Lucky for you I don't have to work in the morning because of tonight's benefit show. So I'll make a deal with you. You put your pretty little self right back to bed, go to sleep, and I'll see about getting those cookies made. Deal?"

Jessie flung her arms around his neck and squeezed him so tightly it hurt. "Thank you, Daddy."

MICHELLE FLUFFED the pillow on the end of her couch and settled down against it—again. She couldn't sleep. Usually, when her demons drove her from her bed, she'd be out as soon as she lay down on the sofa. There was something soothing about being in the living room. There were no expectations there. But it wasn't working this time.

She turned over, closed her eyes and tried to will herself to sleep, but a restless energy hummed through her. Her traitorous mind replayed the scene that had taken place hours earlier in this very room. She could still feel Jacob's arms around her, pulling her against the solidness of his body.

She reached for the picture on the end table, gazing at Brian's likeness in the moonlight. Not that she needed the picture to remember every line of his face, every expression, every smile. She didn't need to see his laughing green eyes to imagine them gazing at her lovingly—or burning with desire the way they had the last time they'd made love.

Dear God, how could she continue just existing like this? She was young and passionate. She needed a man. And Brian had been gone for so long.

Rolling over, she hugged Brian's picture to her breast. Tonight Jacob had been warm and solid—real. He was more than just a memory. She remembered the compassion she'd seen in his eyes when she told him about the baby she'd lost. She had a feeling that underneath his irreverent facade was a deeply caring man. And a passionate one.

But none of that gave her the right to be unfaithful to her husband. She'd rather die a dried-up old maid than take the chance that Brian might come home to find that she'd given her body, her heart, to another man.

JACOB COULD THINK of a lot of things he'd rather be doing at one in the morning than looking through cookbooks. Like going to bed, for instance. And not necessarily alone.

Sugar cookies. That sounded doable. He had sugar. He looked at the picture in the book and figured he could cut out a pretty mean heart with a paring knife. Then scanned the list of ingredients, hoping he wasn't going to find something like chocolate squares or coconut. He didn't stock many baking supplies. Flour, salt, butter. Vanilla he had for when he and the girls, mostly he, cranked out homemade ice cream. And baking soda. Jacob opened his refrigerator—yes, he still had that open box of baking soda Nonnie had told him to put there when he'd forgotten to throw away the bologna before leaving on vacation last summer. He was set.

He dumped the ingredients into his biggest bowl, determined to make the best damn cookies Lomen Elementary had ever had. Maybe then his little girls could just go about living their lives like the happy kids they should be. He'd bet there weren't too many mothers who'd stay up half the night baking cookies simply because their daughters had forgotten to say they needed them. Unless of course that mother were Michelle. He had a feeling she'd stay up *all* night to bake cookies if she had to.

Not that he had any business thinking about Michelle. Nope. He was going to make life easier on himself and keep thoughts of Michelle strictly off-limits. There would be no more spurts of jealousy, no more hormonal reactions. She wasn't the type of woman a guy had a casual affair with. And casual affairs were all Jacob had.

Besides, he didn't have a chance in hell of starting an affair with Michelle, casual or otherwise, even if he chose to, which he wouldn't. Brian's hold on Michelle went much deeper than the loyalty of young love Jacob had originally thought it was. She'd made a pact with fate to hold on until Brian returned. Just hold on. She wasn't really living at all, just existing. It sounded as if she hadn't even yet begun to grieve for the baby she'd lost. She was waiting for that, too.

Jacob cracked an egg on the side of the bowl. After what he'd witnessed and heard that evening, he didn't think Michelle was ever going to get on with life until she had her answers—one way or another. And by the sounds of things, those answers might never be found.

He spent the next few minutes picking eggshell out of his cookie dough.

CHAPTER FIVE

"JACOB, CALL FOR YOU on line six." Bob Chaney, their producer, poked his head into the sound room during a commercial break Friday morning.

Michelle pushed a button on the telephone and handed Jacob the receiver. He looked so different this morning than he had on Wednesday night, and she'd hoped the return to his usual uniform of sweats and T-shirt would have a grounding effect on her growing obsession with him. It hadn't.

"Of course I remember. I never forget a beautiful woman," she heard him say into the receiver. His voice, usually deep and clear, had taken on a low sexy tone.

Michelle studied the program sheet in front of her. They had three promos coming up, a telephone interview, a weather spot, sport scores to announce again and six songs to play. What did she care if Jacob was talking to a beautiful woman? It certainly wasn't anything new.

"Tonight?"

Please say no.

"How late?"

You have children to watch.

"I only stay up past my bedtime on special occasions."

He was grinning. Damn him.

"You're on. I'll pick you up at eight."

Michelle had never felt lonelier in her life.

JESSIE, ALLIE AND MEGGIE dragged in from school Friday afternoon, the oversize 49ers T-shirts they were wearing seeming to weigh them down. They walked through the kitchen, their multicolored backpacks still across their shoulders, not even stopping to take a sip from the three glasses of milk he'd set out on the table.

"Hi," Jacob said, smiling at them.

"Hi," they answered in identically unhappy voices as they continued on out of the kitchen, traipsing down the hall to their room.

Jacob looked at the untouched peanut-butter sandwiches still sitting on the table while a knot formed in his stomach. The only time Allie had ever passed up food was that time she'd reacted to her diphtheria inoculation and run a fever of 103. Enough of this mind-reading routine—he was going to trust his own judgment. Leaving the sandwiches on the table, Jacob turned and strode down the hall.

The girls were sitting on Meggie's bed, their backpacks dropped haphazardly in the middle of the floor. Jacob stood in the doorway, wishing he was a hell of a lot more sure of himself. He could hardly believe he was intimidated by three pint-size seven-year-olds.

"Who's going to tell me what's going on?" he

asked glancing from one to another. They looked so small and vulnerable as they sat there huddled together. But he managed a relentless stare, anyway.

"We promised Ms. Wilson we'd do our best on everything from now on," Allie finally said solemnly.

"That doesn't sound so bad." He didn't see the problem yet.

"I have to be Cinderella, Daddy," Jessie said, looking wistfully excited and ready to cry all at once.

"You got the part?" he asked. He'd thought the triplets had either skipped the auditions or blown them.

"And we're her evil stepsisters," Allie said, pointing to herself and Meghan. Meggie's hair was loose, hiding her face. Jacob hoped she wasn't crying.

He went in and sat down on Allie's bed. "I don't get it. You guys loved acting in the Christmas play. It's all you talked about for months. And now you're upset because you got picked for the starring roles of a story you all three know by heart?" He tried not to panic as it occurred to him that his daughters weren't just his children—they were females. This was what Eleanor Wilson and, later on, Michelle had been trying tactfully to point out. That just by the nature of the beast—male versus female—there were going to be times when he missed the boat.

Allie's little chin trembled. "If I gotta tell you something, you promise you won't get mad enough to go away like Mommy did?"

"Go away?" Jacob was completely unprepared for that. He joined the girls on Meggie's bed, pulling them all into the circle of his arms. "I'm not going anywhere, ever—at least not without you three. You could lie and cheat and steal, and I'd punish the heck out of you, but I'd never leave you. Never. *I love you.*"

Three little pairs of arms wrapped themselves around Jacob, and his words of love echoed back to him in triplicate. Jacob sought the gaze of his eldest daughter by nine minutes. "We're a family, Allie, you and Meggie and Jessie and me, and nothing's going to change that. You guys are stuck with me until you're all grown-up and so sick of me you'll be begging for your own apartments."

Jacob felt an extrahard squeeze around his middle. "I'm going to live with you forever, Daddy," Jessie said.

"You can't, Jessie," Meggie said. "Not when you get married and have babies."

"Then I won't get married."

"Don't you ever want to be a mommy, Jess?" Allie asked.

"Not if I have to leave Daddy."

"That's dumb." Meggie scooted off the bed and sat on the floor by the bookcase.

"It's not dumb, is it, Daddy?" Jessie asked, climbing onto his lap.

"It is kinda dumb, Jess," Allie answered for him, playing with the fringe of his cutoff denim shorts.

"Is not," Jessie said, burrowing her head into his chest.

"Is too," Meggie said. She was leafing through *Green Eggs and Ham*.

"Is n—"

"Okay, girls. We're kind of getting off the subject here. But for the record, whether Jessie's feelings withstand the test of time or not, they aren't dumb— not if Jessie's feeling them. Now, back to *Cinderella*. What's the problem? You don't like acting any- more?"

"I do," Jessie said.

"Me, too," Meggie agreed, still thumbing through the book.

"It's the costumes, Daddy. Ms. Thomas—she's the boss of the play—says they all have to be homemade and we don't even have a sewing machine," Allie said, frowning up at him.

"And Cinderella has to have *two* costumes because of being a maid *and* going to the ball," Jessie added.

Jacob's mind was spinning as he tried to find a way to reassure his daughters and find a solution to their problem at the same time. "So we'll learn how to sew," he said, knowing that was going to be a near impossibility. A sure impossibility considering the time he had to work with.

"Even we know you can't sew, Daddy," Meghan informed him. She was no longer turning the pages of her book. Glancing down he read silently, *Would you could you?* He had a feeling Meggie hadn't stopped there by coincidence.

"So we'll find someone who can," he said, real- izing he knew someone who both could and probably would. He remembered the homemade curtains at her windows, the throw pillows on her couch.

"But we can't just go take them to somebody, Daddy, 'cause we have to help," Allie said.

Jacob shifted Jessie more firmly onto his lap. "Then we'll have to find someone to come here just like Nonnie does."

"We could ask Nonnie," Jessie suggested.

"Nonnie can't *sew*, Jess," Meggie said, clearly irritated with her sister's naiveté. "Her fingers hurt her all the time and she has to look through those funny glasses just to read our papers."

"I'll find someone, girls, I promise," Jacob said before another argument flared up.

"There's more, Daddy," Jessie said timidly.

More? "Well, now's the time to lay it on me." Jacob injected an extra note of cheer into his voice. He wanted them to trust him with their troubles, which meant that one way or another he was going to have come through for them when they did.

"Ms. Thomas said to tell you we need someone to help us change during the show," Meggie said, closing her book with a snap.

"Yeah, she said we couldn't have another incibent like the one at the Christmas play where you came into the girls' changing place. The other girls and mothers didn't like it 'cause you're a boy," Jessie said.

Jacob figured he'd been more embarrassed than anyone else present that night. "I'll tell you what. When I ask someone to help with the costumes I'll make sure she can be there on play night, too. How's that sound?''

Meggie's smile transformed her usually serious face. "That sounds real good, Daddy."

"Yeah," Jessie and Allie chorused.

"Laurie's coming over to baby-sit later tonight, but how about we play a game of hoops before dinner?" Jacob asked.

"Yeah!" All three girls scrambled up, their worlds all right again.

Jacob shook his head and wondered how much his promise was going to cost him as he followed his daughters out to the small basketball hoop he'd installed beside the garage. He knew who he had to ask to help them—someone who'd already offered her services; someone who'd looked longingly at strangers' children the other night.

It was the perfect solution. The girls would have some female companionship; they'd get their costumes made and still be safe from emotional disaster. Michelle was already married, committed elsewhere. It would be no reflection on the girls when she moved on. They'd know going in that she'd already promised her life to another family. If only Jacob could trust himself to remember the same thing.

HE WAITED until Monday to approach Michelle. He could have called her at home over the weekend, but he'd wanted to keep things as impersonal as possible. He chose his moment, the two-minute commercial break in the middle of their show. Short and simple, that was how he planned to keep things.

Leaning forward on his stool, he rested his arms on the counter in front of him. "Remember what you said the other night about me never asking for anything?" he asked, turning his head to glance at her. She looked good. Hell, she looked gorgeous.

"Yeah." The one word brought him back with a snap.

"Well, I'm about to change that." *Get a grip, Ryan.*

"Congratulations." She slid off her stool and headed for the door.

Jacob sat up and stared at her. "Where're you going?" The words came out more sharply than he intended.

She turned back with a startled look. "We only have another eighty seconds and my throat's dry. I need a drink."

"So that's your answer, then?"

She walked back to the counter. "My answer to what?" she asked, clearly perplexed.

"I just took you up on your offer to spend some time with the girls." And it was much harder than even he'd thought it would be. If she said no...

She started to smile. "You did?"

He suddenly felt pounds lighter. "Yeah, I did." He smiled back at her.

"Five, four, three, two...go!" Bob's voice piped over the speaker from the control room.

Michelle mouthed yes as Jacob started in with the

weather report. It was going to be a bright sunny day in Los Angeles.

MICHELLE DIDN'T second-guess her decision to take on Jacob's girls even once, though she thought of little else all morning. Spending time with Jacob's daughters would certainly entail spending more time with him, and considering the way she'd been obsessing about him lately that might have been a problem. Except that she'd just spent the longest weekend of her life picturing Jacob in the arms of some new beauty. When she realized she was actually jealous, she'd been reminded of just why she'd never been tempted by Jacob before. His womanizing and his inability to commit himself to a long-term relationship were basic flaws that were sure to prevent her from seeing him as anything more than a friend. But mothering his children for a while was another ball game entirely. Michelle knew they were just what she needed—and suspected they might very well need *her* a little bit, too.

"So when do we start?" Michelle asked the minute they were off the air.

Jacob started gathering up the material they'd used for that morning's show. "Maybe you'd better wait until you find out what you're getting into before you commit yourself," he said.

Michelle's smile faded as she watched him. "You don't want my help now?" she asked. She should've expected he'd change his mind. Jacob never let himself rely on anyone.

"That's not it," he said, throwing newspapers in the trash. "But I should explain a few things first. You want to go for coffee or something?"

He wasn't meeting her eyes, and she had a pretty good idea why. She just wished it wasn't so hard for him to ask for a little help. "A diet cola would be great," she said.

They went to the deli next door to the station and ordered bagels to go along with Jacob's coffee and Michelle's cola. The girl behind the counter obviously approved of the way Jacob's T-shirt stretched across his chest. Or maybe it was the challenging tilt to his lips that fascinated her. All Michelle knew was that the girl looked at Jacob more than she did her cash register; she was flirting so obviously it was embarrassing. But though Jacob flirted right back, his response seemed somewhat mechanical. Michelle wondered if that was how he managed to keep his women from getting too close.

"Allie, Meggie and Jessie are great kids," he said after he'd emptied three packages of sugar into his coffee.

"You don't have to tell me that, Jacob. I've seen them at the company picnics the past three summers. They have wonderful manners and they certainly seem to mind you."

"But they're also an awful lot of work. Everything has to be done in triplicate, and I mean *everything*. If one gets a hug, they all need a hug. If one asks for a drink, they're all going to want one." He glanced up, the look in his eyes warning of difficult times ahead.

Michelle thought it sounded heavenly so far. "If you're trying to scare me off, you're going to have to do a lot better than that," she told him.

He set his bagel down, uneaten. "Okay, here it is. The girls are in a school play. They need costumes, four of them, homemade by the end of April."

"Okay." Michelle liked to sew. And making costumes sounded like fun.

"They have to help."

"All right." It might take a little longer that way, but considering her lonely evenings that made it all the better.

"And they need a woman to be with them on play night to help with changing and hair and things."

"Fine."

He pushed his untouched coffee aside.

"You don't even know when play night is."

"I assumed you'd tell me, Jacob. It's not like I have a demanding social schedule." She placed her hand over his. "Relax. If you knew how much I wanted to do this, you'd be charging me for it."

He pulled his hand away from hers. "I just don't want any surprises. For either of us," he said, grabbing his cup to take a sip of coffee. "And I need to know that if you agree to this, you're not going to turn tail and run when you have three voices coming at you at once demanding three different things that all have the utmost urgency."

She couldn't hold back her smile any longer. "If only you knew how good all this sounds to me. I've got enough patience and love to go around, Jacob, trust me.''

He looked startled for a moment. "I guess I do trust you or I wouldn't have asked in the first place. I just don't want the girls disappointed."

She understood his concern. "I'll never knowingly do that. You have my word on it."

He nodded. "There's one other thing… You'll be spending some time at the beach house."

"I figured as much."

"I live there."

Michelle thought she was beginning to understand. She felt like sliding under that table as it dawned on her that Jacob might have caught on to the way she'd been responding to him. How humiliating! It could ruin everything—not only their camaraderie on the air but, even worse, her chance to give a little bit of the love she had stored inside to three children who needed it almost as much as she needed to give it.

"And I'm married," she said maybe a little more forcefully than necessary. "Don't you see? It's like I told you the other night. I look for good things to make the waiting easier. Helping Allie and Jessie and Meggie is a good thing. But I'll still be waiting, Jacob. Faithfully. Every minute of every day. Especially now that Frank is finally getting some leads."

Jacob nodded. "And the girls need to understand that. Right from the beginning. I don't want them to start weaving impossible dreams of 'happy ever afters' in their naive little heads."

"You'd like me to tell them about Brian?" Michelle didn't really want to do that. She didn't want to have to start their time together with such an unhappy story.

"I'll do it. But it wouldn't hurt for you to drop reminders now and then."

"If you think it's necessary," she said.

"I know my girls. They'll have us married an hour after you're in the house."

And they both knew how completely impossible that was.

JACOB HAD LET MICHELLE talk him into bringing the girls over for dinner that night so she could start getting to know them. He hadn't been prepared to jump into things so quickly, but she'd convinced him otherwise by detailing what was involved in sewing a gown. And she had four of them to do. He could see that she probably needed to get started as soon as possible.

"Is it time to go yet, Daddy? Is it?" Jessie asked, bouncing up and down in front of the bathroom mirror as he tried to fix her hair.

"Almost, punkin. Where're your sisters?"

"In the bedroom. They just need hair done, too."

Working his way from the bottom up, Jacob attacked the day's worth of tangles. He never could figure out how Jessie always managed to get twice as many knots in her hair as her sisters. "They're wearing their jean skirts and Mickey tops like I asked?"

"Yep. And you're wearing jeans, too, Daddy. We all match."

GET 2

HOW TO GET YOUR
2 FREE BOOKS AND FREE GIFT!

1. Peel off the MIRA sticker on the front cover. Place it in the space provided at right. This automatically entitles you to receive two free books and an exciting mystery gift.

2. Send back this card and you'll get 2 "The Best of the Best™" novels. These books have a combined cover price of $11.00 or more in the U.S. and $13.00 or more in Canada, but they are yours to keep absolutely FREE!

3. There's <u>no</u> catch. You're under <u>no</u> obligation to buy anything. We charge nothing – ZERO – for your first shipment. And you don't have to make any minimum number of purchases – not even one!

4. We call this line "The Best of the Best" because each month you'll receive the best books by some of today's hottest authors. These authors show up time and time again on all the major bestseller lists and their books sell out as soon as they hit the stores. You'll like the convenience of getting them delivered to your home at our special discount prices . . . and you'll love your *Heart to Heart* subscriber newsletter featuring author news, horoscopes, recipes, book reviews and much more!

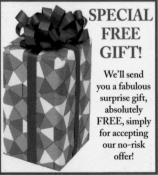

SPECIAL FREE GIFT!

We'll send you a fabulous surprise gift, absolutely FREE, simply for accepting our no-risk offer!

5. We hope that after receiving your free books you'll want to remain a subscriber. But the choice is yours – to continue or cancel, anytime at all! So why not take us up on our invitation, with no risk of any kind. You'll be glad you did!

6. And remember...we'll send you a mystery gift ABSOLUTELY FREE just for giving "The Best of the Best" a try.

Visit us online at
www.mirabooks.com

® and TM are trademarks of Harlequin Enterprises Limited.

QUIET MOMENTS™

Introducing a guilt-free way to pamper yourself and restore the healthy positive balance in your life.

Indulge yourself by mailing the Free Bath Spa Experience order form. We'll send your beautiful gift box overflowing with an array of delights. It's your guilt-free reward for always being there for others.

Let Quiet Moments pamper you from head to toe. Literally!

Mail in the order form, along with two proofs of purchase from specially marked Harlequin novels (and your shipping and handling fee), and we'll send you your introductory Free Bath Spa Experience Kit.

See offer terms on previous page.

HNCPBS2

FREE Bath Spa Experience
With two proofs of purchase from specially marked Harlequin novels.

Special Limited-Time Offer

IN U.S., mail to:
Harlequin Quiet Moments Bath Spa Offer
3010 Walden Ave.
P.O. Box 9023
Buffalo, NY 14269-9023

IN CANADA, mail to:
Harlequin Quiet Moments Bath Spa Offer
P.O. Box 609
Fort Erie, Ontario
L2A 5X3

YES! Please send me my FREE Introductory Bath Spa Experience Kit so I can savor Quiet Moments without cost or obligation, except for shipping and handling. Enclosed are two proofs of purchase from specially marked Harlequin novels and $3.50 shipping and handling fee.

Name (PLEASE PRINT)

Address   Apt. #

City   State/Prov.   Zip/Postal Code

FREE SPA KIT OFFER TERMS

To receive your free Bath Spa Experience Kit, complete the above order form. Mail it to us with two proofs of purchase, one of which can be found in the upper right-hand corner of this page. Requests must be received no later than August 31, 2001. Your Quiet Moments Bath Spa Experience costs you only $3.50 for shipping and handling. The free Bath Spa Experience Kit has a retail value of $16.99 U.S./$24.99 CAN. All orders subject to approval. Products in kit illustrated on the back cover of this book are for illustrative purposes only and items may vary (retail value of items always as previously indicated). Terms and prices subject to change without notice. Sales tax applicable in N.Y. **Please allow 6-8 weeks for receipt of order. Offer good in Canada and the U.S. only.**

Offer good while quantities last. Offer limited to one per household.

425 UDN DAL9

He made it through one section of hair. "You need to stand still, Jess, or we'll never get there."

"She's pretty, isn't she, Daddy?" Jessie's big innocent eyes caught his in the mirror, reflecting her excitement.

He pulled gently at a tangle at the back of her neck. "Who's pretty?"

"Michelle. When we saw her last summer at the picnic she smiled at us a lot."

"Sure Michelle's pretty. That's why she's married. Brian Colby saw how pretty she was years ago and snatched her right up."

"Ouch!" Jessie's hand flew to the back of her neck, covering the spot where Jacob needed to put the brush.

"Just a little bit more, honey. We almost got it," he said, gently removing her hand. He'd thought about cutting the girls' hair shorter a time or two, but he could never bring himself to do it. He loved it long.

"Do you think she'll let us pick our own material?" Jessie asked, wincing.

Jacob worked the tangle free and moved on to the next. "I'm sure of it. What color do you want?"

"Blue! No, green!"

Jacob finally made it all the way through Jessie's hair. He pulled it up into a ponytail and had it in a scrunchie in record time, a testimony to the fact that he could do most anything when he put his mind to it.

Meggie wanted her hair in a braid, but finally al-

lowed Jacob to stick it in a ponytail when he pointed out that he wasn't nearly as good at doing braids and it might make them late for dinner. Allie had to go to the bathroom just after he'd locked the door behind them, but finally, with fifteen minutes to spare, all three girls were buckled into the Explorer.

They chattered nonstop all the way over to Michelle's condo. There was no doubt his daughters were excited about the advent of a woman in their lives. Chalk up another point for Eleanor Wilson.

JACOB WAS HAVING DINNER with four strangers. He'd done his darnedest to initiate a couple of conversations, but when his efforts fizzled, he figured he just had to ride this one out. He didn't have a hope in hell of understanding it. Michelle had barely looked at him since he'd walked in her door. And the triplets were acting like robots from a *Miss Manners* book.

They'd been their loud bouncy selves right up until they'd pulled into Michelle's driveway. But the minute they'd climbed out of the 4×4, they'd become polite little mice. He wondered if he could bottle up some of Michelle's air to take home with him. Only for special occasions, he amended quickly. Most of the time he welcomed the life the girls brought into his home.

Thank goodness for Michelle's cat. Noby had taken to the girls as soon as they stepped in the door, wrapping herself around their legs and earning herself three slaves for life. Even Meggie demanded her turn to hold the fluffy Persian. Noby had managed to keep

things rolling until Michelle had announced that the hamburgers were ready.

"Can I have some more catsup, please?" Allie asked, her hands in her lap.

"Here you go, Allie. You need some help with that?" Michelle was responding to his daughter's needs before Jacob could reach for the bottle.

"What?" Michelle asked when she caught him staring at her in surprise.

"You called her Allie," he said, impressed.

Michelle frowned. "Isn't that what you call her?"

"It's just that people usually mix us up," Allie said in her most adult voice.

Meggie reached for a piece of bread. "It mighta been a lucky guess," she said.

Michelle grinned. "Need some help buttering that, *Meggie?*" she asked.

"Nope."

Michelle's effort with Meggie's name went unrewarded. Jacob could have told her that would happen, simply because she'd offered to help the most independent of his children, though he'd have given his right arm to hear Meggie say yes. He watched as his daughter butchered her bread, leaving more butter on the knife than anywhere else. Michelle sent him an expectant glance, her smile replaced with a frown when he didn't take over the buttering. Which would have been the worst thing Jacob could have done at the moment. It was far more important for Meggie to complete the task herself than for the bread to be edible when she was finished.

Meggie's bread ripped and balled into pieces, but she ate it, anyway. Michelle gave him a disapproving glare.

Michelle had a lot to learn.

CHAPTER SIX

"FRANK STEELE HERE, Mrs. Colby."

Michelle's heart rate doubled as she recognized the detective's raspy voice. It'd been almost a week since his last call.

"What'd you find out, Frank? Did they recognize his picture? Does anyone know where he went from there?"

"It's not that easy, ma'am. I had to rely on a translator, and according to him, your husband was never in that village. And yet everyone got real nervous every time I pulled his picture out. So I figure Brian was there all right, but for some reason they don't want me knowing that." He paused, and Michelle heard him take a long drag on a cigarette. Scooping up Noby, she sank into the nearest chair.

"So now what?"

"We'd be back to square one except that last night, on a hunch, I spread the word I was leaving in the morning. I figure there's always an odd one out, and maybe, if someone had something to say to me, I could push their hand a little. So sometime past midnight, I'm in my tent and I get this visitor. It's a young woman called Jazmin. I'd seen her watching

me a couple of times in the village. Anyway, as it turns out, she speaks English. She tells me about this guy Karim, who's threatened to level the village if anyone ever speaks about the American who lived with them for so many months. She says the American looked different from the picture I showed her—he had a beard and wore his hair in a ponytail—but she'd know his eyes anywhere. She says he called himself Ahmed and that she worked as his translator while he learned Arabic.''

Michelle's chest was so tight she could barely breath. ''Did this woman say what happened to him?'' After all the years of waiting she wasn't sure she was ready for the truth.

''Only that while he'd lived in the village for about a year, he'd been gone far longer and there was nothing to be gained by my hanging around. It was obvious my questions were more painful to her than frightening. She was affected in a personal way. I'm sorry to have to say this, ma'am, but you're paying me to find out what I can—I was left with the impression that Jazmin was in love with your husband.''

Michelle didn't want to hear that.

''She didn't say anything else? Like why he was there or what he did during that year?''

''She did say that he helped a lot of the villagers, like fixing things that were broken. They were all very fond of him. She said he made them laugh a lot.''

''That sounds like Brian.'' The ache inside Michelle was almost overwhelming.

"As far as I can see we have two options left," Frank said in his emotionless tone.

"Which are?"

"Either find this Karim or give up."

"Then find Karim."

"You may be asking the impossible, ma'am. Whoever this Karim guy is, he's got enough power to scare an entire village, and it's my guess he has other such villages under his thumb. If he doesn't want to be found, he won't be."

"I don't care how long it takes, Frank. I have to know."

"I've always had a fascination with this part of the world, ma'am, so I'm willing to stick at it, as long as you're sure…"

"I'm sure, but, Frank?"

"Yeah?"

"Be careful."

"Always. I'll be in touch…"

MICHELLE PLAYED racquetball with her father late that afternoon—sort of. She lost to him so badly he didn't even tease her about it. And she was preoccupied all through dinner. She knew her parents were worried about her, but she just couldn't confide in them. Not yet. Not until she'd come to terms with the fear—the jealousy—that was threatening to rise up and engulf her.

She kept seeing Brian, her Brian, looking at some village beauty the same way he'd looked at her, smiling, laughing. Brian's laugh was contagious. And

somehow, although she'd tortured herself with visions of him in endless situations—hungry, holed up in the dark with rats, locked in chains, running, hiding, suffering from amnesia—never once had she pictured him laughing.

And never once with another woman.

Michelle stopped in at a craft store on the way home from her parents and walked up and down every aisle before leaving empty-handed. She went to the grocery store and bought a basketful of things she didn't need. She didn't go near the ocean or look at the Hollywood sign. She didn't go to any of the places that reminded her of Brian—the places that usually gave her comfort.

But he followed her everywhere.

She finally pulled into her driveway some time after nine, her mind still screaming with questions. *Did he hold her? Did he touch her like he touched me?*

Carrying in her groceries, she locked up for the night. Had another woman made love to Brian? Since she had? While she'd been here missing him so badly she was only half-alive?

She avoided her bedroom. She refused to take the other woman in there....

Had Brian loved her—this unknown beauty? Had he given her his heart, as well as his body? That possibility hurt worst of all. His love was sacred to Michelle—hers alone. It had transcended thousands of miles, endured years of deprivation and loneliness. It had kept her alive during the loss of their son. But

was this relationship she honored with her loyalty, her life, a sham?

Michelle twisted the solid gold ring on her left hand. Maybe she was being ridiculous. Maybe *she* was the one endangering their love by allowing doubts to intrude. If she only believed in Brian when believing was easy, then her loyalty meant nothing. Frank could be wrong. And even if he wasn't, even if the young woman had fallen in love with Brian, it didn't mean Brian had either encouraged or returned her feelings. Michelle sat down on the couch next to Noby.

Brian's picture was smiling at her from the end table. She picked it up, meeting the loving look in his eyes with her own. But he wasn't looking at her. He was gazing at some young village beauty....

Michelle reached for the phone.

"HELLO?" JACOB GRABBED the phone after the first ring so it wouldn't wake the girls. He'd learned to cherish the hour or two of quiet he got each evening almost as much as he cherished the chaos of his days.

"Hi. Am I interrupting?"

His newspaper landed on the floor beside the couch as he sat up. "Michelle? No. Of course you're not interrupting. Is something wrong?"

"Everything's fine," she said, and he wondered why she didn't sound fine. "I just wanted to get started on those costumes."

"Tonight? The girls are eager, too, but they've been in bed for more than an hour."

She laughed, self-consciously, he thought. "I didn't mean tonight, Jacob," she said, sounding more like herself. "But tomorrow would be a good time for me if the girls don't already have other plans. I could pick them up after school and take them to the fabric store. We'll need patterns and material."

The girls? As in, all three of them at once? Jacob hadn't figured on that.

"We're going in-line skating tomorrow, but I guess we can do that after dinner," he said. He couldn't let her take all three of them at once. Not on a first outing. Maybe not ever.

"You take the girls in-line skating?" she asked.

"Yeah."

"With training blades?"

"No. They haven't needed them for over a year." He was rather proud of that fact.

"Aren't they a little young for that? They could sprain an ankle or something."

"They could sprain an ankle walking in the yard."

"I just thought little kids still did roller skates, you know, with four wheels and all."

She really sounded worried. "Some do. But the girls wanted in-line skates last year for Christmas. It seemed like fun, so we all went and learned how to do it. You ever done it?"

"Yeah. I've got my own blades."

"There's a track down by Lomen Elementary. You ever been there?"

"No. I usually just stay around here."

"So why not take Allie to the fabric store after

school while Jessie, Meggie and I make dinner, and then we can all eat and go skating together.'' Jacob was quite pleased with the plan. It left him with two-thirds of the disaster-waiting-to-happen. "The girls would love it," he added for good measure.

"Sounds good, except that I need to take all three girls with me if they're going to choose their own materials and patterns."

"So, do Allie tomorrow, and Jessie and Meggie can each have a day later in the week."

"But then we're that much further from getting started. It would really be easiest to just take them all at once."

Jacob thought of the triplets in a store—any store. "No, it wouldn't."

"What's the matter, Jacob? Are you regretting asking for my help?" She was really making this difficult.

"No. I'm just trying to prevent you from running out on us before you even get started."

"I don't understand."

He was sure she didn't. "Michelle, taking a seven-year-old into a store is a serious endeavor. You're so busy reminding the child not to touch and answering the million and one questions she comes up with that it's hard to concentrate on what you went in for. Now multiply that by three and add in the little extra ingredient of needing their opinions to complete your mission. You get the picture yet?"

"I think the fabric store will survive."

"It's not the store I'm worried about."

"You don't think I can handle it."

"Their mother couldn't."

"I'm not Ellen."

"No, you're not. But neither do you have any idea what you're getting yourself into. Trust me on this one, okay?"

"It sounds to me like you're the one who needs to do some trusting, Jacob. We're only talking about a trip to the store here. It's not like I want to take them off for a weekend or something."

"I know what we're talking about. Far better than you do. Believe me, partner, doing for three isn't as easy as doing for one. And doing for three at once is sometimes so chaotic nothing gets done at all."

"I could use a little chaos in my life, Jacob. It's so dull right now I'm surprised I don't sleep right through it."

Jacob smiled. He couldn't help it. "Okay, lady, you're on. You take the girls. I'll make the dinner. But don't you dare come in here tomorrow night and tell me you have other plans for the next couple of months."

"Don't worry, I won't. You might as well face it, Jacob. You're stuck with me."

Her words rang in his mind long after he'd hung up. She hadn't meant them the way they sounded. Logically he knew that, even if for a minute there he'd wanted them to be true more than anything he could remember wanting in a long, long time.

"HERE'S A GOOD PATTERN for you, Jess. See, she even has a little crown and everything like a real prin-

cess." Allie held the picture so her sister could get a look at it.

Jessie gazed at the picture. "Michelle, Allie found my princess dress. See?" Jessie began twirling as if dancing at a ball. "I'm a princess, see?"

Trying to keep one eye on Meggie, who was sitting at the other end of the table looking in a McCall's book, Michelle leaned over the Simplicity catalog Allie had open, catching Jessie's princess act in her peripheral vision.

"Be careful, Jessie," she warned. "There's a..." She raised her head just in time to watch Jessie knock over a display of thread. Spools rolled in every direction, under the pattern table and out into the aisles.

"Oops," Jessie said with a grin, running to catch some spools that were rolling under a row of chairs.

Thankful that the display had only been half-full, Michelle hurried to help Jessie gather up the thread before one of the employees came over and kicked them out of the store. Allie sat in her chair and watched.

"You missed one under there," she said, pointing to a round table full of fabric remnants.

Michelle reached for the spool.

"I want this dress," Meggie suddenly announced.

Michelle took a second to go look over Meggie's shoulder. Of Jacob's three children, Meggie was the hardest one to get to know. The little girl didn't seem to like Michelle much.

She'd chosen a bridal gown.

Michelle returned the last spools of thread to the rack and took Jessie's hand. "We'll come back to the patterns, girls. Let's look at some material."

Holding on to Jessie's hand, she had the other two walk in front of her as she directed them to the organza display.

"Don't touch, girls," she said as Allie and Meggie reached out to run their fingers through bolts of material along the way.

Michelle heard a thunk beside her. Jessie had her face buried in a bolt of fake fur she'd already pulled off the rack.

Michelle righted the bolt. When she turned back, the triplets were no longer in sight. She heard them, though, and followed their voices over to the organza.

"I want this one!" Jessie said, pulling at a bolt of shiny red material. "I want this one, Michelle, okay? Can I have this one?"

"You can't have that one, Jess. Everyone knows Cinderella wore a blue gown," Allie said. She grabbed the end of a bolt of royal blue organza. "You have to have *this* one."

"I want the red one," Jessie said, her bottom lip jutting out. "Cinderella wore red."

Meggie walked silently around the display of material.

"I'm telling you, Jess, Cinderella wore a blue dress. Don'tcha remember that plate we got that broke?"

Michelle wondered if she was supposed to intervene. But how could she without choosing sides?

"I want a red dress. Red's my favorite color. And Cinderella's dress was red."

Allie stomped her foot. "You have to wear the blue." Jessie's eyes were filling with tears.

Letting her instincts guide her, Michelle stepped between them. "Okay, girls, what's the problem?" She was glad Jacob wasn't here—he'd fire her on the spot.

"Cinderella has to wear blue, and Jessie wants red," Allie said. Jessie sniffled, looking to Michelle to save her from heartbreak. But clearly Allie expected Michelle to back *her* up, too.

Jessie sniffled again, and Michelle made a note to carry tissues in future. "I don't think it would hurt if, just this once, Cinderella wears a red gown to the ball," she said. "What color do you want for *your* dress, Allie? Meggie, stay over here, please," she called as the little girl began to wander off.

Allie walked around the display, studying all the colors. Jessie pulled the bolt of red fabric down, hugging it in her arms.

"I already know what I want," Meggie said, coming up to point out a bolt of white fabric. "I want this one. It's just like the one in the picture."

Allie looked at Meggie's choice. "You can't have that one. It's white. White's for brides. And Cinderella's the bride. Hey, Jess, you should have white."

"Uh-uh. I'm having red," Jess said, clutching the material against her.

Meggie pulled the bolt of white down. "I want white," she said, her voice firm.

"You're not *allowed* to have white. Anyway, purple's your favorite color. You should have purple," Allie said, grabbing the end of the bolt, trying to pull it away from her sister.

Meggie wouldn't let go. "We're each s'posed to choose our own, Al. You heard Ms. Thomas."

Michelle noticed a clerk hovering nearby.

"Meggie's right, Allie honey," Michelle said, taking the bolt of cloth. "The rule was that each of you has to help make your own costume. It'll be okay if the colors don't match the movie exactly. You know, there are actually quite a few movies about Cinderella, and the characters wear different clothes in all of them." She handed the bolt of material to Meggie before turning to Allie. "So what color do you want?" She put her arm around Allie's shoulders and led her back to the display.

Allie shrugged. "I dunno," she said, fingering the fabric.

"Well, what's *your* favorite color?" Michelle asked.

Allie shrugged again.

Michelle knelt down in front of the little girl. "This yellow's a pretty color. We could trim it with gold sequins. How does that sound?" she asked.

"I dunno."

It would be one thing if Allie was just being uncooperative because she didn't get her own way, but Michelle didn't think that was the case. It was as if Allie was lost, not sure what to do. Michelle didn't know what to do, either.

Taking Allie by the shoulders, Michelle guided her toward the front of the rack. "Let's walk around one more time and you take another look," she said. "We have to hurry because I'm going to need you to help me find the thread to match these materials and your daddy's got dinner waiting for us."

Allie's shoulders straightened. "I'm a real good thread chooser, aren't I, you guys?" she said, looking to her sisters for confirmation.

Jessie and Meggie nodded obediently.

Michelle breathed a sigh of relief. All she needed was a little time and she'd get this mothering thing down pat. She grabbed Allie and twirled her around in a hug.

WHEN SHE GOT THE URGE to hug Allie's father later that evening, Michelle's apprehensions returned. They were skating, all five of them, staying on the right side of the course to let faster skaters get by. The girls were in front, with Allie in the lead. And without the triplets knowing it, Jacob was watching them like a hawk. It was amazing how he surrounded them with a security that set them free.

He'd pulled a handkerchief from his pocket earlier to wipe Jessie's scraped knee, but sent her right off to try again. He'd sat patiently, giving Meggie all the time she needed to try to tie her own laces; after four tries she asked him for help. And then when he'd tied them for her he'd made it seem as if she hadn't really needed his help at all.

Michelle was seeing another side to the Jacob Ryan

she'd thought she knew so well. A side she liked—a lot.

She glanced over at him as he skated next to her. He was wearing blue sweats that were cut off at the thigh and a white tank top. His skin was browned by years of exposure to the California sunshine, and his muscles rippled with each thrust of his leg. He was every woman's fantasy man. Or at least hers. But that didn't mean she could start hugging him—or even start wanting to. She was married to another man.

"See, I told you they were pretty good," Jacob said, unaware of the disturbing road her thoughts had taken.

Michelle watched the triplets round a corner of the track. Allie turned to say something to her sisters and Meggie and Jessie grinned.

"They're incredible, Jacob, just incredible." And they were. This arrangement was the best thing that had happened to her in a long, long time. She wouldn't let herself screw it up.

MEGGIE WAS PLAYING POGs with her sisters a couple of nights later. They'd just finished dinner and still had a while to go before bedtime. Michelle was helping their daddy with the dishes. She'd come for dinner again. That was twice in one week.

They heard Daddy's voice saying something and then Michelle laughed. All three girls glanced up from their half-dollar-size disks on the living-room floor to gaze at the hallway leading to the kitchen.

"Michelle's nice," Jessie said.

Allie nodded. "Yeah. She smiles a lot."

Meggie had noticed that, too.

"I'm glad we got picked for the play, after all, and have to make costumes," Jessie said.

Allie turned back to the game, raising her rubber slammer and throwing it down on the stack of cardboard POGs. The entire stack flipped over, and Allie gathered up every one of them.

Allie always won all Meggie's and Jessie's POGs. But it was okay, 'cause she always gave them right back afterward.

"I didn't know Daddy would bring Michelle home to make costumes," Allie said.

Meggie wondered why her sister said things sometimes. Of course Allie didn't know. How could she?

"But he did and I'm glad," Jessie said. "Let's do three this time." She picked up three of her remaining four POGs and put them in the center of the floor. Meggie waited for Allie to add three and then put her three on top.

"Yeah, me, too," Allie said.

Meggie knew Allie was still talking about Michelle. Meggie was secretly glad, too, but she wasn't going to say it. She was afraid to.

Jessie threw her slammer down on the stack. Two POGs flipped over. "Maybe if we're real good Michelle will want to stay and we'll be a whole family just like Katie Walters's," she said, her eyebrows all crinkly like Allie's got when something was serious.

Meggie's heart started to beat hard.

"Yeah! If we're real good I bet she will," Allie said.

They both looked at Meggie. She looked back at them. She wanted to hope for a mother. She wanted to so much. But she couldn't. Sometimes when she wished it made things go bad. Like the time she'd wished her mother would come for Christmas. She'd wished every night for days and days. And that was the year their mother forgot them altogether. Meggie'd always wondered if it was her fault, for wishing for too much.

"Meggie, it's your turn," Allie said, still looking at her. "Don't you think if we're good Michelle will want to stay and make us a whole family?" she asked as Meggie threw her slammer.

"I'll be good," Meggie said, picking up the POG she'd flipped over.

Allie took her turn, tossing her slammer onto the remaining POGs. Every one of them flipped over. "You guys wanna play again?" she asked.

"Sure," Jessie said. "How about you, Meggie?"

"Okay. Only I get to go first this time."

"IT'S EIGHT FORTY-THREE on this gorgeous Monday morning—"

"Already?" Jacob leaned toward his mike to interrupt.

Michelle wrinkled her nose at him. "But before we say goodbye, we need to tell everyone what we have planned for tomorrow..."

"I don't think Bob wants us saying stuff like that on the air."

"I'm talking about tomorrow's show, Jacob," Michelle said, grinning at him.

"Then can we talk about...you know?" Jacob asked. He'd always enjoyed baiting Michelle, but especially now that he was getting to know her better.

"I guess if talk's all you can do..."

Jacob gave her a glance promising retribution. "Psychic Alisha Shane will be joining us tomorrow morning, along with City Councilman Richard Butler, who is, I hear, thinking of running for senator," he said. He looked up from the sheet he was reading. "You think she'll have some insights into his future?"

"He's a politician, Jacob. You think he'll listen?"

Jacob burst out laughing. "That wasn't nice, Michelle."

"I know, and I'm sorry. I'll be nice to him tomorrow, I promise."

Jacob felt good about the morning's show. He'd been a little apprehensive about how their new arrangement might affect their work, maybe make their banter stale, but to the contrary, things just seemed better all around.

The "on the air" light went off in their sound booth. Michelle smiled at him. She was pleased with the show, too. But there was something more to her smile than a sharing of professional success, something warmer, something almost...intimate.

"Hey, you guys were great!" Bob Chaney barged into the room. "Your ratings have been up all week."

Jacob gathered up the papers in front of him. "That's always nice to hear," he said. Why did their producer have to pick this moment to bear his good tidings?

"It sure is," Michelle added. She seemed to be giving a lot of attention to the stack of compact disks in front of her.

Bob leaned against the door frame, crossing one leg over the other. "So tell me, what's going on between you two?"

Jacob wasn't sure who sent Bob the sharpest look, he or Michelle, but he had a feeling if looks could kill Bob would have died twice.

"Nothing," they both said at once.

"Nothing?" Bob laughed incredulously. "Tell me another one. The air's been crackling around you two for days."

"We work well together, Bob. You know that. We always have," Michelle said, as calm as always.

"I can guarantee if there was anything more than that, it *wouldn't* work," Jacob added. "You know me. I love 'em and leave 'em." It was one thing for *him* to fantasize about having a relationship with Michelle, because he knew it would never be anything more than a fantasy, but he couldn't allow anyone else to get ideas.

Bob laughed. "Come on, you two. Anyone with eyes can see that something's changed over the past week or two. What about that crack a couple of days

ago, Michelle, something to do with the stuff growing inside Jacob's refrigerator? And what about you Jacob? How'd you know that Michelle does in-line skating with her hands on her hips? Now come clean, you guys. After all, I'm the one who got the two of you together, so to speak." He grinned knowingly.

Michelle stood up, her face tight with anger. "There is nothing—absolutely nothing—going on between Jacob and me besides a completely platonic friendship. I am a married woman in case you've forgotten. I resent the insinuation that I would be unfaithful to my husband."

And there you have it, folks, Jacob thought. The reminder, if he needed one, that he and Michelle were never going to share anything except his daughters. Not that he'd ever thought otherwise.

Bob straightened abruptly. "But he's… I'm sorry, Michelle, it won't happen again." He looked across at Jacob with an apologetic shrug. "Whatever the reason, thanks for the ratings." He let the door to the sound room close behind him.

Jacob reached for the phone. He needed a date.

CHAPTER SEVEN

MICHELLE GLANCED at the clock. Eleven-thirty. How could Jacob stay out so late when he knew they had to be at work in six and a half hours? She, for one, needed to sleep. Not that he had any idea his late hours were keeping *her* up. As far as Jacob knew, Laurie was sitting with the girls.

She picked up a magazine, leafing through a couple of pages. Although her sewing machine beckoned from across the room, she'd promised Meggie she wouldn't start sewing her sisters' dresses before Meggie's was cut out. And that wouldn't be until after they made another trip to the fabric store to buy more material. But at least Meggie'd agreed to let Michelle cut out the gown this time.

Restless, she glanced at her watch again. What was Jacob doing out this late? No, scratch that. She didn't want to know. But it wasn't as if he hadn't been out in a while. As a matter of fact, he'd been out three times that week. Not that she was counting—it wasn't any business of hers if he was off with a different woman every night—but she couldn't help it if his daughters chose to fill her in on their father's social life.

She heard a rustling sound coming from the girls' room and glanced up, wondering if one of them was awake. Maybe she'd better check.

She walked quietly down the hall toward the door she'd left open at Allie's instruction after she'd tucked the girls into bed. Slipping into the room, Michelle glanced from one bed to the next, assuring herself that all three children were accounted for. Jessie's teddy bear was on the floor. Michelle tiptoed over, picked up the bear and laid it down gently next to the sleeping child.

Crossing to Allie's bed, she saw that the little girl was lying flat on her back, still tucked in just as she'd left her. Then she moved hesitantly toward Meggie, half-afraid that Jacob's self-contained middle child would sense someone trespassing in her space and wake up.

Meggie's covers were hanging off her bed, and Michelle leaned over to rearrange them. Giving into temptation, she kissed Meggie's cheek. The child stirred and Michelle froze. But Meggie settled more deeply into her pillow, a trace of smile softening her face.

With one last longing look, Michelle returned to the living room. She threw herself down on the couch, picked up her magazine, then stared into space. She loved Jacob's girls, and yet there were times when being with them made her feel lonelier than ever. Tonight was one of them.

Would she ever have a child of her own? Would there ever be someone who turned to her with inno-

cent eyes and a hundred questions, trusting her to have all the answers? Would she ever be the one a child ran to for comfort?

Michelle didn't know. And she didn't know if she was doing the best thing, spending so much of her free time with someone else's children. Being on the outside looking in. She only knew that she wouldn't trade her time with Jacob's girls for anything. For as long as they'd include her in their lives, she would be there.

A car pulled into the driveway, its headlights shining through the front window before turning toward the garage. Her heart started to beat a little faster, and her fingers tightened around the edges of the magazine she wasn't reading. He knew she was here; he'd have seen her car out front. So what was he thinking? That she was keeping tabs on him? That she was taking advantage of their arrangement to invade his privacy?

Michelle forced herself to breathe normally and put the magazine down. She was being ridiculous. She had a perfectly legitimate reason for being here. It would've been silly to keep the sitter when Michelle was here, anyway, working with the girls on their costumes. And Jacob was the one who'd told her, when she'd moved her sewing machine into his living room, that she could come over anytime.

She heard his key in the lock, heard him close the door. "Michelle?" His voice sounded so formal. It was worse than she'd imagined.

She stood and slipped into the flats she'd kicked

off a couple of hours before, then turned to face him. But the explanation she'd prepared died before it ever reached her lips.

Damn, damn, damn! Tongue-tied, embarrassed beyond belief and so jealous she wanted to scream at him, she tried to look anywhere but at his face—but she couldn't stop staring. His lips were swollen, and his hair, bearing the unmistakable imprint of a woman's fingers, was standing up in tufts; his eyes had that sleepy unmistakable look of a satisfied male. She recognized it from the times she'd seen it before. Right after Brian made love to her.

"Where's Laurie?" He remained in the doorway, one hand in his pocket, the other fiddling with his keys.

"The girls and I walked her home earlier. There didn't seem to be much point in having both of us here."

He nodded, looking over at the material spread out around her sewing machine, at the magazine she'd left lying open on the coffee table, anywhere but at her. "You paid her?"

"I tried, but she said she'd settle up with you later."

He slid his keys into his pocket. "You never said anything about coming over tonight. I thought you were having dinner with your parents."

Michelle shook her head. "That was Tuesday. They have a standing bridge game on Thursday nights."

He nodded again.

Michelle hated this awkwardness between them. It wasn't supposed to be this way. They were friends—partners.

"The girls went to bed right at eight o'clock, though they did try the old glass-of-water routine I used to pull with my parents," she said, walking toward him.

"Yeah, they still try it on me from time to time, too. My mistake was in falling for it the first time. That's the way it is with them. If you give in once they forever hope you'll do it again."

Michelle smiled. "I'll remember that."

She slid past him, heading for the front door.

Jacob followed her. "I'm sorry it's so late. It looks like you're only going to get a couple of hours' sleep."

She turned around, once again ready to defend her presence there, to tell him that making costumes was a time-consuming business, that she didn't want to leave things till the last minute. Again her words died on her lips. His gaze met hers for the first time since he'd walked in the door. He was rubbing the back of his neck, looking remarkably unsure of himself.

It was so unlike Jacob she froze with one hand on the doorknob. His heavy-lidded eyes were filled with all the words he wasn't saying. There was anger there, the ready defense for finding his home invaded without his prior knowledge. But she saw regret, too. For what? For keeping her out so late? Or for coming home to her straight from the arms of another woman?

She couldn't look away as he moved closer, almost hypnotized by the changing expression in his eyes. He reached out, fingering the strand of her hair that lay against one shoulder. His gaze left hers to settle on her lips.

Michelle had never been so tempted to throw herself at a man in her life. At that moment she wanted him so badly it felt like a matter of life and death. She needed to be crushed in his arms until she felt nothing but him, to be kissed until she was too breathless to think, to feel what the woman he'd been with that night had felt. She ran her tongue along the edge of her lips as he stood there, looking at her mouth, his eyes still slumberous with spent passion, but filled with intent, too.

His head came down, his lips parting. So this was what she'd come to. Was she really so desperate for a man's touch that she'd take him straight from another woman's arms? She didn't try to stop him, but her eyes filled with tears.

Jacob backed away immediately. "Maybe you should call before you come next time," he said as if nothing had happened. "That way I'll know not to stay out so late."

If he was trying to make her feel better, he'd failed miserably. Michelle nodded and pulled open the front door. And that was when she remembered Meggie's ruined costume.

"If it's all right with you, I need to run Meggie back to the fabric store tomorrow," she said as soon as she was safely on the porch.

"You forget something?" he asked, leaning on the frame.

Michelle shook her head, gathering her usual composure about her like a cloak. "She didn't want any help cutting out her costume. She did it herself, with her school scissors, while I was helping Jessie with hers."

Jacob grinned. "I assume it didn't turn out too well," he said.

Michelle smiled back, thinking of the mangled material in his trash can. "You could say that," she said.

Jacob shook his head, the gold highlights in his hair glinting under the porch light. "I promised the girls I'd take them to the Hard Rock Café tomorrow night. Why don't you first take Meggie to the store and then come with us, since you're making the trip over here on a Friday night? I know the place is touristy, but the girls love it."

And suddenly, in spite of everything, the evening was turning out okay. "I'd like that," Michelle said. "And by the way you might want to take some stain remover to the lipstick on your collar before you throw that shirt in the wash..."

JACOB HAD KNOWN it was a mistake to invite Michelle to spend the evening with the girls and him the minute he'd issued the invitation. She was starting to make him crave things he had no business craving— that he'd resigned himself to never having. Things like a warm body in his bed all night, rather than in his arms for a few hours. Things like laughter over

breakfast and loyalty even when he was a grouch. Things like mutual respect and love. Even knowing that she considered herself a married woman, even after his spending an evening in another woman's arms, he still wanted her.

As he waited with her for a table at the Hard Rock Café the next night, he regretted the invitation again, but for a different reason. He should have foreseen the crowd of people waiting for tables.

He wouldn't have minded so much if just he and the girls had been here. While it wasn't easy keeping three energetic and excited seven-year-olds entertained, he was, after all, used to it. But with Michelle here, everything was different. He was on edge, afraid the triplets' enthusiasm was going to wear on her, expecting one of them to do something embarrassing or, worse, all three of them to do something embarrassing.

"Can I have another soda, Daddy?" Meggie asked, bringing him her empty cup.

"I want one, too, Daddy," Jessie said, bobbing up and down in front of him.

"Me, too," Allie said, taking Jessie's cup and handing it to Jacob with her own.

He glanced at Michelle. Her glass was still full, but she was smiling at the girls. Deciding not to risk the unpleasantness that could occur—in triplicate—from the word *no,* he said, "Sure," and headed back to the bar.

As he waited for the bartender he wondered what he was doing trying to avoid the inevitable. At some

point the girls weren't going to be perfect angels. Hell, right this minute he was probably creating the situation that was going to ruin things. As a single father he'd discovered years ago that public rest rooms were the ultimate challenge. He couldn't very well take the girls with him into the men's room. And he sure as hell wasn't sending them anywhere on their own. That was why he never took his daughters anywhere without making sure they went to the bathroom just before they left home. But after the long wait to be seated tonight—and after two large sodas—he expected to hear, "Daddy, I have to go right *now,*" at least three times before the evening was over.

The girls all knew what they wanted to eat, and they placed their orders almost as soon as they were seated at the table. Jacob sat between Jessie and Allie trying to restrain their excited chatter. Being with the triplets had never been so exhausting.

"Look at that guitar, Michelle. Isn't it cool?"

"I like the motorcycle. Did you see the motorcycle, Michelle?"

"Daddy, what's that record hanging over there? Can I go see?"

Jacob wished he were at home. "Girls, girls, one at a time, please," he said, afraid to look at Michelle. Had she had enough yet?

"Well, can I, Daddy? Can I go see?" Meggie was halfway out of her chair.

"Meggie, sit," Jacob said. "We'll look after we're done eating."

"See that guitar, Michelle? It's Elvis Presley's," Allie said, pointing to a corner of the room.

"Yeah, and the motorcycle's his, too," Jessie said, sitting up on her knees.

Michelle's head spun as she tried to keep up with the girls.

"Are they really Elvis Presley's?" she asked Jacob.

He shrugged. "I doubt it, but you never know."

"I'm hungry, Daddy. When's our food coming?" Meggie asked fifteen minutes later, long after the girls had tired of the sights in the room.

"Soon," he said, hoping he was correct. He must have been out of his mind to have invited Michelle on an outing like this—his family was an accident waiting to happen.

Jessie grabbed the saltshaker and turned it over, spilling salt in her palm.

Jacob snatched it from her. "You know better than that, Jess," he said, brushing her hand off with his napkin.

Watching Jessie, Allie and Meggie took an interest in the condiments, too.

"I'm counting the sugars," Meggie said, pulling the dishful of packets toward her.

"What's this, Daddy?" Allie asked, shaking a bottle of steak sauce.

Jacob lunged for the steak sauce, praying the lid was on tight. "Put the sugars back, Meg. People don't want to use them after you've played with them."

Jacob was surprised that Michelle still looked so unruffled. Ellen would've insisted on leaving.

"Anyone know how to play hangman?" Michelle asked, taking a small notepad and pen from her purse.

"What's hangman?" Allie and Jessie chorused. Even Meggie looked interested.

"I think of a word—I'll make it one you guys can spell—and draw blanks like this. Then you try to fill in the blanks by guessing letters. But each time you guess wrong, I get to draw another part of a stick figure up here. If he's complete before you guess the word, then I win."

"What happens if we guess the word before he's done?" Jessie asked.

"Then we win, silly," Allie said. "Okay, let's start."

"Be nice to your sister, Al," Jacob said, relaxing just a bit. Michelle flashed him a quick smile—and the game began.

With Jacob as referee, Michelle kept the girls entertained for another fifteen minutes until their food came. And she helped dispense catsup and salt to the three plates of burgers and fries as naturally as if she'd been doing it all her life.

A second of silence fell over the table while the three children dug into their meals. Jacob figured there was something to be said for keeping their mouths full.

He'd just taken the first bite of his cheeseburger when things started to go wrong. "I have to *go*," Jessie announced, bouncing in her seat.

Jacob groaned inwardly. What now? He glanced down the hall that led to the ladies' room. He could stick his head around the door and make sure the coast was clear before he sent Jessie in, then stand guard outside until she came out. It wasn't the way he liked to do things, but it didn't look as if he had much choice. He'd just have to hope that he didn't offend some poor woman in the process.

"I'll take her," Michelle said easily.

Jessie jumped up and slid her hand into Michelle's. Jacob groaned again—audibly this time. Michelle was putting up a good front, but her food would be cold by the time she got back.

"Allie, Meggie, you go with them," he said. At least he could insure that this only happened once.

"I don't have to go," Allie said, her mouth full of hamburger.

"Me, neither," Meggie added.

Jacob gave the two his sternest look. "This is your only chance, girls. If you have to go, you better do it now."

"I don't," Allie said, looking toward her sister for confirmation.

"Me, neither," Meggie said again.

"I gotta go *now*," Jessie said again, hopping up and down.

Jacob watched her head off with Michelle. Then, flagging down their waiter as he passed, he asked him to try to keep Michelle's meal warm.

Three-quarters of the way through dinner, Allie had to go to the bathroom.

"Me, too," Meggie said when she heard her sister's announcement.

Normally patient with his daughters, Jacob had to bite his tongue to keep from snapping at them. He looked across at Michelle, prepared to see the irritation or, worse, the resignation he'd come to dread seeing on Ellen's face every time one of the girls needed something she'd just done for one of the others.

Michelle was standing there grinning. "Come on, you two. You won't believe what's hanging on the wall right outside the bathroom."

Allie and Meggie jumped up, flanking Michelle as they traipsed off to the bathroom giggling excitedly. Allie was holding her hand, and Michelle was keeping Meggie within grabbing distance, as well.

Jacob stared after them, shaken by a wave of desire. More than her sexy body or silky skin, it was Michelle's obvious fondness for his girls that moved him the most. It almost made him believe he might yet find that happy-ever-after he used to dream about. Until he remembered Brian Colby.

"What's the matter, Daddy? Don't you like your french fries?" Jessie asked, putting her hand on Jacob's arm.

"Sure, sport, I like them just fine," he said, looking down at one of the females who owned his heart.

"Then why did you have such a bad look on your face? Like this." She scrunched her eyebrows together and jutted out her chin.

Jacob smiled and tweaked the end of her nose. "Just to see if you'd notice," he said.

Jessie didn't look convinced. "I love you, Daddy," she said, her small features solemn.

"And I love you, too, Jess," he said, knowing he was lucky beyond belief to have his three beautiful daughters. Somehow he was just going to have to make them be enough.

JACOB EXPECTED Michelle to leave just as soon as they got back to his place that night. But she followed him into the house, offering to make him a pot of coffee while he got the girls tucked into bed. He could tell she had something on her mind. He wondered if she was about to turn tail, after all. Allie and Jessie insisted on hugging her good-night before they'd go to bed. Meggie didn't hug her, but she smiled and thanked Michelle for the trip they'd made to the fabric store that day.

Michelle was gazing out the kitchen window when he came into the kitchen fifteen minutes later. "There's diet cola in the fridge," he said, pouring himself a cup of freshly brewed coffee.

Michelle whirled around as if she hadn't heard him come in. "Thanks," she said, and filled a glass with ice.

"The girls said to tell you good-night, again," he told her when she joined him at the table. He'd had a talk with himself while he'd waited for the girls to get into their pajamas and brush their teeth. Whatever Michelle had to say, he'd deal with it unemotionally.

If she was going to leave them, so be it. He'd find
another way to get the costumes made. In fact, maybe
that would be for the best. Her tears the night before
when he'd tried to kiss her had really thrown him for
a loop. But not as much as the guilt that had plagued
him for coming home to her after sleeping with another woman. He'd felt like an unfaithful husband,
for God's sake. Yeah, maybe it was for the best that
she call it quits before he did anything foolish—like
fall in love with her.

"Can I ask you something?" Michelle said softly.

"Sure."

Her eyes were serious as she looked at him. "You
seemed pretty on edge tonight, and I wondered if I've
done something to upset you. Because if I have I
think we should talk about it now before it becomes
a problem."

"Hell, no!" he said, setting his cup down so forcefully the coffee splashed over the rim. "I wasn't upset
with you."

She shrugged. "Well, what then? I've never seen
you so uptight before. If it bothers you having me
around your girls, I can make the costumes myself at
my house," she said.

Jacob felt as if he was surfing on a wave that was
about to become an undertow. "The girls have to
help, I told you that." He'd said the quickest thing
that came to mind. Now that it seemed she wasn't
leaving, he forgot all about wanting her to go. After
all, who else would he get to make those costumes?

She nodded, still looking serious. "I just don't

want you to think I'm trying to butt in, like when I came over last night."

"Butt in already. It's working out okay, isn't it?" he asked, suddenly wondering if this was a round-about way to get out of helping him.

"That's the problem. I don't know if it's working out or not. You never tell me what you're thinking, and it's driving me nuts to keep guessing, wondering if I'm getting in your way. It wouldn't kill you to open up a little bit, you know."

He wasn't so sure. But he didn't want her to walk out that door and never come back, either. Even if she was only in his house as a friend. He wanted her there. He'd finally admitted it. To himself at least.

He leaned forward, resting his forearms on the table, cradling his coffee cup. "The last time Ellen and I took the girls out to dinner, we'd barely been seated when Jessie spilled her drink. They're good kids most of the time, but they're still kids. And Ellen seemed to bring out the worst in them. That night, Jessie had to use the bathroom before we'd even looked at the menus. Then when Allie started to cry because we wouldn't let her have ice cream for dinner and her sisters joined in, Ellen insisted that I take them home, get a sitter and take her—Ellen—out for a real dinner. She yelled at the girls all the way home, telling them that they didn't have the right to publicly embarrass her, that she deserved to be able to sit down and enjoy a meal at least once in a while, that she wasn't going to let them steal her life away. They were only three at the time, and I don't suppose they understood half

of what she was saying, but they knew she was angry and was blaming *them.* And when I intervened, Ellen went ballistic. She claimed I always sided with the girls, and she took that out on them, as well. There was no reasoning with her. I drove as fast as I could, but the girls were all crying hysterically by the time we got home. It took me the rest of the evening to get them calmed down enough to eat a sandwich and climb into bed. I've never felt so helpless in my life. I should have seen it coming, should have been able to do something more than I was doing, but damned if I knew what it was.''

When he realized how much he'd just revealed, Jacob clamped his mouth shut. Hell, he hadn't even known he remembered that night in such detail.

''She ought to be hung.'' Michelle's fierce look brought a smile to his lips.

''I gotta admit to having had that thought a time or two myself, but it was a lot more complicated than that. She was partially right. I did side with the girls a lot.''

''It sounds like you may have had good reason.''

''Some of the time. But Ellen wasn't a bad person. She just wasn't mother material.''

''Then she shouldn't have had children.'' Michelle's voice was as fierce as her expression. She reminded him of a mother bear protecting her young. Except they were *his* young she was defending. It was a new experience for him, one he could probably get used to with very little effort.

''You're right of course. And she probably

wouldn't have had children if I hadn't pressured her into getting pregnant. I wanted kids. A whole houseful of them.''

"Didn't you two talk about raising a family before you got married? I know Brian and I did.''

"Yeah, we talked. I told her how badly I wanted kids. She said okay. What we didn't talk about, until after she was pregnant, was that she wanted a baby to show off but not to care for. Her idea of parenting was as far from mine as it was possible to get. She'd been raised by a nanny. Her mother was a social butterfly who always looked immaculate, who only saw her child when she stopped home in between appointments. I'd thought that Ellen of all people would understand how hard it is to grow up with parental neglect. Instead, she thought that was the only way to raise children. She was shocked when, once she got pregnant, I refused to consider hiring a nanny. Frankly I didn't have the greatest childhood, and I was determined that my child was going to be raised by his parents, not by strangers.'' Jacob knew that ultimately the fault for his divorce—for his children's motherless state—lay with him. He'd been too unbending. He expected too much. But where his children were concerned, he wasn't going to change. And he wasn't sorry for that.

Michelle laid a hand on Jacob's forearm. "It's not wrong to expect your wife to help raise your children.''

"No, but I was so busy listening to my own needs I never really considered hers, or at least not honestly.

I kept telling Ellen that once she held her baby in her arms everything would change. I was banking on that old mother's instinct kicking in. I hired someone to help her as soon as we knew the triplets were coming, but I insisted that Ellen and I would be the primary care givers. I really thought she'd want it that way, too, once the babies came. She never did.''

"How could any one look at those three precious little girls and not love them instantly?''

"That's just it. She did love them. More than she imagined she would, I think. But their care was just too overwhelming for her. She didn't find any satisfaction in it. She told me once that she was choking on ABC's. She wasn't fascinated by all the simple things that I found so exciting. When Jessie blew bubbles, it wasn't cooing to Ellen, it was drooling. When the girls started to walk, they weren't taking first steps, they were constantly on the brink of falling and hurting themselves. She was repelled by dirty diapers, and the girls' crying made her nervous. And to further complicate matters, they kept Ellen from doing the things she enjoyed, like shopping or playing tennis or heading up some committee. She felt like life was passing her by. And I couldn't agree to putting the girls in day care so young or having a live-in care giver. They weren't going to be shoved aside like I was. I kept telling myself that Ellen would adjust in time, that once the girls got a little older she'd start enjoying them. My immediate solution was to take her out more, but while she enjoyed that, our late

nights left her tired the next day, which meant she
had even less patience for the girls.''

Jacob fell silent, thinking back over those days,
wondering where he'd made the first mistake, looking, always looking, for the solution that would have
been right for both of them. And he came to the same
conclusion as always. Maybe they'd found it.

"All women aren't like Ellen, you know." Michelle's words fell softly into the late-night silence.

He thought of Jenny, his former on-air partner.
She'd said she loved him, but she needed time to
herself, too. Not just an evening without the girls, but
evenings at home alone in front of the television set.
Jacob had never understood why they couldn't watch
television together. And she'd grown tired of having
the triplets as part of the package. She'd liked the
girls. She just hadn't wanted them on a full-time basis. And then there was Katie Walters's mother. What
was it the triplets had heard? Something about she'd
have left, too? Apparently wanting a full-time mother
for his children was asking for too much. But then he
always had wanted more than he should. His own
mother had told him so often enough. Couldn't he see
she had other children to care for besides him?

"I know," he finally said.

"So relax, partner. I think I can handle anything
your girls can dish out. Trust me."

Jacob wished it was that easy.

CHAPTER EIGHT

JACOB AND MICHELLE were in the station lunch room getting their caffeine fixes when Bob Chaney handed them an envelope.

"You guys had the best ratings this week, so enjoy the promo," he said as he walked away. He'd been keeping his distance ever since Michelle had blown up at him the week before.

Michelle opened the envelope, half expecting to find a gift certificate for dinner for two at some romantic out-of-the way spot. She was surprised when she pulled out four tickets to Disneyland.

"What is it?" Jacob asked, sipping his coffee. His T-shirt was blue this morning, depicting a beautiful Colorado skyline. The color looked good on him.

"Four tickets to Disneyland. Two for you and two for me."

"Seems like he got our message. We get to take dates," Jacob said with a grin.

Michelle wondered why that didn't please her as much as it should have. "I guess. Here." She handed him the tickets.

He handed two back. "You get these."

Michelle turned back to the pop machine. "You go ahead, Jacob. Take the girls."

"Don't be ridiculous, Michelle. I'm not taking your promo."

She faced him, a can of soda in hand. "And what am I going to do with two tickets to Disneyland? Take Noby? You know I don't date, and I can't think of a single friend who would choose to spend an entire day with me, rather than with the man in her life." She smiled to take the sting out of her words. It wasn't Jacob's fault she didn't have anybody of her own to take to Disneyland. "Take the girls, Jacob. They'll love it."

"Then you'll have to come with us."

"We only have four tickets."

"So we'll buy one more. I'm not taking these tickets unless you come along with us. Think of it as research. You can get a good look at Cinderella and her evil stepsisters while we're there."

As weak as it was, she accepted the excuse. "Okay, sounds like fun. When should we go?"

"How about Saturday?"

"Saturday's fine. Around eight?"

"Why don't we pick you up at seven and have breakfast on the way. My treat. We can tell the girls tonight."

It was only later that Michelle wondered if they'd both been a little too eager to spend the day together. She was in this for the kids. Period.

"YOU GONNA SEW Jessie's other sleeve on when you finish sewing that one, Michelle?" Allie asked

Wednesday night after supper. She was holding the sleeve in question.

"As soon as I trim the threads on this one," Michelle said. She took her foot off the sewing-machine pedal long enough to turn the sleeve currently under the needle. She was finding it a little difficult to maneuver the material with Jessie hanging on her arm.

"I can trim the threads for you," Allie said.

"How do you make it go so straight?" Jessie asked, leaning to get a better look.

"See that line?" Michelle asked, pointing to a plate on her machine. Jessie nodded. "I just keep the edge of the material even with it, like this."

Meggie wandered over to peer at the sewing machine.

"You get that lace measured out like I showed you, Meggie?" Michelle asked.

"Almost," Meggie replied, returning to her task.

Michelle pulled one of the pins out of the sleeve before the needle hit it.

"Here's the pin cushion," Allie said, taking the pin to put it in the cushion herself. "How about if I take all of the pins out for you?" she asked.

"What can I do? It's my sleeve," Jessie said, still holding on to Michelle.

"You can help me guide the material," Michelle said. "See, take the bottom edge, and help me keep it on the line."

"Like this?" Jessie asked. She'd let go of Michelle's arm but was having a problem getting a good hold on the material.

"Here," Michelle said, lifting her foot from the pedal again to move Jessie onto her lap. "Now we can do it together."

"And I'll do the pins, all right?" Allie asked.

"Okay, you can be the pin lady," Michelle said, trying to slow the machine down to a speed Jessie could handle. "How's the lace coming, Meggie?"

"Fine."

Jessie started to slip off Michelle's lap and tried to right herself, pushing one foot against the floor. But she missed and pushed against Michelle's foot.

The sewing machine whirred loudly as the needle sped into triple time, pulling the material out of Michelle's grasp. There was a loud cracking noise, and everything stopped.

"What happened?" Jessie and Allie asked at once.

"What was that noise?" Meggie asked, coming over to see what was going on.

Michelle leaned around Jessie to get a closer look at the sewing machine. "I think we just broke a needle."

"Uh-oh," Allie said, backing up.

Jessie scooted off Michelle's lap.

Meggie went back to cutting lace.

After Michelle removed the broken needle, she turned to the girls. Two of them of them were watching her carefully, their faces puckered with worry. Meggie was hunched over her lace.

"Hey!" Michelle smiled. "It's no big deal, you guys. Needles break all the time. That's why I have extras. Allie, bring me my sewing basket."

Meggie handed the basket to her sister, who hurried over to Michelle with it. Jessie scooted closer.

It took Michelle only a couple of moments to realize she'd left her extra needles at home.

Allie looked worried again when she heard the news. Jessie started to cry. Meggie's scissors were snipping away.

Michelle cuddled Jessie under one arm and went over to Allie, pulling her under the other. "So I guess we'll just have to take a trip to my house," she said. "You girls can come along and say hi to Noby. You remember Noby, don't you?"

Meggie stopped cutting. All three girls nodded.

"She's probably pretty lonely, so it's good to be able to take a break and go see her. Allie, why don't you run out and tell your daddy where we're going?"

Allie hurried outside to where Jacob was waxing his 4×4. Jessie hopped up and down, obviously eager to get going, her tears forgotten. Meggie went back to cutting.

"Come on, Meggie, you can finish that when we get back."

"I'm staying home with Daddy," she said, concentrating on her task.

Michelle frowned. "Don't you want to see Noby?"

"I wanna stay home with Daddy," Meggie said, neatly sidestepping Michelle's question.

Michelle walked over to the little girl. "You don't *have* to come, Meggie. I just want you to know that I'd love to have you along if you *want* to come."

"I'll stay with Daddy," Meggie said, still not looking up from her lace.

"How about if we bring you back some ice cream?" Michelle asked, determined to reach the little girl.

"Okay, if you want."

And with that, Michelle knew she had to be satisfied.

ALLIE THOUGHT Saturday was never going to come. All day Friday she kept waiting for school to be over, but it was taking forever. Every time Allie looked at the watch her daddy had bought her for Christmas, the numbers had barely changed at all. She thought maybe the battery wasn't so good anymore, but if it wasn't, then the clocks at school weren't working, either, 'cause when her teacher dismissed them for lunch, it was the exact time on Allie's watch that lunch was s'posed to be.

Lunch was hardest of all. She kept being afraid that Meggie or Jessie was going to need her for something, and then she'd blab everything and one of them would ruin it. This was one plan she was just going to have to do on her own. She could, too. And then it wouldn't matter if her sisters found out that she'd almost ruined things by wishing so hard for a mommy that it made Daddy sad, because then her wish would just come true and her sisters would be happily ever after.

She and Jessie and Meggie had been to Disneyland lots of times, and Allie knew plain and simple that

five people couldn't sit together on the rides. So she was going to make sure her sisters sat with her. Then her daddy and Michelle would have to sit together and after a whole day of being next to each other they'd fall in love. Now all Allie had to do was keep her big mouth shut and not tell her sisters that Michelle was going to be their new mommy. Not yet. Not until they got back from Disneyland. Then she'd tell them. After all, she wanted them to know she was the one who got Michelle for them—just in case they ever found out she was the one who started the whole trouble in the first place. But keeping such important stuff a secret was the hardest thing she'd ever done.

FRIDAY NIGHT, Michelle dropped Noby off at her parents for the weekend, worried that her pet was getting depressed at being left alone so much. Her mom and dad seemed delighted to cat-sit, but Michelle knew, as fond as they were of Noby, it wasn't her cat they were worked up about.

She wanted to tell them not to read more into her time with Jacob and his girls than was there, to remind them that she was a married woman, that until Brian was found, one way or the other, she would remain a married woman. But she'd been telling herself the same things all week, and if she hadn't managed to curtail her own excitement at the thought of the next day, she knew she'd fail miserably with her parents.

Sometimes she wondered if she wasn't overdoing her loyalty to a man she hadn't heard from in almost

five years. She wanted to put her life back on track, to have babies, to raise a family. She didn't want to grow old alone. And yet each time she thought about putting the past to rest, there was something inside her holding her to the vows that she and Brian had made. She was certain he hadn't left her by choice. And until she knew for sure he'd left her for good, she couldn't stop being married to him. There was a bond between them—forged many years ago by their young idealistic love—that refused to be broken. Michelle suspected that the reason she still felt that bond so strongly was because Brian was alive somewhere, willing her to wait for him.

And she'd wait forever if she had to, she told herself as she drove home later that evening. But she was going to do what living she could while she waited. Her mother had been right to claim that Michelle had quit reaching out to people. She'd forgotten how good it felt to help someone else, how much less time it left for worrying about her own problems. Now Jacob's girls were filling up some of the empty spaces inside her; she just had to be careful not to let their father do the same.

SHE WAS READY and waiting at seven o'clock Saturday morning when Jacob's Explorer pulled into her driveway. The triplets were buckled up in a row in the back seat, looking absolutely adorable in their identical denim overalls, red T-shirts, high-top tennis shoes and their hair up in ponytails. But it was their differences that stole Michelle's heart as she told

them all good-morning and slid into the front beside Jacob.

"Michelle, guess what? We're stopping at Mc-Donald's for breakfast on the way," Allie piped up from the middle of the back seat.

"I get to sit next to you," Jessie confided.

"At McDonald's, she means," Allie added importantly.

"Hi," Meggie said, not quite containing her smile.

"I missed you guys yesterday, you know that?" Michelle said, smiling at them. The day was perfect already, and it had only just begun.

They arrived at the Magic Kingdom just as the gates were opening. Jacob pulled into one of the few vacant parking spaces in the Thumper lot, and by the time he'd turned off the ignition the girls had unfastened their seat belts. Meggie tugged on one door handle and Jessie on the other, while Allie bounced impatiently between them.

"Come on, you guys," Allie said.

"Whoa!"

Michelle was startled by Jacob's stern tone—and by the reaction he got. The girls froze in their seats, three pairs of dark eyes trained on their father.

"I want the rules one more time," Jacob said, turning around. "Jessie?"

"We stick together and always hold someone's hand."

"Good. And?"

"If we have to go, we tell you *before* we get in a long line."

Jacob smiled. "You got it. Meggie?"

"No running."

"Right. Allie?"

"*If* we get lost, we go to the castle and wait there."

"Right."

"But we won't, you know, Daddy. We never do."

"I know, sport, but I'm supposed to worry, anyway," he said, giving Allie's ponytail a tug. "Now let's get this show on the road."

The girls climbed out of the 4×4, not one ounce less excited, but much more contained. Michelle was impressed.

She was having trouble containing her own excitement as they entered the park and headed down Main Street. The sun was shining, glinting off the lampposts lining the street. The shops beckoned with their colorful displays of candy and stuffed renditions of every Disney character ever to have graced a motion-picture screen. And best of all was the magnificent blue-and-white castle that stood tall and proud at the end of Main Street. Michelle figured even the staunchest scrooge couldn't look at that castle and not feel, just for an instant, that dreams really did come true.

They decided, at Allie's urging, to tackle Fantasy-land first and work their way around the entire park. Michelle thought the plan seemed a bit too elaborate for seven-year-olds, but by the sounds of the chatter between the girls and Jacob, doing Disneyland—all of it—was nothing new to them. She hoped *she* would be able to hold out.

The girls skipped between Jacob and her talking as fast as their little tongues could manage. Michelle wondered if they even heard each other, as none of them seemed to stay quiet long enough for a single word to reach them.

"We'll do Snow White's Scary Adventures first, Daddy, okay?" Allie asked, glancing up at her father.

"Fine, sport." Jacob nodded. Though he was watching the girls like a hawk, he looked more relaxed than Michelle had ever seen him. If she wasn't mistaken, Jacob Ryan was as affected by the magic around them as she was.

Another family brushed past, and Michelle saw the mother turn around, do a double take and then nudge her husband. Michelle smiled, not yet used to the attention the triplets attracted wherever they went. She supposed to these strangers she was the mother who completed Jacob's family unit, and she wished suddenly that it was true. She could only imagine how it would feel to be the nucleus of a family, but she figured that this day with Jacob and his children was the closest she'd come to it. It might be the closest she'd *ever* come to it. And she was going to enjoy every minute, she determined as she followed the girls toward Snow White's Scary Adventures.

"Jessie and Meggie 'n me'll go in the first car, so you guys can see us, okay, Daddy?" Allie said, pulling on the sleeve of Jacob's Lakers jersey.

Jacob smiled down at her "Yep."

She grabbed the map of the park from the back pocket of his jeans. "Where're we going next?" she

asked, scanning the pages of the map as if she could read every word. "How about Pinocchio's Daring Journey? Let's do that next."

"If it's okay with your sisters," Jacob said.

Jessie and Meggie were leaning over the railing trying to see what was going on ahead of them.

"They don't care," Allie said with certainty.

He turned to Michelle. "How about you? You have any special requests? If so, you better get them in quick before Allie has the whole day planned."

Michelle grinned. "I wouldn't dare interfere with the expert," she said, happy just to be standing in line with the four of them.

The line moved forward, and Jacob urged his daughters along, leaving Michelle to bring up the rear. She found herself fixating on his snugly clad backside. She'd known Jacob for years—why was he suddenly so appealing?

"Michelle, come on!"

Allie's voice jerked Michelle out of her reverie and she hurried to catch up. She hadn't even noticed that they'd reached the front of the line.

"Okay, girls, hands inside, no standing, wait for us at the end and have fun."

Michelle was amazed that Jacob had the time to get in all his instructions as he fastened the safety bar across his girls and waved them off.

"This is ours," he said as the next automated carrier came along.

It wasn't until then that Michelle realized she would be sharing a very small space with Jacob. Her

hands felt a little clammy as she slid across the seat.
It got worse when Jacob sat down beside her. His hip
pressed against hers and his arm brushed her breast
as he reached to fasten their safety bar. Michelle shivered, horrified when her nipples tightened. She
hunched her shoulders and prayed the ride would be
a dark one.

Jacob leaned toward her. "You cold?" he asked as
their car jerked forward.

"A little," Michelle said. Jacob grinned at her in
lazy satisfaction. He had a look about him that said
he knew exactly what was happening—and was
pleased by it. Dear Lord, how was she going to get
through the next two minutes, let alone the next several hours?

They rode on a boat through the storybook canal,
went through It's a Small World twice at Jessie's request and screamed their way through the Matterhorn
Bobsleds. And through it all, whether sitting next to
Jacob or not, Michelle was aware of every inch of his
healthy masculine body.

"I wanna sit with Michelle," Jessie said three lines
later. "I don't wanna sit with you on this one, Allie.
I wanna sit with Michelle."

"That's fine with me, honey," Michelle said. She
hoped she didn't sound as eager as she felt to change
the seating arrangements. At this stage, the impression
of Jacob's shoulder and hip must be permanently im-
printed on hers, and the touch of his hand was af-
fecting more than her concentration.

"When we're done with Peter Pan can we go to Tomorrowland?" Allie asked.

"Sure, Al, as long as no one objects," Jacob said. He smiled at Michelle over his daughter's head, and even though his sunglasses hid his eyes something told her that Jacob was just as affected by their close confines as she was.

"I'm thirsty, Daddy. Can I have money for a soda?" Meggie asked half an hour later as the five of them headed for Tomorrowland.

"I could use a drink myself," Michelle said. "I'll go with you."

She took orders from the other two girls and Jacob, then remembering Jacob's rule about hand-holding, reached for Meggie's hand and headed toward the drink line. She felt a rush of happiness when Meggie's little fingers curled around her own. There really was magic in Disney's kingdom. She'd scale Meggie's walls yet.

They stopped for lunch halfway through Tomorrowland; afterword, Michelle suggested that they do some of the "old folks" rides like the Monorail and the Submarine voyage. She didn't want to take any chances that their day would be ruined by upset stomachs.

The girls were good sports on the tamer attractions, but as soon as Michelle announced that they'd waited long enough for their food to settle, they were back to their daring adventures. About three-quarters of the way around the building in the line at Space Mountain

was a sign that said it was a forty-five-minute wait from that point, but the girls weren't daunted.

"Please, Daddy," Jessie said.

"You don't mind waiting, do you?" Allie asked Michelle at the same time.

Jacob and Michelle looked at each other over the girls' heads, passing silent messages of acquiescence before they gave in with resigned shrugs. Michelle hadn't been on Space Mountain in years, but if she remembered it correctly, it was one ride on which she wouldn't mind being paired with Jacob—for moral support. She'd always been a little bit nervous of roller coasters, and this one was in the dark.

All in all the wait wasn't so bad. There were four people to a cart, two in front and two in back, and Allie was directing traffic as usual as they approached.

Meggie walked up to the cart in front of the one Allie had picked for her and her sisters to share. "I'm riding by myself," she said.

Allie turned to Jacob. "Is that okay, Daddy?" she asked.

Jacob looked at Meggie standing resolutely in her spot. "Yeah, it's okay," he said. "You keep your hands in and hold on tight, Meg, got it?"

"Got it," she said, grinning back at them.

Allie told Jessie to take the first seat in the next cart and then climbed in beside her, leaving Michelle and Jacob together once again. The carts rolled forward, and Michelle was thrown almost into Jacob's lap with the force of the turns. They climbed and

dropped, spun and swerved, but none of it was as exciting as the feel of Jacob's arm around her shoulders, as they hurtled through the darkness.

CHAPTER NINE

THE GIRLS' ENERGY seemed endless. As the day wore on, they left Tomorrowland behind to hike over to Mickey's Toontown. They traipsed through Mickey's house and had their picture taken with the host himself, visited Minnie's house, climbed onto Donald's boat and laughed at the goods for sale in the Gag Factory. Michelle was busy trying to explain a particularly zany contraption to Meggie when suddenly Jacob grabbed her arm.

"Have you seen Jessie?"

Michelle glanced around the store, searching for the little girl. "She was over there with Allie a second ago," she said, pointing to the display where Allie was standing.

Jacob crossed to Allie with Michelle and Meggie right behind him. Jessie was probably just hidden by the display.

"Al, where's Jessie?" Jacob asked.

Allie turned. "She said she was going over to where you were, Daddy."

Jacob spun around, retracing his steps. "Jessie?" he called.

"You two stay right here and don't move," Mi-

chelle said, stationing Allie and Meggie by the checkout counter before following Jacob.

The store was full of patrons, most of whom ignored them. Michelle suspected that a lost child at Disneyland wasn't all that unusual. Or that alarming, either. At least she hoped that was the case.

"I'm sure she's here someplace," she said, as much for her own sake as for Jacob's. Her stomach knotted, even though she kept telling herself she was overreacting. Jessie knew the rules. She wouldn't run off alone.

"Jessie?" Jacob called again. He was striding up and down the aisles, looking beneath racks of hanging clothes, searching every spot big enough to hold a seven-year-old. Michelle searched with him, feeling sicker by the second. What if Jessie hadn't run off by herself? What if someone had *taken* her?

Telling herself to get a grip, Michelle kept an eye firmly on Meggie and Allie. The girls stood by the counter where she'd left them, playing with a display of pencils. Michelle should take her cue from them. They didn't seem worried at all. They probably went through this all the time.

"She's not here," Jacob said from behind her.

Michelle whirled around. It was time to panic.

"I'm going to ask the clerk if she saw anything," Jacob said.

Michelle went with him, her gaze darting over the store one last time. Where could Jessie be? Would she really have disobeyed her father and wandered off her own? Michelle had a hard time believing that.

Jacob guided Meggie and Allie over to the clerk. "My daughter seems to be missing. She looks exactly like these two. You didn't happen to see her walk out of here, did you?" Michelle didn't know how he could sound so calm. Always a rock, that was Jacob. But she knew him well enough now to know he had to be a wreck on the inside.

"I'm sorry, sir. This is my first day here, and as you can see, we're really busy," the clerk said, motioning to the people in line waiting to pay for purchases.

"Are you sure you didn't see her?" Michelle asked. She couldn't believe this was happening.

The clerk shook her head. "Did you check outside? She's probably waiting for you out there." She flashed a harried smile.

Jacob ushered his family outside. They searched the immediate vicinity, but there was no sign of Jessie. Something was wrong. Very wrong. And as frightened as Michelle was, she could only imagine what this was doing to Jacob.

"Where *is* Jessie, Daddy?" Allie asked, her voice thick with tears. Michelle hugged the little girl, trying to comfort her. Jacob didn't need to contend with a hysterical child right now. She looked around Toontown. There were people everywhere. How were they ever going to find one small-for-her-age seven-year-old?

"Do you think something bad happened to Jessie?" Meggie asked quietly, her voice laced with fear. She slipped her hand into Jacob's.

"No! I don't think anything bad happened to her," Jacob said, studying the compound.

Allie and Meggie stood between the adults looking lost themselves as they gazed at the people milling all around. "Let's go back to Minnie's house. Jessie liked it best," Jacob said, heading off in that direction with Meggie in tow. Michelle gripped Allie's hand and followed him, looking at every short person she passed.

"You're hurting me," Allie said, tugging on her hand.

Michelle looked down. "I'm sorry, sweetie. How's that?" She lightened her grip.

Allie nodded and sniffled. Michelle reached into the pouch at her waist, pulled out a tissue and handed it to Allie, searching the area around them all the while. There were children everywhere, some accompanied by adults. But there was no sign of Jessie.

"Are you worried, Michelle?" Allie asked softly, staring at her father's straight back in front of them.

"She'll be fine, Al. Disneyland is one place kids are still safe without their parents."

"Daddy's worried."

"Your daddy's just concentrating on finding her, honey. I'm sure she'll turn up really soon."

Allie looked at Michelle with teary eyes. "Then how come your voice sounds all wobbly like you're gonna cry?"

Michelle forced a smile, putting her arm around Allie to hug the little girl as they walked. "Because

I'm being silly,'' she said. ''Now come on, let's catch up to your father and Meggie.''

Jessie wasn't at Minnie's house.

And she wasn't at Donald's Boat or Chip 'n Dale's Tree Slide, either.

Jacob's lips grew thinner as the minutes passed, his stride more and more determined. Michelle was having a hard time not thinking about some demented person carrying Jessie off. Her skin grew cold as they continued to search.

''Let's head to the castle,'' Jacob said after they'd been around Toontown twice.

''She knows she's s'posed to go there if she's lost,'' Meggie said.

Michelle prayed all the way to Jiminy Cricket's bridge.

''Do you think she'll be there?'' Allie asked. Her tears had stopped, but Michelle knew they weren't far away.

''I hope so, honey. I sure hope so,'' Michelle said, guiding Allie around a slow-moving family as they made their way to Main Street.

Jacob's pace had quickened and Meggie was having a hard time keeping up.

''I'll take her if you want to go on ahead,'' Michelle called to him.

He hesitated as if he didn't want to let go of his daughter's hand. And then he nodded, handing Meggie off to Michelle before jogging away through the crowd.

"Daddy's awfully worried," Meggie said as they hurried after him.

"He's not," Allie said, sniffling again.

"He is, too, Al. He just doesn't want us to know it. He didn't even hear me when I asked him what happens if Jessie's not at the castle."

Allie digested that in silence.

"If she's not at the castle then we keep looking till we find her," Michelle said. She'd never seen so many people in her life, and every last one of them was getting in her way as she tried to maneuver the girls through the crowd. She could see the castle up ahead.

"Jessie's gonna be in big trouble," Meggie said.

Michelle hoped so. But only because that would mean she'd been found safe and sound.

Her heart was pumping so hard she found it difficult to breathe as she approached the castle. Jessie had to be there. She just had to be.

"She's not here," Jacob said as soon as he spotted them.

Michelle shuddered. Images of the horrible things that could happen to children flashed through her mind. And not only was Jessie a beautiful little girl, she was far too trusting.

"Aren't we ever going to find her?" Allie started to sob. Michelle lifted Allie up, cradling her small body.

"Shh. We'll find Jessie, honey," she murmured in Allie's ear.

Meggie watched Allie sobbing in Michelle's arms.

She looked around at all the strangers passing by. Then she tugged at the bottom of Jacob's jersey. "What are we gonna do, Daddy?" she asked, bursting into tears.

Jacob swung Meggie up, perching her on his hip. "I'll find her, girls," he said.

He didn't look as sure as he sounded. In fact, he looked a little lost himself. Michelle turned away, swallowing her tears. They had to keep searching.

"What's the problem here, folks?"

Allie and Meggie both turned to see the owner of the muffled voice. But even a life-size Goofy wasn't enough to dry their tears.

"Their sister is missing," Jacob said, tight-lipped.

"Have you checked the lost-child center?" Goofy was suddenly all business.

"I didn't know there was a lost-child center," Jacob said, glancing at Michelle. She shrugged. She hadn't known, either.

"Follow me." Goofy headed through the plaza toward the end of Main Street. "Most folks don't know about the lost-child center unless they've needed it before. Your daughter's probably there right now, ma'am, having the time of her life."

Michelle smiled tremulously, hugging Allie's small body more securely against her as she carried the child through the crowds. Goofy turned left at the Carefree Corners gift shop with Jacob walking purposefully beside him. She could only imagine the thoughts that must be running through Jacob's head.

They reached a building with a Red Cross emblem,

and Goofy held the door open for them. Jacob went in first, still carrying Meggie.

"Daddy!"

Michelle heard Jessie's happy cry before she'd even gotten inside the door. Her arms went limp with relief and she set a scrambling Allie down, allowing the little girl to rush to greet her sister.

Jacob was there already, checking Jessie over, hugging her, then checking her over again. Tears started to Michelle's eyes as she watched him, knowing he'd never forget the past forty-five minutes. Meggie and Allie finally pushed by him to take their turns hugging their sister, and then Jessie, looking at Michelle, held out her arms. And that's when Michelle's composure snapped. "Oh, baby!" she cried, a sob breaking free when she finally held the little girl in her arms. *Thank you, God. Thank you.* The words played over and over in her head.

"Where'd you go, Jessie?" Allie's voice broke into Michelle's litany, reminding her that Jessie had a whole family waiting to find out what had happened. After a final hug, Michelle moved aside.

"Yeah, what happened?" Meggie asked, her voice accusing.

The girls stood right in front of Jessie, grilling her, but Jessie took it in stride. "I saw Minnie, Al. She was right outside the door and I just went to say hi, I promise." She looked from Allie's unforgiving frown to Meggie's. "I was going to come right back. But by the time I catched up with her, I couldn't find which store we were at."

"Why didn't you go to the castle, Jess?" Jacob asked, kneeling beside Allie.

Jessie looked up at her father, her face completely serious. "I forgot."

"Jessie," Jacob said, his exasperation drawing out the one word.

"I know, Daddy, but it was okay. A nice lady was picking up trash by me, and when I cried, she helped me come here and I got to watch a cartoon on TV and then Roger Rabbit came and played with me and I met a friend, Susan, except her mommy and daddy just came and found her."

Jacob looked as if he was about to tell Jessie just how okay it was not, but Goofy stepped forward as Jessie was finishing her explanation.

"Everything all right now, folks?" he asked.

Jacob's stern look faded, replaced by a grateful smile. "Fine. Thank you very much," he said.

"And you, young lady—" Goofy put his big paws on Jessie's shoulders "—you mind your mommy and daddy and stay with them from now on, okay?"

Jessie's dark eyes grew bigger as she listened to the life-size cartoon character. "Mmm-hmm," she said, nodding solemnly.

"Enjoy the rest of your day at the park, folks," Goofy said, holding the door open for them.

"Did you hear that, Daddy? He called Michelle my mommy," Jessie said as if, because it came from Goofy, it must mean something.

Michelle held her breath, looking anywhere but at Jacob. This was just what he'd warned her about from

the very beginning. He didn't want his girls weaving impossible dreams around her. She looked at the other two triplets. Allie had an odd, almost conspiratorial grin on her face. Meggie appeared engrossed in the double-decker bus making its way down Main Street.

"Goofy doesn't know that Michelle's already married to someone else," Jacob said.

"But her husband doesn't live with her, so why can't she live with us?" Jessie demanded. Allie looked expectant and worried at the same time, and Michelle felt awful. Jacob didn't need this on top of everything else.

He frowned down at Allie and Jessie. "Look girls, I told you—"

"Can we ride that, Daddy?" Meggie interrupted, pointing to the bus.

Michelle couldn't stand there quietly anymore. Afraid that Jacob might be pushed to the point of calling off their arrangement, she gathered the three girls around her, kneeling to meet them eye to eye. "Here's the thing, girls. I can't be your real mommy, like living with you and your daddy out at the beach, 'cause I already have a house and a husband. But I don't have any kids of my own, and so I kind of thought we could borrow each other for as long as you want to."

She was probably going to be in trouble with Jacob but, dammit, she wanted the girls to believe they could count on her even if he didn't. She'd realized when Jessie was missing just how much she'd come

to care for these children. She wasn't going to desert them ever—not even if, or when, Brian came home.

Jessie's brow furrowed. "Borrow?" she asked.

"Yes, like a loan, except we can make it a kind of permanent borrow."

Jacob stirred restlessly but Michelle wasn't going to let him intimidate her. He was just going to have to trust her.

"Kind of like puppies are on loan from their mommies when they go to live with people, only you won't be living with us?" Allie asked.

Michelle smiled. "Yep. Kind of like that. For as long as you guys want me you've got me."

Meggie shifted, backing away from the circle a little. "But what about when your husband comes home and you have your own kids and don't need to borrow us no more?" Meggie was certainly her father's daughter.

"Even if Brian comes home, even if I have my own children someday, I'll still love being there if you need me. That's how love works. It doesn't run out—it just keeps growing."

"You mean you love us?" Allie asked, frowning.

Tears welled in Michelle's eyes again. "Of course I love you guys. You're a pretty special threesome."

Allie and Jessie grinned, throwing their arms around Michelle. "I love you, too, Michelle," Jessie whispered, while at the same time, Allie left the same soft message in Michelle's other ear.

Meggie stood back, watching them, her face still

solemn. Even Jacob, standing behind her grinning, was melting more than she was.

"Come here, Meggie," Michelle said, her heart breaking as she saw the little girl looking so alone.

Meggie moved forward slowly and joined in the hug. But Michelle didn't miss the fact that Meggie's small arms hugged her sisters, not Michelle.

"I WORRY ABOUT MEGGIE, sometimes," Jacob said later that evening. He and Michelle had just put the triplets to bed and were having a drink at the kitchen table before Michelle left. She was driving Jacob's Explorer home and would return with it the next morning when she came to work on the costumes.

"Because she's so independent?" Michelle asked.

Jacob shrugged. "She's always been that way. When the girls were babies, Meggie was the first one to hold her own bottle, the first one to insist on dressing herself, even the first one potty-trained. But it's more than that now. She's so withdrawn."

"I've noticed."

Hearing Michelle's hurt, Jacob said, "Believe it or not, she's more open with you than she is with most people. Meggie's teacher put her arm around Meggie a couple of months ago, and Meggie told the woman to never touch her again."

"Do you have any idea why?"

Jacob shook his head. "She's still affectionate with me and her sisters, and Nonnie gets a hug now and then. But that's as far as it goes. She doesn't seem to trust anyone else."

Michelle eyed him across the table. "Sounds like someone else I know."

Jacob drained his glass. "Maybe," he said, getting up to rinse it and set it in the dishwasher.

"I guess I should get going so I can be back here bright and early tomorrow," Michelle said, following him to the sink.

"Yeah." Jacob didn't want her to leave. He walked with her into the living room.

"It's going to be weird going home without Noby there." She picked up his car keys from the coffee table.

Jacob approached her slowly, tentatively. Something had changed between them that day. Running his fingers across her cheek, he held her startled gaze. "You don't have to go, you know."

She stared up at him. "I don't?"

Jacob shook his head, still watching her closely. He kept hearing her words to the girls that afternoon. She'd said *if* Brian returns, not *when*. "You could sleep on the couch. It pulls out into a bed. The girls would love to wake up and find you here in the morning." He trailed his fingers down her neck.

She started to say something but looked away from him, instead. He could feel her pulse beating in her throat and knew she was feeling some of the same things he was. He just wasn't sure whether she was ready to admit it. Or what, if anything, he should do about it.

"I've even got a spare toothbrush around here somewhere. The girls have a tendency to lose theirs."

She leaned toward him, turning her face into his hand. Her lips brushed his palm.

"And I fix a mighty mean breakfast," he said. She'd reduced him to rambling. He slid his hand down her silky blond hair to her shoulder as a flame of desire threatened to burn up what little self-control he had left. He'd been imagining this for far too long.

Her eyes—filled with confusion, but not fear—met his. "You're tempting me," she said. Jacob knew she wasn't talking about his offer of breakfast. It was all the encouragement he needed.

With his thumb under her chin, he guided her face slowly upward until her lips were just beneath his. She didn't resist. She didn't turn away. Most importantly she didn't cry.

Jacob lowered his mouth and finally tasted her lips. She dropped his keys.

She was everything he'd ever fantasized—and more. Her lips were hesitant at first, as if unused to the intimate contact, but as Jacob caressed them with his own, they slowly opened for him and his tongue met hers for the first time.

He lowered her to the floor, breaking the kiss only long enough to follow her down, before recapturing her lips. With his fingers in her hair, he held her still as his kisses grew bolder, her passion driving him on. He'd never needed a woman the way he needed her.

Michelle's hands were everywhere, gliding over his shoulders, his back, touching his face, his hair. When her fingers crept slowly down his back, sliding into

the pockets of his jeans, he thought he might lose his mind.

With a groan, he spread her legs with his knee and settled himself between her thighs. She rose to meet him. "Yes," she whispered. "Please, Jacob, yes."

He yanked on the waistband of her jeans and opened them, burning with his need. She gasped and moved against him, but her sighs had changed. He slowly raised his head to stare into her beautiful face.

She wanted him…yes. But she hated herself for it. He could see it in her eyes.

His movements were jerky as he sat up, his back to her. He wasn't sure what had just happened or where they went from here.

"I'm sorry," she said from behind him.

"Yeah, me, too." His hands clenched into fists.

The rasp of her zipper was loud in the too-quiet room. "You're angry," she said.

"Maybe." He wasn't sure what he was feeling, but it wasn't good.

"I led you on."

"No, you didn't."

"I let it go too far."

He turned to face her then.

"Don't worry about it. Sex isn't the problem here, anyway."

She watched him pace to the window and back. "Then what is?"

"Your loyalty to a man who was declared dead more than a year ago. Why do you do it, Michelle? Why do you hide behind him?"

She stood, gathering his keys up off the floor. Her hands were trembling. "I wasn't all that loyal a few minutes ago. But it's just like you to call being faithful hiding, Jacob."

"Don't turn this back on me, Michelle. You're so scared of losing again, you're never going to risk loving again, either, are you? That's what this is really about."

"Loving?" She laughed incredulously as she headed for the door. "What do you know about loving, Jacob? The more the merrier? Let's see, who was it last week? Gwen, Darlene and Yvonne. Tell me that you didn't date three different women in one week and then we'll talk about loving."

Jacob clamped his jaw shut before he said something he'd regret. The woman made him madder than anyone else ever had. What did she know about his dates? He wasn't about to tell her that while each of those women fulfilled something inside him, he was looking for more than they had to give. And fool that he was, he couldn't stop looking.

"I'll see you tomorrow," she said, letting herself out.

Jacob watched through the window until she was in his Explorer and pulling out of his drive. He wondered if she'd show up in the morning.

CHAPTER TEN

"YOU DO THE SPOT on Cruise's new movie. I'll take the trial." Jacob marked the program sheet in front of him. He hadn't looked at her in days, not since the night they'd almost made love on his living room floor.

Michelle studied her copy of the day's program. "What about the seismologist, Morgon? We've got him on from seven to eight. How was he when you talked to him?"

Jacob shrugged. "He's all right. Not much of a sense of humor, but he's got some interesting stuff on earthquake survival. He said he'd bring some up-to-date predictions, and we can always open up the phone lines if we need to."

Michelle nodded then reached for a newspaper. Jacob did the same. The silence in the booth was interrupted only by the rustling of paper and the occasional sound of scissors clipping as one or the other of them found something worth mentioning on the air.

"There's a good piece here about a mountain rescue over the weekend," Michelle said.

Jacob looked over the article. "Let's do it," he said, handing it back to her. His fingers were long and tanned and—

"You guys ready?" Bob's voice piped into the room from the control booth next door.

They slid their earphones into place and clicked on their mikes. "Ready."

"Ready."

They watched the seconds tick down and waited in silence for the on-the-air globe to light.

"Good morning! This is Jacob Ryan along with Michelle Colby getting your day started for you, and a great day it's going to be...."

Michelle listened to Jacob, waiting for her cue, and sailed through the show saying all the right things at all the right times. At least on the air she and Jacob were still magic. He went for a coffee refill during their first commercial break, bringing a diet cola back for her. He set it down beside her, rather than handing it to her. She knew she should be thankful that he was respecting her choices, that he wasn't pressuring her to explore the possibilities that had sprung up between them over the weekend. But her gratitude didn't quite cover the hurt. She missed him.

"I won't be coming over tonight," she said finally, breaking the silence that had fallen over the booth.

"The girls can't expect you every night."

"I have a lot of mail to catch up on."

"Fine."

If Jacob saw through the flimsiness of her excuse, he was gentlemanly enough not to mention it. Either that, or he just plain didn't care.

MICHELLE DROVE straight home after the show, shutting herself in the home she'd made with Brian, hop-

ing to recapture the certainty she'd always felt about
the love they shared. She didn't let her silent answering machine discourage her. Frank had said it
might be a while before she heard from him again.
She reminded Noby of that when the cat jumped up
on the desk beside the answering machine, purring.

Taking the cat into the bedroom with her, Michelle
changed out of the slacks and sweater she'd worn to
work, then pulled on a pair of Brian's running shorts
and one of his old Southern Cal sweatshirts. She
dusted the tops of his shoes while she was in the
closet and on a sudden impulse decided to climb into
the attic for the box of college memorabilia she and
Brian had packed.

Noby watched as Michelle carried in the ladder,
pushed open the ceiling panel in the guest room and
climbed up to retrieve the box. The cat continued to
stare, unblinking, when Michelle struggled to get
back down with the heavy box in her arms.

Two hours later, surrounded by pictures and ticket
stubs, programs and awards, Michelle still felt torn,
incomplete. She picked up a letter Brian had written
her from San Francisco. She smiled when she saw his
decisive handwriting and started to cry when she read
the part about how much he missed her. Sitting on
the living room floor, she leaned back against the
couch and remembered the summer, shortly after she
and Brian were married, they went there together.
They'd spent three days in that city made for lovers,
strolling down on the wharf, exploring Chinatown and

making love in their hotel room overlooking the Golden Gate Bridge.

Noby started to meow at Michelle sometime after six that evening. She wasn't loud in her demands, but she was persistent. It was time for dinner. Michelle opened a can of tuna, emptying half of it into the cat's bowl before adding mayonnaise to the rest. She wondered what the triplets were having for dinner.

Eating her sandwich, she carried on a desultory conversation with Noby. But while Noby did her best to be captivating company, no matter how Michelle tried to deny it, she was lonely. She rinsed her few dishes, thinking of the times she and Jacob had shared the same chore at his beach house. She remembered other things they'd shared, too. Forbidden things.

She spent the rest of the evening watching videos. She had two of her wedding and at least one from every trip and major event she and Brian had shared. There was his graduation, and her graduation, their honeymoon trip to Hawaii, the time they'd rafted down the Colorado River and move-in day at their house. No matter where they were or what they were doing, one thing was obvious in every video she saw—she and Brian were very much in love.

But none of the movies, none of the letters or pictures, none of the memories stopped her from wondering as she climbed into bed that night if Jacob had missed being with her that evening anywhere near as much as she'd missed being with him.

''GOOD NIGHT, SLEEP TIGHT and don't let the bedbugs bite.'' Jacob leaned against the door and watched as

Michelle bent to kiss Allie good-night.

"'Night, Michelle." Allie looked like the cat who'd swallowed the cream.

Jessie was next. "Sweet dreams, punkin." Michelle tucked Jessie's stuffed bear under the covers.

"I love you, Michelle."

"I love you, too." As Michelle hugged Jessie again, Jacob had to fight the feeling of contentment settling over him. The scene was one he'd imagined a hundred times when he'd been planning his future. Except for one very wrong thing. Michelle wasn't here to stay.

She sat down on the edge of Meggie's bed, one hand on each side of his daughter's small body. "Try and keep your covers on tonight, 'kay, Meg?"

Meggie nodded, her wide dark eyes set on Michelle. Michelle leaned down and whispered something in the child's ear. Jacob had no idea what, but as she got up and slipped past Jacob, Meggie snuggled into the covers with a smile on her face.

Jacob did his rounds and enjoyed the nightly ritual more than he had in a long time. He wished his girls pleasant dreams, just as he did every night, but for once the burden wasn't entirely his. Someone else was wishing with him.

He thought about the evening they'd all shared, about the costumes that were far from finished. He wasn't any expert, but he could count. Although Michelle had been working on the dresses for weeks, there was only one completed ball gown hanging in

the girls' closet. Jacob had a suspicion her helpers were "helping" a little too much. And she still loved them. Amazing.

When Jacob returned to the living room, he discovered Michelle with her jacket on, her car keys in hand. "I'm going to the gym in the morning, and then Mom and I are going to a craft fair tomorrow afternoon, but I could come back on Sunday if the girls are going to be around," she said.

Jacob didn't know why he was surprised. She loved his daughters, not him. That much had become obvious in the past two weeks. He'd never thought two people could spend so much time together and yet be so far apart.

"Why don't you stay awhile tonight? It's Friday. We don't have to work in the morning, and you'd probably get three times as much done with the triplets in bed."

Michelle shook her head. "I'm teaching the girls how to sew. They're supposed to be involved in making the costumes, remember?"

"They've already helped you finish one of them. They don't have to *help* in triplicate." He was tired of their cold war. He wanted his friend back.

"Still, they'll probably be upset if I don't wait for them."

Jacob thought of the number of interruptions Michelle had put up with that night. "Michelle, they have the attention span of seven-year-olds. They've seen it all once, which means all that's left is getting

in the way. Why do you think we spent half an hour picking pins out of the carpet tonight?''

Michelle grinned. ''Meggie was sorting them by color.''

''Exactly.'' She hadn't smiled at him in weeks. ''So stay already. Unless of course you're afraid to be alone with me.''

He'd been teasing her. Just as he'd been doing for years. But he knew he'd made a mistake as soon as saw the frozen look on her face.

''It's just like you to bring sex into it,'' she said. Jacob felt as if he'd been slapped.

''What's with you, Michelle? You've been avoiding me for two weeks and now you can't even take a little teasing. Where's your sense of humor?''

''I haven't been avoiding you. I've spent more evenings here than I have in my own home. Noby's going to put herself up for adoption pretty soon.''

''You *have* been avoiding me and we both know it. And to be honest, until now I've been just as happy to avoid you, too. But...''

She looked at him, her eyes pleading. ''Then why can't we just leave well enough alone? It's worked for the past couple of weeks. It can keep on working.''

He wanted to shake her. ''It's not working, Michelle. I feel like I'm walking in a mine field. What happens if it explodes when we're on the air?''

''I won't let it.''

''We're going to have to face this sooner or later.''

''There's nothing to face.''

"There you go, avoiding the issue again. So I'll say it straight out. I want you, Michelle. And what's more, I think you want me, too."

"Your ego amazes me, Ryan."

She was driving him crazy. "There's a difference between truth and ego. You think if you pretend long enough that we're not attracted to each other it'll just go away?"

"I'd hoped." Her tough act was gone, leaving her vulnerable.

Jacob clasped her shoulders, caressing them with his thumbs. "Is it so awful to live again, honey?"

She stared at him for a long silent moment, and then shrugged off his hands. "I've been alive all along, Jacob," she said, swinging the shoulder strap of her purse onto her shoulder. "If I were already dead, I couldn't be dying of loneliness. But I'd rather do that than be unfaithful to my husband. Which is the problem in a nutshell." Her laugh was bitter. "Because for the first time since Brian's disappearance, I'm not sure I'm strong enough to resist."

She was out the door before Jacob had a chance to reply. He wanted to run after her. He didn't want her going off into the night by herself, hurting. He knew what it was like to be alone and in pain. But he didn't go. He couldn't help her.

Locking up, he wondered why his life was one irony after another. He'd just been told by the woman he wanted above all others that she wanted him, too. And he was still going to bed alone.

THERE WAS A MESSAGE from Frank when Michelle got home from the gym the next morning. Sweaty and uncomfortable in her workout clothes, she listened to the message a second time.

"Frank Steele, here, Mrs. Colby. I managed to track down Jazmin's younger sister. She's been living away from the village since she was a child, but Jazmin confided in her some. According to her, Karim paved the way for Brian's acceptance into the village four years ago, and then Brian left on Karim's orders. Still nothing on Karim's whereabouts. I've put out word that I'm looking for him, but he's showing no signs of surfacing. Guys like Karim have been known to disappear for years, so you may want to reconsider my employment. I'll be in touch…"

Clicking off the machine, Michelle picked up Noby and headed for the bedroom. Her mother was going to be here in half an hour and she still had to shower. She opened her closet door and then just stood there, her tears once again soaking Noby's coat.

MICHELLE TRIED to enjoy the day with her mother, but she didn't fool either one of them. By the time Grace pulled into Michelle's driveway late that afternoon she was wearing a worried frown.

"I wish you'd let your father and me take you out to dinner, honey. Choose anywhere you'd like."

Michelle smiled and leaned across the car to hug her mother. "Thanks, Mom. Maybe next weekend."

"It bothers me to think of you all alone on your birthday. It's not right."

"It's the way I want it, Mom, honest. I'm going to spoil myself rotten, eat everything in sight, watch a couple of old movies and work on the Cinderella cross-stitch I'm doing for the girls."

Michelle knew it was her last statement that convinced her mother to go. She saw Jacob's girls as the beginning of Michelle's journey into the future. Michelle knew they were the only things getting her through the present.

She grilled herself a steak for dinner, drank a glass of wine and faced the fact that life was passing her by. Frank had said his investigation could take years, and where would she be then? Still sitting alone in her too-small home in a run-down neighborhood, too old to bear children but too young to be at peace with that fact?

She poured herself another glass of wine, swatting Noby's nose as the cat tried to share her libation. She wondered if Brian knew what day it was, if he was thinking about how she'd spend it, if he ever wondered how the years were treating her. She wondered how she'd look to him after all their time apart. Wrinkles were starting to form in the corners of her eyes— how pronounced would they be when he came home? And how long would it be before gray started to take the place of blond in her hair?

After her third glass of wine, Michelle picked up Noby and went to bed. She hadn't played the movies or stitched a single stitch. And she hadn't touched the cake her mother brought her that morning. She just

wanted to go to sleep and forget that another year had passed her by.

JACOB GAVE HIS PILLOW an extra punch. The damn thing was too lumpy. He laid his head back down, willing himself to relax. He should've bought one stuffed with feathers. Cursing, Jacob threw his pillow off the bed. He'd go without.

Lying flat on his back, he stared at the ceiling. He didn't know why he'd ever thought that Michelle was easygoing. Hell, she was the most stubborn woman he'd ever met. In the week since she'd admitted to wanting him, he'd seen her outside of work exactly once. It was amazing the way they could both spend so much time in the same house and still have no contact. Jacob had been doing the voice-over for a set of commercials the past week, and knowing that, Michelle had used the time to sew the costumes. She'd worked it out like clockwork. She picked the girls up from rehearsal, took them home, gave them a snack and then sewed until Jacob came back. At which time, she hugged the girls goodbye and left.

Jacob didn't know whether to kiss her or strangle her. Either way, he knew something was going to have to give soon. She was starting to look like hell, with dark shadows under her eyes and a forced smile on her lips. And he was starting to climb the walls. He'd snapped at Jessie that evening when she'd spilled her milk at the dinner table. He'd made her cry, and he hated himself for it.

Giving up on sleep, Jacob wandered out onto the

deck to cool down. He knew there was more to his wanting Michelle than just sex. He'd dealt with sexual frustration before. This was different. He didn't just ache for physical release; what he craved was a way of life. A life with Michelle. But she'd made it plain that she already had plans and they didn't include him. When was he going to accept that?

IT WAS THREE DAYS before the play was due to open, and Jacob knew that whether Michelle liked it or not she was going to have to stay late at the cottage to get the last costume done. A week ago Jacob would've been delighted at the prospect. Now, it only depressed him. Because as soon as she finished that costume she wasn't going to have any reason to come back.

He was reminded of that when the silence that fell in the cottage after his daughters went to bed was broken by the soft whir of Michelle's sewing machine. He sat back on the couch and tried not to enjoy the sense of peace—of completion—that filled his home when she was there. Michelle wasn't a part of his life, of his family. Hell, she wasn't his at all. And it was time he came to terms with that.

He knew he hadn't succeeded when, an hour later, Michelle finally stood up from her machine holding a miniature white ball gown.

"What do you think?" She rubbed the back of her neck and then one of her shoulders.

"Beautiful."

She frowned at him. "The dress, Ryan."

"Meggie'll be the most beautiful woman at the ball."

"You've got your stories mixed. Jessie's the most beautiful woman at this ball." She put the dress on a hanger.

"They're all three going to look great, Michelle. You did a wonderful job. We owe you."

She shrugged. "I enjoyed doing it." She started to tidy up.

"It's late. Just leave it," Jacob said, moving behind her.

"But…" Her protest died on her lips as Jacob started massaging her shoulders.

Her muscles were so tight he was surprised she didn't cry out at his touch. "Come here," he said, pulling her over to the couch.

He worked on her knotted muscles, gently but relentlessly until he could feel her starting to relax.

"Mmm. That feels wonderful," she said, rolling her head forward.

It felt so good to be touching her again. Her skin was soft and silky, everything he'd been dreaming about for weeks. Slowly, almost of their own accord, his fingers trailed over her collarbone. Her eyes closed as she leaned back against him.

She raised her hands and covered his, not to pull them away as he'd half expected, but to guide them down to her breasts.

He turned her slowly to face him, then lowered his lips to hers.

It had never been like this before, this need, not to

consume, but to give. As her lips parted, he wrapped his arms around her, lifting her onto his lap. Her weight was a sweet agony against him as he kissed and caressed her, knowing that any second she might freeze and push him away.

"Oh, Jacob." He heard the confusion, as well as the longing, in her voice.

"It's okay, darling," he murmured, wanting her to believe that as much as he did. He'd give anything to be able to fight her battle for her, to help her bury the past once and for all.

She unbuttoned his shirt with shaking hands, sliding her fingers over his chest. Her touch was tantalizing and oh, so feminine, arousing in him a need to cherish her, to protect her, to love her. It gave him hope.

"You're so beautiful," he said, taking her face in his hands. Her long blond hair fell over his fingers like a silken veil, and he lowered his lips to hers once again.

"Hold me." He felt her plea more than he heard it—her first sweet invitation for loving—and his arms tightened around her.

"Daddy?"

CHAPTER ELEVEN

THE SLEEPY LITTLE VOICE from the hallway registered with Jacob right about the time Michelle pushed his arms away and slid off his lap. He was sitting uncompromisingly alone on the couch when Jessie came into the room.

"What's the matter, sweetheart?" Michelle asked, scooping the little girl up.

"Had a bad dream," Jessie said, her voice wobbly. "The pumpkin turned into a dragon, 'stead of a carriage, and ate Daddy."

"Shh. It's okay. It was only a dream. Your daddy's right here." Michelle pushed Jessie's tumble of hair away from her face, then dried her tears and kissed her.

Jacob appreciated the time she gave him to recover. He'd never even considered the possibility of this type of interruption.

"I'll take her," he said at last, standing and reaching for Jessie.

The little girl wrapped her arms around his neck, laying her head against his shoulder. "Will you rock me, Daddy? Please?"

He looked at Michelle over Jessie's shoulder, try-

ing to tell her how sorry he was, asking her to wait for him. She smiled faintly, shook her head and collected her things. The regret was back.

Holding Jessie, he watched out the window long after Michelle's taillights had disappeared. When at last his daughter's weight grew heavy with sleep, he took her back to her room. But he didn't put her to bed right away. He sat with her in the rocker, instead, the one he'd bought when Ellen had first told him they were expecting a baby. He wondered if Jessie's timing had been horrendous or a gift from the gods. She might just have saved him from making the biggest mistake of his life.

Then again, it might already be too late for that. Making love with Michelle wasn't the mistake. It was falling in love with her in the first place that would cost him.

JESSIE SNUGGLED HER FACE into Daddy's neck. He smelled good. Kind of like a mixture of him and Michelle. She could hardly remember what her bad dream was about as Daddy rocked her and rubbed her back. She counted his heartbeats for a while. One, two. One, two. Daddy's heartbeat was strong, just like he was.

She wondered if Michelle had noticed that about Daddy. She thought for a minute about what she'd seen when she'd first come down the hallway. Daddy had been holding Michelle on his lap, and at first Jessie had thought that something was wrong, that Michelle was hurt or crying like she and Meggie and

Allie sometimes did. She'd been really scared. But she knew as soon as she opened her eyes all the way that Daddy was holding Michelle different. And he was kissing her. Just like the daddies and mommies did in the movies. Jessie smiled. Now maybe Daddy wouldn't be sad and Allie wouldn't be so mean about being good all the time and Meggie wouldn't be so afraid that Daddy was going to leave them, too.

Jessie's eyes got too heavy to keep open. She would love to have Michelle for a mommy. It made her feel all warm and good inside to think about telling the kids at school that she had a mommy at home, too. Michelle always made her feel like she didn't have to worry about stuff, because it would be okay. She guessed that was what mommies were supposed to do.

She could hardly keep herself awake to think of all the good things about Michelle being their mommy. She'd bet, when they went to the grocery store, Michelle wouldn't pass by those cake-decorating things like Daddy always did. Maybe, when they had their next birthday, Michelle would even...

JACOB GAZED DOWN at his sleeping daughter. If life never gave him another thing, he had more than his share already in his three little girls. His gaze trailed over the sleeping forms of his other two daughters. When he thought of Michelle heading home to only a cat for company, he knew he was a very lucky man.

He continued to rock Jessie long after the child had fallen asleep. He should put her to bed—he needed

to get some sleep—but he just wasn't ready to give up the comfort her weight brought him and walk down the hall to his empty room.

MICHELLE DROVE ALL NIGHT. She went down to Long Beach and then followed the ocean highway all the way to San Diego. She was too distraught to sleep, but too tired to think. She just couldn't go home. She couldn't face the reckoning waiting there.

She couldn't put it off forever of course. Arriving home early Tuesday morning, she had just enough time to get ready for work. And looking in the mirror to apply her makeup, she finally had to admit the truth: if it hadn't been for a seven-year-old child, she'd have broken the vows she'd made to Brian. If thoughts were as bad as deeds, if *wants* were a consideration, she was already an adulteress.

Because, in spite of everything—her love for Brian, her five years of faithful vigilance, the weeks of self-loathing—she still wanted Jacob.

God, how she wished she could hate him. She'd tried to blame him for what had happened, tried to cast herself as his victim. But she'd never knowingly lied, to herself or anyone else. She couldn't start now.

JACOB WASN'T SURE what to expect when he arrived at work Tuesday morning. He saw Michelle's car in the lot and pulled his Explorer into an empty space next to it. He wished to hell he knew what to do about their situation. Part of him just wanted to wash his

hands of the whole thing. But he didn't have that option.

"Morning," he said as he pushed into the sound booth.

He passed by Michelle's stool to get to his own, sat down, picked up the day's program sheet and only then realized she hadn't said a word since he'd walked through the door. She wouldn't look at him, either.

"You okay?" he asked, wanting to kiss her and shake her at the same time.

"I didn't get much sleep last night," she said.

"Me, neither. I guess we need to talk about that, huh?" He willed her to look at him. He needed to know what was going on in that head of hers. Was she really as in love with her husband as she claimed even after all this time? Or had her loyalty to Brian become a habit? A way to keep her heart safe.

She turned her face towards him but her eyes only made it to the level of his cheek. "There's nothing to talk about," she said.

Jacob was starting to get angry. He knew she felt *something* for him. This hunger that was consuming him wasn't completely one-sided. "Michelle—"

She busied herself with the papers in front of her. "We have a show to do, Ryan."

Jacob clenched his jaw. Somebody definitely needed to shake her. "Then by all means let's do it," he said. If she wanted to pretend last night had never happened, it was fine with him.

Only it wasn't fine. With either of them. For the

first time in the three years they'd been on the air together, Jacob Ryan and Michelle Colby were *not* like clockwork. They did their show, announcing everything that was required of them, interviewing the chef of a new restaurant in Beverly Hills, giving away free movie passes and KOLR T-shirts, and repeating weather reports and station call letters at all the right intervals. But there was no magic between them, no give-and-take. They followed their program sheet exactly, like a couple of robots, without a single editorial comment or burst of laughter. Jacob knew even before he saw Bob's frown as they signed off that he and Michelle had to talk whether she wanted to or not. If they couldn't fool Bob, they'd certainly never fool Allie, Jessie and Meggie.

He let her leave the station without even saying goodbye. He had a hunch the KOLR staff had sufficient grist for the gossip mill to keep their tongues wagging for the rest of the week as it was. Then, maintaining enough distance so Michelle wouldn't see him, he followed her home.

He told himself he was only doing this for the sake of their careers, but he knew, as he pulled into her driveway behind her blocking her escape, that there was a lot more to it than that. He was angry as hell, though he'd be hard put to say why, and he was worried about her.

"Go home, Jacob," she said when he met her at the front door. She looked tired enough to collapse on the spot.

"Not until we get this settled," he said, standing his ground.

"I don't want to talk about it."

"I think we need to."

She opened the front door and turned to face him, still not quite meeting his eyes. "It'd be beating our heads against a brick wall, Jacob. There's nothing we can do."

Reaching out a hand, Jacob lifted her chin until she could no longer avoid his gaze. The shame he saw reflected in her soft blue eyes was like a kick in the gut. It made something dirty out of the best thing he'd felt in his life. "We need to talk, Michelle. If for no other reason than the sake of our careers. Another show like this morning, and we'll both be out of jobs."

She nodded wordlessly, then entered the house, leaving the door open for him to follow. The first thing he saw as he trailed her to the living room was the picture of her husband she kept on the end table. He looked away, unable to face the other man's smiling countenance.

"We didn't do anything wrong."

Michelle stood by the window staring out at the sunshiny day. "I did." The words cut into him.

He walked over to her, taking her shoulders in his hands, pulling her back against him. "What I felt last night when I held you in my arms was like nothing I've ever felt before, Michelle. It was different, special."

She jerked away from him. "I wonder how many other women you've said that to."

The words were ugly, but he thought he understood why she'd said them. She was punishing herself. It wasn't bad enough that she believed herself capable of infidelity. No, now she was accusing herself of betraying her husband for no more than a cheap fling.

He turned her to face him, holding her teary gaze with his own. "None. I've never felt it. I've never said it. I'd never have believed myself capable of forgetting the presence of my three daughters down the hall, Michelle. Last night meant something."

She gazed up at him for a long silent moment as if some part of her desperately needed to know she meant more to him than all the women she'd seen come and go in his life over the years.

And then she pulled away again, crossing to sit on the couch. "It was still wrong, Jacob. There aren't any pretty words to excuse the fact that I was going to be unfaithful to my husband."

"It wasn't like that, Michelle. For God's sake, Brian was declared dead more than a year ago." How much longer was she going to hide behind a dead man?

"And you think that's going to matter if someday when I've given myself to someone else—to you— Brian comes home to claim me? It's happened before, Jacob. Just last year a man was found living in a remote village in Korea. He'd been declared dead, too. Instead, he'd been suffering from amnesia for fourteen years.

"The government's decision that I'm a widow doesn't prove anything, at least not to me. Brian could come walking in that door any day. And to what? To find another man in his wife's bed? And what if he got beyond that, was willing to forgive me and wanted me back? Who would have first rights? My husband or my lover? Who do I choose to hurt? Don't you see, Jacob? It's not just me or even Brian I'm thinking about. It's you, too. I can't make love with you, not knowing if someday I'll have to walk away with another man. I can't do that to you."

Jacob might have been willing to take the risk for himself, but he couldn't stand to see Michelle tearing herself up this way. Her compassion, her loyalty, were qualities he'd grown to cherish in her. That they were the same qualities that would keep them apart seemed ironic. If he fought her on this, if he won, the prize wouldn't be worth having. He'd be satisfying his own needs at the expense of hers.

"Can I ask you something? How can you be so certain he's still alive?"

"Because he didn't say goodbye."

Jacob stared at her.

Her eyes pleaded with him to understand. "I don't mean verbally. It's just something I feel. Like he's still holding on to me. I can't get rid of the feeling he's trapped in some nightmare somewhere trying every way he knows how to make it home. And I can't bear to think of him finally making it back only to find that there's nothing left for him here."

"You're something else, you know that?" he

asked. He wanted to go to her, to hold her, but he wasn't going to do that—to either of them. He reached into his pocket for his keys. "Brian Colby is one lucky man."

She stood up. "Yeah, right. He has a wife who can't seem to keep herself out of another man's arms."

"You're being too hard on yourself, Michelle. I touched you first, not the other way around."

"I could have told you to stop."

"It was late. You were tired. And being with the girls has put us into an unusually intimate situation." Making excuses for what they'd shared went against his grain, but he'd do just about anything to take that look of self-reproach off her face. "You've been alone a long time, honey, and unfortunately your husband's disappearance doesn't erase your very normal needs. Everyone has to have a little human contact now and then."

She listened to him, but judging by her unchanging expression, he didn't think she'd believed him. "It was more than 'a little human contact.' If it weren't for Jessie I would've committed adultery last night."

He'd been calling what they'd almost done something else. "You wouldn't have, you know."

"How can you say that?"

"Because I know you, honey. You'd have stopped me just like you did the first time I kissed you." He reached out, placing his hand just beneath her breast. "Something in here would have kept you loyal to the man you love."

Michelle's grateful smile hurt most of all. Jacob left her, swearing to himself that, other than his daughters, he was never going to care for another human being again. He never seemed to get it right.

SOMETHING IN HERE would have kept you loyal to the man you love. Michelle studied her reflection in the mirror as she got ready for the triplets' big night. Jacob's words had been replaying themselves over and over in her head. He'd said them to comfort her. She knew that. But he'd failed to consider one very frightening possibility. What if the man she loved wasn't Brian? The idea was unconscionable, but even more, it scared her to death.

Checking the suspenders holding up her gray pin-striped slacks, Michelle's eye was caught by a glint in the mirror. Her wedding ring. Holding out her hand, Michelle studied the wide gold band. The ring was a symbol of faith, of hope—of love. If she was going to continue being true to it, then she might just have to stop seeing Jacob Ryan, which meant that she wouldn't be seeing the triplets, either. She wondered how many times her heart had to break before it couldn't hurt anymore.

THE GIRLS WERE a cyclone of excitement when Michelle climbed into Jacob's Explorer twenty minutes later.

"Did you remember the bobby pins, Michelle? We gotta have our hair not fall down," Allie said by way of greeting.

Michelle grinned. "I got 'em right here, Al." There was nothing like children to put life in perspective.

"We get to wear makeup, Michelle! Ms. Thomas said we had to so we would show up and Daddy said it was okay!" Jessie bounced up and down as much as her seat belt would allow.

"And we get flowers after the show," Meggie added, not to be outdone by her siblings on this important occasion. "We saw them in the back. Daddy bought them for us and everything..."

"...and we all practiced our parts just like you said, didn't we, Daddy?" Allie piped up.

"Yeah, and I got almost all of them right," Jessie said before Jacob had a chance to reply.

"We didn't eat much dinner, though," Meggie said. "Daddy said we can have another dinner after the show if we want to."

"You can have it with us, Michelle, can't she, Daddy?" Jessie asked.

Jacob looked at Michelle, shrugging apologetically. "Sure, if she wants to, Jess," he said.

Michelle could think of few things she wanted more than to go home with them after the play, but she knew she couldn't risk it. It would be late. The girls would be tired. They'd be in bed before she knew it. She looked at Jacob, not used to seeing him in a suit and tie, and thought of the way such an evening would surely end.

"We'll see," she said.

Michelle was run off her feet during the next two hours, applying makeup, fixing hair and getting the

girls zipped into their costumes. Several of the other mothers offered to help her, probably thinking Michelle couldn't possibly manage all three of Jacob's girls on her own, but she refused them happily. This was *her* time with the girls and she cherished every second of it.

And then the girls were called to take their places backstage, and Michelle made her way to the front of the auditorium and the seat Jacob was saving for her in the second row. Nonnie was there, too, and Michelle smiled, greeting the elderly woman just as the house lights dimmed and the curtains opened.

Jessie was the most precious Cinderella Michelle had ever seen. She remembered all her lines and instilled just the right amounts of sadness and joy into each scene. Meggie and Allie were superb in their wickedness.

"They're wonderful," Michelle whispered to Jacob.

"I know," he said, smiling with pride.

Michelle elbowed him gently. "Your ego's showing, Ryan."

He grabbed her hand, squeezed it and brought it with his own to rest against his thigh. "So sue me," he said, not taking his eyes off the stage.

He held her hand for the rest of the play, and Michelle let him, as if by some unspoken agreement they'd both enjoy this one last evening pretending they were a family. And then they were standing to applaud as the young cast members took their final bows. The lights came up in the auditorium and it was over.

Michelle met the girls back in their dressing room. Allie and Jessie threw themselves into her arms, beside themselves with excitement.

"Did you see us, Michelle? Did you see us?"

"Of course I saw you, Jess, every second. You were wonderful. Now stand still while I get you out of this dress."

"Did you like the way my eye switched, Michelle? Did I do it good?"

"That's twitched, Allie honey, and yes, you were magnificent."

"I tried to sound real wicked," Meggie said, trying to unzip the back of her dress.

"You were terrific, Meg. You made the whole audience shudder. Here, let me get that zipper for you."

"What's shudder?" Allie wanted to know while Michelle handed them the jeans and sweatshirts they'd worn to the school.

"It's this," Michelle said, shivering and making a face as if she'd tasted something sour.

Meggie was the first one dressed and, still bouncing with excitement, stumbled into Michelle as she handed over her costume. Michelle's arms came out to steady the little girl, her breath stilling as she felt Meggie's quick hug.

"Thank you, Michelle." Then Meggie hopped off to urge her sisters to hurry so they could go see Jacob and get their flowers.

And just like that, Michelle knew she could no more stop seeing Jacob's children than she could cut out her heart. She owed Brian many things, but she'd

made promises to Allie and Jessie and Meggie, too. Promises she meant to keep.

She led the girls out to meet Jacob, promising herself, and her husband, that she would stay away from any situations that might leave Jacob and her alone together. She could make this work. She had to make it work. She was afraid she might just curl up and die if she had to go back to the lonely existence she'd had before Jacob and his family had come into her life.

ELEANOR WILSON stood in the wings and watched the Ryan girls come out of the dressing room. They were all talking at once, excited by their performances, bouncing around the woman accompanying them. Eleanor listened unashamedly as the little girls all vied for attention. It was obvious they were happier than they'd been in a very long time. And that Mrs. Colby was just as happy to be with them. Eleanor smiled. She could rest easy now, knowing her darlings were in the right hands.

JACOB'S MESSAGE LIGHT was blinking when he got home that night. The girls had talked Michelle and him into a celebratory dinner at McDonald's before dropping Michelle off at her house, and all three of them had finally fallen asleep during the drive back to the beach. He carried them inside one by one, got them tucked into bed and poured himself a scotch and water. Then he went into the living room to play back his messages.

"Hi, Jake, honey." Jake choked on a swallow of scotch. "I'm back in L.A. staying at the Beverly Hills Maison de Maison. Call me."

He played the message a second time, listening for any nuances in her voice that might give him a clue to what she wanted. She sounded sweet as honey, just the way she'd been when they'd first met ten years before. A small part of him remembered that time with affection. Mostly he remembered everything that came afterward. Grabbing the telephone book, he turned to the hotel listings, then punched out the numbers for the Maison, wondering why he was returning the call, because for the life of him, he just couldn't think of one good reason for him to care that Ellen was back in town.

CHAPTER TWELVE

ELLEN WANTED to see him. For old times' sake, she'd said. Jacob didn't think there was anything in their old times that called for another meeting. Except, maybe, his three motherless children. They were beginning to bring Michelle into every conversation. And after the talk he'd had with Michelle the other morning, he had serious doubts that she'd be a part of their lives for very much longer. Because, despite what he'd told Michelle, there was no way they could continue to share his daughters without, sooner or later, betraying Brian Colby. The attraction between them was simply too strong.

Which left him with the same problem he'd had before. Allie, Jessie and Meggie needed a mother. Did Jacob have the right to deny them this chance? If Ellen was going to make an effort to see them, didn't he owe it to the girls to find out if she'd changed?

"...SO CALLER NUMBER NINE wins a chance at the Hawaiian Tropics all-expense-paid trip to Hawaii on Delta Airlines. The number's 555-8484. That's 555-8484...." Jacob watched Michelle snap off her mike as Bob put on the Hawaiian Tropics commercial in the other room and manned the phone lines.

A Michael Bolton tune was set for right after the commercial. They had five minutes. Now was as good a time as any. "Ellen's in town. I'm having dinner with her tonight," Jacob said, tapping his pen against the program log in front of him.

Michelle's hand froze above her mike switch. "Ellen?"

"My ex."

She looked at him, the hurt in her eyes quickly masked.

"The girls' mother," she said, as if that summed it all up.

"There was a message from her when we got home last night. She wants to see me."

"Do the girls know?"

"No."

She digested that bit of information in silence. Jacob wished he knew what she was thinking. What a crazy situation. He valued her advice, yet he could hardly ask the woman he'd fallen in love with what she thought about him seeing his ex-wife.

"I don't know what Ellen wants or what this is all about. And until I do, the girls aren't going to even know she's around. They were hurt badly by her desertion, and I'm not going to risk it happening all over again."

Michelle nodded. "Will Laurie stay with them tonight?"

"Probably. It was too late to call her last night, but she usually doesn't mind short notice. Unless you

want to stay with them," he offered, responding to the look of yearning in her eyes.

"Could I?"

Jacob didn't see why it should matter. The girls already adored her. One night more or less wouldn't change that.

"Of course," he said. "You're a part of their lives for as long as you want to be, Michelle. I thought we'd established that much at least."

She smiled, the hint of tears in her eyes saying far more than words. "Thanks," she said, turning to break into the last bars of the song. "That was Michael Bolton with a cut off his new CD...."

Jacob wanted to take her away and make love to her until all the pain she'd suffered was nothing but a memory. Frustrated as hell, he called the mother of his children and confirmed plans to take her out to dinner. This time around he wouldn't expect too much. He'd learned the hard way not to expect anything from Ellen at all.

ALLIE CALLED A MEETING with her sisters that afternoon after school. Daddy had told them about Michelle coming over when they'd been eating their snack. Allie'd been worrying since Disneyland that her plan for Daddy and Michelle to be in love hadn't worked, but if Michelle was coming over not to sew or anything then it must've. Finally she was gonna get to tell the others her secret.

"Come on, Allie. Daddy said he'd take us bike

riding," Meggie complained as soon as Allie shut the bedroom door behind the three of them.

"Shh. He'll hear you," Allie said, climbing onto Meggie's bed. "This is important."

"What is?" Jessie asked, climbing onto the bed beside her.

Meggie sat on her pillow. "Yeah, what?"

Allie felt all excited inside. Her sisters were going to love this.

"Daddy and Michelle are in love and Michelle's going to be our mommy."

"I already know that," Jessie said, rolling her eyes at Allie.

"How do you know?" Allie asked. She'd thought this would be a surprise.

"Because. I saw them kissing on the couch."

Meggie sat forward. "When?" she asked, her dark eyes wide.

"One time when I had a bad dream. It was the middle of the night and they were kissing on the couch."

Allie nodded, satisfied. She was actually relieved to know she was right. It was too important to make a mistake about. "Okay, so now we have to be really good tonight."

"Again?" Jessie asked, frowning. "How come?"

"Because this is a pretend time for Michelle to be our mommy and we don't want to make her change her mind."

"That's dumb, Al. Michelle's been around lots already."

"Yeah, but that was just to sew and stuff. This is the first time she's coming just to be with us. It's important or Daddy would've just called Laurie like he always does."

Meggie looked scared all of a sudden. "What if Daddy's going on a date? If Michelle's going to be our mommy she won't like that."

Allie shook her head. "He's going to do business," she said. He hadn't said so, but Allie knew that people in love didn't do dates with other people.

"Is this the last time we have to be so good?" Jessie asked, sounding resigned.

"I don't know. But maybe," Allie said. "Come on, let's get our tennis shoes on so we can ride our bikes. Maybe Daddy'll take us to the park."

"I get to swing first if he does," Jessie said, sliding down off the bed.

"And I'm second this time," Meggie said, joining her sister in the doorway of their closet.

Allie came up behind them. "Those are my shoes, Jess. That's my 'nitial on the heel."

Jessie tossed Allie her shoes. "Do you really think Michelle's going to be our mommy, Al?"

Allie noticed that Meggie was looking at her, too. She loved it when her sisters asked her important stuff. "Yep, I'm sure," Allie said, crawling into the closet to find Jessie's shoes.

ELLEN WAS AS BEAUTIFUL as ever. Jacob sat across from her at a secluded table in the restaurant at the

top of the Maison de Maison, remembering how he used to tell her she was made for loving.

"So how long are you in town?" he asked.

Even her shrug was sexy. "Maybe permanently. I'm between jobs at the moment."

"Do you have any leads?"

"I've had an open-ended offer. I'm just not sure I want to stay in politics. I, uh, kind of thought I'd like to, you know, pursue something else that once mattered to me."

Her blatant look made it clear that that something was Jacob. He just wasn't sure why.

"I've grown up in the past few years, Jacob. I've learned to be a little more flexible." She smiled across at him, her dinner fork poised above her plate. She was wearing a black silk jumpsuit, and it looked as expensive as she did.

"You mean I could've worn my sweats and you still would have been seen with me?"

"I said flexible, dear, not uncouth. Besides, that suit looks good on you. It matches your eyes. You clean up very nicely, you know."

He recognized that come-hither smile. "So do you, but then you always did."

"I used to wonder sometimes if you even noticed."

What? "Of course I noticed! Our sex life was never the problem."

"Not before the babies were born."

"What's that supposed to mean?"

"Just that you lost interest in sex after we had the girls."

"That's ludicrous! I've been interested in sex since I turned twelve. It was just harder to make the time after the girls were born. But we still managed. Remember that weekend in San Diego?"

Ellen's face softened. "Yeah. It was the best, Jacob. I was amazed you'd go to all that trouble just to make me feel good. You even got the honeymoon suite. I never knew you could be such a romantic. As I recall, we didn't leave that suite all weekend."

"I never stopped finding you attractive, Ellen."

"Not even when I was as fat as an elephant?"

"Especially not then. I thought you were beautiful. And afterward, too. But with the girls waking up on three different schedules all night long, sleep had to be our priority. If you remember, I took turns getting up with them, too, and still had to be at work at five o'clock in the morning. It was all I could do to keep my eyes open some days. I thought you understood that."

"I suppose I was a little inflexible on that score. I wanted to come first all the time, not just an occasional weekend. But you could have tried harder, too, you know."

Jacob shrugged, seeing those years in a new light. The triplets had consumed so much of his time and energy then, perhaps he'd forgotten he needed to be a husband, not just a father.

They finished dinner and Ellen was charming throughout. She didn't talk much about her life in Washington, but whatever had happened there appeared to have been good for her. She'd grown up.

But she hadn't changed completely. She was still a little too interested in appearances, in material things. And other than a brief inquiry the night before, she still hadn't asked about her daughters.

"So, do you have anybody special in your life?" she asked after their waiter had cleared their dinner plates and brought their desserts.

He thought of Michelle at home with his children. "I date."

"But no one steady?"

"Not right now."

She slid her fork into a three-inch slice of chocolate mousse, a smile curving her lips. "We were very good together once, you and I," she said.

"I thought so." His dessert fork still lay on the table beside him.

"I bet we could be again."

He nodded, his forearms resting on the pristine white tablecloth. "Probably."

She stopped eating, studying him across the candlelit expanse, her expression assessing. "You know, I have to commend you, Jacob. We've been together almost two hours and you haven't mentioned the girls once."

"I wondered if you were ever going to get around to asking about them."

She shrugged. "I guess I just wanted to see if you've changed as much as I have. In the old days, you never talked about anything else. It was always the babies this, the babies that. If one of them hadn't

gotten a new tooth or learned how to drink from a straw, then someone had a runny nose.''

"They're our children, Ellen. Who else would I talk to about them?"

"Well, nobody of course, but it's nice to have adult conversation once in a while, too, you know. There were days there when I felt like little ropes of ABC's were going to wrap around my neck and strangle me to death.''

One thing hadn't changed. She still had that knack for making him feel guilty. "I guess I should have listened to you a little more closely. Maybe a full-time nanny wouldn't have hurt.''

She smiled, looking more grateful than victorious. The old Ellen would have gloated. "So how are they?" she asked.

And Jacob suddenly found himself not knowing what to say. He'd love to be able to spill out all his worries to the mother of his children, to have her share them. He'd love to tell her about Ms. Wilson's warnings, about the play, about Meggie's withdrawal. But he wasn't sure she really wanted to hear them.

"Good. They're doing fine.''

"They're in first grade now, aren't they? How are they doing in school? Do they like it?''

"School's good. Allie's separated from Meggie and Jessie this year.''

Ellen's eyes shadowed. "Is it hard for her? She was always kind of the leader of the three, wasn't she?''

"She still is. And yes, it's been a little difficult, but for the best, I think. She's adjusting. And their grades

are all pretty good. Jessie's dip every now and then, but she'll come around.''

Ellen smiled. "She never was a good listener."

"She still isn't." Jacob grinned back at her.

"Remember that time she fell in Rick Morris's pool right after we'd both warned her to stay back from the water?"

Jacob wasn't likely to forget. The station manager hadn't been too pleased to have his wedding reception interrupted by a wet screaming child.

They talked about the triplets for a few more minutes and then Jacob paid the bill. He didn't want to keep Michelle out too late.

He walked Ellen to the elevator and pushed the button. "Can we do this again sometime?" she asked.

Jacob slid his hands into his pockets. "Sure."

"Soon?" She ran her tongue across her lips.

The elevator arrived. "I'll call you," he said as she disappeared inside.

IN SPITE of the relatively early hour, Michelle was asleep on the couch when Jacob let himself into his beach house forty-five minutes later. As he stood gazing at her sweet gentle face, he had to consciously restrain himself from touching her.

Slipping out of his suit jacket, he wondered if maybe it wouldn't be better for both of them if he simply joined her there. If she woke up in his arms, surely she'd forget her resistance and make love with him.

Yes, maybe that was the way to end this insanity.

Maybe then he could get on with his life, have dinner with his ex-wife and actually consider the invitations she was sending out.

It might even be good for Michelle. Maybe all she needed to be free from her past was to take that first irrevocable step. Because he just didn't believe she was as in love with her husband as she claimed. If she had been, she wouldn't have responded to his kisses as she had.

He took a quiet step forward. What if he was wrong? How could he be sure she *wasn't* still in love with her husband? What if her response to Jacob was a substitute for what she couldn't have? What if Michelle hated herself afterward? Could he live with that? Was one night of passion worth losing the friendship of the woman he loved?

He leaned over her, bracing his weight on the back of the couch as he smoothed her hair away from her face. With a sigh, she turned over, flinging her arm out over the edge of the couch. Something glinted in the light from the single lamp she'd left on. Her wedding ring.

Jacob straightened and backed away. It wasn't for him to decide whether or not Michelle loved her husband or to determine what was best for her. Even if she *was* hiding behind her marriage vows, he couldn't make love to another man's wife. And as long as Michelle wore Brian Colby's ring, that was exactly what she was—another man's wife.

Jacob went down the hall to check on the girls, giving himself a couple of minutes to pull himself

together before he woke Michelle. As he kissed his three sleeping daughters good-night, he promised himself he'd call Ellen first thing in the morning. They'd reached some new understandings tonight. Maybe, for the girls' sake, they'd be able to salvage some of their old love.

MICHELLE MISSED another easy shot and knew there wasn't any way she was going to win the match.

"You wanna call it quits?" she asked her father.

He picked up her towel and locker key and handed them to her. "I don't think I've ever seen you so distracted," he said.

"It's been a rough week."

He looked at his watch. "I'll bet your mother's home by now. She has a way of making almost anything look better."

Michelle stood on tiptoe to kiss her father's cheek. "I love you, Pop."

"I love you, too, baby. Don't ever forget that."

GRACE WAS OUT BACK with a pitcher of lemonade when Michelle and her father got home.

"Everything okay?" she asked, looking from one to the other for an explanation of their early arrival.

"Everything's fine," James said, answering for both of them, but Michelle didn't miss the silent communication that passed between her parents as her father leaned down to kiss his wife. "I think I'll go fix that drip in the guest bathroom before I take my

shower,'' he said, taking a glass of lemonade with him.

Grace poured some of the freshly squeezed fruit juice for Michelle as her daughter sat down beside her in the lounge chair. "You want to talk about it?"

"Jacob's ex-wife is in town."

"The girls' mother?" Grace asked, frowning.

Michelle nodded. "He's seen her three times in the past week."

"Is she here to stay?"

"I don't know. I haven't asked."

"Why not?"

"I figure if he wants me to know he'll tell me. It's not like I have any hold on him."

Grace nodded. "Is Jacob happy to see her?"

"He doesn't seem unhappy."

"So where does that leave you? Are you still spending time with his girls?"

"Some, and I don't know where it leaves me. Part of the problem is I have no idea where it *should* leave me." As fast as she blinked them away, tears welled in Michelle's eyes. She didn't want to break down in front of her mother. Grace worried enough about her already .

A bird flew over to the patio table and perched on the pitcher of lemonade. Michelle swished it away. "How can I want the man's children and have nothing to do with the man? I keep telling myself that a relationship with Jacob is wrong, and yet it's eating me up to think of him out with that woman."

Grace cast her a motherly glance. "Why do you think that is?"

"Because I'm jealous, that's why. I can't have him, but I don't want anyone else to have him, either. Doesn't make me a very nice person, does it?"

"It makes you human, honey."

Michelle stared out at the lush green lawn wishing she were a little girl again, able to climb into her mother's lap and wait for her to make everything better.

"I'm scared, Mom."

"I know, sweetie. It may be time for you to make some decisions."

"I'm afraid I'm going to lose the girls, and I love them so much." Michelle gazed at her mother. "I don't know when I started feeling as though they were part mine, but I do know I can't bear the thought of losing them. If their mother comes home to stay, they aren't going to need me anymore."

"Has she been spending a lot of time with them?"

Michelle shook her head. "I don't think Jacob's even told them she's in town. Allie thinks he's out doing business when he's with Ellen."

"But she's their mother! Doesn't she want to see them?" Grace asked, her usual calm manner gone.

"I'm not sure Jacob's given her the chance. She may not want to see them for all I know, but I think that even if she did he wouldn't allow it. Not until he's sure she's not going to hurt them again."

"He'll never have that guarantee. Not from anyone."

"I know. But in Ellen's case I can see him being especially careful. After all, she deserted them once, so who's to say she wouldn't do it again? The last time, she took them to a neighbor while Jacob was at the station and drove off without a backward glance. They were too young to realize what was going on, but something like that would kill the girls now."

"If it was that bad I'm surprised he's even seeing her again."

"Apparently she's changed. But it still doesn't seem fair that she can suddenly waltz back into their lives and claim them as if she'd never left. Just because she gave birth to them doesn't make her their mother, not in the ways that count."

"No, it doesn't. But it does give her some legal rights. And the truth of the matter is, honey, if Jacob decides to get back with Ellen, if the five of them become a family again, there's not a lot you can do about that."

Michelle's voice trembled. "Are you saying you think I should just give up?"

"No, sweetheart." Grace reached across the table for Michelle's hand. "I'm saying you need to think long and hard about what you want and what you're willing to do to get it. Answer me this. Are you in love with Jacob?"

The denial that rose automatically to Michelle's lips froze there. She couldn't lie to her mother, even if she was still trying desperately to lie to herself. "Maybe," she whispered, ashamed.

"It's not wrong to love someone, Michelle."

"It is when you're married to someone else."

"Brian's been gone a long time, honey. You're a different woman now. It's only natural for your feelings to be different, too. If Brian had been here, you two would probably have grown together through the changes the years have brought. But apart, who knows?"

"I've always thought the love Brian and I shared was like yours and Daddy's. I thought it would last forever."

"If Brian had been here it probably would have. Michelle, your father and I have been together more than thirty years, and yes, we've been very lucky to be able to maintain our love throughout our marriage, but a lot of that comes from growing together and coping with life's challenges as a team. Who's to say what would've happened if we'd been apart for years, dealing with life's hardships separately?"

The quiet of the afternoon settled around them. "Are you telling me I should forget Brian and tell Jacob I love him?"

"No. Whatever decisions you make have to be ones *you* can live with. And only you can decide that. I wish with all my heart I could help you, but this time I just can't."

Michelle leaned over, hugging her mother. "You already have, Mom. Just by being here."

"That's one thing you can count on, sweetie."

"OKAY, GANG, CLIMB IN." Jacob stood in the school parking lot, opening the Explorer's front and rear pas-

senger doors.

"It's my turn to sit up front, Meggie," Jessie said, trying to push her sister aside.

Meggie didn't budge. "It's not, either. You sat in front on the way to school."

"I did not. Allie did."

"She's right, Meg. Hop in back with Allie. You're first tomorrow morning," Jacob said. He never forgot the seating schedule.

"How come you came and got us today, instead of the bus?" Allie asked, climbing in beside her sister.

"Because we need to do some shopping. We're all out of bread and milk."

"We coulda goed later. I'm hungry for my snack."

"Me, too. What's for a snack, Daddy?" Jessie asked.

Jacob checked to make sure all seat belts were fastened and then put the Explorer into gear. "We'll stop for ice-cream cones, and we couldn't go later because I have a date tonight."

"Another one?" Allie asked.

He glanced at her in the rearview mirror. Her face looked like a disapproving schoolmarm's. "I was home with you guys last night, Al, and for the most of the weekend, too. You've never minded my dating before."

He caught the look between Allie and her sisters. "We don't mind, Daddy," she said. For an actress, she did a pretty poor job of lying.

"Is Michelle coming to stay with us?" Meggie asked.

"Michelle's having dinner with her parents tonight, punkin. Laurie's coming."

"I don't want Laurie."

Jacob pulled into the parking lot of the grocery store. "What's the matter with Laurie?" he asked, turning to face Meghan. His middle child was wearing the stone-faced expression he recognized all too well.

"I want Michelle."

Allie and Jessie exchanged worried glances. The girls knew better than to talk that way to their dad.

"I already told you that Michelle's busy tonight, Meghan. Laurie's coming and I expect you to be good for her."

Meggie didn't argue but she didn't agree, either. She climbed out of the Explorer silently and didn't say a word for the rest of the outing. Jacob felt as if he was walking a tightrope that was about to shred.

CHAPTER THIRTEEN

THE FEELING WAS STILL with Jacob a couple of days later when Nonnie came out to the garage to find him. He was working on Jessie's bicycle, realigning the chain that had come loose when she'd sideswiped a curb the last time she'd been riding.

The housekeeper stopped just inside the door, her face lined with concern.

"Meghan pinched her fingers in the step stool. I don't think she's broken anything, but they're bleeding and she won't let me attend to them."

Jacob dropped his screwdriver and headed toward the house. "What was she doing with the step stool?"

"Trying to reach a puzzle up on her closet shelf." Nonnie wrung her hands as she hurried beside Jacob.

"Let me guess," he said, holding the kitchen door open for her. "She didn't ask for help with that, either, did she?"

"No, Mr. Ryan. I'd have reached it for her if I'd known she wanted it."

"I know you would've, Nonnie. Don't worry about it." He headed down the hall toward the sound of running water in the girls' bathroom.

"Let me *see*, Meggie." He recognized Allie's commanding voice.

"I wanna see, Meggie. Is it bad?" Jessie asked.

Both girls stepped aside as Jacob entered the room. "Meggie hurt her hand, Daddy," Jessie said, wide-eyed.

"On your step stool," Allie supplied.

Meggie looked at him as he lowered himself to one knee beside her. Fresh tears welled in her big brown eyes. By the look of things, she'd shed more than a few before he'd gotten there.

"What's the problem, sport?" he asked, removing Meggie's hand from the water. Her little fingers were icy cold.

"I'm sorry, Daddy."

"I'm sorry, too, Meg," he said. The skin had been stripped away just below the knuckles of her index and middle fingers, and the surrounding area was already black-and-blue.

"Can you bend them?" he asked, holding up her hand.

She sniffled, but very slowly all four of her fingers bent forward into his palm.

Jacob reached into the medicine cabinet for some antiseptic cream. "No bones broken, but your hand's going to be pretty sore for a while. We'll put some ice on it as soon as we get you cleaned up."

"Okay, Daddy," Meggie said, subdued.

"Does it hurt real bad, Meggie?" Jessie asked, watching from the side of the sink.

"Not too bad."

"She's not in trouble, is she, Daddy?" Allie wanted to know.

"No, Al. She's not in trouble."

But *he* was. Ever since he'd begun going out in the evenings regularly, Meggie had begun withdrawing more and more. First from Laurie and now from Nonnie. The problem wasn't going to go away. It wasn't going to take care of itself. And he couldn't ignore it any longer. He was going to have to have a long talk with Ellen. It was time to bring her home and introduce her to her daughters.

MICHELLE WENT to the gym after work on Thursday, needing to release some of the tension building inside her. She was no closer to making any decisions about her life. How could she, in good conscience, forge ahead in a new relationship while she still believed Brian was alive? And yet she dreaded waking up each day and going in to work, afraid Jacob would tell her that he and Ellen were getting married again.

She'd just walked in the front door after an hour at the gym when the telephone rang. Ms. Wilson, the principal from the girls' school, was calling. A truck had run into a hydro pole by the school, bringing down the power lines. School had to be let out early for the day and Jacob couldn't be reached.

"I called Mr. Ryan's housekeeper, Nonnie Moore, but she's out for the day, as well. Allie suggested we give you a call," Ms. Wilson said.

Michelle thought of the traffic between her part of town and Jacob's. "I'll be there in twenty minutes, half an hour tops," she said, hanging up as soon as

she'd assured herself that the principal would wait that long.

Still wearing the gray sweats she'd put on after showering at the gym, Michelle hurried out to her car. She didn't want the girls waiting around like unwanted puppies. As she drove down the 405, she tried to remember if Jacob had said anything about where he was going after work. She couldn't remember him mentioning anything. She wondered if that meant he was with Ellen; he'd stopped telling Michelle when he was going to be with his ex-wife.

The girls were in the cafeteria with a handful of other students when Michelle arrived. Allie and Jessie were sitting across a table from Meggie, their backs to the door, trying to color by the dull light filtering through the windows. Meggie was watching the door.

She leapt from her seat the second she saw Michelle.

"You really came!" she said, running over to take Michelle's hand.

Meggie's grip was like a vise, nearly cutting off the circulation in Michelle's fingers. "Of course I came," Michelle said, bending to press a quick kiss on Meggie's cheek. It was a statement of how distraught Meggie was that she allowed Michelle's kiss. She'd been limiting their tokens of affection to hugs only.

Allie and Jessie bounced out of their chairs with a flurry of goodbyes to their schoolmates, and Michelle herded the girls out to her car.

"All the lights went out, Michelle, and it was really

dark,'' Jessie said as Michelle pulled out of the school lot. Jessie and Meggie were strapped in the back seat. The girls had told her that it was Allie's turn to ride in the front.

''It *was* a little scary,'' Allie said.

''And Meggie said you weren't coming to get us, even though Allie told Ms. Wilson to call you,'' Jessie said.

Michelle stopped at the corner and glanced back at Meggie. She was looking out her window.

''Why would you think I wouldn't come, Meg?''

Meggie shrugged, her head still turned away.

A car honked behind Michelle, and she pulled through the intersection, turned into the parking lot of a convenience store and stopped.

''I told all three of you I'd be here for as long as you needed me, Meg. Didn't you believe me?''

Meggie nodded. Allie and Jessie were watching the exchange, silent for once.

''So what's changed?''

''Maybe you didn't want us anymore.'' The words were so soft Michelle could barely hear them. But they hurt. A lot.

She reached back and tapped Meggie's shoulder. ''What would make you think such a thing?'' Michelle asked, holding Meggie's solemn gaze with her own.

''Daddy's been doing dates. A lot. And not with you.''

Michelle felt a rush of fear.

"And you thought that would make a difference to the way I feel about you three?"

"You won't marry Daddy if he's doing dates with other people."

"I can't marry your daddy, anyway, Meg. I thought you understood that. I'm already married. But remember what I told you? Even if my husband comes home, even if I have other children someday, nothing's going to change the way I feel about you. And that works the same if your daddy ever gets married to somebody else. I love you guys. *Nothing's going to change that—ever.*"

"Even if we're bad?" Jessie asked.

Michelle smiled at the little girl, barely holding her tears at bay. "Even if you're bad."

Allie turned, placing her hand on Michelle's arm. "Don't you think you could love our daddy, too?"

"I think your father's a pretty special man, Allie, but I already promised to love someone else, and your daddy has the right to date anyone he wants to date."

Allie chewed her lip, pondering that.

"She's just like all the rest."

Michelle looked into the back seat. Meggie was staring out the window again.

"Who is, Meg?"

"The lady. She doesn't want to meet us, just like all the rest."

"You don't know that, Meggie."

Meg looked at Michelle, her eyes too old for her age as she nodded. "Uh-huh. That's why Daddy always has to go places to be with her without us. Peo-

ple say we're too much trouble, 'cause there's three of us all at once, and it's true 'cause no one ever wants us. They just want to be with Daddy.''

"No, Meggie! It's not like that at all." Michelle could hardly believe what she was hearing.

"Meggie's right, Michelle," said Allie. "We heard Katie Walters's mommy say it. And even our own mommy didn't want us, and not Jennie or all of Daddy's other girlfriends, either. Besides, people always look at us when we go places and say things to Daddy like 'You sure have your hands full.'" Allie's voice grew very adultlike as she mimicked.

"Have you talked to your daddy about this?"

"He told us we're not too much trouble and it wasn't our fault Mommy didn't want to stay with us, but he has to say that, 'cause he's our daddy, doesn't he, Allie?" Jessie looked at her sister for confirmation.

Michelle had had no idea things were this bad. "Well, I can't speak for anyone else, girls, but *I* don't think you're a handful at all. I think you're a heartful. Do you know what that means?"

All three girls shook their heads, their eyes trained on her. "It means that you fill up my heart until it's full of love. And that's an awful lot of love, because my heart's been almost empty for a long time."

Allie leaned over, hugging Michelle. "We sure wish you were our mommy."

Michelle took the girls home, and while they waited for Jacob she did everything she could to convince them they were the light of her life. But nothing

could stop Meggie's words from running around and around in her head. There were some home truths Jacob Ryan was about to hear just as soon as Michelle had him to herself.

MICHELLE WAS STILL UPSET as she drove to work the next morning. Jacob had invited her to stay for dinner the night before, but she'd been too angry with him to pretend, even for the girls' sake, that nothing was wrong. So she'd gone home, instead, and gotten madder and madder. Jacob had to know what he was doing to his girls. Ms. Wilson had pointed it out to him months ago. He'd told Michelle so himself. So why did he continue to foster the triplets' belief that no one wanted them? Why was he keeping even their own mother from them?

The radio show was a nightmare. Part of her knew that her attitude was irrational, but her anger continued to fester inside her regardless. And no matter how hard she tried to banter with Jacob as usual, her words kept sounding more like nasty barbs than playful darts.

"You gonna tell me what's wrong?" Jacob asked as soon as they'd signed off the air. Even in his baggy sweats and T-shirt, he looked pretty intimidating.

Michelle tossed the CD she'd been holding onto the counter. "Yeah, I'll tell you what's wrong. You. You're what's wrong." She had no idea where the words came from. She'd never talked to anyone like this before.

Jacob stood up so fast his stool spun. "*I'm* what's

wrong? And how's that?'' His voice had grown soft, deceptively soft.

Michelle stood, too, her back stiffening as she thought of her conversation with the girls. ''Your daughters think they're nothing but trouble—that nobody wants them. Do you realize Meggie didn't believe I was coming to get them yesterday even after Ms. Wilson told them I was on my way? I know you're aware of their problems, Jacob, because we've talked about them. Is seeing Ellen so important to you that it's worth your daughters' emotional stability? Where are your priorities? How can you be so insensitive to their needs?'' *And to mine?*

Jacob's jaw clenched, his eyes like flint. ''*My* priorities are right where they need to be, right where they've always been—with my children. I may not always get it right, but I *always* put them first. And right now what my girls need is a mother. One who's willing to live with them, not just visit occasionally. And it looks like Ellen might be interested in that.''

''She's so interested they don't even know she's in town?'' Michelle asked, sarcastically.

''They don't know she's in town because I think it's in their best interests not to tell them yet. I'm not bringing Ellen back home until I'm certain she's here to stay. I can't risk putting them through another one of her dramatic exits.''

''I'm not so sure you're sparing them anything. They're already feeling rejected.''

''It would be worse if they grew to love Ellen again and then lost her. At least now they think they aren't

wanted by someone who doesn't know them. And maybe my way isn't right. I've never claimed to be an expert at this. But at least *I'm* trying.''

''And you think I'm not?''

He slid his hands into the pockets of his sweats. ''I guess that is what I think.'' His eyes were as hard as a rifle barrel as he delivered his blow. ''You claim to care, Michelle, but you wear your wedding band like armor, and whenever things get too much for you, you retreat to your shrine of the past. You tell the girls you love them, but you're really too frightened to risk loving anyone.''

Michelle hid her trembling hands in her pockets. They were talking about more than his daughters now. ''You don't understand.'' Her voice was barely more than a whisper.

Jacob reached for his keys and wallet. ''I understand, probably better than you do,'' he said, going to the door of the studio. ''You'd rather cling to the five-year-old image of a dead man than risk giving yourself to a flesh-and-blood one again. At least Brian can't expect too much from you, can he?''

He opened the door and walked out.

Michelle stood in the empty room, shaking, hurting so badly she could hardly think. Finally she sank onto her stool. She leaned on the counter, resting her head in her arms, and willed herself to get up and go to her car.

''You okay, Michelle?'' Bob Chaney poked his head in the door.

She swung around, embarrassed. ''Fine, just tired,''

she said, hoping the words didn't sound as unlikely to him as they did to her.

He nodded, but didn't look completely convinced. "Well, if you ever need a shoulder I've got an extra," he said hesitantly.

She smiled and tried not to cry. "Thanks. I may just take you up on that sometime," she said. But she knew she wouldn't. The only shoulder she wanted to lean on had just walked out on her.

JACOB CHANGED into his swim trunks and headed down to the beach the minute he got home. He plunged into the water, eager to battle the white-capped waves. This was something he understood. Nature wasn't forgiving, but at least he knew the rules. And this time, at least, he knew he could win.

He wasn't so sure with Michelle. He'd had no right to lash out at her as he had. Hell, her loyalty was one of the things he admired most about her. It was just so damn frustrating that her loyalty was all for another man, one who probably was no longer alive. But what if Brian Colby *wasn't* dead? What if Michelle fell in love again and then Brian came back into her life? What would she do? What would Jacob do in her position? He didn't have any answers. So where did he get off judging her?

He swam as far out as he dared, slicing into the waves, conquering them. And then, when his skin was numb with cold, he turned over, letting the waves carry him back toward shore. He'd been a fool to fall in love with Michelle. Knowing that she cared for

him, too, was no excuse. Because it wasn't enough. And that was what had goaded him into his outburst that morning. He couldn't forgive Michelle for not loving him enough to let Brian go. She'd stood there and preached to him about the girls, telling him what he was doing wrong, not even seeing that she was the one who could make everything right. All she had to do was say goodbye to a memory. Was that too much to ask?

Jacob's feet scraped the sand and he stood, welcoming the warmth of the sun on his chest. He was doing it again. Expecting too much.

He waded onto the beach, wiping himself down with the towel he'd left lying there. The girls weren't due home for several hours yet. That meant he had time to go to Michelle and apologize, to try to salvage something of the friendship that meant more to him than she'd probably ever know.

THERE WERE TWO MESSAGES waiting for Michelle when she got home. One was from Grace, telling her that Amanda Blake had just delivered a healthy eight-pound baby girl; the other was from Frank Steele, asking her to call him. Her fingers trembled as she punched in the numbers he'd left.

"There's still no word from Karim, Mrs. Colby, but I've found some people here in Sana with information for sale. And from what I gather, I'm not sure your husband's worth the money you're spending on him."

Michelle wanted to hang up the phone. She couldn't face this. Not today. "What do you mean?"

"If you want my professional opinion I think he's probably dead, just like the government said, ma'am. Three years is a long time to hide."

"Karim's doing it, though."

There was a pause as Frank took a long drag on his ever-present cigarette.

"So let's assume that he is alive. It still doesn't look good. He lived of his own free will in that village, ma'am. From all accounts, no one was holding him hostage. No one was under any direction to watch him or detain him."

Michelle swallowed. "Go on." Her throat was so dry she almost choked.

"I've found out quite a bit more about this Karim. The man is a legend on the streets. From what I can tell, he runs some kind of elite terrorist group that works for hire. Everyone fears him and everyone has stories about the murders, the stealing, the bombings he's been involved in. I'd guess that some of it has been exaggerated, but probably not much."

"So what does this have to do with Brian?"

"The village people believe Brian was working with him, sort of a second in command, if you will. Which would explain why Jazmin was afraid to admit she loved Brian. These people don't want to be tied to Karim any more than they have to be to stay alive. Of course some of this is speculation. Without Karim, we don't know for sure Brian's exact role in things, but I'm certainly convinced we've found enough."

"I'm not."

"Mrs. Colby, I love the money I'm making here, but—"

"Keep looking, Frank."

"If you're sure...."

"I have to know..." Michelle's voice faltered. She barely got the phone hung up before she collapsed in tears.

Her sobs were harsh and hopeless, but they didn't last long. Frank had to be mistaken. He was missing something. There was an explanation—there had to be. The villagers knew what Karim wanted them to know. If the man was so powerful he could make people see only what he wanted them to, couldn't he? Not only would Brian never be involved in bombings and murder, he'd never have willingly deserted his wife. Of that, she was absolutely certain.

She got up from her desk and went in to change her clothes, Frank's words replaying through her mind all the while. She was looking for the hole in Frank's reasoning that would prove Brian's innocence. Brian smiled up at her from her nightstand, his face innocent, boyish and unlined. She picked up the photo and stared at it for a long time, as if the answers she was seeking were hidden there.

And maybe they were. She got out her wedding pictures and looked through them, remembering the moment when Brian had pledged his love to her, his young voice strong and clear enough to be heard in the back of the church. She remembered the feel of

the cool gold band sliding up her finger as he made her his wife.

And she remembered their wedding night, Brian's tenderness, his unselfish loving, his gentleness—and again, his youth. There was just no way Brian was a willing partner in any terrorist organization. He was too intrinsically gentle to be capable of senseless violence.

But neither was this young man still capable of filling Michelle's needs. She was no longer the naive girl Brian had married. The past five years could have destroyed her, but they hadn't. Instead, they'd matured her, tempered her. And with that new maturity had come desires stronger than anything she'd ever felt for Brian. She'd come to love as deeply, as passionately, as she'd suffered.

Michelle went through the house slowly, systematically, collecting all of Brian's pictures. She cried for each one of them, for the dreams lost, and stacked them carefully in a box.

Her answering machine caught her eye as she headed toward the bedroom, and she stopped, coming back to play the recorded outgoing message. She listened one last time to Brian's youthful voice saying, "This is the Colbys..." Then she pushed the record button, cleared her throat and said, "This is Michelle. I can't come to the phone right now..."

Brian's clothes came next. She pulled his shirts off their hangers, folding them neatly, and with every one of them was a memory. She brought in another box

and loaded it with his clothes, until the only thing left of Brian in the home they'd had together was the shiny gold band on her finger.

and leaned it with his thmb, until the only thing left of cabin in the house they stood . and structure was the scent gold band on her finger.

CHAPTER FOURTEEN

JACOB KNOCKED on Michelle's door, shoving his hands into the pockets of his jeans as he waited for her to answer. He knew she was home. He'd pulled his car behind hers in the driveway. Mind you, he wouldn't blame her for not wanting to see him. His words to her that morning had been more than cruel. They'd been unforgivable. But he was going to apologize, anyway, if he had to camp on her doorstep until she came out.

He was surprised when her door opened almost immediately and she pulled him inside. He could tell she'd been crying.

"Michelle, I'm—"

"Shh." She put her finger against his lips. "Dance with me?" she whispered. It was only then that Jacob noticed the soft saxophone music playing in the background.

Unsure what was happening, he looked into her eyes hoping to see a glint of humor—some indication that this was merely an elaborate joke. Instead, all he saw was desperation.

He wrapped his arms around her, pulling her up against him, and started to sway slowly to the music. *What the hell's going on?* he wondered.

She nestled her face against his neck. *She's seeking comfort,* he decided—until he felt the flick of her tongue against his skin.

Her fingers slid to the front of his shirt and freed the buttons at the neck before skimming down his body to slide the shirt off. Her hands were torturing him, arousing him and— *Dear God.* Why was she doing this? She was worrying the hell out of him, and he wasn't sure what to do about it.

Undaunted by his lack of response, Michelle continued to caress him. Jacob knew he was going to have to stop her, make her tell him what was going on. But something held him back. There was a desperation in her touch—mirroring what he'd glimpsed in her eyes.

Still slowly dancing, he looked over her shoulder, hoping to discover some clue what was prompting her to act like this. Then it hit him. Brian's picture wasn't in its usual spot on the end table. He noticed the empty mantel above her fireplace, the empty spaces on her bookcase where her wedding pictures used to be.

And suddenly Jacob understood. Michelle wasn't making love to him, Jacob Ryan. She was using him to say goodbye to Brian Colby.

He tilted her head up, intending to reason with her. But then her lips met his and all hope for a rational discussion was lost. Her kisses were too hungry, his passion too long denied.

He pulled her T-shirt over her head, trailing his hands across her ribs and breasts before reaching be-

hind her to unfasten the catch on her bra. And then she was back in his arms, pressing her warm full breasts against his chest.

Leaving their shirts where they'd dropped them, she took his hand and led him down the hall to her bedroom. Jacob didn't need to look to know that this room, too, was bare of reminders of her husband. He wanted to ask her if she'd had word that Brian was dead, but when he started to speak her eyes pleaded with him not to.

She released his hand, then unzipped her skirt, sliding the material over her hips to pool at her feet. *Oh, Lord, she was beautiful.* Jacob throbbed with need as he unbuttoned his jeans and stripped them off. Then, still without saying a word, she lay down on the bed and pulled him on top of her. As he lowered his head to kiss her he realized with a sense of fatality that making love to Michelle like this wasn't enough. Not for him. But what he needed was more than she had to give.

Yet he'd come too far to stop. They both had.

Driven by needs he barely understood, Jacob made love to Michelle with a single-minded passion that precluded conscious thought. He was only aware of their bodies straining together, thrusting urgently.

And when it was over, when he finally looked directly into her eyes, he wasn't surprised by the regret he saw in their soft blue depths, nor by the tears trickling down her cheeks. Damn it to hell. It shouldn't be like this. It was more than he'd ever had before—

but it still fell short of what it could have been. What it should have been.

She looked up at him silently, apologetically, and stroked his face with her hand. It was then that he saw her wedding band. No matter what she'd done with Brian's pictures, in her heart she was still married to another man.

Jacob slid his body off hers and rolled onto his back. As much as he wanted to be gone, he couldn't just get up and leave her. She snuggled against him.

He held her until she was sleeping soundly, and then, as silently as they'd made love, he rose, dressed and went home to his girls.

IT WAS THE LONGEST weekend of Jacob's life. He took Ellen to a preview screening of a new Tom Cruise movie and afterward over drinks tried to get a few things settled.

"When are we going to talk about the future, Ellen?" he asked, his hands on the glass of scotch in front of him.

Her eyes lit with pleasure. "I wasn't sure you thought we had one." She slid her hand across the table to his.

"You're the mother of my children. It seems to me only natural to consider a future together." *Great, Ryan. Think you could sound a little more excited about it?*

"You don't know how relieved I am to hear you say that. Your insistence on keeping this just between the two of us really had me worried."

He wished he could be sure he was doing the right thing. "You haven't seemed overanxious to see the girls."

"They *are* my daughters, Jacob. I may not be your ideal of a mother, but I do love them. I just didn't want to push things. You were always protective of the girls, but you've guarded them like the crown jewels since I left."

"You've had access to them."

She covered his hand with hers, lines creasing her beautiful brow. "And I knew I'd have you to answer to if I said one wrong thing. You seemed to think I would just know automatically what all the right things were. And I don't. Whoever hands out that natural mother's instinct when children are born wasn't in the delivery room when I had the triplets. No matter what I did, it always seemed to be the wrong thing. I'd make them cry or make them mad— it got to the point where I was afraid to do anything at all."

Jacob thought of Michelle's relationship with his children, her instinctive ability to provide for their needs. Looking at the woman across from him, he reminded himself that Ellen was his future. She was the one who'd borne his children. She was the one who wanted him.

"You'd probably be a lot easier around them if you'd just relax a little," he told her. "Maybe it would help if you saw them more as miniature adults than little aliens," he added with a smile. He'd been happy with Ellen once. Maybe he could be again.

She smiled back. "Perhaps. I'm certainly willing to try."

And with that, he *would* be satisfied.

ALLIE WOKE Jacob from a restless sleep at three o'clock Sunday morning, climbing into bed beside him.

"Have a bad dream, punkin?" he asked, his brain still fogged with sleep. He'd been dreaming that Michelle had told Ellen that Brian had come home.

"Uh-uh," Allie said. "I'm cold." Her teeth chattered.

Instantly awake, Jacob felt her forehead. His little leader of the pack wasn't cold at all. She was hot. Too hot.

Telling himself not to panic, Jacob settled Allie in the middle of his bed, pulled the covers up to her chin and told her to stay put.

"I don't feel so good, Daddy," she said meekly.

"I know, punkin. Can you tell me what hurts?"

"Everything hurts," she said, starting to cry.

Jacob brushed the hair back from her brow. "Shh. Don't cry, honey. I'll make it better in a jiffy. Does your throat hurt?"

She shook her head.

"How about your tummy?"

"Uh-uh."

"You have an earache?" The girls had had their share of them over the years.

"Uh-uh."

What else was there?

"Just everything hurts, huh?"

She nodded, her little mouth pursed as if she was going to cry again.

"Okay, we'll get you fixed up in no time. I'm just going to check on your sisters and then I'll be right back with something to make you feel better, okay?"

She gave him a weak smile and snuggled into his pillow. "Okay, Daddy."

Jessie and Meggie were both sleeping soundly. Jacob laid his hand against each of their cheeks and was relieved to find that both girls were as cool as the night air could make them. With any luck, they'd stay that way.

Allie was still awake when he returned to his bedroom with the thermometer and children's Tylenol. The girls had had their share of illnesses through the years, and he'd become pretty adept at recognizing the symptoms. But other than her fever, Allie didn't seem to have any. He hoped that was good news.

She held the thermometer under her tongue, but she squirmed under the covers the entire two minutes he made her keep it there.

"I'm itchy, Daddy," she said the minute her mouth was free.

He stared at the thermometer. She had a fever of 102 and she itched. His stomach sank as he realized what was bothering his daughter. He hoped he was wrong.

"Where does it itch, sport?" he asked.

"All over, but especially here and here," Allie

whined, pushing away the covers to point to her stomach and her armpits.

After a quick inspection Jacob's suspicion was confirmed. Allie had chicken pox. And judging by the number of nasty-looking red spots on her body, she wasn't going to have an easy time of it. He went back to the bathroom and located the calamine lotion he'd bought the time Jessie had fallen into a patch of poison ivy. Resigned to a long haul ahead, he returned to his bedroom and covered Allie's skin with the soothing lotion. There was no way the other two were going to escape this unscathed.

The Tylenol took effect shortly after that and Allie fell into a restless sleep. But Jacob knew his vigil had just begun. Lying down beside her, he wondered how long it would be before Jessie and Meggie started itching, too. It was times like these that the loneliness inherent in being a single parent hit him most of all.

By four o'clock Sunday afternoon Jacob was at his wits' end. He'd spent the day catering to three cranky, itchy little girls and he was exhausted. Allie's fever had risen to 103, and by midafternoon, Jessie and Meggie had fevers, as well. He called their doctor, only to be told he was already doing all that could be done for the girls and should continue administering the analgesic. The doctor told him he'd have to keep the triplets out of school for several days until they passed the contagious stage of the disease. When Jacob asked for something to help make them more comfortable the doctor suggested cool baths and lots of tender loving care.

"I itch too much, Daddy," Jessie whined when he returned to the girls' room.

"How about a cool bath, Jess? Maybe that'll make you feel better."

Jessie sat up slowly. "Okay," she said, as if agreeing to give her favorite doll to the poor.

"Can I have some juice, Daddy? I'm thirsty," Allie said, scratching at her stomach.

"Just as soon as I get Jessie in the tub, Al. Try not to scratch so much."

Meggie wrestled with her covers. "I can't get to an itch, Daddy!" she cried. "It's back here over my shoulder."

Jacob went over to rub Meggie's back. "Dad-de-e-e, my bath," Jessie wailed from across the room.

"What about my juice, Daddy?" Allie asked hoarsely.

Jacob wished he was four people. He considered calling Ellen but dismissed the thought almost immediately. Ellen didn't tolerate sickness very well.

But as soon as he had Jessie settled in the bath, got Allie her juice and put a fresh batch of calamine lotion on Meggie, he headed for the phone. Right or wrong didn't matter anymore. He needed help.

"I SLEPT WITH JACOB, Mom," Michelle said, telling her mother over the phone something she'd probably never have been able to say in person. But she'd needed to talk with somebody. Her guilt was eating her up.

"I expected that would happen sooner or later," Grace said, surprising her.

Michelle stopped fiddling with the phone cord. "You did?"

"You're a normal healthy adult, Michelle, and sex is a normal healthy need," Grace said, sounding like the doctor she was.

"Mother!"

"It's all part of facing the future, honey."

"Maybe. I just wish I could be sure."

"You of all people should know that life is never a sure thing, Michelle. Your feelings for Brian felt right five years ago but they don't anymore, do they?"

Michelle's eyes welled with tears. "No," she said softly. Grace was putting into words what Michelle had only just discovered for herself. Somehow Michelle had outgrown the love she and Brian had shared.

"So how did you feel when you were with Jacob? Were you thinking about Brian?"

Blushing, Michelle remembered Jacob's hands, large and sure on her body. "Not once," she said. Making love with Jacob had been better than she'd dreamed it could be. She'd spent the past two days cherishing the memory, reliving it over and over, and hating herself for it at the same time. She couldn't imagine what Jacob must think of her.

"Have you talked to Jacob since then?" Grace asked.

Michelle shook her head, then realized her mother

couldn't see her. She dried her eyes. "I called him last night, you know, to talk about things—seeing as we do have to work together. The girls' baby-sitter said he was out—with Ellen." She wasn't going to cry about it again. She wasn't.

There was a long pause on the line. "You may have to accept that he's made his choice," Grace said gently.

"I know."

"I'm sorry, honey. So sorry."

"Yeah, me, too..."

Grace invited Michelle over for dinner, but Michelle declined, preferring to lick her wounds in private. She and Grace talked awhile longer, her mother telling her that Amanda Blake had found a job in a day-care center so she could support her daughter and still be with her all day. Michelle was happy for the young woman, if a bit envious, and even more pleased for the baby who was going to have a fair shake at life, after all. She was proud of the work her mother did and told her so.

She'd just hung up the phone when it rang again.

"I've been trying to get you for over half an hour." Jacob's voice was disgruntled. Michelle's heart sped up in spite of herself. The last time she'd seen him they'd... And he'd been... But the next night he'd been out with his ex-wife.

"I was talking to my mother. What's up?"

"I need your help. You've already done so much and I'm a heel to ask, but I don't know who else to call."

Michelle frowned, immediately concerned. He sounded exhausted. "What's wrong?"

"The girls have chicken pox."

"All three of them?"

"Yeah. All three. Allie started in the middle of the night, Jessie woke up with them around seven, and by noon, Meggie was down with them, too. They're all running fevers, they're itchy and cranky, and…"

"I'm on my way," Michelle said, hanging up the phone.

She fed Noby and sped out the door, a smile on her face. He needed her. Not Ellen. She reminded herself all the way out to the beach that Jacob's choice was the only logical one—she'd been around so much lately the girls would be more comfortable with her than with the mother they hadn't seen in years. But by the time she arrived at the cottage she still hadn't managed to convince herself that there wasn't something significant in Jacob's plea for help.

GOD, SHE'S BEAUTIFUL. Jacob stood in the doorway of the cottage and stared at Michelle, only then realizing just how much he'd missed her.

"Can I come in?" she asked, a shy smile curving her lips.

"Of course. Sorry," Jacob said, stepping aside. She smelled like California sunshine and fresh air. She tasted that way, too, he remembered.

"Where are they?" she asked, looking around the living room, avoiding his gaze.

"In the bedroom." He wondered if she'd been thinking about Friday afternoon as much as he had.

"Daddy?" Meggie's voice trailed weakly down the hall. Michelle looked relieved as she glanced toward the sound.

"Coming, punkin," he called back. He and Michelle headed down the hall together.

"Allie and Jessie are sleeping, but I just promised Meggie a soak in the tub. They're all three due for Tylenol again in another hour," he said softly. Even if she wouldn't look him in the eye, he was damn glad she was here.

She paused just outside the girls' bedroom door.

"Why don't you try to get some rest now, and I'll see to Meggie."

He could only think of one thing that sounded better, but he knew there was no hope of that. "If you're sure..."

She pushed him toward his room. "Go," she said, and went in to cluck over Meggie.

He heard his recalcitrant daughter's happy greeting as he shut his bedroom door behind him.

To say the next twenty-four hours were grueling was an understatement. Michelle called Bob Chaney Sunday afternoon while Jacob slept and arranged to have the weekend morning announcer cover for Jacob and her until further notice. She let Bob draw his own conclusions about her presence at the triplets' sickbeds.

Jessie and Allie were both awake and fussy by the

time Michelle got Meggie tucked back into bed after her bath, but they were happy to see her, too. Michelle anointed and fetched, rubbed hard-to-reach places and read stories. And as much as it bothered her to see the girls so miserable, she was delighted to be able to care for them. It felt wonderful to be needed again.

Jacob finally awoke late that evening. All three girls were asleep for the moment, Jessie in Michelle's arms.

"Want me to take her?" he whispered, walking into the bedroom.

Michelle wanted to hold the little girl forever, but her arms were numb and she needed something to drink. She nodded, feeling chilled as Jacob lifted his daughter away from her and laid Jessie gently in her bed.

He followed Michelle into the hall. "Thanks for the rest," he said.

She glanced up at him. He'd obviously had a shower—his hair was still wet. "I'm glad you could sleep," she said, wishing she could touch him.

He trailed her into the kitchen, helping himself to a cup of coffee from the warm pot on the counter. "Did the girls eat?"

She poured herself a diet cola. "Some. They wanted macaroni and cheese, but no one had much of an appetite once it was cooked."

They sat down at the table together quietly, the intimacy of their situation wrapping around them. Now was the time when mothers and fathers shared

a tired but still passionate kiss. Michelle wondered why she continued to torment herself with images of things she might never have.

"I called Bob," she said. "Rhonda's covering for us."

"Hell, I forgot all about work tomorrow," Jacob said, his brow creasing. God, he looked handsome! "I suppose you're about ready to head home."

"I can stay a little while longer. They'll need Tylenol again in another half an hour, and once they're awake they're probably going to need lotion, too."

Jacob grinned. "Tell me about it," he said, and then grew serious again. "Have you checked their fevers? I forgot to tell you the thermometer's in the bathroom cabinet."

"I found it. Allie's has dropped to 101, but Jessie's and Meggie's are both hovering around 102."

Jacob nodded and took a sip of his coffee. "They'll probably be a lot more comfortable once their fevers break."

Michelle grimaced. "I don't know. I have a feeling the itching gets worse." She couldn't believe how much she still wanted him. Sitting there with him, close enough to touch, was harder than she would've believed now that she knew how incredible their lovemaking could be. She wondered if they were ever going to talk about that afternoon, but before she could broach the subject, he drained his coffee cup and stood up.

"Let's get this done," he said. "The sooner they're awake, the sooner they'll go back to sleep."

He reached into the refrigerator for a bottle of apple juice, and Michelle took three plastic cups from the cupboard. She'd learned the last go-round that the triplets would only take their pills with apple juice. She followed Jacob down the hall a couple of minutes later, careful not to spill any of the juice she carried. Waking the girls, they gave them their Tylenol, rubbed lotion on them and had them settled back into bed, if not back asleep, within twenty minutes. Even when they weren't on the air she and Jacob worked together like naturals.

MICHELLE ENDED UP spending the night, taking a turn in Jacob's bed—alone—while he crashed on the couch for the couple of hours all three girls slept. And though she fell asleep almost as soon as her head hit his pillow, Michelle's dreams were all about the two of them together in bed. Waking up, she was hit with a wave of desire so strong she actually considered asking him to come and make love to her.

But she didn't. She wasn't going to repeat her mistake. If she ever made love to Jacob again, it would only be when she was sure Brian was out of her life—one way or another. And it would only be when their lovemaking included promises for the future. She'd discovered the other day that she didn't like waking up alone when she hadn't gone to bed that way.

The girls' fevers broke on Monday, but things didn't get any easier. For the girls' energy came back full force. Their complaining was louder, their requests more frequent, their need to be entertained al-

most constant. They'd spent so much time in bed over the past forty-eight hours none of them wanted to sleep.

Michelle had finally coaxed them all onto Meggie's bed to play a game of Candyland when the telephone rang.

"I'll get it," Jacob said, abandoning his role of kibitzer.

Michelle wondered if it was Bob calling from the station. Rhonda's husband, a pilot, was due to fly in unexpectedly sometime that night, which meant that Michelle might have to go into work in the morning—she glanced down at her watch—just a little over eight hours from now. She sure hoped not. Leaving the girls to their game, she followed Jacob out to the telephone.

"I just don't think tomorrow's a good time. They've been sick for two days, and I'm not sure we're through the worst of it," she heard him say. He was looking out the living room window. He hadn't seen her yet.

"I appreciate your concern, Ellen, but I'm not sure this is a good time for your first visit. You know how you hate sickrooms."

Ellen.

CHAPTER FIFTEEN

MICHELLE FELT THE BLOOD drain from her face. Somehow over the past twenty-four hours she'd managed to forget the other woman. Or at least she'd started to believe that Ellen wasn't a threat.

"I *do* believe you've changed. I'd just feel better if the girls weren't at their worst the first time you see them." He sounded tired.

Michelle stood frozen in the doorway.

"Okay. If you insist. But on one condition."

He's agreeing? With me right here in his home? He's going to let that woman just walk in and take my place? Michelle panicked as another though occurred to her. *Will the girls be just as willing to replace her?* Fear raced through her, making it hard to breathe.

"I don't want them given any indication this might be permanent. As far as the girls are concerned you're just in town on a visit and want to see them." He was going to give in to her. After all that woman had done to those children he was letting her come back to them.

"All right. Ten o'clock'll be fine. See you in the morning."

Jacob hung up, turned and saw Michelle. She hoped she didn't look as upset as she felt. She had to get through this, and then go home where she belonged.

"I didn't know you were there," he said, looking like a child caught with a hand in the cookie jar.

"I thought it might have been Bob." *Go home now. There's no more reason for you to stay.*

"That was Ellen," he said, watching her. She hoped it wasn't pity she saw in his eyes. The last thing she wanted was for him to feel sorry for her.

She folded her arms. "She wants to see them now?"

He nodded. That was all.

Something inside her wouldn't let her leave it alone. "And you're going to let her?" She hadn't meant to sound so accusing, but how could he do this to her? She'd just spent two days caring for those girls as if they were her own. And hadn't Friday afternoon meant anything to him? Without even talking to her, he was going to resume his relationship with that other woman?

"She's their mother, Michelle."

"She lost the right to that title when she deserted them."

"She's changed since then, grown up."

So now he's defending her. "Maybe."

"I won't ever know if I don't give her a chance."

"I thought you wanted to protect the girls." Even she knew she was being unfair. She'd heard his conditions for the visit.

"They aren't going to know we're considering making this permanent." That was the second time she'd heard that word. *Permanent.*

Michelle felt cold all over. She welcomed the sensation, knowing from experience that numbness would follow. So Jacob and Ellen were considering making it permanent. In spite of the fact that he and Michelle had made incredible love only the other day, he was still considering a reunion with his ex-wife. Not that Michelle had any right to blame him. She might have put Brian's things away, but didn't he still have a stranglehold on her heart?

"You love her, then?" She didn't know why she was torturing herself, but she couldn't help asking.

He turned around, facing the window. "She's a beautiful woman," he said.

"So you do love her."

"I enjoy her company."

"But are you in love with her?" Michelle asked harshly, having reached the end of her tether. It was time to go home to Noby.

She was unprepared for Jacob's response. He swung around, his face taut with anger. "No! I'm not in love with her. How can I be when I'm in love with you?"

"Then why…" She couldn't finish the question. She just stood there, staring at him, filled with an equal mix of wonder and fear.

"Because my children need a mother and she's willing to try to be one for them."

"And I'm not?" *The man has just said he loves*

you. She willed herself to be calm. To try to understand. "What's this been, then? A holiday?"

"You're wonderful with the kids, Michelle. We both know that. But the girls and I are a package deal."

He was only across the room from her, but she felt as if there was a world between them. "What about Friday? What was that if not trying?"

Michelle's heart sped up as she watched him move toward her. She wanted him—needed him—to hold her. But she was so afraid to love him that she was choking on her fear.

He reached out to her, but instead of taking her in his arms, he grabbed her left hand and held it up.

"And what's this? A friendship ring?" he asked. "I can't share you, Michelle. I'm not that giving a person."

Tears filled her eyes as she looked at her wedding band. She wanted to pull it off, to be free of five years of anguish. She wanted to walk into Jacob's arms unencumbered and whole. But she wasn't whole. She'd loved before with all her heart. And she was terrified to risk loving that way again.

Jacob dropped her hand and turned away.

"COME ON, YOU GUYS, hurry up." Meggie stood in the door of the bedroom she shared with her sisters, wondering why it always took Jessie so long to tie her tennis shoes and why Allie always had to make it take even longer by helping. Daddy was driving them to Michelle's for the afternoon, and Meggie was

sure she was going to die if she didn't get there soon. She'd figured it all out in the middle of the night when her eyes wouldn't stay closed even when she told them to. She had to talk to Michelle.

"Hey, you guys, don't tell Michelle about Mommy, okay?" she said as an afterthought. She didn't want to have to ask Michelle in front of them. Just in case.

Jessie looked up from her tennis shoe. "Why not? She always wants to hear about everything that happens to us."

"You don't want to hurt her feelings, do ya?" Allie asked, tugging on Jessie's foot.

Meggie was glad Allie had the answer. Allie always knew what to say.

Allie finished with Jessie's shoe, and it looked kind of loose to Meggie. It probably wasn't going to stay tied very long, but Meggie wasn't going to say anything about it now. They had to go.

"Do you think we should bring a game or something?" Allie asked, staring at the shelves filled with toys and puzzles and games in their closet.

"'Course not. Michelle'll have stuff," Meggie said, afraid Allie would take forever deciding what to bring. Meggie didn't know if Michelle had anything to do over at her house or not, but she didn't care. She just had to get there. There was something she had to know.

"I'm bringing the pet shop," Jessie said, pulling down the case filled with plastic miniatures.

"Okay, and I'll bring the travel desk," Allie said, lugging it from its corner in the closet.

Maybe it was a good idea for her sisters to bring stuff, 'cause then Meggie could have some time alone with Michelle. Besides, they'd decided quick. "Okay, let's go."

Jessie stood by the closet door. "Aren't you bringing anything, Meggie?" she asked.

Meggie stomped her foot. "I'll just play with yours," she said, gritting her teeth so they'd know she was getting mad and start listening to her. "Now let's *go*." This was just as important for them as it was for her, even if they didn't know it yet.

Meggie couldn't wait to see Michelle. They'd been sick for two more days after Michelle left and then their mommy had been coming to visit, so Meggie hadn't seen Michelle in days. But Michelle had called and talked to them every evening they were sick and afterward, too. And now she'd invited them over to spend the day with her because she'd promised them she would as soon as they were better. They still itched some, but Allie was the worst and even her bumps were almost all just scabs.

Daddy turned onto Michelle's street and Meggie looked out the window. She wasn't sure she'd know which house was Michelle's because they all kind of looked alike on Michelle's street, but she found it right away. It was the one with Michelle outside on the step.

Meggie waited just until Daddy turned off the car so she wouldn't get yelled at, then she unbuckled her

seat belt and scrambled out of the car. Jessie and Allie always got the first hugs, but today Meggie wanted the first one. Just for once.

"Hi, Michelle," she called, heading up the walk. She felt a little funny just running up and hugging her. What if Michelle didn't hug back? Or worse, what if she just patted Meggie on the back like Mommy did?

"Hi, sweetheart, how are you feeling?" Michelle asked. She didn't even wait for Meggie to reach her. She came down the walk and grabbed Meggie right up.

"I've missed you," she said softly, her breath tickling Meggie's neck. Michelle squeezed so hard it almost hurt, but Meggie didn't care. She was just glad that Michelle was hugging her.

"I've missed you, too," Meggie said, even though she was kind of scared to say the words. And she had more to say. Right now, before she chickened out and before she didn't have a chance with her sisters around.

"I need to tell you some stuff in private, okay?" She hoped Michelle would understand how important it was.

Michelle pulled away and looked at her kind of funnylike, but Meggie made herself stare right back even though it made her tummy cramp up like when she ate too much candy.

Then Michelle smiled. "I'll make sure we have the time," she said—just to Meggie, even though Allie and Jessie were running up the walk toward her.

It took a long time to get alone with Michelle because Allie and Jessie had missed Michelle an awful lot, too, probably as much as Meggie had. And, anyway, Meggie was hungry and Michelle had made sloppy joes, and Meggie wanted to play with Noby, too. But finally Michelle put on a movie of Bugs Bunny cartoons and gave them all cards to sew on. And as soon as Allie and Jessie were busy, she called Meggie to help her clean up in the kitchen. Michelle sure was smart. Allie and Jessie didn't like dishes any more than Meggie did, so they'd stay right there in the living room where they didn't have to help. If she'd called Meggie to her bedroom or something, her sisters probably would've wanted to come along.

Meggie's tummy started to cramp up a little again as she dropped her sewing card, and she wished she hadn't had seconds at lunch. She followed Michelle to the kitchen and forgot the words she'd rehearsed the night before. Michelle was an adult and she didn't want to make her mad. Maybe she'd made a big mistake. Allie and Jessie laughed at something in the living room, and Meggie wished she was in there, too. The sewing cards were really neat.

Michelle turned around then and smiled—all warm and soft, just like she had when Meggie was so sick and itchy—and lifted Meggie up onto the counter, making her as big as Michelle so her neck didn't get tired looking up. That's what was so neat about Michelle. She was always doing that stuff, like she knew what it was like being seven.

"Okay, sweetie, what's up?" Michelle asked, giv-

ing Meggie her full attention. Meggie wondered for the millionth time why God hadn't made Michelle their mommy.

Meggie thought about what Allie said about hurting Michelle's feelings. She didn't know what she'd do if she made Michelle cry.

"Mommy's here visiting us." She said it real fast to get it over.

Michelle didn't look like she was going to cry, but her eyes weren't all smiley, either.

"I know, honey," she said, surprising Meggie.

"You do?"

Michelle nodded. "Your daddy told me."

"Oh." Meggie hadn't figured on that one.

"I'll bet it was great to see her."

Meggie didn't know what she was supposed to say. If Daddy and Michelle were talking about Mommy, then Michelle might tell Daddy what Meggie said. But if she didn't talk to Michelle, she would just go on being afraid. And she'd thought since that day Michelle had come and gotten them from school that she wouldn't have to be afraid anymore.

Michelle put her hands on the counter on either side of Meggie's legs. It made Meggie feel like Michelle was kind of holding her.

"Meggie? Isn't it great to see your mother?" Michelle asked, looking at her like Ms. Wilson did when she'd better tell the truth.

Shrugging, Meggie stared down at Michelle's hands.

"Is she nice to you?" Michelle asked.

Meggie nodded. As hard as she tried, she couldn't make herself say the words she wanted to say.

Michelle lifted her chin. "So what's the problem?"

"She likes Daddy better than us." Meggie was surprised to hear her words come out, but she felt better when they did.

"Oh, honey, I'm sure she doesn't. What makes you think that?"

Meggie had never even considered the idea that Michelle might not believe her. "She does, Michelle. Even Jessie knows it. She always sits by Daddy and talks to Daddy at the table, and she only smiles at us sometimes when we say something or when Daddy talks to us. And she mixes us up."

"What does your daddy say about it?"

Finally Meggie was getting somewhere. She stared into Michelle's eyes and talked real fast so she could get it all in. "Nothing. He prob'ly thinks we don't know. But he's in a bad mood a lot and me and Allie figure it's because he's stuck with us and maybe Mommy will go away again like she did last time and then he'll be mad at us 'cause he has to stay with us. Allie and me talked about how we could maybe take care of ourselves 'cause I know how to make sandwiches and Allie ran the washer once when Daddy was sick, but we don't think they're allowed to let us stay alone, so I was wondering if, maybe, Mommy doesn't want us, you do."

There, she'd said it. Meggie held her breath.

"Oh, baby, of course I want you—always." Michelle pulled Meggie off the counter and into her

arms, just like the day Jessie got lost at Disneyland and Michelle held Allie all close. "But don't give up on your daddy yet, okay?" she asked. "I think he wants you three more than anyone else in the whole world."

Meggie laid her head on Michelle's shoulder, hugging her as tight as she could. She sure hoped Michelle was right.

IT WASN'T GOING TO WORK. Jacob looked at Ellen's smiling face on the dance floor and knew there was no way he could reconcile with her. She was having the time of her life in this swank nightclub. He'd much rather be at home with the girls. It didn't matter that they were sound asleep in their beds; he just liked having them close. Taking a sip of his drink, he raised his glass in a toast as Ellen glanced over at him. She'd had more partners among this Saturday-night crowd than he could count, and he didn't even care.

She'd tried several times to get him to dance, but he hadn't wanted to join her on the crowded floor. Not that he minded dancing, as long as he was partnering the right woman.

And there was the crux of his problem. He couldn't marry Ellen when he was in love with another woman. Not even for his girls, though he had a feeling they weren't going to suffer overly much without their birth mother. Eventually they were going to figure out that Ellen's main interest was in him, anyway.

"It's great out there. You sure you won't change your mind and join me?" Ellen asked, sliding into

her chair. She'd chosen their secluded table when they'd first arrived, and now Jacob was thankful for the privacy.

"I'm sure. Why don't you sit this one out, have a drink, catch your breath." *Why don't you sit still for a moment so I can get this over with?*

She smiled at him, leaning back in her seat. "You've always been so solicitous, Jacob. It's one of the things I missed most about you when I left for Washington."

That was his opening. "Speaking of which, have you thought any more about that job offer you've had?"

She frowned at him. "Well, I kind of thought that was a decision we might make together," she said. She was pouting, just like Jessie did when she didn't get her way.

"What you do with your career is something you're going to have to decide on your own, honey. You're the one who has to work at it."

She leaned forward, sliding her hand across the table to cover his. "There's plenty of time to make those decisions later, don't you think? I didn't plan to go right back to work if we remarried."

His eyes narrowed. "You thought you might stay home with the girls for a while? Make up for lost time?" *Had he misjudged her so completely?*

She sat back. "I'll spend time with them, sure. But I've already been approached about resuming my old positions on the charity boards. It seems they miss my organizational skills."

"So things would be just like they were before. You running off here and there, or frustrated with the girls because they kept you from running here and there."

"No! I'm older now, Jacob. And so are they. I'm a lot more tolerant, and they're hardly likely to need as much of my time as they did when they were three."

He drained his glass. "That's the problem, Ellen. The girls don't deserve to be tolerated—they deserve to be loved. And while I'll grant you their needs are different now that they're older, they still have needs. The next time they have a mother, it's going to be someone who'd rather carve a pumpkin than play bridge, who'd willingly give up tickets to the ballet to string popcorn for the Christmas tree—and who won't yell at them for messing up their clothes when they go skating in the park."

Ellen's face hardened, reminding him of the many times they'd argued in the past. "You're living in the Dark Ages, Jacob. Women aren't satisfied with baking cookies and wiping noses anymore. They have careers. They have equality. They have nannies to raise their children."

Jacob thought of Michelle, his partner, who didn't hesitate to work nights to finish four beautiful little ball gowns. "And who do you think those nannies are, Ellen, if not women who find satisfaction in baking and mothering?"

Ellen's look was sincere as she leaned toward him. "They're career women, too, Jacob. They're making

a living, probably the only way they know how, but at least they have the satisfaction of earning a paycheck each week. You're looking for something that just doesn't exist anymore. You want a woman of the fifties, someone from the days of 'Leave It to Beaver' and 'The Donna Reed Show.' You want someone who'll be happy to be at the beck and call of your children, run your household, still look good when you come home from work and do it all for love. You didn't have that growing up, so you think you're going to make up for that by providing it for our kids. But you're not being fair. Women aren't expected to live like that anymore.''

Jacob digested Ellen's words in silence. The damnable part was a lot of what she said was true. Not all of it. He was happy to share in every bit of the work involved in caring for his home and children. But he did want a woman who would put family above everything else in her life. He did expect too much. But he couldn't seem to be satisfied with less.

"Which is exactly why I'm all done asking others to live up to my expectations," he said.

Ellen sat back in her chair. "What are you saying?"

"I don't think it's going to work between us any better the second time than it did the first, honey."

Her smile was poignant, regretful, but just a little bit relieved. "That's your last word?" she asked.

Jacob nodded. This was one thing he was sure about.

"I don't suppose I could talk you into an hour or two in my room for old times' sake, could I?"

He shook his head.

THE GIRLS WERE ASLEEP when Jacob got home an hour later. He locked up the cottage and tried not to notice the silence surrounding him. If he was destined to live the rest of his life alone, so be it.

Stealing into the triplets' bedroom, he picked up Jessie's teddy bear from the floor, tucked it back under her covers and kissed her gently on the brow. He hoped she never got too old to be his baby.

Allie was lying flat on her back, the covers up to her chin. Jacob bent to kiss her good-night, loving the strength he saw in her young face, even in sleep. A few more years, and he wasn't going to have to worry about being lonely. Allie would organize his life for him, just as she was already doing for her sisters.

Meggie's leg was hanging off the side of her bed, and Jacob slid it back beneath the covers. Some difficult times lay ahead for all of them these next few years, but he suspected they would be the hardest for Meggie. She was so determined to be independent, but after seeing her open up to Michelle, he knew she was the one who missed having a mother most of all.

But maybe he could do something about that. He kissed Meggie good-night, then left the girls and headed down the hall to his bedroom, stripping off his clothes as he went. He stepped into the shower, remembering something Ellen had said weeks before. She'd accused him of giving up too easily. She might

as well have called him the coward that he was. Maybe the reason he didn't know how to be satisfied with less was that he'd never hung in there long enough to try.

There was no doubt in his mind that Michelle cared about him, especially after the afternoon he'd spent in her bed. But more importantly he was certain of her attachment to his girls. Yet as usual he'd asked too much of her. He hadn't been satisfied to have her in his life as a mother figure to his children. No, he'd expected her to want to be a wife to him, as well.

Maybe it was time to try to settle for less. If Michelle only offered him friendship, so be it. He'd be a fool not to take what he *could* get. And he'd been a fool long enough.

MEGGIE'S PLEA for acceptance haunted Michelle all weekend. The children needed her. So what was she going to do about it? She'd assured the triplets of her love many times over the past couple of months, but now, as she lay in her bed watching the sun come up on a new day, she realized she'd only been mouthing words.

Afraid of where her thoughts were taking her—of the jumble of emotions twisting her stomach into knots—she got up and showered. But as hard as she tried to concentrate on her routine, to plan the day ahead, she couldn't keep her thoughts from straying to the those three little girls who needed her, or the man who'd fathered them.

Allie, Jessie and Meggie needed a mother. She'd

been telling herself there was nothing she could do about that, but she knew in her heart that there was. The girls needed someone who enjoyed being with them, who considered herself lucky to see to their needs, who loved them. They needed *her*.

Michelle had run long enough. It was time to do more than proclaim she loved the Ryans. It was time to do something about it. That thought brought on the biggest panic attack she'd ever had in her life. Right there in the shower her skin turned cold and then hot and she was afraid she was going to pass out.

But suddenly as she leaned against the shower stall telling herself to breathe, she finally faced the truth she'd been hiding from for months. It wasn't guilt or loyalty to her husband that was keeping her from loving Jacob; it was plain old fear. She was afraid—no, she was terrified—to love again, to open herself up to the possibility of the pain that went hand in hand with trusting her heart to someone else.

Turning off the water, Michelle dried herself and slipped into the first clothes she came across. Fear had robbed her of five years of her life. Looking back, she didn't know when her love for Brian had faded, to be replaced by cowardice. Her emotions had been frozen for so long she supposed she'd never know. But if she was half the woman she thought she was, her days of running were over. It was long past time to get on with her life.

THERE WAS SOMETHING different about Michelle on Monday. Jacob noticed the change as soon as he

walked into the sound booth. Although she greeted him normally she looked as if she was on the verge of a grin.

At first he thought she'd heard from Brian—that her husband was finally coming home to her—and hated himself for wishing it was anything but that. He loved Michelle. He wanted her to be happy. But still, as the morning wore on and she said nothing, the relief he felt was immense. If Brian Colby was on his way home, Michelle wouldn't keep it a secret.

She didn't sit still once all morning. Her fingers fluttered through program sheets, newspapers, CDs and AP bulletins. When she reached up to punch off her mike after announcing a commercial break about an hour into the show, she knocked over her diet cola in her eagerness. Fortunately there hadn't been much in the cup.

"What is it with you?" Jacob asked, half amused, half exasperated. She reminded him of Jessie on the day before Christmas.

She glanced over at him, that grin still hovering on her lips. "Nothing," she said cheerily, picking up her cup. "Want me to warm yours? Your coffee, I mean."

Jacob slid his mug across the counter. "Sure," he said, watching her through narrowed eyes. Her cheeks were flooded with color. He wasn't used to seeing Michelle flustered. Something was definitely up. And she obviously wasn't going to tell him what until she was good and ready.

He'd planned on talking to her about Ellen after

the show that morning. He was all set to lay his cards on the table, to tell Michelle she was welcome to be a member of their family free of charge, no marriage vows required. He'd thought about little else all weekend. The way he figured it, divorced people shared parenting all the time—so why couldn't he and Michelle? They'd even have the added benefit of not having the bitterness of a divorce between them.

"Here you go, all nice and hot." She breezed back into the room carrying two cups. One was filled with diet cola. The other one she set down in front of Jacob.

"Thanks," he said, pushing the mug aside. Maybe he'd better wait to have his talk with Michelle. What he had to say was important, and he wanted her to be all there for the conversation. He didn't know where she was this morning, but it definitely wasn't at KOLR. She'd just brought him someone else's coffee mug. He wondered where his Number One Dad mug had ended up.

Michelle grew more jittery as the morning wore on, but the couple of times he brought it to her attention she denied acting out of the ordinary. He segued into their last commercial, determined to pin her down to an explanation as soon as the show was over. He glanced her way, intending to tell her just that as she reached for the last CD. She wasn't wearing her wedding ring.

Jacob froze as he stared at her bare left hand, telling himself not to make too much of it, just as the commercial came to an end. He was supposed to cue in

the last song of the show. He reached automatically
for his mike button, still staring at Michelle's hand.
He was almost afraid to look up, to look into her eyes,
for fear of what might *not* be there.

"Welcome back..." She was speaking into her
mike. Jacob's gaze flew to hers. *What are you doing,
Michelle? Don't you know I've got the last cue in
front of me?*

"...and before we leave you this morning, we have
one final bit of business to take care of." Her eyes
never left Jacob's as she spoke. He didn't know of
any last-minute announcements.

"As you all know, from time to time Jacob and I
take personal announcements from our listeners and
broadcast them on the air. I have one of those announcements this morning. Except that this one is a
little different. This one is from me, and since all of
you have been so loyal to the pair of us doing this
show, I thought maybe you'd like to help me. With
all of you behind me, I figure I stand a much better
chance. So here goes. Jacob, there's no other way to
say this except straight out. I want to get married."

Jacob's heart beat rapidly, but the rest of him froze.
What in hell...? She was on the air. What was she
going to do—take the ninth caller? He glanced from
her to the phone. It was lit up like a Christmas tree.

Michelle reached over and gently grasped his chin,
turning him to face her. "To you," she said, looking
directly into his eyes.

Jacob's grin spread slowly across his face as, without a word, he pulled her off her stool and into his

arms. Forgetting where he was, forgetting everything but her, he crushed Michelle's lips in a kiss that held all of the promises he'd been waiting a lifetime to make.

"Does this mean yes?" Michelle asked when he lifted his head.

"Yes," he said, then realized he'd forgotten to turn off his mike. The show's producer and technician were on the other side of the glass making enthusiastic "okay" signs with thumb and forefinger and grinning hugely.

Michelle snuggled closer, reaching up to pull his mike down in front of her mouth. "This one's for you, Jacob," she said, cuing in their last song herself.

The song was half-over before Jacob stopped kissing her long enough to hear what was playing. It wasn't Sade's latest tune, which was what their program sheets had stipulated. Instead, he heard the hauntingly beautiful "I Am Your Lady" filling the room.

He looked down at the woman in his arms, at the happy tears filling her eyes, and knew that even though they still had some things to work through, this moment of happiness had been worth the wait.

"Let's go home," he said, keeping his arm around her all the way to the parking lot.

CHAPTER SIXTEEN

"I WANT TO MAKE LOVE to you, Michelle," Jacob said the minute they were inside the beach house. He pulled her into his arms and kissed her so tenderly she was afraid she was going to start to cry.

"I love you, Jacob Ryan," she said, smiling up at him. His arms felt glorious around her, so strong and sure.

His brown eyes glistened with emotion as he held her. "And I love you. Always. Enough to let you go if you ever—"

Michelle placed two fingers against his lips. "Shh. Not now. This time I want it to be just you and me." She took his hand and started down the hall to his room.

He stopped her just outside his bedroom door, and lifted her chin to kiss her slowly, gently, almost chastely. "Are you sure?" he asked.

Her heart ached at the hesitation she saw in his eyes. She'd put him through so much, and all he'd ever wanted to do was love her. She planned to spend the next fifty years making sure he didn't regret it.

"Absolutely."

"No regrets?"

"None."

She loved the wicked grin that spread across his face, feeling giddy with freedom as he swept her up and carried her to his bed. She'd told him the complete truth. She had no regrets, only impatience.

She didn't know whose clothes came off first, only that they all came off quickly. Jacob's body was as glorious as she remembered it, and she caressed him as she'd never done before, hardly daring to believe he was hers to love.

Her body was on fire for him, her nerve endings sensitized to his every touch. His hands slid up her arms and she shivered. He stroked her breasts and she moaned.

"You like that?" he asked, smiling down at her.

"Oh, yes," she whispered.

She couldn't stop looking at him, amazed that this was really happening, that after years of imagining him with other women, she finally had him for herself. And the biggest miracle of all was that she had something that none of those other women had ever had. His love.

Their union was quick and fierce, erasing any that had come before. Their gazes locked as their bodies joined, and they stayed that way as she met each strong thrust of Jacob's hips, their eyes speaking of their love as they climaxed together in a perfect melding of body and soul.

And never once, not even for a second, did Michelle have any doubts. Loving Jacob was right, des-

tined. He was the other half of the person she'd become, the man meant to share her life.

Jacob brushed her hair back from her face with gentle fingers, their bodies still linked. "Your eyes have gone cloudy. Having second thoughts?" he asked softly.

She shook her head. "Not one."

"You don't feel like you've just been unfaithful?"

"How could I? I'm lying in the arms of the man I love. And for the record, I didn't feel unfaithful the last time we made love."

Jacob moved away, lying on his side beside her, his head propped on his elbow. "Don't do that, Michelle."

"Do what?"

"If this relationship is going to work we've got to have total honesty between us from the very beginning. The last time we made love you were eaten up with guilt."

"Of course I was. I'd just treated you like little more than a gigolo, making love to you when I knew I wasn't free to love you. I'd made it all so cheap. But never did I feel unfaithful to the man I love."

"So what's changed? Why are you suddenly free?" he asked.

Michelle sat up, not wanting to talk about another man in the bed she planned to share with Jacob for the rest of her life.

She reached for her tank top. "Can we do this somewhere else?" she asked, putting on the rest of her clothes.

"How about a walk on the beach?" Jacob asked, pulling on the shorts he'd worn to work and poking his feet into a pair of old sandals.

Jacob didn't know if it was a good sign or a bad one that Michelle wasn't willing to talk about Brian while in his bed. Now that he'd had some time to recover from the shock of her proposal, doubts were crowding in on him. Michelle had been loyal to her first husband for five long years. How could she suddenly just be over him? Unless—his skin grew cold as a thought occurred to him—unless she wasn't. It was possible that Michelle was doing this because she didn't want to lose the girls, not because she'd come to grips with her past.

"I've put my house up for sale," she said, her bare toes sinking into the wet sand as they walked.

"I'm glad to hear that. The area's been going down-hill for years. You shouldn't be living there alone," he said. But selling her house didn't mean she wasn't still wedded to Brian Colby in her heart.

"And I've arranged for a headstone to be erected in Brian's memory." Her fingers stole into his. Jacob threaded their fingers together, welcoming the contact as if, with possession being nine-tenths of the law, he could claim her heart merely by holding on to her.

"So you believe he's gone, then?" he asked, choosing his words carefully. If Michelle had loved Brian anywhere near as much as Jacob loved her, he could only imagine how much it must have hurt to finally say goodbye.

She shrugged. "We may never know what hap-

pened to him. But after five years he's no longer the man I married. That's the Brian I'm burying.''

He could hear the tears in her voice and stopped walking to pull her into his arms. "I'm sorry, sweetheart. I'm so sorry," he said, feeling helpless.

She didn't make a sound, but he knew she was crying. She held on to him, her hands clenching into fists against his back.

"I won't rush you if you're not ready...."

She raised her head, her teary eyes filled with conviction as she looked up at him. "I'm ready, Jacob. I've spent five years pushing away the pain, refusing to believe Brian was gone so I didn't have to mourn him. I've only just realized that I lost five years of my life. And I realized something else I'm not proud of."

Keeping his arm around her waist, he started walking again. The waves lapped their feet. "What?"

"That you were right. I was hiding behind my wedding ring so that I didn't ever have to hurt like this again."

Jacob was beginning to believe she really was ready to commit herself to him. "And what brought about that realization now?"

"Meggie."

Jacob stopped, turning to face her. "Meggie?"

"The other day when the girls came over, Meggie was afraid that you wanted to be with Ellen and that she and her sisters were standing in your way. That if Ellen went away again, you'd be mad because she

and her sisters were keeping you from going with her.''

Jacob felt sick to think that Meggie had been so worried and he hadn't even known it. And then something occurred to him.

''She was worried I'd be mad that Ellen left, not sad about her mother abandoning her again?''

Michelle bent her head and said something, but her words were too soft to be heard over the surf.

''What was that?'' Jacob asked, tilting her face up to his.

''She wanted to know if I'd take them,'' Michelle said, obviously concerned about how this news was going to affect him. But she couldn't hide the joy Meggie's request had brought her.

Jacob didn't like to think that his daughters were making plans to replace him, but he was confident enough in their love to know that their plans were only in case *he* chose to leave *them*.

He pulled Michelle back into his arms, grinning. ''She did, did she? And what did you tell her?''

''That there was no way you'd ever leave them, and that I'd always want them. It was then I realized what I'd been doing all these months.''

''And what was that?''

''Telling the girls how much I loved them while moving aside to make room for Ellen—when I knew darn well she'd never love them as much as I do.''

Jacob's grin grew wider. ''She wouldn't, huh?'' he asked, amused at Michelle's defensive tone.

''How could she? She left them. And that's when

it hit me that I'd done the very same thing. I'd run home to my memories every time I was afraid of getting too close, of opening myself up to that pain all over again. Well, I'm not running anymore, Jacob. I don't want the rest of my life to slip by without a single memory to make it worth having lived. Besides, could you look Meggie in the eye and run away?''

Jacob laughed. ''Nope. That's why I'm saddled with three identical little witches who have me wrapped around their little fingers.''

''Well, it's two against three now, and we're bigger than they are. You think we have a chance?''

''Nope,'' Jacob said again, sealing their fate with a kiss. He still had a niggling doubt or two, but he was certain of one thing: Michelle loved him every bit as much as he loved her.

''So, when are we going to get married?'' she asked as they headed back up the beach toward the cottage. The girls were due home from school shortly.

Jacob had been thinking about that. ''I think we should wait awhile,'' he said. He couldn't get away from the fact that no matter how much Michelle loved him, there was always going to be a doubt in her heart about Brian's death. He could imagine her taking second glances every time they passed someone who resembled Brian Colby. But his worst fear was that Brian would return someday and that Michelle, forced to choose, would feel obligated to her first commitment, no matter how much she loved Jacob.

"We don't have to get married at all," she said. "I guess I did kind of pressure you into it."

Jacob stopped in his tracks and turned her to face him, surprised to see the hurt in her eyes. "What on earth are you talking about?" he asked.

"You don't sound too eager, that's all." She looked like she was going to cry again.

Jacob pulled her up into his arms. "Sweetheart, I'd marry you tonight if I had my way. It's you I'm concerned about. I just think we should wait until Frank Steele finishes his investigation before we say our vows. I want you to feel as unencumbered as possible. No guilt."

Michelle reached up to kiss him. "I'd feel that way if I married you right now, but we can wait until we hear from Frank again if it makes you feel better. Except…"

"Except what?" he asked, liking the flush that stole across her cheeks.

"Do we have to actually live in two houses until then?"

Jacob wasn't going to send her away even for one night. "I'll sleep on the couch," he said, wondering how many times he'd have to steal into his bedroom after the girls were asleep before he could join his wife there on a nightly basis. "Now let's go home. I think there'll be three little urchins arriving momentarily who've waited long enough to have their mother welcome them back from a hard day at school."

Michelle's face was alight with happiness as they

resumed walking. She'd never looked more beautiful to Jacob then she did at that moment, anticipating his daughters' reaction to their news.

"They will be glad, won't they?" she asked, sounding nervous all of a sudden.

Jacob still didn't understand women, which meant that it was lucky he'd have four of them living under his roof. Sooner or later, with that much practice, he was bound to get it right. "Of course they'll be glad. Where've you been these past months?"

"Well, they've never had to share you before. They want a mother, but will they like your having a wife?"

"They're smart kids. They'll see the advantages. Besides, if we tell them they might have a little brother or sister someday, you'll be a shoo-in."

He felt her steps falter beside him. "I wasn't sure you'd want more children. You already have three."

"And I'd take three more in a second if they were yours," Jacob assured her, stopping for a kiss they didn't really have time for. "Speaking of which, we haven't used protection. Is there any possibility we have something to hope for?"

Michelle gave him a saucy grin that earned her definite retribution, he decided, as soon as the triplets were down for the night. "Maybe," she said, continuing toward the cottage. Jacob saw the girls clomping up the driveway, the miniature work boots they'd talked him into buying for them too heavy for their feet. He hurried after Michelle. He was anxious to introduce his daughters to their new mother.

WORD CAME from Frank Steele two weeks later. He
left a message for Michelle to call him, which she did
from Jacob's house. Jacob was there with her. They
were planning to take the girls swimming as soon as
they got home from school.

"I've got your answers, Mrs. Colby, but I'm sorry
to say the news isn't good." Michelle listened to
Frank's gravelly voice, feeling again that freezing of
emotion that had kept her strong during the long or-
deal of Brian's disappearance. And then she glanced
over at Jacob, sitting in a chair beside the couch,
watching her, loving her, and she knew she was ready
to hear whatever Frank had to tell her.

"You've found him?" she asked, hoping that Brian
was alive. She knew now that whether he was or not
would make no difference to her plans.

"He died three years ago, Mrs. Colby. I'm sorry."

"Three years ago?" she repeated. Jacob got up and
crossed to her. He stood behind her and Michelle
leaned against him, glad for his strength. No matter
how solid her plans for the future, it was still a shock
to hear that the young man she'd loved was dead.

"He'd been mistaken for a government official and
taken hostage by some of Karim's men, who planned
to use him as a bartering tool. When they found out
their mistake they took him to the village where I'd
traced him, trying to pass him off as the official they'd
thought he was. They bought his cooperation with
threats to the village, ma'am. After two years of ne-
gotiations, Karim agreed to trade his hostage for a
couple of his men who'd been sent to prison the year

before. Karim's men, and Brian, were killed when his
deception was found out. If it's any consolation he
was loyal to you until the end, ma'am, apparently
crying out your name when he was shot.''

"Thank you, Frank. Thank you." Michelle was
barely aware of what she was saying as she hung up
the phone.

She turned into Jacob's arms, pressed her face into
his chest and cried away five years of almost unen-
durable anguish. She cried for the young man she'd
known, the young man she'd loved with all her heart.
She cried for the tragedy of his last two years, and
for the love they'd shared, the love he'd carried with
him to his grave. She cried for herself, for the years
she'd spent waiting, while he'd still been alive trying
to get home to her, and for the years she'd wasted,
waiting for him to come home when he was no longer
alive. And she cried in relief, glad to know that her
vigil was over at last.

Looking up at the strong handsome features of her
husband-to-be, she smiled through her tears.

"I think the girls are home."

"SHH. YOU'RE GONNA get us in trouble."

"But Allie, Mommy says she's our baby, too."

Meggie barely heard her sisters' whispers as she peeked over the edge of the crib in the nursery Daddy'd had built onto the side of their cottage. He and Mommy were in the kitchen, supposedly doing the dishes, but Meggie could tell by Mommy's giggles that the dishes weren't getting done as fast as they could be.

At first she'd been a little hurt that Mommy sometimes wanted to be with Daddy more than her and her sisters, and a lot hurt when Daddy paid attention to Mommy and didn't always hear everything she and her sisters said, but her parents had gotten better about not going off in that funny way where they forgot that somebody else was in the room, and besides, Mommy said Noby was hers and Allie's and Jessie's, too, and Noby slept on Meggie's bed. So now Meggie was mostly just glad that Mommy and Daddy loved each other so much. None of her and her sisters' friends had parents who smiled at each other like Daddy and Mommy did. And secretly Meggie thought that none of them had parents who smiled at their

kids as much as Mommy and Daddy either. And Daddy and Mommy didn't go out and leave them alone a lot, or read the paper all day or do chores all the time they were home. Daddy still played basketball with them, and Mommy had even played, too, until the baby made her too big.

Little Brianna made a sound and bunched her bottom up in the air. Meggie hoped that meant she was waking up. It was her turn to pick her up and take her to Mommy and Daddy.

"How long till you think she can play?" Jessie whispered.

"Shh. Not for a long time, silly," Allie whispered back.

Meggie thought Allie's whisper was just as loud as Jessie's, but she didn't care. She hoped her sisters *would* wake up the baby. Brianna had been sleeping ever since they got home from school and Meggie'd been waiting hours for her turn to hold her.

Meggie had never felt anything as good as holding Brianna. Her baby sister was so warm and cuddly, and made her feel like she was really important even though she was only eight. Nobody knew it, but Meggie had made a promise to Brianna the first day she was born, when Daddy had taken them to Mommy's hospital room to see her. That was the first time Meggie had gotten to hold her, and while everyone had been talking to Mommy, Meggie had told Brianna she'd never have to worry about not having some-

body, because Meggie'd be her person for her whole life.

Jessie ran around to the other side of the crib, jolting it as her foot knocked into one of the legs. Brianna stirred and Meggie held her breath, hoping the baby wouldn't go back to sleep. Nobody had ever told her that babies slept so much. It was the only thing she didn't like about having a baby sister.

One of Brianna's eyes popped open and then closed again. Her little mouth yawned and Meggie had never seen anything so cute in her life. Meggie reached down, sliding her arms beneath the baby.

"Wait, Meggie, she's not awake yet," Allie said, her voice warning of dire outcomes if the baby was woken up.

"She is too. She opened one eye," Jessie said.

So, she wasn't the only one who'd seen it. That was enough for Meggie. She lifted the baby into her arms.

Allie and Jessie walked on each side of her as she carried the baby into the kitchen, and Meggie knew the best part was coming. Mommy and Daddy quit kissing and moved toward her and her sisters as they came into the room. Michelle smiled, looking at each one of them so no one felt left out, and everybody cooed over baby Brianna for a few minutes while Meggie held her and then, right before Michelle lifted Brianna up to go change her, Daddy pulled them all into their nightly group hug, just as Meggie had known he would.

"I must be the luckiest man alive to have five such beautiful girls," he said.

Meggie figured he was right.

Coming June 2001

Three stories
written for the heart of every mother...
by bestselling author

TARA TAYLOR QUINN

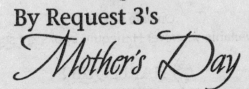

By Request 3's
Mother's Day